YESTERDAY

YESTERDAY

FELICIA YAP

MULHOLLAND
BOOKS

Little, Brown and Company
New York Boston London

Mulholland Books/Little, Brown and Company
Hachette Book Group
1290 Avenue of the Americas, New York, NY 10104
littlebrown.com

First Edition: August 2017

Mulholland Books is an imprint of Little, Brown and Company, a division of Hachette Book Group, Inc. The Mulholland Books name and logo are trademarks of Hachette Book Group, Inc.

The publisher is not responsible for websites (or their content) that are not owned by the publisher.

The Hachette Speakers Bureau provides a wide range of authors for speaking events. To find out more, go to hachettespeakersbureau.com or call (866) 376-6591.

Library of Congress Cataloging-in-Publication Data
Names: Yap, Felicia, author.
Title: Yesterday / Felicia Yap.
Description: First edition. | New York: Mulholland Books, 2017.
Identifiers: LCCN 2016056953 | ISBN 978-0-316-46525-0 (hardback) /
978-0-316-51484-2 (int'l pb)
Subjects: LCSH: Married people—Fiction. | Social classes—Fiction. | Memory—
Fiction. | Murder—Investigation—Fiction. | Identity (Psychology)—Fiction. | BISAC:
FICTION / Mystery & Detective / Police
Procedural. | FICTION / Technological. | GSAFD: Mystery fiction. | Fantasy fiction.
Classification: LCC PR6125.A6 Y47 2017 | DDC 823/.92—dc23
LC record available at https://lccn.loc.gov/2016056953.

10 9 8 7 6 5 4 3 2 1

LSC-C

Printed in the United States of America

For Alex and Han Shih

YESTERDAY

Chapter Zero

A VILLAGE NEAR CAMBRIDGE
TWO YEARS BEFORE THE MURDER

Let me tell you a couple of horrible secrets. I'll start by showing you a photograph.

This is me, a long time ago. I had a flat chest and protruding ears. If you look closely, you can see that I once had hope in my eyes and fire in my soul. Today, both the hope and the fire are gone. Wiped out by years of institutionalization.

Here's a second photograph. Oh, I see you flinching. That's understandable. It is, after all, a photograph of *you*. Your own mug shot, taken recently. You don't look too bad here. Blond hair cascading down your shoulders, impressive tits. Guess what? I'm going to transform myself so I'll look *exactly* like you. I'm going to bleach my hair and get boobs like yours.

Is that a frown I see on your forehead? You don't get it, do you? You're wondering: Why would I want to look like you?

Let me explain. I remember *everything*. Really, I do. I'm the *only person in this world who remembers her past*. All of it. Mostly in vivid detail. I'm not kidding. And that makes me pretty damned special.

You don't believe me, do you?

That's understandable, too. Like the five billion Monos around us, you only remember what happened yesterday. You wake up each morning with *facts* in your head. Carefully curated information about yourself and other people. You stagger from your bed to the iDiary on your gleaming kitchen counter. To that electronic device of yours, your meager lifeline to the past. Desperate to learn the few pitiful details you've written down the night before. Eager to add them to your memories of what happened yesterday—and to the other cold, sterile facts you've learned about yourself.

Pretty rubbish, isn't it?

And you're even used to this, aren't you? Because you've been doing it since the age of eighteen, after your hapless little brain switched itself off. No wonder you're envious of the few Duos whose short-term memories are slightly better than yours. But you are all the same.

Equally pathetic.

Let me add a simple truth, since you're getting to know the real me.

When you remember everything, you recall what other people have done to you (even if they don't remember it themselves). Down to the smallest, most gruesome detail. Which causes you to desire vengeance if they've hurt you bad. Like, really, really bad. Like, say, if they caused you to end up in a mental asylum for seventeen years. It makes you yearn, during the darkest hours of the night when the moon's smile has faded and the owls have fallen silent, to set matters straight.

When you remember everything, you will also get away with everything. Like revenge, for instance.

Fucking convenient, isn't it?

This is precisely why I, Sophia Alyssa Ayling, will get away with it.

Vengeance would be nice. Especially in view of what you've done to me. All the terrible little things you've been guilty of over the years. I recall each and every one of them. It's the *sum total* of remembered grievances that makes hatred potent. Oh, yes. The act of revenge will be easy.

Because no one will remember what I'm going to do to you.

Except for me.

Happiness is a process. Unhappiness is a state.
—Diary of Mark Henry Evans

CHAPTER ONE

CLAIRE

A man is whimpering in the kitchen. He is also blocking my way to the marble counter where my iDiary lies, its LED indicator still flashing electric purple. I squint; he's clutching his left hand and wincing in pain. Blood is dripping from his forefinger. He's surrounded by the remains of a teapot.

"What happened?" I ask.

"It slipped," he says, mouth taking on a stricken line.

"Let me have a look," I say, stepping around ceramic shards. As I move towards him, the gold ring on his left hand mocks me with a sharp glint. It causes the main facts I've learned about my husband over the years to spin back to mind. Name: Mark Henry Evans. Age: forty-five. Occupation: novelist hoping to be the next MP for South Cambridgeshire. We got married at 12:30 on 30 September 1995, in the chapel of Trinity College. Nine people attended our wedding. Mark's parents had refused to come. I promised Chaplain Walters that I will tell myself each morning that I love Mark. The cost of the wedding was £678.29. We last had sex more than two years ago, at 22:34 on 11 January, 2013. He was done in six and a half minutes.

I haven't yet worked out if these multiple facts I've retained about my husband should make me feel bad, sad—or mad.

"Tried to catch it midfall," says Mark. "But it bounced off the dishwasher."

I study the gash on his forefinger. It's almost an inch long. I lift my eyes to Mark's face, taking in the heavy creases above his brow. The troubled wrinkles fanning out from the corners of his eyes. His twisted lips. I remember him tossing about in bed last night, as if he was pursued by something in his dreams.

"Looks nasty," I say. "I'll get a bandage."

Turning my back on him, I hurry up the stairs. Fact: The first-aid kit is stored in the cabinet next to the bathroom mirror. Before I reach up, I pause in front of my reflection. The eyes staring back at me are different from the haunted eyes I saw yesterday. Today's face has clearer pupils. Yet its cheeks are swollen. The skin around its eyes is puffy.

I cried myself to sleep last night. I spent most of the day in bed.

I wonder why. I stare hard at the distended image in the mirror, willing the relevant facts to come to my mind. But the reasons behind yesterday's misery are flitting beyond reach, like the wings of an elusive butterfly. I only remember hiding, sobbing into my pillow, and refusing to eat. I grimace in defeat; the face in the mirror frowns back. Yesterday's unhappiness must have been caused by something that happened two days ago. But what?

I don't recall what occurred the day before yesterday. Because I can't. I only remember what happened yesterday.

My husband needs me, I tell myself with a sigh. I remove the kit from the cabinet and head downstairs. Mark is sitting at the kitchen table, nursing the injured finger in his right hand. His lips are still pulled back in a tortured grimace.

"Let me see to it," I say, opening the kit.

Mark winces as I wipe the blood away with a cotton swab. The cut's much deeper than I thought.

"I ought to disinfect it first." I pull out a small bottle of antiseptic from the kit and uncork its stopper.

"No need to fuss."

"I'm not having you walking around with an infected finger."

"It's just a small cut."

I ignore Mark; I dab a generous amount of antiseptic on the wound (he winces again) and wind a bandage round his finger. He opens his mouth to say something, but closes it again with a frown.

I kiss his finger before rising from the table and picking up my iDiary from the kitchen counter. I place my right thumb on its fingerprint-recognition sensor, causing its purple LEARN YESTERDAY'S ENTRY NOW diode to stop flashing. I scroll down to the final entry. Last night, I wrote:

11:12: Woke up feeling awful. Burden of knowledge hangs on shoulders. Spent hour crying in bed. Found Mark asleep in study at 12:25; woke him up and gave him present I bought—even though his birthday's a week from now. Broke down in tears again, went back to bed. Neglected all household chores—even gardening. Skipped lunch and dinner. Mark kept coming to bedroom with worried face to tell me that everything will be back to normal tomorrow. He's right. Yesterday's nightmare will be gone in the morning. Surfaced for a banana, usual pills, and two large single malts at 21:15 before returning to bed.

An accurate if skimpy description of what happened yesterday. But the entry does not explain why I cried. It only suggests that yesterday's unhappiness was triggered by something that happened two days ago. Something nightmarish. I scroll over to my penultimate entry:

Thunderstorm until 9:47. Took Nettle for walk afterwards. Lunch consisting of roast beef and potatoes at 13:30, taken in conservatory on my own. Mark wanted lunch in study so he could continue writing. Headed over to Grange Road at 16:50 for long chat with Emily over tea and crumpets. Evening uneventful. Mark headed back to study to do more writing. Curled up in front of television with microwaved leftovers.

I'm disappointed, even bemused, by the entry. I'd assumed that it would shed some light on the reasons behind yesterday's misery. But the entry is terse, even opaque. I scour its contents again only to draw a blank once more. Mark might know what happened two days ago. Unlike me, he's a Duo who remembers *both* yesterday and the day before. This is what makes him different from most of us. This is why he thinks he's superior.

"I remember spending most of yesterday crying," I say, noting that the frown on Mark's face has not lifted. "But I can't figure out why."

Our eyes meet. There's a dark glint in Mark's pupils, one I'm unable to fathom. Is it anger? Grief? Or fear?

He turns away from me and stares at my moth orchid for several seconds before replying.

"You forgot to take your medication two evenings ago," he says. "This caused a relapse yesterday."

He must be right. Fact: I've been taking two types of drugs since 7 April 2013, as prescribed by Dr. Helmut Jong of Addenbrooke's Hospital. Lexapro and Pristiq. Two of the former and one of the latter, each day. I reach for the medicine container on the counter, sifting through my mind again for more relevant details. Fact: I traveled to Newnham Pharmacy at 14:27 on 1 June 2015, to pick up the most recent round of pills, bearing another prescription from Dr. Jong. Sixty and thirty respectively, enough for a month.

I count the pills inside the gray container. There should be fifty and twenty-five of each. Instead, there are fifty-two and twenty-six remaining.

"You're right," I say, sighing. "I forgot to take my pills."

Mark grunts before getting up from his chair. I detect a slight softening of the tension around his shoulders.

"I'll clear up," he says.

As Mark bustles around the kitchen with a dustpan and brush, I move to the fridge and pull out a bottle of milk. My stomach's growling. I heap cornflakes into a bowl. I settle down at the kitchen counter with a spoon before turning on the radio. Static crackles in the room; a jingle for a car-insurance-comparison website chimes moments later. Mark has swept away the last of the shards. He has also decided that he still wants his tea; he's taken out a mug and plopped an Earl Grey tea bag into it.

"Good morning, East Anglia," says a male voice on the radio. "This is the news at eight. The queen has given her royal assent to an act of Parliament designed to encourage more mixed marriages between Monos and Duos, who, as the 2011 census has shown, now form seventy and thirty percent of the population respectively. Entrenched cultural prejudices have long deterred these unions from taking place. Only three hundred and eighty-nine mixed marriages were registered in Britain in 2014."

I steal a glance at Mark. He's stirring in a lump of sugar with a more cheerful upturn of his lips, though only by the tiniest of fractions. I know why he's pleased. The news must bode well for his ongoing MP campaign. Fact: He had the guts to wed Mono Claire Bushey twenty years ago despite strong opposition from his family. He's a Duo in touch with the needs, hopes, and fears of the Mono masses of Britain. He is *married to one*.

"Recent scientific studies have proved that a Mono-Duo couple has a seventy-five percent chance of conceiving Duo children."

Children. Fact: I want a baby. My heart's crying out for a little one to care for and love. But how will I have a baby when sex has dried up in my marriage?

"The government believes that an increased proportion of Duos will heighten Britain's economic competitiveness and productivity," continues the newscaster. "It has supported the Mixed Marriage Act, a piece of legislation granting tax advantages to Mono-Duo partnerships. The act is expected to come into effect on the fifteenth of February in 2016."

If only they knew. Facts matter. I've forced myself to learn them, whether I like them or not.

Fact: Monos married to Duos are subjected to daily reminders of their memory limitations. This dooms them to a state of chronic inferiority. This is probably why I've been on antidepressants for years. Yet I dare not contemplate the thought of leaving the man who ignored society's biggest taboo to marry me, as my prospects would be poorer if I did. Fact: Mark received an advance of £350,000 for *On Death's Door*, his most successful novel. We live in a Newnham mansion overlooking the Cam. Six bedrooms, a conservatory, and a 1.4-acre garden. Two vacations to the Caribbean each year, flying first class. If I'd married a fellow Mono, I'd still be a waitress at Varsity Blues.

The newscaster is now gabbling about the result of yesterday's football fixture between England and Germany.

I sigh, taking another spoonful of cereal. I crunch the flakes; their syrupy sweetness coats my tongue. My life is idyllic—but only on the surface. The facts say as much. If only there were a child in my life. The void is getting wider as the years pass—I'm thirty-nine now. And if only I could remember things as Mark does. Our memory gap separates us like an unbridgeable chasm.

The newscaster is saying something about Cambridge. I prick up my ears.

"…the body of a middle-aged woman was found in the River Cam at dawn today, in a nature reserve near the village of Newnham…"

The words are drowned by a crash. I look up from my cereal. Mark has dropped his mug. It's now in a dozen pieces on the kitchen floor. A steaming puddle of Earl Grey lies in front of him. A limp tea bag has draped itself over his foot.

"A spokesman for the Cambridgeshire Constabulary says the police are treating the death as suspicious and an investigation is now under way," the newscaster is saying. "Moving to the weather forecast, the Met Office says the day will be windy…"

I switch off the radio. The resulting silence seems twice as unsettling.

"What's the matter?" I say.

Mark does not respond. His eyes are out of focus. His shoulders are strung in a tense line.

"Was it the report about the dead woman?"

My husband blinks; I must be right. It *is* about her. But why?

"I was…just shocked by the news," he says, stumbling over his words. "They probably found her in the Paradise nature reserve, down the road. How dreadful. So that's why I heard police sirens this morning."

I study his face. His jaw is clenched.

"I don't understand why you look so agitated."

"I'm not," says Mark, although the tautness around his shoulders suggests otherwise. "I'm just careless. First the teapot, now the mug. Sorry. I'll clear up again."

He turns away from me and marches out of the kitchen.

I stare at the remainder of the cereal in my bowl. I'm no longer hungry.

Mark has swept away the remnants of the mug and retreated to his study at the end of the garden. I'm tempted to take Nettle for a walk in the nature reserve. While sections of the park are likely to be cordoned off, I might catch a glimpse of what the police are up to.

I place Nettle on a leash and head out into the sunshine. The morning air is crisp, even chilly. Faint notes of honeysuckle perfume the sidewalk. We proceed in the direction of the kissing gate at the end of Grantchester Meadows. Nettle bounces forward, sensing a rabbit or two. I tighten his leash. The kissing gate squeaks; we step through into the reserve. The ground underfoot is soft, even boggy in places. It's pockmarked with footprints, mostly fresh ones. A speckled wood butterfly dances up ahead, a flickering silhouette against rays of sunlight.

I hear muffled voices as we head down the woodland path, past several mature willows and a murky offshoot of the Cam on the right. Black helmets bob in the distance. I move closer. Several people are gathered on a strip of boardwalk, their heads turned away from me. They are held back by three policemen. A long ribbon of yellow tape winds between two trees, its ends fluttering in the wind.

Pulling Nettle's leash tight, I join the crowd. A denim-clad man with a green padded jacket is operating a camera. A suited newscaster with a pronounced quiff is speaking into a microphone. Most people are staring at the riverbank. Thrusting myself upwards on my toes, I peer over their heads.

"No smartphones." One of the policemen is shaking his finger at a boy.

The spectacle that greets my eyes is disappointing. I do not see a body—or a body bag. Only two men in white protective suits and blue rubber gloves. One of them is sealing something into a plastic bag. The second man is taking photographs of a large tree overhanging the Cam. Its enormous main trunk, partially submerged, protrudes over the waterway for about twenty feet before branching upwards into leafy boughs.

"What's going on?" I turn to a man in fluorescent orange running shoes.

"They found a dead body in the river earlier this morning."

"Can't see it."

"They took her away some time ago, down that lane." He points in the direction of a second woodland path, opposite the place where Nettle and I have come from.

"Must have been an awful sight."

"They were zipping her up into a bag when I first jogged by. That was a couple of hours ago. Blond. Long-haired. Couldn't quite make out her face."

"Do you know how they found her?"

"I overheard that man." He turns his finger to the newscaster with the microphone. "A jogger apparently saw her wedged in the reeds, floating in a facedown position. Right at the base of that large tree."

"Oh, dear."

"Wish I'd got up earlier this morning. Would have spotted her first."

"I wonder if they know who she is."

"The newsman said they found a driving license in one of her pockets. But he didn't mention the name."

I nod.

"I'm off now. It's getting boring. Nice dog."

He turns and jogs away, his orange shoes flashing between the trees. I can see the newscaster putting his microphone away. The camera is no longer rolling. I loosen Nettle's leash and begin tugging him in the direction of home, between willows rustling in the wind.

Poor woman. I wonder what happened to her.

Mark isn't around when I get home. He must be in his study. I unfasten Nettle's leash and pour a generous helping of biscuits into his bowl. As he crunches them down, I put on my overalls and gloves. My diary tells me that I have not done any outdoor work for at least two days. The garden must be crying out for some pruning and weeding. All 1.4 acres of it.

I push the door of the conservatory open and head out into the sunshine again. The wind has picked up. I troop down the paved path that slopes downwards in the direction of Mark's study. The thunderstorm of two mornings ago has left a trail of destruction across the garden. Broken twigs and snapped branches are strewn about everywhere. Hundreds of leaves whirl in circles, swept up by the wind. The storm has even uprooted some of the polished black and white pebbles along the garden path. Dark, grassless indentations mark the stones' absence.

I do not see the dislodged pebbles anywhere nearby. Nettle must have carried them off. He has a history of squirreling things away, because my diary says I found two stones and a manky tennis ball in his basket last Christmas Day. I'm good at learning small random facts, despite what Mark thinks.

I get to work at once, grabbing a rake from the garden shed. Before long, I've accumulated a stack of wilted leaves near the hedge at the front of the house. A comforting, earthy smell wafts from the pile.

Gardening is therapeutic; this must be true, as the unease in my stomach is evaporating. Or perhaps it's because the hefty pile of leaves testifies that I've accomplished something useful this morning. Homemakers like me are reduced to measuring their daily accomplishments by the number of items they have cleaned or cleared away. It is probably the only thing that keeps us sane (or less depressed). Unlike Mark, I do not have book sales in the millions to be proud of.

And, unlike my husband, I have done very little to be proud of in my lifetime. My diary says as much.

Things are not improved by the fact that Mark, like most other Duos, secretly thinks Monos are stupid. That we are mentally circumscribed by our inability to remember what happened two days ago. That we have a myopic understanding of the world around us. He lacks the courage to say this to my face. But whenever I open my mouth, I can see Mark thinks as much. My diary indicates that I've endured twenty years of patronizing jibes from my Duo husband.

But I shall not dwell on these matters. I shall not think of my own inadequacies, either real or imaginary. Not when my spirits are finally lifting.

I grab a couple of large refuse bags from the garden shed and begin shoveling the leaves into them with renewed energy. Something rings in the distance. It sounds like the doorbell. It must be the postman.

I unlock a side door in the garden hedge and walk around the corner of the house to the front. A man is standing on the porch, his face turned at an angle away from me. He isn't the postman. His face is chiseled thin, with a strong, angular jawline. Hints of gray abound on his temples. His snowy button-down shirt is immaculate, pressed to perfection. His Oxford brogues are polished to a high sheen.

"Can I help you?" I say.

The man jumps before turning to look at me.

"Oh," he says.

His eyes settle on me, taking in my dirty overalls and shoes. His irises are steely gray in color, almost magnetic in focus. He reaches into his breast pocket and pulls out a photographic badge attached to a black folding wallet. It's in the shape of a snowflake with a crown on it.

"DCI Hans Richardson, Cambridgeshire Constabulary. I would like to speak to Mark Evans."

"Why?"

"We would like him to help us with an investigation."

"What are you investigating?"

"The death of a woman."

I gape at the detective.

"Surely not...er...the woman on the news this morning? Whose body was found in the Cam?"

"Actually, yes," he says with a nod. "I'm the senior investigating officer on the case. I'll be grateful if you could get Mr. Evans. He's your husband, I presume."

I nod. Something isn't right with the universe this morning, but I'm unable to place my finger on it. My eyes dart past Richardson; his checked blue-and-yellow patrol car is right outside our house. A uniformed driver is behind the wheel, his mustached face blurred by the tinted windows. A couple of neighbors are poking their heads out; one has even emerged onto her front porch to stare at us, still in her purple dressing gown. It's a shame a pesky row of terraced houses lies on the other side of the road.

"Mark's at work in his study," I say, eager to remove Richardson from my neighbors' line of vision. "Follow me."

I lead the detective around the corner of the house, noticing that his silk tie bears a small repeated motif. It looks like the Greek pi symbol I learned in school ages ago. Nettle bounces up to us. Richardson stoops down to scratch the dog's head, eliciting a vigorous wag in return. As we step through the side door leading into the garden, I decide to be brave and ask:

"What was her name?"

The detective purses his lips before answering:

"Sophia Ayling."

The name does not ring a single factual bell in my mind.

"Why is her death...er...being treated as suspicious?"

"I cannot say." He shakes his head. "Sorry. Your garden's lovely, by the way. Really interesting."

"Thank you. I'll get my husband."

Richardson nods. I begin walking down the garden path to retrieve Mark. Alarm rushes into and floods my heart, blotting out everything else. Mark surely cannot be linked to Sophia Ayling. I've not learned any facts about her. To confirm this, I pause in my tracks to pull out my iDiary and tap in her name. Nothing shows up.

I reach the door of Mark's den and tap its surface. A loud groan issues from within.

"I'm writing, Claire." Mark's voice is muted, but I hear a distinct note of exasperation in it. "I've told you not to disturb me whenever I'm writing. You should type this down in your diary tonight. Spend a bit more time learning this fact."

"It's urgent, Mark. Please come out."

I hear a muffled curse, followed by an eventual patter of footsteps in my direction.

The door swings open with a loud creak, revealing Mark's neatly ordered study. My husband is standing before me with unfocused eyes. There is even a slight wildness in them. If he had been writing over the past hour, the act must have caused him great agitation.

"A detective wants to speak to you. DCI Hans Richardson of the Cambridgeshire Constabulary. He's investigating the dead woman on the radio this morning."

Blood is draining from Mark's face. His left hand is trembling.

SCIENTIFIC AMERICAN

It's All Down to Our Genes

Scientists Have Found the Gene and Protein Responsible for Society's Memory Divide

15 September 2005

Scientists at Harvard University have identified the genetic switch responsible for short-term memory differences between Duos and Monos. The gene regulates the production of a protein, cyclic AMP response enhancement-binding protein, more easily remembered as CREB.

Blood samples taken from five thousand volunteers confirm that both adult Duos and adult Monos have very low levels of CREB, in contrast to adolescents younger than age eighteen. Yet Duos still have more CREB in their blood than Monos do, thus giving Duos two days' worth of short-term memories instead of one.

Scientists are certain that this protein is inhibited at the age of twenty-three for Duos and eighteen for Monos, thereby accounting for society's memory divide. They are trying to understand how and why this is so, and whether this has always been the case.

Duo Patrick Kilburn, the project's lead researcher, believes that this genetic trigger may be switched on by a synchronized combination of physical and emotional stressors. Both forms of trauma must be present at the same time for this to occur, he insists. Mice subjected to simultaneous physical and emotional shocks, he says, have elevated levels of CREB and better short-term memories.

A spokesman for the International Memory Fund (IMF), the organization financing the research, says, "The discovery of this genetic switch raises the delicious possibility that humanity can be helped to acquire better memories in the future. At the very least, all Monos may be converted into Duos someday."

Chapter Two

MARK

I thought that things couldn't get any worse when I heard the news on the radio this morning. But they have.

They say that ignorance is bliss. I look back into Claire's eyes, the eyes that first entranced me twenty years ago when I gazed into them at Varsity Blues (as my diary says). Her pupils are crystal clear today, unsullied by the burden of knowledge. What a difference a day can make. Yesterday, torturous agony was spilling from them. Today, she has the lavender irises of a serene woman, one secure in the comfort of *not* remembering, exempt from the *punishment of knowing*.

The wind begins to howl above the treetops.

For once, I would give anything to be a Mono like Claire. Especially today. I know she's envious of me. Deeply so. It's an issue that crops up repeatedly in our marriage—and in my diary. I've lost count of the times I've written sentences beginning with "Claire's latest rant about Duos is that they are…"

Little does Claire know that being a Mono is what gives her the *right* to be a happier person.

I take a deep breath, trying to calm my racing thoughts.

"How odd," I say.

"Inspector Richardson's waiting, Mark." Claire crosses her arms, fastening vexed eyes on me.

I'm left with no other option but to follow her up the garden path to the spot where the detective is waiting. Even from a distance, I see that he's tall and well built, with powerful shoulders. No-nonsense, I-mean-business shoulders.

I squint; the man's slipping something into his pocket. It looks like a camera case. Damn. What has he been photographing in my garden? I hasten my stride over the remaining yards.

"Morning, Inspector," I say. Up close, I realize his features are marred by a hawkish nose.

"Good morning, Mr. Evans."

"I understand you wish to speak to me."

"I'm sorry to trouble you, sir; I know you're busy. But I have some sad news about Miss Sophia Ayling. I'm sorry to say that her body was found in the Cam earlier this morning."

"What?"

"Now, sir, it's standard procedure in a case like this to take witness statements from family and friends. We need to piece together the deceased's movements prior to her death, to make sure the coroner's inquest has all the facts it needs. You were acquainted with Miss Ayling, it seems. Do you mind coming with me to the Parkside station, where I'll take your statement? It shouldn't take long."

I hear Claire sucking in her breath.

"Did you...did you say Mark and Sophia were *acquainted?*"

"I did." The inspector nods.

"Mark..." Claire turns back to me, pupils wide and accusing. "Is this a fact?"

Damn. I really ought to defuse the suspicion smoldering in my wife's eyes.

"I'll check," I say, pulling out my diary and examining it with the most innocent expression I can muster.

"My diary says I ran into Sophia in York, at a writers' conference two years ago," I say. "An aspiring novelist writing about...er... patients in a mental hospital. Their drug-addled fantasies, in particular. She asked me to sign her copy of *On Death's Door*. Said she was a massive fan of my books. How did you know we were acquainted, Inspector?"

"Miss Ayling wrote about you in her diary."

Shit. What is Sophia's diary doing in the inspector's hands?

"I'm surprised you have access to her diary," I say, trying to keep my voice calm. "If I learned my facts correctly, the United Kingdom Human Rights Act of 1953 protects a person's right to privacy. This includes correspondence and diaries."

"That is correct, sir, but only in general terms."

The detective pauses, his mouth taking on a curl.

"The 1998 Data Protection Act has been amended to enable the police to obtain 'personal data revelation warrants' when necessary. We may seize or inspect e-diaries in the interest of national security. Or when we are investigating serious crimes such as murder and child abduction. You know, the very serious offenses."

I swallow hard.

"We've since obtained one of these warrants for the inspection of Sophia's diary. Its contents, we feel, might aid our current investigation into her death."

"What did Sophia say about me?"

The detective shakes his head in silence, thrusting his jaw forward.

"Inspector." I look him in the eye. "You've just told me that poor Sophia has been found in the Cam. And you're standing in my garden asking me to help you. I wish to know the context."

"Do you *really* wish to?"

"I absolutely insist."

"Well, if you insist..." He holds my gaze with unflinching eyes.

I hear Claire sucking in her breath once again.

"Sophia suggested in her diary that the two of you became *quite close* after your first meeting in York." The corner of the detective's mouth twitches.

Claire takes a step backwards. She looks as though she has been punched in the gut. But the horror that first registered on her face is replaced by something else. Her cheeks are a thunderous flush. Her eyes are blazing over pinched lips.

Damn. I've just made a terrible mistake. The best course of action would have been to deny any factual memory of Sophia in the first place. But I was thrown off balance by Claire's initial reaction. I have to dig myself out of the hole I've created. Make sure I won't slip up again.

I have four options:

(A) deny an affair occurred;
(B) cast doubt on Sophia's character;
(C) find out what Sophia wrote about me in her diary, preferably not in front of Claire;
(D) all of the above.

"That's a lie," I say, bunching my fingers into a fist. "Sophia made it up. She said she was crazy about my books. Crazy about *me*, even though we'd never met before."

The detective does not look convinced.

"She wrote down what she wanted to believe. She was desperately unhinged. You're wasting your time here, Inspector."

"I'm obliged to follow all possible leads." The detective's jaw is rigid. "They include the men whom Miss Ayling was *quite close* to."

I glance at Claire. She's clenching her fingers, as I am. Molten lava is still surging to her eyes. But she is, thankfully, amenable to persistent persuasion, as my diary jottings over the past twenty years have tended to suggest. Fact: One of my June 1995 entries, for instance, says that Claire is partial to crimson roses and that "dogged pleading is the key to her stubborn heart."

Yet I can't help but shudder. If the tabloids ever hear I *may* have strayed from Claire, I can wave good-bye to my dream of becoming an MP.

"Inspector," I say. "I hope it isn't your intention to arrest me—"

"Dear Lord, no. Of course not, sir. We merely require a witness statement."

I'm not sure if I should be alarmed or relieved by this.

Richardson clears his throat, tilting his chin a little.

"You wanted to know what Sophia wrote about you," he says. "Well, under the terms of our warrant, we may disclose the contents of her diary to those directly affected by the investigation. I may share some details at the station."

The detective must suspect that I would give anything to know what she wrote about me.

"I'll come with you, Inspector," I say with a groan. "I'm willing to help your investigation, even though Sophia was completely delusional about the nature of our relationship."

"Thank you."

"Trust me, Claire," I say, looking into her eyes with the most imploring expression I can muster.

But Claire does not reply as I follow the detective up the garden path and in the direction of his car.

I thought I would be led to an interrogation room. One of those rooms you see in police movies, with nothing but a table and chair and a powerful halogen lamp aimed at the eyes of the hapless suspect.

Instead I'm ushered into Richardson's office. His worktable is mostly bare, featuring a computer, an iDiary (I wonder if it's Sophia's), a digital recording device, and a giant stapler. A wooden chess set occupies a prime position on the left-hand corner of the table. The pawns are engaged in a vigorous skirmish. There are no papers stacked up in large piles, no files strewn about in haphazard fashion, no coffee mugs containing moldy five-day-old dregs. But the shelves behind the desk are revealing for what they tell me about Richardson's personality. They are full of color-coded notebooks, arranged in impeccable rows according to the precise shade of their markers.

I should be careful.

I will not appear terrified, even if I am.

My eyes settle on an inscription etched on a metal plaque pinned onto the back wall. It states:

You can't force genius. It happens.
Nor can you force inspiration. It strikes when
you are least prepared.
But you can force solutions to problems within a day.
You merely have to go after them with a giant club.
—Anonymous

I definitely need to be wary. Careful to the extreme. I smell an unrelenting Inspector Javert type who will leave no stone unturned in his quest for answers. He looks like the sort of person who inhales his job with every breath. A hawk-nosed detective who will not rest until he ferrets out the truth.

"Thank you for coming," says Richardson. He points to the uniformed sergeant who has accompanied us into the room, an earnest-looking young man with thick caterpillar eyebrows. "Sergeant Donald Angus will be typing your witness statement on the requisite MG11 form. We'll need you to sign a copy afterwards."

I nod.

"So you are a Duo, Mr. Evans."

"Of course."

"How long have you been married?"

"Twenty years."

"Children?"

"None."

"You're a successful novelist. But you hope to be the next MP for South Cambridgeshire and will be running as an independent candidate at the upcoming elections."

"Correct."

"What did Sophia Ayling say when she approached you after your talk in York?"

"Let me check."

I pull out my iDiary and tap its keyboard before looking up at Richardson.

"She said she loved my novels. She had been reading them for years.

She hoped her unpublished manuscript would be just as successful. My diary says so, at least."

"Anything else?"

"Nope."

"Wait a minute. Didn't Miss Ayling also mention she was crazy about you?"

He's a sharp one, this Inspector Richardson.

"Ah, yes. She did."

"How did you respond?"

"Said I was flattered."

"What happened after that?"

I pause. I would give anything to know what Sophia wrote in her diary about our first encounter.

"She invited me to dinner. I refused."

"You said *no* to a beautiful blonde?" Incredulity darts across Richardson's face.

"I did." I meet his gaze, knowing that it's Sophia's written word against mine. But I have an advantage over Sophia, because a dead woman no longer has words to defend herself. Unlike me.

"But why?"

"I do not accept invitations from everyone I meet at writers' conferences. Even if they are beautiful blondes."

"Why not?"

"If someone claims to be crazy about me, an alarm goes off in my head."

"And why so?"

Stymied for an appropriate answer, I type "crazy + conference" into my iDiary. To my relief, a single hit surfaces. I scan the words before looking up at Richardson.

"You get the occasional loony at these events, Inspector. Last year's diary says that I saw a woman with lurid pink lipstick attacking a literary agent with her handbag."

The detective raises a skeptical eyebrow.

"So what happened next?" he says. "After you refused Miss Ayling's invitation?"

"She looked disappointed. But she went away."

"What do you mean *went away?*"

"Left the room," I say, trying not to sound impatient.

"To sleep with you in another room?"

"Course not."

"You sure?"

"Look here, Inspector." I have to struggle to prevent irritation from edging into my voice. "I understand you're eager to get to the bottom of Sophia's death. But you're barking up the wrong tree as far as I'm concerned."

"What happened *after* the conference?"

"Nothing." I shake my head. "Does her diary say we've had a torrid affair for years?"

The detective does not answer. I can see him thrusting his jaw forward again. I brace myself for the next question.

"Did you have any contact with her afterwards?"

I prod my diary in response.

"I received a couple of gushing e-mails from her. Messages implying she was still obsessed with me. I deleted them. My agent, Camilla, regularly forwards similar e-mails from other female fans."

"It must be gratifying to have women fawning over you."

"My diary tells me it can get a little annoying at times."

"Your name crops up a few times in Miss Ayling's iDiary," says Richardson to my surprise. "One hundred and eighty-four times, to be precise."

"Was she *that* obsessed with me?"

"Her diary has rather…shall we say…vivid contents," says Richardson, fixing his eyes on mine. "I'm still digesting them. It's unlike any other diary I've read under warrant in a murder case."

I sit up in my chair.

"It reads like a volatile stream of consciousness," he continues. "Or perhaps more like a raging river of semiconsciousness. It's a fascinating tangle of thoughts."

I always knew that Sophia was mercurial (my diary says so), but I never realized she was *that* batty.

"What did she write about me?"

"I cannot say."

"But...but...you said you'll be happy to share some details at the station."

"I said I *may*."

"Did she write that she was madly in love with me?"

"I'm supposed to be the one asking questions here."

"Sorry, Inspector," I say. "I'm just curious, that's all. You've just told me that my name crops up one hundred and eighty-four times in her diary."

"Let's move on." Richardson's lips are a grim line. "Could you give me a precise account of your movements over the past three days? Let's start with yesterday."

I have four options:

(A) tell Richardson the truth about what I did;
(B) give up the truth about what Claire did;
(C) lie;
(D) none of the above.

"My wife woke up feeling awful, as she forgot to take her prescription pills the night before," I say. "That's why I decided to stay at home. I even canceled my meeting with a group of campaign volunteers so that I could keep an eye on her. Thankfully, she decided to stay in bed for most of the day, and all remained well."

"What was wrong with her?"

I groan. Fact: Claire's condition has been a considerable source of vexation to me over the years.

"If you must know, Inspector," I say with a sigh, "my wife suffers from depression. Her behavior can get a little erratic at times. I'd be grateful if you could keep this confidential, by the way. I do not wish the press to learn about my wife's…er…health problems."

Richardson nods before jotting something in his notebook with a frown.

"Did you and Mrs. Evans stay at home all day yesterday, then?"

"Yes."

"What else did you do, apart from keeping tabs on her?"

"I tried to do some writing at the kitchen table while Claire rested upstairs. But I wasn't too productive in the end. So I decided to do some admin work in my study, while checking on Claire every hour or so."

"What sort of work?"

"Spreadsheets. E-mails. Things that do not require inspiration."

"And what inspires you, Mr. Evans?"

"Everyday life. The simplest things."

"Like marital turmoil, say? Did it inspire that scene in *On Death's Door*? The one in which your protagonist, Gunnar, quarrels with his wife, Sigrid, only two days before the death of their child?"

So the detective has read my novel.

"It's impossible to say how novels are shaped by real life." My sentence comes out more curtly than I had intended.

"How do you keep track of what inspires you?"

Fact: For one reason or another, only Monos have ever asked me that question at writers' conferences. I don't know why: it must be a Mono inferiority thing. But surely the detective isn't a Mono. At any rate, I should give him my stock answer, the one I dredge out each time.

"By writing it all down in my diary, of course. *Everything*. The shocking, the heart-wrenching, and the absurd."

"How do you keep track of what you have already written when you are working on a novel?"

"I just page back to what I don't remember."

"Then why does Gunnar come from Valberg on one page and Varberg on another? One's in Norway, the other's in Sweden."

I gape at the detective. Fact: I only discovered that typo two months after publication; it somehow evaded all the editors who worked on the book. Yet none of my readers has spotted the error—until today. Richardson must have read the novel *really* carefully. This makes me twice as nervous.

"You clearly know your Scandinavian geography, Inspector."

"I'm one-quarter Swedish and one-quarter Danish."

I blink.

"You haven't answered my question," he says.

"All novels have ... er ... mistakes in them. Do you spend all your time trying to spot errors in books?"

"My job is to find cracks in what appears seamless on the surface." The detective's gray eyes are mutating into iron gimlets. "How would you describe the state of your marriage, by the way?"

"Happy, of course." My words spill out in a quaver despite my best attempt at sounding confident.

"And what do you mean by *happy?*"

I rack my brains for an appropriate factual answer before deciding to borrow a couple of lines from *On Death's Door*:

"It depends on how happiness is defined. My personal definition is that you know you were happy only afterwards."

Richardson raises an eyebrow before scribbling a couple of things down in his notebook.

"What happened the day before yesterday? Thursday?"

This is where it gets trickier. I ought to watch my words.

"I stayed in, too. I spent most of the day writing in my study. Unlike yesterday, it was a reasonably productive day. I wrote around eight hundred words. I then dealt with e-mails in the afternoon."

"So you didn't leave your home."

"Nope."

"Did you speak to anyone during the day?"

"I was on the phone in the late afternoon, to my agent, Camilla, and my campaign manager, Rowan."

"What happened in the evening?"

"Nothing much. I fell asleep in front of the television in my study."

"Two days before? Wednesday?"

I reach for my iDiary and scan Wednesday's entry:

I spent a frustrating morning battling with *The Serendipity of Being,* but I did manage around eight hundred words by lunchtime. At noon, I trooped to the kitchen to make a sandwich for myself before Claire's return from the Cambridge Flower School. I enjoyed wolfing down the sandwich without having to make meaningless lunchtime conversation with my wife. It's a shame her company's so unstimulating these days. I called Camilla after lunch to reassure her that *The Serendipity of Being* is coming along well.

—Thank God for that! Novelists and deadlines seldom go together. That's a fact. But you'll deliver, won't you?

—I'm glad the shit storm over my *Sunday Times* article has died down over the past couple of days.

—Shit storms are what we need to sell your book. That must be the best promotion piece you've ever written. Maybe you should do a follow-up next month.

Camilla added that our publicist, Ben, is attempting to secure a prime-time TV interview slot ahead of the novel's release next spring. He's pretty confident about getting one, she added, in the wake of the uproar caused by my *Sunday Times* article. Rowan phoned later to confirm the time of our press conference at the Cambridge Guildhall—12:00 p.m. this Saturday—to coincide with the Mixed Marriage Act, due for royal assent on Friday. I should make the most out of the fact that I've been in a mixed marriage for twenty years.

—Always seize an opportunity when it presents itself, Mark. This is a cardinal rule of politics. Although timing's just as important, if you haven't yet worked this out.

Rowan's right. I spent the rest of the afternoon drafting out answers to possible questions from journalists, saved as "Press-conf.doc." I then dealt with e-mails and other campaign-related correspondence. (God, I hate bureaucracy—perhaps I should get a secretary.) Dinner with Claire, who had spent the entire afternoon preparing my favorite rabbit stew. I feel bad whenever I see her slaving away in the kitchen: Why does she always try so hard to please? I feel twice as guilty whenever she tries to be nice. The rabbit was spectacular, but the conversation was again devoid of intellectual sparkle. Why isn't Claire into fine art or classical literature? Ibsen plays, Wagner operas, or Virginia Woolf? What on earth does she see in those ditzy women's magazines on her bedside table? Why must I bite my tongue whenever I'm tempted to discuss plot twists for *The Serendipity of Being,* certain that a Mono like her will never get it? Spent the rest of the evening sprawled before the television in my study, making greater headway with a bottle of Château Lafite Rothschild (1996) than with *The Serendipity of Being.*

"I spent the morning writing," I say, looking up from my diary. "I had a lunchtime sandwich before speaking on the phone with Camilla and Rowan. I then dealt with e-mails and other nuisances in the afternoon before spending the evening in front of the television."

"Your days appear to play out in remarkably similar fashion." The detective cocks his left eyebrow at me. "What you did on Wednesday sounds exactly the same as what you did on Thursday."

Damn. I've screwed up again.

"I'm a novelist," I say, trying to keep my voice controlled. "I've learned to recognize the symptoms of creative mania over the course of my career. I try to make the most of them. This is why I spent the week at home, writing. My diary says as much. I surface only when I need to."

"*Creative mania,*" Richardson repeats after me with a thoughtful crease of his brow. "I recall reading the phrase in Sophia's diary."

I'm not surprised, as I had borrowed the phrase from Sophia in the first place. Fact: She had used it on me the first time we met. I was so taken by it—because it encapsulated the phases of productive output I occasionally experience—that I'd jotted it down and learned it the following day.

"Sophia was, of course, an aspiring novelist," I decide to remind Richardson. "Most writers, I'm sure, hope to experience a bout of creative mania at some point or another."

"But *nothing* in her diary suggests she regarded herself as a novelist."

The detective's eyes are burning into mine.

"She did not refer to any unpublished manuscripts," he adds. "Nor did she say that she was working on any literary masterpieces, for that matter."

"How odd, Inspector," I say, still desperately attempting to stay unruffled. "She did mention a manuscript about patients in a mental hospital."

"Funny you should say that." Richardson's mouth twitches. "Miss Ayling did appear to know a thing or two about these hospitals. Her diary practically revolves around them."

A sudden rancid taste surges into my mouth.

"What do you mean?"

"It implies that she was in a mental institution for a long time before she was released, two years ago."

"She was *institutionalized?*"

"Yes. Seventeen years."

"I did not know this, Inspector." The detective must have heard the slight tremor at the end of my sentence, because he leans forward with unflinching, relentless eyes. He reminds me of a leopard full of coiled tension, a hungry cat eyeing its prey.

"Someone *murdered* Miss Ayling," he says with a growl, his face inches away from mine. "I sense it in my bones, even though my deputy thinks it was suicide. At any rate, the coroner's report is due before the end of the day. I'm sure it will vindicate my suspicions. Sophia Ayling did *not* put on an overcoat, fill its pockets with stones, walk into the River Cam, and drown herself like Virginia Woolf did. I know my literary figures, too. I'm going to establish the identity of her murderer before the day's end. Mark my words, Mr. Evans. *I will.*"

HOW TO CONVERT DETAILS IN YOUR DIARIES INTO FACTS

From the Official Guidelines for Transitioning Monos and Duos on Their Eighteenth and Twenty-Third Birthdays

1. Write in your diary at the end of each day, even if you are a Duo with a grace period of two days. You should write down what matters to you—details you think may be significant.

2. Understand what facts are. Facts are details that you have learned from your diaries, details that will never be forgotten. Facts surge immediately to mind because these details have been transferred to the long-term storage compartments of your brains.

3. Read the previous night's entry as soon as you wake up each morning. This should be the first thing you do each day. The more effort you put into learning your diaries, the more you will retain. Studies have shown that Monos who work hard at learning their diaries are able to retain just as many facts about themselves as Duos. When it comes to learning diaries, Monos and Duos are equals.

4. Relax. You won't be able to convert all details in your diaries into facts in your heads, no matter how hard you try. Scientific studies have suggested that both Monos and Duos can retain as much as 70 percent of what they have written in their diaries (there are, of course, exceptions to this norm).

CHAPTER THREE

SOPHIA

2 September 2013

Hot. Stifling. Aspiring authors everywhere, packing the room. Hiding their ambitions behind polite smiles and shabby clothing. He stood on the podium, bearing the touches of middle age. A thicker midriff. Hair no longer luxuriant, even thinning a little at the front. But no one in the room would have guessed. Unless they knew him when he was a skinny lad of twenty-five with a generous shock of hair on his head.

Oh, they cheered for him. They did. No one writes like Mark Henry Evans. No one sells books like Mark Henry Evans. At the back of the room, I hovered. Even applauded like the others. I had to. It was important to blend in. Look normal, as Mariska had advised.

He spoke about inspiration. Concentrated phases of creative output. The trappings of literary fame and success. But all I could think of, as he spoke, was that tricky little business of trapping *him*.

I approached him after his talk. Smugly confident about my appearance. Hair down in sleek platinum waves. Eyebrows preened to perfection. Nails the color of blood. Lips painted a ravishing scarlet. I had even dressed for murder. Slinky little black Alexander McQueen, décolletage hinting at the ample possibilities below.

Enjoyed your talk, Mr. Evans, I said, giving him a smoldering, megawatt smile. He smiled back. Eyes immediately straying downwards. Burning my curves. Not the slightest flicker of recognition. Thank God for that. So my plastic surgeon pulled off a great job in the end.

Your discussion of creativity *really* resonated with me, I purred. It's all about the joys of creative mania, isn't it? Madness, after all, occasionally manifests as mania. Aren't creativity and insanity two sides of the same coin? And doesn't literary genius like yours, Mr. Evans, lie at the intersection between the two?

His eyes said it all.

He was hooked by my looks. Captivated by my words. Mine for the taking.

Men are so fucking easy.

How about dinner together? I asked, curling a lock of per-oxided hair around my finger. Casual. Coquettish. Yet moving in for the kill. Let's discuss this fascinating little business of creative mania at length.

I can think of much better things than dinner, he said with a chuckle. Eyes fixed on my tits.

He delivered that night.

Ate me up.

Licked cream off my boobs.

Oh, yes, he did.

5 September 2013

God, my head's fucking killing me again.

Six days since our York encounter. Not a single phone call or text message.

He must have lost my number.
Why hasn't that idiot called?

6 September 2013

They released me from St. Augustine's nine months ago today. Gaunt. Haggard. Hair shorn like a sheep's coat, thanks to one of my predecessors, who managed to hang herself from the rafters by her braids. Twelve years before I got there. They had been cropping the hair of all inmates since. At least that was what Mariska said, hair in god-awful spikes like mine, during one of her calmer moments in the back garden. The only outdoor space where some of the "lesser basket cases" were permitted to roam. Beneath gnarled, stunted poplars in the late-summer afternoons.

Shame she's dead now. Cardiac arrest. Only thirty-six. Once beautiful.

If only the warders could see me now. None of them would recognize me. Gained a few curves since. Cheeks filled out again. Complexion no longer pinched or sallow. Porcelain veneers. Hair trimmed in soft waves, right below my shoulders. As it was when they first threw me on the boat to St. Augustine's. I look feminine again. Nose is definitely an improvement. Dare I say refined? Ears finally pinned back. Chin and cheeks resculptured à la *Venus de Milo*. Lips a little fuller, thanks to hyaluronic acid. Tits perky and impressive, thanks to the joys of silicone padding.

The vanity tag, instead of the insanity tag, suits me better.

They stole seventeen years of my life. Seventeen fucking years. I can't get them back.

But I can get my looks back.

And I *will* get my revenge.

7 September 2013

Raindrops slither down the windowpanes outside.

Darkness swallows them.

Terrible dream. The same one, too. Warders pressing down on me. Hands everywhere. Insistent. Restraining. Suffocating. Whirls of light above their heads. Shards of darkness everywhere. Stars dancing about as twinkling elliptical forms, like van Gogh's *Starry Night*. But the stars are not whimsical. Nor are they playful. They conceal a malevolent presence. They harbor unforgiving hands. Hands forcing me down. Hands robbing me of my freedom.

Hands strangling me.

There are many consolations in being free. I can drink as much as I want. Shag anyone I want. Both drinking and shagging weren't exactly routine occurrences at St. Augustine's. Booze was only attainable if one had the appropriate means to bribe the orderlies. Shags were only achievable if one's tastes were limited to women. Damaged women.

Plus I can type whatever I like into this little diary. No need to maintain a facade for the warders. A bloody charade. The pretense that my brain's "normal." So those little fuckers had been monitoring the contents of the iDiary they gave me. I ought to have written what they wanted to see. I wouldn't have ended up spending seventeen years in St. Augustine's. I would have cut my sentence short. I would have freed myself from their evil, restraining hands much earlier.

I should thank poor dead Mariska for the revelation. But better late than never.

We were in the back garden that day. Sunshine was streaming through the stunted poplars. Whitecaps were rippling across the ocean in the distance. She was sitting on the lawn, blade of grass in hand. Studying it with interest. As if she had never seen grass before.

How are you? I asked, deciding to make conversation. She gave me a silent, scornful glance. Began twirling the blade of grass in her fingers. Slowly at first. Then rapidly.

As well as I can be, she said. What about you, sweetheart?

What do you think? I said.

Aren't we both on fire? she shot back, aiming a searing glare at the poplars. The ones that grew around the island's perimeter, standing between us and freedom.

Then she leaned forward, a conspiratorial glint in her eye, before tossing the blade of grass back down on the lawn.

Overheard two warders discussing your case late yesterday night, she said. How Sophia's unique. How Sophia's different.

I always knew I was special, I said.

You don't write in the iDiary they've given you, she continued with narrowed eyes.

I don't bother with diaries, I agreed.

Why not? She tossed her question at me with a nonchalant shrug of her shoulders. But curiosity glimmered on her face.

No need to, I said.

But don't you want to hold on to your past? Facts that may matter in the future? She raised a quizzical eyebrow at me, running her fingers through her shorn hair. Everyone keeps diaries, sweetheart. Because everyone needs a few vital facts about themselves. Because everyone needs something from the past.

I pointed to my head.

The facts are right there, I said. All of them. I still remember everything that happened to me after the age of twenty-three.

She cocked her head, staring at me with interest. Digesting my words. Perhaps even taking them seriously. Most inmates of St. Augustine's tended to do so. After all, we had to live with each other's plagues. Paranoia. Schizophrenia. Hallucinations. Delusions. Psychotic episodes. We had to suffer together. No way of bailing out. Not when we were locked up together on a wretched island.

How nice to have it all in your head, Mariska said. Deadpan. Couldn't tell if she was being sarcastic. Hope you didn't mention this superhuman ability of yours to the warders, sweetheart.

I snorted.

Why would I even think of doing so? I said.

Good, she said. Because three inmates who bragged to the warders that they have full memories are now six feet underground at the far end of the island. A rather inconvenient fact for them.

I narrowed my eyes in the direction she pointed, past a gnarled poplar swaying in the wind.

What happened to them? I asked.

No one knows, she said with a shrug. Or maybe no one really wants to know. Because my diary says the warders hushed everything up afterwards, making sure no one raised the subject. So you really ought to write in your diary, sweetheart. Every night. Like everyone else. Like a normal person. Like me.

Waste of time, I said with a sniff.

Not a waste of time, she said. Not a waste at all. The warders are also reading our iDiaries.

You're fucking kidding me, I said.

Mariska rolled her eyes. Threw me a pitying look. As if I was the stupidest person she'd ever met.

The warders have our fingerprints, she said. They monitor our diary entries for continued signs of lunacy. Or for promising markers of normalcy. Even though the difference between lunacy and normalcy, as we both know, is slight. If you wish to be free, you should at least *try* to appear normal. *By writing a diary, sweetheart.* The sooner you do so, the sooner you'll be out of here. Deinstitutionalized. You do wish to be free again, don't you? She chuckled, a hoarse rumble at the base of her throat. After being locked away in purgatory for so long, the only way out of here is either in a coffin or a boat. You still have a chance at getting a return ticket. If you play your diary card right.

I sat up straight.

Your diary should document the crucial facts of your existence, Mariska said with a long-suffering sigh. As if she were explaining things to a child. Dates, times, and events that matter. Facts you may need in the future. So that it sounds convincing enough to the warders.

I can even show you my own diary if you wish, she offered with a puckish smile. Lips curling up in slight amusement. If you ever require inspiration.

But it was the next thing she said that made me gasp:

Your stepmum told your dad that she found your paper diaries in the trash bin all those years ago. Your dad thought you'd gone mad. That's why he decided to drag you to a psychiatric ward in Cambridge. That's why you eventually ended up here. That's why the orderlies are eager to read your diaries. That's why they've kept you here for such a long time, fearing that you were one of those delusional full-memory sorts. That's why they've taken special pains to make sure you didn't escape. Except you never bothered to write in the iDiary they gave you later. Thought I should tell you this, sweetheart. While yesterday's conversation between the two warders remains clear in my mind. You surely don't wish to join those three fools buried on the far side of the island, do you?

Something clicked in my head. The weak sunlight filtering through the poplars took on a sudden sinister tone. Everything made troubling sense. I felt enlightened, if threatened. Grateful to Mariska for opening my eyes to the realities of St. Augustine's. To possibilities beyond its perimeter.

Like vengeance, for instance. The revenge I both desired and deserved.

I mumbled my thanks. Because she had prodded me into action. Made me desperate to get out.

Now I sit under rain-sodden eaves. Haunted by nightmares. Consoled by a giant bottle of vodka.

But at least I'm free, thanks to Mariska. Shame about the cardiac arrest. Pity she never got back to Amsterdam. Kissed her cold lips before they took her to the mortuary. She was right about getting out of the Outer Hebrides in a coffin.

I will not repeat the mistakes that led me to St. Augustine's. If you can't remember the past, you're bound to repeat your errors. But if you can, you shouldn't be making too many of them. I have plenty to do from now on. I should stay focused. Go back to sleep. After I've finished my vodka, of course.

I'm going to start by screwing the man who screwed up my life.

Regularly.

I woke up this morning and realized I can't remember what happened two days ago. What a catastrophe. It feels as if someone has just thrust a large knife into my heart. Spent most of the day walking around in a daze. I've always thought that I'm a Duo. Everyone was sure I would take after Duo Dad (and not Mono Mum); after all, I've been the top student in every class I've attended since the age of seven. I have to register with the Department of Monos tomorrow as per the Class Registration Act (1898). I will also have to tell my superiors at the Cambridgeshire Constabulary. My future career is dissolving into wretched pieces: I will still be a lowly constable when I retire. (Note to Self: I'm going to keep quiet for a while and see what happens. How would anyone know that I'm a Mono if I decide to keep this a secret? There must be a way out, I'm sure. They say that when it comes to learning the contents of diaries, Monos and Duos are equals. I'll write really detailed entries from now on and learn them carefully. Wake up early each morning to do so; I'm sure I can retain more than 70 percent if I work hard enough. I'm not going to let my dreams and ambitions evaporate.)

—Diary of Hans Richardson, 1990

CHAPTER FOUR

HANS

13¼ HOURS UNTIL THE END OF THE DAY

I had to let Mark Henry Evans go, regrettably. Though I would have loved to clap him into a cell at the back of the station.

The man was a liar. He was so fishy he reeked.

But I had nothing on him. Apart from a muddled and incoherent diary left behind by a dead woman who had embarked on an affair with him despite bearing some sort of a grudge. A Botox-addled, ex-bulimic female who had spent seventeen years in a mental asylum. Who had apparently opened her eyes one day to discover that she remembered *everything* about her past. It wasn't exactly the sort of compelling, in-your-face evidence I needed to pin Evans down.

I study the alignment of forces on my chessboard and edge a white pawn forward.

The man's a liar. I don't believe him. But the woman's worse. I can't trust a single word in her diary. Fact: The protein responsible for short-term memory is inhibited after the age of twenty-three. Sophia Ayling's claim to full memory defies both scientific explanation and logic.

It must surely be the most ridiculous thing I've ever heard.

I push a black pawn forward in turn. The move looks positively suicidal.

What happened yesterday is crystal clear in my head. I remember *everything* about the day. In vivid color, too. Every single snapshot, from when I woke up in the morning with a slight hangover to when I fell asleep reading "Ten Things You Should Know About Getting Ahead in Your Job." What happened before my eighteenth birthday is just as vivid. Like the contents of those criminology courses I took, down to the minutest detail. I can even visualize the pores on the face of the grizzled professor who taught Introduction to Criminal Investigation (and who wrote the accompanying five-volume textbook). He had also reeked of stale tobacco, unwashed corduroy, and burned sausages.

But how on earth does one remember *everything* after the age of twenty-three? That's impossible.

I prod a white bishop on a forward diagonal and knock the suicidal black pawn out of the fray.

If something sounds like undistilled fantasy, it probably is. I am of two minds as to whether I should finish reading Sophia's diary today. Or leave it until tomorrow. Fact: Concrete, indisputable evidence is what should interest me in the first twenty-four hours after a crime comes to my attention. Especially when it involves a *murder*. Besides, I hope to work out the killer's identity before the end of the day.

I rise from my chair, itching for another dose of coffee. But as I take my first step in the direction of the vending machine, young Toby hurtles in through the door of my office.

"I've run her fingerprints through various databases," he says. "Nothing shows up at all."

I'm not surprised. Sophia did not look like someone with an existing criminal record.

"I've also double-checked her DVLA details," he continues. "They confirm that Sophia Alyssa Ayling was a Duo born on 20 November 1970, in Bermuda. She obtained her driving license in August of 2013. But HM Revenue and Customs are adamant they do *not* have a Sophia Alyssa Ayling on their database. I've also drawn blanks as far as General Register Office, Home Office, and Electoral Registration Office records are concerned. That goes for the Ministry of Memory and the Department of Duos, too."

"Keep digging, will you? Her name should eventually crop up in one database or another."

"Okay," he says with a nod. "I also ran checks on her vehicle registration number. She bought her car from a dealership in Camborne on 22 August 2013. A secondhand black Fiat for twenty-nine hundred pounds."

I freeze.

"But I'm still unable to find her medical records," he continues, flinging up his hands. "The NHS does not have a Sophia Alyssa Ayling on file. Neither does Addenbrooke's Hospital. I've even gone back as far as ten years before her birth date, just to be sure. Nothing, I'm afraid."

Sophia's diary must have been even more delusional than I thought. Toby's findings discredit its contents further. But I should perhaps obtain concrete confirmation of my suspicions.

"I need two more things from you," I say. "One, the full particulars of Ayling's financial records."

Toby nods.

"Two: Could you find out if she was ever at a mental hospital named St. Augustine's? I do not have much on this establishment apart from the possibility that it may be located somewhere in the Outer Hebrides."

"The *Outer Hebrides?*" Toby narrows his eyes at me.

"A long shot, I know." I shrug. "But off you go."

Toby shakes his head before disappearing through the door. I pull out my Dictaphone, tap on the Sophia Ayling file, and recite "Born in Bermuda," "20 November 1970," and "secondhand black Fiat with tinted windows." Fact: Every little seemingly insignificant detail helps when one is trying to solve a mystery.

I hit the Recall button to check that the device has correctly transcribed what I've said. Just then I hear a shuffling of feet yards away from my desk. It must be my deputy Hamish, still wearing his heavy boots.

Damn. If only forensics had kept him in the nature reserve for several more hours. I could have done with a longer period of grace.

"If you still think she killed herself, I suggest you stick around for the postmortem report," I say.

"I decided to visit the mortuary on my way back to Parkside. Marge and company had begun their external work on the body. I begged her for an informal prelim, saying that it's necessary for our investigation. She obliged."

Smugness expands on Hamish's face.

"And?"

"They still can't rule out suicide as a possibility. Not at this stage, at least. They haven't yet found any signs of external injury."

"Hmm…"

"I don't understand why you remain so adamant that foul play was involved—"

"In case you didn't notice, the trench coat she was wearing was massive." Exasperation creeps into my voice. "It was way too large for her. It wasn't her coat in the first place."

"But—"

"Someone had put it on her. Someone who panicked. Someone who wanted to get rid of her body as quickly as possible. The stones in the coat's pockets were merely a clumsy afterthought."

"I don't get you."

"The facts say that the Cam has been flowing faster than usual this week. We've had lots of rain recently."

"So?"

"The current must have dislodged some of the stones weighing her down. Her body surfaced and became entangled in those reeds."

"Even so, she could have killed herself." Hamish's voice is mulish. "We shouldn't read too much into an oversize coat. They're fashionable this season, it seems. I saw a few on the last train from Cambridge to Ely two evenings ago, swallowing up their owners. Even my wife has one. She wore it yesterday to the concert at the Corn Exchange."

I sigh. Fact: Hamish can sometimes be more hindrance than help. This is partly attributable to his rigid self-importance, a common failing of most Duo detectives in the Cambridgeshire Constabulary. A problem exacerbated by his frequent inability to think outside the box, a critical element of detective work. But perhaps I should just feel sorry for my deputy: he has a tendency to miss the obvious. And if he did indeed pay a flying visit to Dr. Sheldon's domain, I should get more details out of him.

"Did Marge find any external residues on the body?" I say.

"I didn't ask."

I'm tempted to groan. Any self-respecting detective would have asked the pathologist this basic question.

"Likely time of death?"

"She's still working on it," says Hamish. "But her preliminary assessment puts it somewhere between thirty-two and thirty-eight hours ago. Judging from the way rigor mortis has set in, she said."

This means that Sophia Ayling was murdered sometime on Thursday evening.

The day before yesterday.

I hope it wasn't a Mono who killed her. This would complicate my investigation in all sorts of undesirable ways. And if it was a Duo who did it, I ought to pin down the culprit before the end of the day. Because the Duo murderer will still *remember* what he or she did. This makes it easier for me to extract an *honest* confession.

"What else did Marge find?"

"The platinum's fake. Ayling was a natural brunette. She'd also had lots of cosmetic surgery. Chin, nose, ears, and cheeks. Silicone boobs, Botox, and fillers."

At least the woman wasn't delusional about the amount of cosmetic surgery she'd paid for.

"Anything else?" I ask.

"That's about it, I'm afraid. Marge hopes to get her report to us before the end of the day."

I would give anything to know the precise cause of death. But I have little option but to wait for Dr. Sheldon's report. In the meantime, I should stop Hamish from stifling my thoughts. I should give him something to do, to keep his hands occupied.

"I would like you to check something for me," I say, pushing a black bishop on a short backwards diagonal and removing a white pawn from the board. "I believe that Mark Henry Evans is scheduled to give a noon-time press conference at the Guildhall. I would like you to attend the event and report back on its outcome."

"Mark Henry Evans?" I detect a note of astonishment in Hamish's voice. "I saw a campaign poster on my way back here. Isn't he running as an independent candidate for South Cambridgeshire?"

"Indeed. He's a slippery one, dear Mr. Evans."

"And how exactly is Sophia Ayling related to Mark Evans?"

"One said they fucked. The other says they didn't."

Before I go any further, I should reacquaint myself with the key facts about my present sorry situation. I fish out my own iDiary, place my right thumb on its fingerprint-recognition sensor, and tap my way to the entry I wrote two evenings ago. Its final section reads:

I did two daft things today. Hamish and I were discussing something trivial when I said that I should consult my diary entry for two days ago, just to be sure. Hamish threw me a puzzled, slightly suspicious look. I corrected my-self, of course. Said that I meant my entry for three days ago, and not two, before changing the subject at once. I can't believe I was careless enough to make an error as spectacular as that.

(NTS: Must watch my words in Hamish's presence. He'll start investigating me if I slip up again. It'll be terrible if everything I've built up over the years comes crashing down on my head. The powers above will demote me at once if they discover that I've been masquerading as a

Duo. Or sack me without a severance package. My excellent track record in the force—and the sheer number of cases that I've solved within a day when I can still hold everything together in my head—would mean nothing to them. After all, the force still has a Jurassic outlook as far as Monos are concerned: none of us is capable enough for higher office. Didn't I write here that Commissioner Mayhew had stated in a 2014 interview that Monos should be thankful that the force is broad-minded enough to employ them as constables in the first place?)

The second daft thing happened later in the evening. I finished work at 18:20 (it was, after all, a quiet day) and decided to undertake a circular jog to Grantchester. I saw a beat-up Fiat at the edge of Newnham village, just before the footpath across the meadows. A blond woman was perched behind the wheel, her face blurred by the tinted windows. She looked up at me as I jogged past; I gave her a curt nod before continuing on my way.

Hey, the woman shouted. I turned around in surprise, only to realize that she had jumped out of her car and was bearing down on me. She was clad from head to toe in black to match her vehicle.

Aren't you Hans Richardson? she said, frowning. I nodded, astonished that she knew my name.

You fucking piece of shit, she shrieked. The next thing I knew, her right hand had flashed forward in my direction.

I ducked just in time. I did not understand why I was a fucking piece of shit. Or why she thought I deserved a slap in the face. I did understand, however, that the woman had tried to assault a law enforcement officer.

I think I've read enough; I flip off my iDiary with shaking hands. I need to do two things today:

1. Beware of Hamish. He'll smell a giant rat if I slip up again, especially because he remembers what happened two days ago with crystal clarity (unlike me). I should keep him at arm's length at all times, if possible.

2. Solve this case before the end of the day, while I can still hold everything together in my head. Fact: While a few Sunday patrol units will still be operating tomorrow, Toby and most of my more capable assistants will be on leave. If I were to pick up the threads of this investigation again on Monday, I would only have a few skimpy facts about the Ayling case in my Dictaphone, notebook, and iDiary. Basically everything I'm able to write down or record today, which won't be sufficient. To make things worse, Hamish will still remember everything about today on Monday, down to the smallest significant (or insignificant) detail. *I won't.*

I grimace at the clock on my wall. I should get going; I have only thirteen hours left until midnight. And I should steer clear of Hamish at the same time.

It sounds like a mission impossible. Especially as I have very little to go on at the moment. Apart from a few telltale black and white garden pebbles and a fibbing novelist-politician.

Maybe I should give the dead woman's iDiary a second chance.

TEN THINGS YOU SHOULD KNOW ABOUT A WORLD WHERE MOST PEOPLE HAVE FULL MEMORIES

By Mark Henry Evans

24 May 2015 | *The Sunday Times*

1. Sex in a monogamous relationship will get more and more uninteresting, causing adultery to be rife. Repetition breeds boredom, especially if people remember that they've deployed the same missionary position twenty years in a row.
2. People in long-term relationships (like, say, those in twenty-year-old partnerships) will understand why they are still together.
3. People will be divided by the color of their skin instead of the number of days they can remember.
4. Children younger than age eighteen will be a little less cocky and a little more respectful to their parents.
5. People won't have any difficulty distinguishing between fact and fiction.
6. People will be collecting experiences instead of objects, and no one will be cluttering his or her home with useless junk.
7. People will be perpetually drunk (or stoned) because they need to escape from both the present and the past.
8. People will be keeping diaries out of boredom instead of out of necessity, and Apple's market capitalization will be half of what it is now.
9. Society will dispose of people who have less than full memories by putting them in proper institutions for the demented.
10. People will understand the true meaning of love and hate.

Mark Henry Evans's novel *The Serendipity of Being* is about a murder that takes place in a darkly skewed version of contemporary

Britain where most people have full memories. The book will be published in February of 2016, priced at £11.99 in hardcover.

LETTERS TO THE EDITOR

31 May 2015 | *The Sunday Times*

Dear Editor,

Mark Henry Evans's "Ten Things You Should Know" (published on 24 May 2015) was an utter load of rubbish. The novelist is asking readers of his forthcoming novel to suspend disbelief and buy into a parallel dystopia where people have full memories. But the "high-concept" premise is so far-fetched it's ridiculous. How could a world like that exist? If people understood the "true meaning of hate" (as Mr. Evans claims), they would be killing each other without restraint. There would be world wars, terrorist attacks, megalomaniacal dictators, religious extremists, and all sorts of other horrible things. Civilization would grind to an immediate halt, crippled by its own hatred. Or humanity would simply wipe itself out in a nuclear apocalypse.

I am appalled that your newspaper would inflict such claptrap on its intelligent readership to promote a novelist's upcoming book. There are better ways of parting with £11.99. I'll be spending the money on a hardware upgrade for my iDiary.

Shame on you, Mr. Editor.

A DISGRUNTLED READER

Oxford

CHAPTER FIVE

SOPHIA

8 September 2013

It was Mariska who provided the spark. But it was a newspaper article that supplied the kindling two days later.

Front page of the newspaper's Arts and Literature section. Photo of Mark Henry Evans grinning back at me. Holding his novel *On Death's Door* at a book signing. Looking as smug as a cat that caught a rat and gulped down an entire celebratory bottle of Champagne.

That same night, I began typing away in the iDiary the orderlies gave me. It wasn't difficult. After all, I knew what being a Duo meant. The words came easily. They flowed like high-grade vodka. I recorded all dates, times, and events with determination. I wrote down all the "facts" of my miserable existence. Each and every one of them. I wrote to free myself. To redeem myself. To avenge myself. After nearly two decades of bottling up my desire for retribution.

It all came pouring out in a torrent of words.

10 September 2013

Shit happens. When you least expect it. That was the sort of shit that happened to me in 1995. When a brute-force tsunami struck. Flashback after flashback of truths once erased by sleep. Truths I tried to forget. Truths I left behind. Truths I omitted from my diaries.

Everything that happened after my twenty-third birthday just unspooled in my head. Came back in a merciless surge.

Bringing their soul-destroying burdens of guilt, fear, and regret.

Guilt. The death of my Persian cat, Catapult, three months after my twenty-third birthday. The grief as I buried my face in his fur. So soft. So velvety. Yet so devoid of life. Truth was, I'd been too lazy to write down the symptoms of his illness in my diary. Even though he had trouble breathing for days, I did not take him to the vet. That's the real reason why Catapult's heart stopped beating.

Fear. The shock of nearly being mowed down by a car on Trinity Street two weeks after my twenty-third birthday. The vehicle barreling in my direction, headlong, nose pointed at me. The sunlight glinting off its chrome fender in diabolical fashion. Tires hurtling forward with malevolent intent. The sickening screech of brakes. The helplessness on my tongue as I lay under my crumpled bicycle. The bleak, terrifying certainty that my life was about to be snuffed out by two tons of steel.

Worse, the flash of realization that I'd brought it upon myself. I only had my own stupidity to blame. I had been dense enough to ignore the one-way-street signs and cycle in the wrong direction.

Regret. My foolish breakup with Alistair six months after my twenty-third birthday. The crushing distress that flooded his eyes when I told him he deserved someone better. Truth was, I'd been seeing my ex-classmate Jack for months behind Alistair's back. The burning regret that consumed me later when I found out that Jack was in fact a two-timing jerk. I had made a big mistake about Alistair. Massive. The boy had loved me. But he had already moved on by then.

It was too late.

The staggering number of times I threw up in the loo. Minutes after eating. Eyes averted from the vomit in the bowl. So I could be as slim as Laura, whom all the guys fancied. God, I was envious of her lithe, slender figure. Her consequent ability to twirl men around her little finger, like one of the locks of hair framing her face. How they would come panting in response. Trousers practically around their ankles.

Truth was, I had omitted each and every toilet episode from my diary. Just to pretend they never happened. Flushing, then forgetting. So that I could keep throwing up. Again and again. Even after promising Dad that I would kick the habit on pain of losing my monthly allowance.

Scars I'd accumulated after my twenty-third birthday. Baggage I thought I'd shed. Lessons I failed to learn. Promises I broke. Secrets I failed to keep. Errors I kept repeating. Things I regretted. Opportunities I missed. Aches that tore my heart apart. Fears that flooded my gut. Horrors that haunted my mind. Reminders of my own stupidity that scarred my soul.

It was the sheer magnitude of those truths surging into my head. Unbidden and unwanted. Terrifying in their immediacy. Overwhelming in their volume. Crippling in their intensity.

It punctured my spirit. Turned me into an emotional wreck. I could no longer hide beneath the cloak of self-delusion. I could no longer tune out the terrible realities that swamped my mind.

I spent days wandering around in a daze.

When I realized there was comfort in forgetfulness.
But I could no longer forget.

11 September 2013

Why can't I be like the other people around me? Like the Mono housewife who lives next door with her cat and husband. Who wakes up cheerful most mornings. Ready to begin yet another page of her life. Emotionally untainted by the previous pages. Blissful in her selective ignorance.

She isn't a prisoner of her unwanted past.

Will I ever be free from bad memories? Free of the traumas clogging my mind. Swamping it. Weighing it down. Free of the baggage of memory. The burden of remembering. Free of knowing what I do not wish to know.

I tried, for a while, to pretend that everything was all right. That I was the girl I once was. Even though the girl was gone. Then I gave up. No point in keeping up the pretense, I thought. That's when I did the stupidest thing I could have ever done. I threw away all my old paper diaries, thinking I didn't need them anymore. After all, those diaries were a mocking reminder of the bliss I enjoyed after my twenty-third birthday.

I was dense enough to think that no one would notice.

Big mistake, as they say.

Huge.

Dad thought he had the right medicine for me, didn't he? The tablet of institutionalization. If he dragged me to St. Augustine's after he found my diaries in the bin, he must have interpreted my act as lunacy. My frustration as insanity.

But all I needed was sense. The understanding that I should conceal my differences from people around me.

Dad meant well, I'm sure.

But fuck him for that one-way ride to St. Augustine's. It took me seventeen years to get a return ticket.

12 September 2013

Why isn't Mark Henry Evans ringing? Yet I'm not going to be the first to call. I won't. Even though I'm tempted to feel sorry for myself. Little Miss Memory sitting in her cottage all alone.

Memory's weird, by the way. Because some recollections are getting fuzzier and fuzzier.

The problem with being able to remember everything is that you don't really remember all of it. Some memories no longer arrive as they once did. A few have even warped into elusive fragments. Wispy clouds of blurry, opaque nothingness. Indistinct bits and pieces, all blunted around their edges. Shadowy shards of darkness and light. Vapid remnants of sounds and colors.

Yet bad memories have a stubborn tendency to stick around. The god-awful ones. They refuse to travel down the fuzzy route. They creep back into my mind at the most inopportune moments. They haunt me in the middle of the night.

And that's the whole fucking problem.

But I should stop feeling sorry for myself. It's pointless to moan about old shit. It's time for a new sort of shit. It's time for *change*. From now on, I will use my memories well. To my advantage and satisfaction.

I will use them to destroy *him*.

13 September 2013

He called. Oh, yes, the mighty Mark Henry Evans finally

did. He was attending a meeting in London at three in the afternoon, he said. But he was free afterwards.

What he wanted from me was clear.

Perhaps, I said.

He had to beg. Oh, yes, he did have to beg.

Foyer of the Kandinsky a few hours later. Small boutique hotel nestled amongst the townhouses of South Kensington. Discreet entrance. Understated elegance. Pretty Polish receptionist behind the marbled front desk. Matthew and Veronica Adams, I said. She checked her computer and nodded. Room 261. Pointed me to the stairs. Plush carpet. Soft atmospheric lighting. Magnolia-scented candles.

He answered the door within ten seconds. Still in his jacket. Tie not yet undone.

So I undid it for him.

It's all going according to plan. I should be pleased by how things are developing.

At any rate, I do enjoy a good fuck now and again. It's been years. Plus he hasn't lost his touch.

I even know what I will do to him tomorrow.

It's something he will never expect.

World Wide Wishful Thinking?

Web to Improve Memory Storage and Change Lives

6 August 1991

A British scientist's creation will be one of the greatest inventions by humanity for humanity, it was claimed yesterday night.

Duo Tim Berners-Lee, 36, has announced the launch of a public memory-storage device called World Wide Web. He describes it as a means of placing and exchanging memories on an "Internet" with no central manager or database.

Berners-Lee, who works at the CERN research lab in Geneva, has created a simple coding system known as HTML (hypertext markup language). He has also worked out a set of rules called HTTP (hypertext transfer protocol) that would allow memories to be exchanged across computers. So far, this Internet has only been used by professionals and academics, but its benefits will eventually be enjoyed by everyone.

Berners-Lee has insisted that he will be taking the nonprofit route in the future development of his brainchild. "Technology is worthless unless it serves the basic human need for the transfer and retention of memories," he said.

One Duo scientist said: "This is going to be massive. The idea of strangers swapping memories on a global scale, at a simple click of a button, is staggering." But another sneered: "They said that the Segway would revolutionize transportation. Today, it is only used by lazy tourists."

CHAPTER SIX

HANS

12½ HOURS UNTIL THE END OF THE DAY

This diary is still the most ridiculous thing I've ever read. Its contents are a blatant, unsettling paradox. She claims to remember everything but *not really*. Her so-called memories tend to get fuzzier over time, she says.

How does one recollect something that's *fuzzy?* That's impossible. One either remembers—or not. One either learns facts that matter—or one doesn't. Well-learned facts spring to mind. Badly learned facts don't. It all depends on how much effort one puts into learning what one has written in one's diary. But either way, people have concrete facts in their heads—or they don't.

It's a simple matter of black and white. Just like those pebbles in the dead woman's overcoat.

I reach forward to rein in a knight.

I do not have any lingering sensorial snapshots in my head from, say, last Monday. But I know what's important. What Monday has taught me. (Fact: Most everyday experiences are mundane and are not worth remembering anyway.) I have a description of what *really* matters from Monday in my diary. In textual black and white. If I learn these facts well, I can dredge them up as readily as, say, the date Hitler shot himself in a Berlin bunker at the end of the Second World War (30 April 1945). They are as clear as my memories from before my eighteenth birthday.

In short, the words in my diaries become clear facts in my head if I learn them carefully enough.

It's as simple as that.

So how can memories be *fuzzy?*

The woman's bonkers. Which suggests that further forays into her diary may well be a waste of time.

I should perhaps check a small point she made, though. I pick up the phone on my desk.

"Hamish," I say.

"Yes?"

"Before you head to the Guildhall, ring the Kandinsky in London and find out if a Matthew Adams ever stayed in room 261. If he ever brought a female companion with him. A woman named Veronica Adams."

My sergeant-driver cruises to a stop in front of Sophia's cottage in Grantchester. I jump out as soon as the car comes to a halt. Our appearance for the second time in one morning is causing a sensation amongst the locals. Even Sophia's next-door neighbor is poking her head out for a closer look.

"Good morning," I say, striding up her garden path and presenting my identification badge. "DCI Hans Richardson of the Cambridgeshire Constabulary. Could I ask you a few questions about your neighbor Sophia Ayling?"

The woman's mouth creases with alarm.

"Please don't be worried. I'm merely conducting a routine inquiry."

She nods, though with a frown on her forehead. I suspect she's a Mono, like Claire Evans, judging from the dimness of her eyes. Fact: Twenty years of detective work have taught me that intelligence is correlated with eye clarity and focus, two attributes some Monos, unfortunately, do not have. It's a shame the lack of intelligence of a few reinforces the bigotry against the many.

"All right, then," she says. "Come on in."

I step into her living room only to be greeted by an overpowering blast of burned grease and stale cooking oil. The space is full of chintzy knick-knacks and floral-patterned furniture. A china bulldog grins down from the mantelpiece near a battered sofa with swirling patterns of forget-me-nots. A ginger-haired Persian cat throws me a suspicious glance from a corner before darting past an ornate grandfather clock.

"Your name, please?"

"Mrs. Martha Brown."

"Class?"

"Mono."

"Have you ever spoken to your neighbor Sophia Ayling?"

"Yes. But let me check my diary to be sure."

She pulls out a diary from the folds of her apron and taps its keyboard before giving me a vigorous nod.

"We've talked a few times, indeed. Usually about Rufus."

"Rufus?"

She points at the ginger-haired animal, happily sharpening its claws on the base of the clock.

"What about your cat?" I ask.

"Sophia drops by often to hand him back to me. Especially before she leaves for London. My diary says he likes sneaking inside her cottage at night. I don't know why he's taken a fancy to her. She must feed him in secret."

"Does Miss Ayling go to London often?"

Mrs. Brown studies her device for a few moments before replying:

"Yes, she spends quite a bit of time there."

"Do you know why?"

My question triggers a void on Mrs. Brown's face.

"I don't think I've...er...ever learned the reason why," she says, flapping her hands in a slight fluster. "But I'll do a keyword search for you."

As Martha Brown peers down at her device again, I find myself studying her sharp-clawed cat. Perhaps Sophia encouraged Rufus's nocturnal visits because she once had a cherished Persian cat. Her diary may not have been completely delusional.

"Inspector." Mrs. Brown interrupts my thoughts. "I've just typed the words *London* and *neighbor*. Nothing shows up, unfortunately."

"Do you know what Miss Ayling normally does in Cambridge?"

She frowns as she taps her diary again.

"It says here that Sophia is a sweet, charming neighbor." She looks up at me with earnest eyes. "Stylish clothes, not a hair out of place. She's always driving about in that Fiat of hers. But she's really secretive about her private life. I've grumbled about this to my husband before. He said that I ought to mind my own business and that I shouldn't really be sticking my nose—"

"When did Miss Ayling move in next door?"

"Let me see…October of 2013. She looked like a nice improvement from the previous occupant."

"Does she ever have visitors?"

Martha Brown's eyes are vacant. She sighs, reaching for her diary once more.

"Tried *visitor* and *neighbor*," she says a few moments later. "Nothing, I'm afraid."

"When was the last time you saw Miss Ayling?"

"Let me see…Sophia handed Rufus back to me two Fridays ago, before catching an evening train to London."

"Did you not see her more recently, then?"

"Er…I *may* have." Consternation flits across Mrs. Brown's face. "But if I did, it must have been a forgettable encounter. The sort not worthy of a diary entry. If anything, I certainly didn't see her yesterday. By the way, you've showed up twice in Grantchester this morning, Inspector. You went inside her cottage the first time you dropped by. Did something happen to her? Something bad?"

"I cannot say. Sorry. Thank you for your time."

"I hope nothing has happened to Sophia," Mrs. Brown calls out behind me as I walk out of her cottage. "She *really* is a sweet, charming thing. Even though she feeds Rufus behind my back."

Best not to reply, I think. Especially as my impressions of Sophia Ayling thus far do not fall within the "sweet, charming" category.

Sophia's heavy front door presents a stubborn challenge again, but I eventually manage to squeeze through into her living room. I'd noticed five main things when I conducted a perfunctory search of her cottage earlier this morning:

1. Her living room contained only two items of furniture: a plush red leather sofa and a lacquered coffee table. There were no paintings on the walls. No magazines on the table. No rugs on the floor. Nothing decorative whatsoever.

2. The oil painting above her bed depicted a nude blonde reclining on a Persian divan with a sultry, come-hither expression and parted legs. The blonde looked very much like Sophia herself.

3. She had placed her iDiary atop her dressing table next to a bottle of Chanel No. 5 and an English translation of the Kama Sutra. To my surprise, her diary did not require a password when I flipped it on. Neither was it fingerprint-protected. This made me wonder if she had deliberately planted it there for someone to read or if she didn't give a damn about privacy in the first place.

4. She kept a small stack of books on her bedside table. All were written by Mark Henry Evans; most had charity-shop price tags. A well-thumbed paperback copy of his novel *On Death's Door* lay on top of the pile, open at pages 44 and 45. My skim of the two pages had confirmed that Evans favors florid, over-the-top adjectives and a liberal use of active verbs.

5. There was a half-empty bottle of vodka on her kitchen counter and a small packet of raspberry-flavored Brie in her refrigerator.

This time, I study the coats hanging on the hooks behind the door. There are three in total, all made of luxurious woolen fabrics. I check their labels. Dior, Prada, and Moschino. All are size 8. This confirms my suspicions about the extra-large Aquascutum trench coat draped around the body: *it did not belong to her.*

I stoop down to examine the contents of the shoe cupboard. Fourteen pairs of killer stilettos are lined up inside, all in bold, brash colors. Blood-red Jimmy Choos with four-inch heels. Electric-blue Manolo Blahniks, just as gravity-defying. Canary-yellow Christian Louboutins, towering as high. The brand names are still legible on the soles. But Sophia was wearing a pair of flat-heeled Lanvin boots when we found her this morning. In sedate black, too. She must have put on her only pair of practical shoes before setting out from her cottage. I wonder why.

I stride into the kitchen, put on a pair of gloves, and begin opening the gleaming white cupboards one by one. Before long, I uncover a small stash of cat food in a bottom drawer. So Mrs. Brown was right about Rufus.

Next up: the bedroom. I head for the giant mahogany wardrobe in the corner and peer inside. Musky bergamot fills my nostrils; the space is crammed with clothes. I pick out a blouse and two dresses at random. Their luxurious, tactile fabrics caress my palms. I check their labels: Elie Saab, Missoni, and Alexander McQueen. All are size 6, which indicates that their owner had favored coats a size larger than her clothes. Certainly not coats of the extra-large variety.

I move over to the mahogany dressing table at the other end of the room and begin rummaging through its drawers. My search reveals the following:

1. An enormous tray of makeup items, featuring two dozen shades of scarlet lipstick and a dozen similar variations of nail varnish.
2. An impressive stash of lingerie. I'm not an expert on this particular front, but Sophia had a clear preference for fancy lace and satin intimates.

3. A drawer of sex toys, including a pair of pink Ann Summers jiggle balls, three bullet vibrators, and two Rampant Rabbits. There are also seven lace eye masks, all in black.

4. A locked wooden box measuring nine by twelve inches. I shake it. Something papery rustles inside.

5. A dusty photo album at the back of the bottom drawer. I flip through its pages to discover numerous photographs, taken in and around Cambridge, of a brunette in her early twenties. She reclines in a punt next to two delirious-looking girls in minidresses, holding a bottle of Champagne. She sprawls on the grass, head nestled in someone's lap. She waves from a bicycle outside the university library, backpack bulging with books. She angles a carving knife at a roast beef, wearing a paper crown from a Christmas cracker and a black college gown.

I recite these discoveries to my Dictaphone before settling down on the armchair next to the bed, album in hand. I study the face of the brunette in the photographs, taking in her high-bridged nose and slightly protruding ears. Her long hair, curling below her shoulders. Her flat-chested body, painfully angled and emaciated in some places. She bears little resemblance to the curvaceous blonde we extracted from the Cam this morning. But she must definitely be a younger, pre-plastic-surgery version of Sophia Ayling. Perhaps even a bulimia-fraught incarnation, as her diary implies. She is, after all, as thin as a cop's baton in these photographs.

I flip through the album once more, studying the girl's appearance. Her eyes are bright, sparkling with the dewy exuberance of youth. Her face sizzles with vivacious energy. She's grinning in many of the pictures, although the camera occasionally catches a more pensive side to her profile. Her smiles are wide, almost always reaching her eyes. It is the face of a young girl relishing her time as a student in Cambridge.

Not the look of a person who writes tortured, twisted diary entries about redemption and revenge.

But as I stare at the photo album, an insistent murmur in my head tells me that I should perhaps go over Sophia's diary again. Something drastic must have happened to her since these photos were taken. A ghastly journey that caused her cosmetically enhanced body to wash up against a tree this morning. If I hope to pin down her murderer, I ought to work out all the cryptic turns of her life's recent trajectory. And precisely how Mark Henry Evans fits into them.

I close the album with a loud snap. It's coming back with me to the police station, along with Ayling's copy of *On Death's Door*. (Fact: I read Evans's novel when it was first published in hardcover, but it's good to refresh one's mind.) Plus the tantalizing-looking wooden box, of course.

It takes Sergeant Donald Angus only thirty seconds to break the latch on Sophia's box after I get back to Parkside. He grins and gives me the thumbs-up sign before lifting its lid.

"What the hell?" he says, peering down at its contents.

He lifts a giant stack of papers out of the box and begins riffling through them. They are mostly newspaper clippings. A 144-GB memory stick occupies a corner of the box.

"She was obsessed with him," he says moments later, bushy eyebrows curling upwards.

"This we already know," I say, peering over his shoulder and realizing that the articles are arranged in chronological order. The first piece is from the Arts and Literature section of the *Times*, dated 17 January 2012. It is accompanied by a photograph of Mark Henry Evans at a book signing. His wife, Claire, is hovering behind him, her face a little blurred. ON DEATH'S DOOR TOPS THE NEW YORK TIMES BESTSELLER LIST, the headline says. The subhead reads: PROVING THAT AUTHORS CAN GET AWAY WITH NOVELS THAT TAKE AT LEAST FOUR HOURS TO READ.

Sophia mentioned in her diary that she saw Mark Evans grinning from the pages of a newspaper.

"But why?" asks Donald, frowning.

"This I do not know." I shake my head.

"Maybe Evans was telling us the truth."

I shrug.

"I didn't realize the man has such lofty aspirations," he says moments later, waving another clipping at me. I catch the headline before Donald returns it to the pile. It states: DUO AUTHOR WITH MONO WIFE EYES SOUTH CAMBRIDGESHIRE SEAT. The article features a photograph of Mark Henry Evans at a political convention, his wife hanging on to his arm. The subhead is a rhetorical question: ARE INDEPENDENT CANDIDATES FINALLY HAVING THEIR DAY IN THE SUN?

"Hmm…" I say as a possibility strikes me. "Could we have a look at the last article in the pile, please?"

Donald riffles through to the final clipping, dated only six days ago. It features a photograph of a blue-eyed blonde frolicking on a yacht with a hairy-chested male companion. The accompanying headline screams: NOT A TAXING DECISION: JUSTIN AND CHANTELLE TO WED SOON.

I snatch the *Daily Mail* article from Donald's hands. It reads:

Justin Winward, Britain's most eligible Duo singer-songwriter, will wed Mono model Chantelle Huston in September. Friends close to the couple say that Winward presented the blond bombshell with a four-carat diamond ring after his sellout concert at the O2 Arena last night.

This will be Winward's second marriage after divorcing Duo actress Gwyneth Langley last October. The singer-songwriter, 32, is number 137 on *Forbes*'s list of the richest men in Britain, with an estimated net worth of £75 million. Huston, 22, first shot to fame in *Big Brother* two years ago, and is known for her 36DD cups and her onscreen fling with the footballer Harold Dwight.

This high-profile Mono-Duo pairing has delighted supporters of the Mixed Marriage Act, due for royal assent on Friday. "Mixed unions work," says the Duo novelist Mark Henry Evans, an independent MP candidate for South Cambridgeshire. "My

Mono wife, Claire, and I have been together for twenty years. Justin and Chantelle have every chance of succeeding as a married couple."

But one of Winward's close Duo friends, who declined to be named, hinted that the singer-songwriter is aware of the generous tax breaks promised to those entering Mono-Duo unions. "Justin's shrewd," he says. "He knows a thing or two about taxes and realities. Those 36DD cups will not blind him to the importance of a prenuptial agreement."

I look up at Donald and chuckle; something has just clicked in my head.

"Sophia Ayling was obsessed with Mark Evans," I say. "But she became equally preoccupied by someone else. A woman who had all the physical attributes she lacked during her younger days. Blond hair, blue eyes, and large boobs."

"Who?" Donald lifts an eyebrow.

I smile before replying.

"Claire Evans."

THE ECONOMIST

Apple Unveils the iDiary

27 January 1998 | San Francisco

Steve Jobs, the CEO of Apple, is a scrupulous diary writer. He also has a reputation for claiming to go where no Duo has gone before. At last week's launch of the iDiary, Apple's latest portable creation, he did not disappoint.

In his presentation, Mr. Jobs made his views of the iDiary's world-historical significance clear. Paper-and-ink diaries are the last bastions of the analog era, he said, and diaries are now entering the electronic age.

This is what Jobs hopes to achieve with his iDiary. It measures six inches (15.24 centimeters) diagonally and weighs just twenty-five ounces (0.7 kilograms). It features a touch screen and a full keyboard with a thumbwheel. It has an LED indicator that flashes electric purple each morning to remind users to learn the previous nights' entries. Its software includes a nifty search function (thereby making it easier to retrieve facts), a to-do list, a daily planner, and an appointments calendar. Entries may be edited or erased with ease. The device is priced at £79 for the basic version and £99 for one with literally more memory, thus bringing it within the reach of the masses.

But the security features of the iDiary are perhaps its unique selling point. It self-locks after two minutes of inactivity and only unlocks upon recognizing the fingerprint of its user. Users may also deploy an additional layer of password protection. After several high-profile diary thefts over the past year, Apple's investors are salivating over the iDiary's market potential. Within three days of the device's launch, the company's share price reached an all-time high.

Chapter Seven

CLAIRE

I cannot lose my head. I mustn't. Even though my husband has been led away by the police for questioning, I'm certain he didn't kill Sophia Ayling. Fact: Mark's not one to harm others. He's the sort of man who winces at violence. He closes his eyes at fight sequences in Quentin Tarantino movies (despite what Mark thinks of me, I *am* good at learning the small random facts I've written in my diaries).

But he definitely slept with *her*.

I stare down at my hands. They look grubby after the gardening I've done. They also seem helpless. They are the hands of a woman who has always remained in the dutiful, colorless background while her husband does bold and brash things. Like selling books by the million and running for Parliament.

Having affairs.

So Mark Henry Evans, the man who promised me in the Trinity chapel that he would love and cherish me to the exclusion of all others, has been cheating on me. That's why he's been spending those weekends away from Cambridge. Fact: He said he had to attend work-related events in London. He even took me along to a few book signings and charity galas. But he was just using me as window dressing.

I'm not stupid. I'm capable of reading between the lines. If Mark can write, I can read.

The bits between the lines say that Mark is a shameless, conniving cheat. A liar who has no compunction about betraying the woman who has shared his bed for twenty years. A Lothario who takes advantage of the bitches who hang on to his every word. I've seen them over the years. I've learned the facts about their existence. They flock to his book readings with adoring eyes. They wait in endless queues for his autograph. They giggle around him like gaggles of excitable geese.

If Mark had an affair with Sophia Ayling, he could have easily slept with several other women over the past twenty years. While I stayed at home, clearing dead leaves from the garden path.

I grab the rake propped alongside the shed and fling it into the distance. It hits a nearby flowerpot with a loud, satisfying thud before clanging onto the ground.

The rattle jars my teeth.

I will not cry. Even though I'm tempted to do so. Even though Mark's unfaithfulness is a figurative slap in the face. A blow to my pride, to my self-worth as a wife and a woman.

But there are no excuses for infidelity. None at all.

How did it ever come to this? I thought that Mark was a faithful husband, despite the flaws and inequalities in our mixed marriage. I'd assumed his political aspirations would prevent him from straying. It doesn't take a genius to work out what will happen to his MP campaign if the press discovers he has been sleeping around.

I stumble up the garden path and let myself into the conservatory. My prized gardenias perfume the air, mingling with the sweetness of queen of the night. The combination triggers a sudden, nauseating lurch in my stomach. Nettle scampers up, greeting me with a wet lick. I pat his ears before slumping onto a nearby chair, next to a cockleshell orchid with two yellowing flowers that must have wilted overnight.

I wrench them off the plant and scrunch them in my hand.

A little voice pipes up in my head. It says that I should have worked harder to *understand* the facts about our marriage instead of just learning them by rote. Why our relationship has become more practical than passionate. More functional than fervid. Why Mark and I last had sex more than two years ago. Why he has stayed away from me since. Why there isn't a child in our lives.

I'm no longer as beautiful as I once was. Twenty years of marriage equals twenty years of aging. Twenty years of cumulative crow's-feet. Twenty years of aggregated skin sagging. Twenty years of the grievous effects of gravity. I shall not even think about the fact that I've put on a whopping three stone and two pounds since my father walked me down the aisle, delirious that his eldest daughter was marrying above her class.

But did Mark ever love me? Was he in love with me when we first met, for instance? Or was it merely a factual illusion on my part? He must have been, otherwise he would not have married me in the autumn of 1995. But perhaps I've always deluded myself by interpreting the facts incorrectly.

Irrational as it may be, I'm consumed by a sudden desire to understand. To work out how and when our relationship went wrong. Did we ever get it right in the first place? Or was our marriage merely a sham from the start?

I rise from the chair and hurry down the hallway. Fact: Before the iDiary was invented, in 1998, I'd accumulated a large stack of paper-and-ink diaries. They are now in an enormous safe in the storage room. I flick the light on and walk over to the safe. Fact: The code is 8412. I key in the number. A green light flashes in response.

I yank the door open and peer at the rows of diaries inside. Fact: I used to write a lot when I was younger, especially right after I turned eighteen. Much more than I do these days. Fairly descriptive stuff, too. It could be a result of the comparative verbosity of youth, as I'm now relatively sparing with words. Or it could be caused by my initial desperation to record *everything* for fear of missing something important. That was before wisdom born of age (and jaded realization) kicked in: I don't need to put it all down because most everyday experiences are pretty trivial anyway.

Fact: Mark and I first met on 26 May 1995. I pull out the volume marked "May–August 1995" and turn its pages to that date:

17:35: Arrived at Varsity Blues to receive serious ticking-off from Jenkins for being late. Emily threw me sympathetic look afterwards (NTS: Must not arrive late again as could lose job). Survived first ninety minutes of service without major mishaps, though I did bring a customer Coke instead of Diet Coke (NTS: Must grab empty plates on way out each time, as per Emily's "full hands in, full hands out" advice).

Was thinking I was finally getting the hang of waitressing when man walked in at 20:17 with redhead on arm. Emily showed them to table. Went over a few minutes later to take orders. He looked up from menu and smiled. Don't know what came over me as pen and notepad fell from hands. Was it his smile? Or his clean-cut looks and floppy bangs? Didn't have time to figure out answers as pen bounced off table and landed on girl's lap, spraying ink across skirt. Gasped apology before grabbing napkin to blot splotches. Ink merely expanded on fabric, prompting her to shriek. Things got worse. Jenkins appeared at side and began yelling head off, while redhead grabbed handbag and stormed out of restaurant with more curses.

Man, however, remained in seat. I turned to him and said first thing that came to mind: I would personally pay for his dinner if he still wanted it (which, in hindsight, would have cost more than daily pay of £12.75). Man smiled and said he wanted small glass of Bordeaux. This placated Jenkins, who retreated to counter with purple face while I scurried off to get order. Brought full 0.75L carafe and basket of bread, face similar shade to wine, before apologizing again and hurrying away.

He lingered at table for twenty minutes or so. Felt his eyes studying me with interest as I bustled up and down. He left when I was in the kitchen. Moved over to clear table afterwards. Discovered £20 note tucked beneath glass, even though wine cost £3.80. Also saw scribbled note on napkin:

"What an evening. I should reciprocate the excitement. Emily tells me that Monday's your day off. I'll be waiting at the Hotel du Vin restaurant on Monday (29 May), from 19:30 onwards. Mark Henry Evans."

Spent rest of service in daze before slinking home at 23:45. Jenkins dispensed long parting glare (and only gave me £11.20 of Mark's tip after docking £5 for "appalling clumsiness"). Am not sure how to respond to dinner invitation (NTS: Should perhaps consider buying new dress on Monday morning).

A disconcerting thought strikes me. Was Mark merely amused by my blistering ineptitude? An amusement that gradually turned to weary contempt over twenty years of marriage? I didn't write that he had smitten eyes that evening. His eyes, if anything, merely studied me "with interest."

Perhaps I should consult that Monday's entry, too. To confirm my suspicions that I've merely been fooling myself over the years. Reading more than I should into facts, especially those that brought us together in the first place.

Taking a deep breath, I flip a couple of pages:

05:41: Woke up covered in sweat. Terrible dream featuring Jenkins and his loud snarl, saying I'll always be useless. Glad I didn't have to go into Varsity Blues today. Jenkins must have really crept under skin if I've started dreaming about him. . . .

19:35: Showed up at du Vin as per Emily's advice that women should be fashionably late for dates by five minutes, feeling self-conscious in new dress and heels (Mum was beside herself and insisted on matching shoes when I rang to say that man had asked me out). Maître-d' showed me to table where Mark was waiting with dozen roses (half were pink, rest were white). Dashing gray shirt with starched collar, top two buttons undone. Smelled of expensive cologne. Thanked me for coming and gave me flowers before lowering eyes to cleavage (NTS: Should buy another figure-hugging, low-cut cocktail dress with next paycheck).

Began apologizing again, but he lifted finger to lips. Said I did him a favor, as he found redhead's attentions "asphyxiatingly cloying." Wasn't sure what he meant, but gathered he wasn't too upset with me. Maître-d' poured Champagne (noticed bottle was labeled Krug Grande Cuvée 1977, which sounded grand) and presented us with menus. Gulped when saw prices, which averaged between £20 and £25 for entrées. Asked for pork belly, cheapest I could see. Mark ordered lobster tail before raising toast to "memorable first meeting," smiling as he clinked my glass.

Found out various facts about him over dinner: Duo (had to gulp) junior research fellow in English literature at Trinity. Finished undergraduate and postgraduate degrees at same college before twenty-third birthday. Tempted to quit academia and hopes to be a writer of some distinction one day. Though the dozen short stories he has written remain unpublished, and he has unsuccessfully submitted them to the *Times*'s £30,000 short-story competition for six years running. Felt sorry for him because I know what it means not to get anywhere. Only son of industrialist who owns Ainsley Manor in Buckinghamshire. Dad hopes Mark will take over family business, but he hasn't the slightest interest. In turn, admitted that VB was my second job since leaving high school after longish stint as apprentice hairdresser. Didn't say I'm Mono, but I'm sure he figured that out.

Worked up the courage to ask him why he invited me to dinner. He looked straight into my eyes and said I was the most beautiful woman he'd ever met. His heart even skipped couple of beats when I came to take his order. A charmer, all right. He definitely has a way with words. So Mark fell in love with me at first sight. Should be flattered.

It's strange how a diary entry can take on such different connotations twenty years later. I'd interpreted Mark's words that fateful evening as proof that he fell in love with me at first sight. At least the younger version of Claire wanted to believe this, even learning this assumption as fact. But nineteen-year-old Claire was a romantic, soppy young idiot. These weary, thirty-nine-year-old eyes now see something different.

It was more lust than love. Mark had never loved me, not even from the start. He'd merely wanted to seduce me, as he thought that I was the "most beautiful woman he'd ever met." That's what he *really* said to me that evening. And I read more into his words than I should have.

I force a couple of tears back and turn to the entry dated 2 June 1995:

22:05: Finished dinner. Foie gras amazing; beluga caviar even better. Mark's world dazzles me. One can develop a taste for these things. Three flutes of Champagne ringing in head as we stumbled out of Midsummer House, twenty-four pink and white roses filling up arms. He invited me back to Trinity room for nightcap, promising to walk me back afterwards. I hesitated. Right then, he gave me another of those smiles. So I said yes. Getting me past porters proved tricky, but Mark soon found unlocked side door. Whisked me to room overlooking dark grassy quadrangle, complete with giant fireplace. Handed me full glass of port, which caused head to spin further.

Next thing I knew, he began kissing me on lips. He'd kissed me before we parted ways yesterday night, but it was a chaste peck, though lingering. This kiss was different. It was urgent, even forceful. He began tugging away at zip on dress. Tried to lift restraining hand, but it was a limb muddled by Champagne and port. Before long, dress and bra had vanished, and he had transferred attention to nipples. Felt brief surge of alarm. But it felt so good. So right. After all, Mark was a gentleman. Not one of those scruffy lads hanging around neighborhood where I grew up. His hands began moving downwards; last piece of cloth on body slid off moments later. Began to feel anxious, as I'd learned from somewhere that it tends to hurt the first time. Tried to push him away, but hands failed to convince even myself.

Then it happened. A sharp tearing pain, followed by general discomfort. But he was gentle, and it was all over in matter of minutes. Can't say I enjoyed it too much, but I suppose it will be better next time. He grunted, rolled off my body, wedged himself under duvet, and began snoring. Not knowing what to do, I studied his profile for several minutes, sore and perplexed. Eventually crept out of bed, put dress back on, and stole out of room at 23:35, leaving roses behind. Thankfully, I did not meet any porters during scamper across quadrangle to side door. The crisp night air and brisk walk back to lodgings in Mill Road helped clear head. Heard Mrs. Perkins stirring as I crept inside at 23:55, but otherwise disturbed no one.

What have I gotten myself into? Mark's Duo, for God's sake. Monos and Duos have no future together. But Mum and Dad will adore Mark if they meet him. Looking forward to his phone call tomorrow, at any rate. He did mention over dinner that he would love to take me to Norfolk this weekend in his Jaguar, for picnic on coastal dunes with large bottle of vintage Bollinger from his dad's cellar.

My tears are in free-flow mode, as I now understand what happened over the days that followed. I flip the pages to my 3 June entry:

04:22: Woke up with racing pulse and sweaty palms. Horrible dream involving Jenkins with purple face. Yelling at me from behind counter, saying I'm useless and pathetic. My entry for 29 May says I've had similar dream before. Awful . . .

22:45: Mark did not call today in the end. But am sure he will call tomorrow regarding Norfolk. Weather forecast for Sunday looks amazing: 28°C and sunny. Am picturing us walking hand in hand along pebbled beach with rustic picnic basket.

My entry for 4 June reads:

21:15: Phone still has not rung. Hopes of picnicking on Norfolk coast under sunny blue skies long evaporated. Still wondering what has happened to Mark. (NTS: Should call him tomorrow. After all, something bad may have happened.)

And I now understand why Mark behaved the way he did when I phoned him on 5 June:

18:04: Called Mark on Mrs. Perkins's phone before cycling over to VB. Said he was sorry he did not call during the weekend; had to attend to urgent family matter. Sounded distant, even preoccupied. Said he had to go. Placed receiver down feeling confused. Suppose I should be relieved nothing bad has happened to him. . . .

I flip a few more pages of my diary, scanning their contents. They confirm my growing suspicion about those early days of our relationship: Mark had pursued me with vigor right up to the night we had sex in his Trinity room, only to lose interest in me afterwards. He did not phone again to invite me to a picnic. Or dinner, for that matter. In fact, he did not ring at all.

Truth I'd failed to see: Mark merely wanted to have sex with me, a once attractive nineteen-year-old virgin.

Nothing more.

Which explains why I spotted him a few days later with another girl. My diary says so, in plain factual terms. Perhaps I should reacquaint myself with what occurred that evening, now that I'm finally realizing the truth about his early behavior.

Using a sleeve to dab my eyes, I turn to the entry dated 12 June 1995:

18:30: First two hours of VB service quiet. Emily said it was because May Balls were taking place at Trinity, Jesus, and Claire.

21:32: Showed customers to seats by window. To my horror, saw Mark walking along pavement across road, wearing white tie and holding hand of girl in stunning peach dress and white gloves. They were clearly going to a ball, probably Trinity. Gaped for several moments before hurrying to Emily and begging her to cover for me (Jenkins was, thankfully, distracted by customer). Shot out of VB only to discover that Mark and girl had vanished from sight. Was determined to confront Mark, so began running in direction they were heading. Failed to spot them along Chesterton Road; backtracked after realizing they could have crossed footbridge over Jesus Lock.

Eventually spotted them on footpath alongside river. Began running in their direction, itching to yell at Mark. But girl stepped forward and did exactly what I wanted to do: she pulled off glove and slapped Mark in face. Raised hand to hit him again only to lose balance. Reeled backwards over stilettos, smashing head on nearby lamppost and hitting ground in tangle of limbs and fabric. Staggered back to knees and tried to slap Mark again, though more feebly this time.

Wondered if I should join girl in attacking Mark. But I told myself he had gotten what he deserved, and Jenkins would sack me if I abandoned duties for too long. Turned and began walking back to VB, but soon felt another hot surge of anger. Pushing Jenkins out of head, did abrupt U-turn on Chesterton Road and ran across bridge again. By then, Mark and girl had vanished from Jesus Green. Was sure they were farther ahead, so continued running along riverside path. Eventually spotted Mark on Magdalene Street. He was alone. Girl in peach dress had vanished

I turn the page and freeze. The subsequent sheets are gone. Only thin strips of paper remain at the diary's spine. The rest have been cleaved away neatly, probably with a blade or a penknife.

My tears have evaporated. I run a trembling finger along the strips of paper. Bafflement mingled with disbelief prompts me to count them: twelve in total. The next diary entry begins a whopping thirteen days later, on 25 June. I must have removed those pages at some point in the past.

But why?

My entry for 25 June might explain why the preceding pages have vanished. I scan the passage with eager eyes:

05:50: Drenched sheets, thanks to dream-version Jenkins and his insults. ("You're useless, Claire. Pathetic.") Struggled to go back to sleep. Checked earlier entries here: I've had this dream four times since I started work at VB. Jenkins is pursuing me both day and night. Am tempted to quit job. But he pays better than Hair & Beauty Solutions.

10:30: Woke up from troubled, post-Jenkins half sleep. A dull, sinking feeling pinned me to bed, so just lay there and stared at spidery cracks on ceiling.

12:30: Decided I should listen to Emily. Hauled myself up from bed and rang Bridge Street Medical Center. Managed to get appointment with GP Arthur Devine at 11:00 on 29 June. (NTS: Should tell Dr. Devine that a black, bottomless hole has swallowed me, that I struggled to fall asleep last night, and that I have terrible, suffocating pains in chest. But I shouldn't tell him that my mind strayed to tempting possibilities offered by Mrs. Perkins's kitchen knife yesterday, before I set out for VB.)

21:58: Dropped wineglass on floor during service. Jenkins snarled and said he will dock cost from next paycheck, adding the two plates I broke yesterday (NTS: Should be careful over next few weeks, otherwise there will be nothing left of salary).

22:53: Stepped out of VB to discover Mark waiting outside with yet another bouquet of roses. After week of ignoring his miserable presence (he did, after all, wait outside for seven consecutive nights with ever-expanding bouquets), I felt sudden twinge of sympathy for him. Perhaps he's really sorry. . . .

The entry suggests that I spiraled into terrible depression after discovering that Mark had been two-timing me with another girl. This prompted me to seek medical help. My depression might have also caused me to do something stupid, like cut out twelve pages from my own diary.

Yet all is not lost as far as these missing pages are concerned. Fact: I'm good at learning my diaries. I spend more time learning their contents than my husband does (I pore over my iDiary each morning, while Mark only gives his device a perfunctory glance; his Duo arrogance blinds him to the fact that he puts in less effort than I do). I should have faith in the facts that persist in my head.

To test myself, I scrunch my eyes shut in an attempt to dredge up some facts I've learned about that twelve-day period. This is what happened on the night of the Trinity ball, soon after I found Mark on his own along Magdalene Street:

"Mark!" I called out behind him.

He froze in his tracks before turning around. As soon as he realized it was me, his shoulders went rigid.

"What are you doing here?" he said.

"I saw you earlier," I said, advancing towards him. "Holding her hand."

Mark's mouth fell open at that point. I noticed that his white bow tie was loose after his scuffle with the girl.

"I saw everything on Jesus Green." My words tumbled out in a torrent. "Everything. You're sleeping with her, aren't you? I thought we were seeing each other."

"I can . . . explain . . ."

"You've been stringing me along. With your roses. Your sugary words. Your lies. Well, you can go to hell, Mark. I don't want to see you ever again."

With that, I turned around and stomped back in the direction of Varsity Blues.

He made no attempt to follow me. Or apologize. Or plead with me to reconsider, for that matter.

And this is what happened on 24 June, the evening before I called Bridge Street Medical Center:

Emily came up to me before I left VB, a deep frown of concern shading her forehead.

"You haven't been yourself recently," she said.

"I'm fine."

"No, Claire. You're not. I can see it in your face and in the way you've been acting."

"You're imagining it."

"You broke two plates earlier. You told Jenkins you were careless. But I saw you sobbing just before you dropped those plates."

"We all have bad days from time to time. Isn't this a fact?"

"I'm still seventeen. I remember small details you may have left out of your diary. Like the way you come in here each day with your eyes fixed on the ground, as if you're hoping it might swallow you up. Trust me, sweetie. You haven't been well over the past two weeks."

I couldn't think of a suitable response.

"You ought to see your GP. He might give you some pills that will make you feel better."

"I don't need a doctor."

"Just think about it, will you?" She patted my shoulder before pointing to the door of the restaurant. "The Duo's waiting outside with more roses, by the way. I can't believe he's been standing there at closing time for a whole week now, with bouquets that get larger and larger each time. Maybe you should listen to what he has to say."

Emily was right. I stepped out of VB to discover that Mark was standing outside with a giant bouquet of crimson roses in his hands.

"I'm sorry, Claire," he said.

I wondered if I should listen to Emily. But I decided to elbow him away before jumping onto my bicycle and pedaling off.

I should be pleased that some facts I've learned about 24 June are still in my head; I must have worked hard to learn these fragments from my diary. I don't really need those twelve missing pages, do I? But are there any other facts from that period that I should be reevaluating today in light of what has happened? Facts that will confirm my growing suspicion that love was never in the equation for Mark and that lust drove our relationship at the start?

I freeze.

There are *no* other facts from that twelve-day period inside my head.

I force my eyes shut, struggling to draw up something. Anything at all. But there's only a dark void within me. I get up and pace the room with a growing sense of desperation, trying to haul up some relevant facts. But much of the period remains a gnawing blank. I can't summon any details about what happened the day following the Trinity ball, after I stalked away from Mark in a fury. Nor am I able to dredge up any more facts from the days that followed. It's as if they never occurred. They've become a gaping vacuum, a black hole within my past.

I must have made little effort—or no effort whatsoever—to learn the contents of those pages before chopping them out. I must have become *seriously* depressed after the night of the Trinity ball if I decided not to learn twelve days' worth of facts. To make things worse, I've vandalized my own diary. Now I know what happens when I don't learn my entries: it feels as if I've erased a part of myself.

Part of my mind, perhaps even part of my soul.

I wonder what I did with those missing pages. I could have flung them into the fireplace and watched them burn. But there may well be other written records spanning the period of 13 to 24 June in this house.

A door slams in the distance. I hear feet shuffling in the hallway outside. I shove my diary back into the safe before keying in the numbers 8412 again. The green indicator light flashes in response.

It's time to confront my husband. That lying spouse of mine.

The path to political stardom is littered with the bodies of those who failed to get their spin right. Ignore this fact at your peril.

  —Rowan Redford, *Spin Your Way to Success*

CHAPTER EIGHT

MARK

I let myself in through the front door with a sigh. Fact: I've written about police interrogations in my novels. But the real thing was more unpleasant than anything I could have ever imagined. After twenty-seven minutes of verbal skewering by a bellicose bulldog, I'm in desperate need of a mug of hot tea.

Especially because my nerves are still jangling from the way the interview ended. I'd terminated the conversation soon after Richardson's outburst about Virginia Woolf, stating that I had to go. Richardson had checked Sergeant Angus's typed statement before shoving it into my hands. The opening and closing paragraphs made me wince:

WITNESS STATEMENT

CJ Act 1967, § 9; MC Act 1980, §§ 5A(3)(a), 5B; Criminal
    Procedure Rules 2005, 27.1
Statement of: Mark Henry Evans
Date: 6 June 2015
Occupation: Novelist
Class: Duo

I have been married for twenty years. I do not have any children. Sophia Ayling approached me after my talk in York and said she loved my novels. She had been apparently reading them for years and hoped her unpublished manuscript would be just as successful. She said she was crazy about me. I said I was flattered. She invited me to dinner. I refused because I do not accept invitations from every people I meet at writer's conferences, even if they are beautiful blonds....

I stayed in Thursday. I spent most of the day writing in my study. I then dealt with e-mails in the afternoon. I did not leave my home. I was on the phone in the late afternoon, to my agent Camilla and my campaign manager Rowan. During the evening, I fell asleep in front of the television in my study. On Wednesday, I spent the morning writing. I then had lunch before speaking on the phone with Camilla and Rowan. I dealt with e-mails and other nuissances in the afternoon before spending the evening in front of the television.

*Signature:*_____

"I can't sign this," I said, waving the sheet of paper at Richardson and putting the pen down on his desk. "There are too many errors in it."

"What sort of errors?" Richardson said, narrowing his eyes at me.

"Grammatical ones, mainly. Spelling, too. *Nuisances* should be spelled with one *s*. The apostrophe's in the wrong place."

Angus's bushy eyebrows twisted upwards, causing him to acquire the expression of an injured caterpillar. I doubt if anyone had ever criticized the position of the sergeant's apostrophes before.

"Ah." Richardson sighed. "I should have known. Literary sorts have a tendency to be pedantic."

"While policemen can't write for toffee."

"Actually, we policemen are quite capable of stringing sentences together. But grammatical errors aside, you should sign the statement if it reflects the truth. And you *did* tell us the truth earlier, didn't you?"

I remained silent.

"Oh, dear. Surely you haven't been lying to us, Mr. Evans. Is this the *real* reason why you aren't signing?"

I grabbed a fountain pen and scrawled my name on the statement before stomping out of the detective's office.

But I'm not the only person marching down corridors today; I hear determined footsteps just a few yards away. I turn around. Claire has emerged into the hallway and is staring at me. Her arms are folded. Her nose is wrinkled, as if something disgusting has just walked in.

"You slept with her, didn't you?"

Her question is more of a statement. It slices through the air between us.

I remain silent. A sudden weariness descends on my shoulders. Pulling off my jacket, I fling it onto the back of a chair before heading into the kitchen. Claire follows me. Although I dare not meet her eyes, I can feel them burning my back.

I flip the kettle on and pull out a mug from an upper cupboard.

"You lied to me."

She plants herself next to the kitchen counter, blocking my way to the tea bags.

"You said you had work to do in London. Turns out your work was sex."

I flinch.

"Your imagination's running wild. Sophia was a crazed fan who made things up. She spent seventeen years in a lunatic asylum. Even Richardson called her diary a 'raging river of semiconsciousness.'"

Claire snorts.

"I can't believe you're still lying to me," she says, eyes flashing red. "You're a *cheat*. A man who sleeps around while telling the world we've been happily married for years."

I'm unable to think of a suitable reply.

"You are a cheat, Mark."

The cereal bowl she had used earlier this morning whizzes across the kitchen. It smashes into a cupboard a few yards away with an almighty crash, splintering into a dozen shards. One of them bounces off my shoe. Nettle springs up from the tiled floor, his bark a terrified yowl.

"*You're—*"

"Claire." I raise my hands, desperate to placate her. She's trembling with the force of her fury, her fingers balled into fists.

"Claire." My voice is a shrill plea. "Just calm—"

"*You're in deep shit.*"

She's absolutely right. Although Richardson has permitted me to return home, I have a feeling the pugnacious detective remains determined to lock me up in a cell at the back of his station.

"And you're going to be in deeper shit soon, as far as your political career is concerned," Claire continues, dropping her voice to a sudden whisper. It merely makes her words twice as menacing.

She throws me a twisted smile, one I never expected her to be capable of. There's murder in her eyes, the sort of expression one associates with a wronged woman.

"I want a divorce," she says.

I rub my eyes before swallowing the rest of the cold tea in my mug. It tastes tannic, even bitter, on my tongue. Claire's words are still pounding in my ears. She has vanished upstairs, slamming the bedroom door in triumph. I'm tempted to run up and reason with her. With luck, she can be convinced of the folly of her decision. She surely needs me more than I need her in light of what has happened today. In the meantime, I'll have to make sure the press does not hear about my recent visit to Parkside station.

The press. Bloody hell.

I've forgotten about my noontime press conference at the Guildhall. Shit.

On cue, my mobile phone begins to ring. With a groan, I pull it out of my pocket. I already know who's calling.

"Where the hell are you, Mark?" Desperation overwhelms Rowan's gruff voice.

"Sorry, I've been held up at—"

"Get your ass over here at once, you dolt. It's already two minutes past twelve."

I rush into the pink marble foyer of the Guildhall with my briefcase, twenty minutes late for my own press conference. My undignified canter across windswept Market Square has, thankfully, restored a few brain functions. I pat my bangs down, wishing I'd smeared some gel onto them before setting out from home. But I barely had time to put on a suit.

Rowan is mincing about at the bottom of the stairs, next to a wooden statue of a melancholic-looking sea horse. His forehead is folded in deep troughs.

"Sorry, Rowan—"

"Count yourself lucky they're still waiting upstairs," he says, giving me a vicious glare. "There's quite a few of them. The *Times*, *Daily Telegraph*, and *Independent*. BBC and ITV. Even that poodle from the *Daily Mail*. The one who keeps writing op-eds about her four ex-husbands, as my diary says. Try not to antagonize her if you can. I'm surprised there's so much interest. But all publicity's good publicity, and I've already handed out copies of your statement."

Rowan's making me nervous.

"Be contrite about arriving late." He shakes his forefinger at me. "Be polite. Be serious but not pompous. Say you'll make an amazing MP. Don't screw up. Don't fucking screw up."

I give him a meek nod as he shepherds me up the stairs and down a corridor. He flings a door open. I plaster a smile onto my face and stride to the front of the wood-paneled room, Rowan trailing in my wake. Three microphones are perched on a stand, two of them labeled "BBC" and "ITV."

"I'm sorry to have kept you waiting," I say in my most apologetic voice. "Rowan's given you my statement. I'll be delighted to answer any questions you may have."

Hands are shooting up everywhere in the room. I decide on a balding man in the back row, who looks harmless.

"BBC," he says. "How do you feel about the successful passage of the Mixed Marriage Act, Mr. Evans?"

"Delighted, of course." My mouth creases into a wide smile. "Especially after throwing my weight behind the campaign and getting lots of support from the fans of my books. I'll be working just as hard for South Cambridgeshire if elected as MP."

Time to move on. I point to a woman with horn-rimmed glasses seated in the middle of the room.

"Diane Tate, *Daily Telegraph*," she says. "Yesterday's royal assent has not dampened the rumblings of Mono discontent in this country. What about the true economic costs of the act? Many are still convinced that the government will be taxing our hardworking Mono masses and enriching Duos even further. You're in a mixed union yourself, Mr. Evans. You'll gain financially from the act. Is this the *real* reason why you've acted as a poster boy for the mixed-marriage campaign?"

Muted titters erupt in the room.

"Thank you, Diane." I smile at her. "The advantages of the act have already been debated at length in Parliament. I'll reiterate the main conclusion: the act bodes well for Britain's productivity in the long term. I believe in supporting what's best for our country. I'll benefit from the tax breaks, of course. But so will my Mono wife, Claire. Mixed marriages benefit *both* Monos and Duos. Some twenty thousand Mono citizens will begin enjoying these rebates over the next fifteen years if the act's a success."

Tate rolls her eyes. I brace myself for another onslaught.

"*Success.*" She emits a derisive snort, getting up to her feet. "Social barriers between Monos and Duos will not come tumbling down overnight, even if the government has managed to rush an ill-conceived act through Parliament. Did your parents attend your wedding, Mr. Evans?"

Damn.

"No," I say with a shrug, deciding to tell the truth. "But my diary says that Claire's parents were present. Her father gave her away with joy on his face. You're right about existing social barriers, Diane. We are all products of our own prejudices. These barriers constrain the progress of our society. But they will only be demolished if we attempt to break them down in the first place. The act's a step in the right direction."

Rowan gives me a surreptitious poke in the back, urging me to move on at once. I pick out a bearded man in the third row, clad in a lightning-blue turtleneck sweater.

"*Cambridge Evening News,*" he says. "Your statement suggests you'll campaign for the mixed children of South Cambridgeshire if elected. What do you hope to achieve?"

Thank God for a benign question. Time for another stock answer, prepared and learned with Rowan's help.

"The 2011 census shows that Cambridge, like London and Oxford, is home to a large number of mixed couples," I say. "Cambridge also has a high number of mixed-marriage children. A recent study suggests that these youngsters, even Mono ones, tend to achieve higher grades at school and are more likely to go to university. Mixed marriages work in all sorts of wonderful, unexpected ways. If elected, I'll campaign for tuition rebates to be granted to these children. They deserve all the help they can get."

A woman with dangling tortoiseshell earrings flings her hand up from the second row. I nod at her.

"Mr. Evans," she says, not bothering to introduce herself. "Does your wife, Claire, work?"

What an odd question.

"No," I say. "She doesn't."

"You said she'll benefit from the tax breaks. But she doesn't work."

Dear God. She must be a Mono. Fact: Dim-witted, myopic people have a tendency to get on my nerves, especially when they become fixated on the irrelevant. But I should be correct in my reply.

"You're right," I say. "Claire isn't a taxpayer at present. But she may go into business someday. If she does, she'll be among the numerous Monos benefiting from the promised tax breaks."

Even though the only business Claire intends to go into at present is the business of divorce, I suppose a white lie or two does not hurt. Rowan gives me a sharp nudge to indicate that I should move on. He's definitely capable of recognizing a lame answer when he hears one.

A woman with cherry-colored lips and a bubble-gum-pink scarf around her neck waves at me. I point at her.

"*Daily Mail,*" Rowan hisses into my ear. "Beware."

"Your statement says you've been in a mixed marriage for twenty years," she says, baring her teeth in a broad yet menacing smile. "That's impressive, Mr. Evans. What's your secret to marital success?"

"Not getting angry with each other at the same time," I say, causing small chuckles to ripple across the room. This prompts me to throw in another one-liner from the repertoire I've learned:

"Earning more than Claire can spend."

This triggers a number of loud guffaws. Excellent.

"The differences between Monos and Duos are smaller than most people think they are," I continue, spotting an approving look on Rowan's face out of the corner of my eye. "My wife and I have learned to live with our *similarities*. We repeat our marriage vows to ourselves each morning—the fact that we love each other."

"You sang the praises of mixed-marriage babies just now," the woman persists, still smiling at me. "But you've been married for twenty years and don't have any children."

"We've tried," I say, hanging my head for greater effect. "My diary says that Claire has been desperate for a little one for years. With luck, there may be an addition to the Evans family someday."

Sympathetic murmurs waft across the room.

"I definitely understand the mental and emotional heartache suffered by childless couples," I continue. "I'll support the recent motion for the adoption process to be simplified. That way, more couples will experience the joys of parenthood. I've learned that one hundred and forty-one couples are on the waiting list in South Cambridgeshire. They deserve to be parents. If elected, *I'll make this happen.*"

Rowan should be proud of me. After all, I've managed to conceal the fact that I've not had sex with my wife for a damned long time (the date of our last sexual encounter eludes me). Fact: Claire will never have the guts to admit in public that our sex life has gone into hibernation. The truth about our relationship should remain a secret known only to the two of us.

A suited man with a flamboyant quiff is trying to get my attention from the right-hand side of the room. He's standing next to a man in a green jacket, hand gripping a television camera. Its lenses are pointed in my direction.

"Mr. Evans," he says. "Bruce Bernard, crime beat, ITV. A dead woman was found in the River Cam this morning."

Shit.

Even though I know Bernard's camera is trained on me, I'm unable to stop blood draining from my face. So that's why so many journalists are lurking around in Cambridge—and at my press conference—this morning.

"The woman has since been identified as Sophia Alyssa Ayling, a resident of neighboring Grantchester," says Bernard. "You were interrogated by the police earlier this morning. Could you explain why?"

Gasps resound across the room. Rowan stiffens at my side; I swear he's also beginning to hyperventilate. I ought to have told him about Richardson's arrival this morning and my subsequent Parkside ordeal, but I didn't have an opportunity.

Did Sophia *really* live in Grantchester? What was she doing there?

"I...I...er..."

I gulp, still casting about for an appropriate answer. The journalists in the room are craning their heads forward, sensing delicious copy. They look like a pack of bloodthirsty hyenas closing in after a kill.

"I was...er...horrified when I heard the news," I continue, trying to sound as much. "I also felt that it was...er...my duty to help the police. My diary says that I met Miss Ayling at a writers' conference two years ago. Her behavior suggested that she was obsessed with me and my books. The police, as far as I understand, are trying to build up her psychological profile. You're a crime beat journalist, Bruce. I'm sure you've learned that every little detail helps in this regard. The police haven't yet dismissed suicide as a possibility, it seems. After all, Miss Ayling was in a mental institution for seventeen years before she was released two years ago."

Dear God. I have waffled on a bit. But I may have averted disaster with that final juicy detail about Sophia. Bernard's scribbling away in his notebook, knitting his eyebrows in concentration. I draw in a surreptitious sigh of relief. Rowan's relaxing a little, too. A woman in the front row is waving her mobile phone at me. I raise a hand, hoping she will steer the subject away from Sophia.

"Jane McDonald, *Woman's Weekly*. I interviewed you and your charming wife, Claire, for an article last year."

Ah, yes. Fact: A journalist named Jane McDonald came to our home for an interview last December. My diary also contains a few rude remarks about her. She had turned out to be more interested in Claire's orchids than the books I've written, even though she claimed to be researching unorthodox sources of literary inspiration.

"My diary tells me that Claire's a remarkable woman," says McDonald. "I was impressed by her mince pies and her ideas for home improvement. We even featured a few photographs of your living room in our Christmas issue. Claire and I have since kept in touch. We both love exotic flowers, you see. In fact, we've been sending each other the occasional text message."

I wonder where this inconsequential ramble is heading. But it's better to have journalists do more of the talking. I should just keep quiet for the moment.

"Your wife's sent me another text," she continues, her tone pregnant with ominous implication. "Just about a minute or so ago. It's an *interesting* one."

Oh, no. I know what's coming. Damn it. I should have interrupted McDonald earlier and moved on to the next person. But it's too late now.

An eager hush has descended on the room. The journalists are leaning forward as a rapt collective, sensing blood again. I retract my right hand behind the podium before spooling my fingers into a fist to prevent them from trembling.

That scheming woman at home.

"She says she's divorcing you, Mr. Evans."

Fury is etched on Rowan's face as he bundles me out of the conference room. I wonder if I've ever seen him in such an apoplectic state before.

"Why didn't you tell me about Claire?" he says, choking on his words. "And about that dead woman?"

"I didn't get a chance—"

"A chance? You're on the fucking verge of ruining everything—"

"I know, but I did try to salvage things when that woman brought up Claire—"

"Salvage?" Rowan's face is getting redder. "You dug yourself an even bigger hole when you said that you and Claire had a 'tiny disagreement.' That things will be 'all right again soon.' At that point, I wanted to reach out and clamp your mouth shut. Do you realize what you've done?"

I remain silent.

"You've gone and screwed yourself. Chopped off your own balls in the process. By admitting you've fucked up with Claire. Which suggests she's dead serious about divorce."

Bloody hell. Rowan's right.

"I can already picture tomorrow's headline: MARK EVANS'S MIXED MARRIAGE COLLAPSES: DO THESE LAUDED UNIONS REALLY WORK? Your political career's dissolving even before it's started."

"But I'm sure that Claire can be persuaded to change her mind…"

"You're a fucking idiot." Rowan gives me another vicious glare. "Even if Claire wakes up tomorrow with a forgiving heart, it's clear to everyone that your marriage is on the rocks. She must be damned pissed off with you if she's getting dramatic."

I gnash my lower lip.

"No one elects a man who can't keep his own household in order. No one."

"But I couldn't think of anything else—"

"You should have said it wasn't Claire. That it's *unthinkable* for her to have written a message like that. People get prank messages and calls all the time. The text was from someone else. Someone with evil intentions. An ulterior motive. A *heinous* one. You're a fucking *writer*, Mark, for God's sake. You can figure out the right adjective. The point is: someone out there is trying to bring you down."

Spin Doctor Rowan is right. I should have said something along those lines. Weariness overtakes me again; I spot a stool a few feet away and collapse on it. Rowan, however, remains standing with his arms folded.

"Denial's the first rule of politics," he says with a growl, spitting his words out. "Especially when you think you might be heading for disaster."

I ought to write these two points down in my diary tonight.

"I'm sorry," I say, hanging my head. "My brain stopped working when that woman brought up Claire. I had a really tough morning. Especially after the police showed up at my door."

"Don't even get me started on the dead woman." Rowan gives me another withering look. "That ITV guy nearly gave me a heart attack. Only *guilty* people get interrogated, mind you. But you did well there, saying she's a suicidal nutcase. You're clearly capable of improvising when you need to. The business about Claire is worse. Much worse."

"So what do we do?"

Rowan sighs.

"You don't need to be a fucking genius," he says, "to figure out that damage has been done. *Serious* damage. This calls for damage-control mode. Pick-up-the-bloody-pieces mode. Wipe-the-shit-you've-made-in-your-own-pants mode. You have two options."

"Go on."

"One. Convince people that Claire wasn't thinking. That she got all emotional when she texted that woman. That it was a massive mistake on her part. She still loves you. She thinks you'll make a brilliant MP."

I shake my head.

"Two. Get her to issue an immediate press statement, within the next two hours if possible, stating that it *wasn't* she who sent the message. Given that Claire brought this pile of shit on your head, she alone can scrub you clean."

"But how do I persuade her to do that?"

Rowan sighs again before sinking down on the stool next to mine.

"She isn't my wife," he says. "You know more facts about her than I do. Like whether she prefers flowers or fancy lingerie. Or whether you should just grovel at her feet. Good luck, Mark. You'll need it."

Monos and Duos should be defined by their humanity rather than their ability to remember one day or two.

—Manifesto of the International
Anti-Discrimination Society, 2015

Chapter Nine

HANS

10¾ HOURS UNTIL THE END OF THE DAY

Mark Evans's neighbors must either be uninterested in their surroundings or only interested in themselves. Or both. I've tried four households already and no one has seen or heard anything of significance. This is damned frustrating; I've already wasted thirty-three minutes of my fast-evaporating time. Yet there are still two doors remaining on the row of terraced houses opposite Evans's home. I knock on the penultimate one: a frazzled-looking woman answers the door, a baby boy in her arms. Dark purple bags frame her eyes; mashed carrot stains pepper her shirt. The child's holding an enormous blue rattle. He must be around a year old.

"Good afternoon," I say, holding up my badge. "DCI Hans Richardson of the Cambridgeshire Constabulary. Could I ask you a few questions about Mark and Claire Evans, please?"

She wrinkles her nose.

"What about them?" she says.

"Your name first, madam, if you don't mind."

"Mary-Jane Rutherford." She winces as the boy shakes his rattle in her ear.

"Duo?"

"Definitely. I'm afraid I haven't got all day, Inspector. Not with Fred driving me nuts. What *precisely* do you need to know?"

I'm going to dispense with all the questions I had originally intended to ask. After all, the *Textbook of Criminal Investigation* says that detectives should display instinctive, fleet-footed agility when responding to each circumstance.

"Why don't you like Mr. and Mrs. Evans?" I say.

Surprise glints on her face.

"How...how did you know that I—"

"Your nose said it all when I mentioned them just now. What do you not like about them?"

She puckers her lips in silence. Young Fred shakes his rattle again, this time in my direction. The noise jars my nerves. One should never arm a crook with a gun or a baby with a giant rattle.

"I shouldn't be saying this..."

"I won't tell anyone."

"I really shouldn't, but hey...I've always thought that Newnham's a select neighborhood for Duos. *Duos.* Even if one half of a partnership is rich and famous. Exclusive areas like this one shouldn't be polluted with...people of a certain class. Do you get my drift?"

"I most certainly do. But do you not like Claire Evans as a person?"

She grimaces.

"Why not?"

"She gives me envious looks whenever I go by with Fred. The fact crops up often in my diary. It's probably because she has always wanted a child. But she really shouldn't..."

She trails off with a scowl.

"Why shouldn't Mrs. Evans want a child?"

"Haven't you heard the news this morning?" she says. "Duo-Mono couples have a twenty-five-percent chance of conceiving Mono children. *Twenty-five percent*, mind you. That's a pretty large percentage, in my humble opinion."

"I don't see why this is wrong."

"There are more than enough stupid Monos in this world, Inspector. Most murders are committed by Monos. That's a fact, no? Monos already create enough trouble for us Duos as it stands. Duos shouldn't be going around polluting their own bloodlines. Don't you agree with me?"

"Not all Monos are stupid."

She narrows her eyes at me, nose flaring.

Damn it. I really should bite back the rest of my blistering reply for fear of giving myself away.

"But I'm sure your feelings are shared by many," I add, trying hard to keep my voice level.

Fact: I meet Duos like Rutherford all the time. I shouldn't work myself up into a fluster, although it's tempting to yell at—

A giant rattle is traveling in the direction of my head; I twist my neck, dodging the missile just in time. It hits the ground in a shrill-pitched crash, prompting young Fred to emit a loud squeal of delight.

Mrs. Rutherford sighs.

"Sorry, Inspector," she says. "Fred's just being naughty. Is there anything else you need to know?"

"Not really." I shake my head. "I've found out everything I wanted to know about what rattles people on this street."

Time for the last door, the one belonging to the curly-haired neighbor in the purple dressing gown who came out on her porch earlier this morning to stare at Claire and me. I tap the polished brass knocker; the woman answers within seconds, dark eyes burning bright. She is wearing large hoop earrings and a flamboyant dress that resembles a caftan. Her manicured fingernails are painted alternately purple and green to match her dress. A shiny faux crystal is embedded in each nail.

"Hello," I say, holding up my identification badge. "I'm DCI Hans Richardson of the Cambridge—"

"I saw you leading Mark away from his home earlier," she says, her words spilling out in a nasal accent. "Did he do something wrong? Something bad?"

"I cannot answer," I say, causing disappointment to flood her face. "What's your name, madam?"

"Carmen Miranda Scott-Thomas."

"That's a grand name."

"My mum's Brazilian; she named me after the famous samba singer. But my husband's English."

"Duo, aren't you?"

"Yes."

"Could I ask you a few questions about Mr. and Mrs. Evans, please?"

"Sure," she says. "Come on in."

I step into her living room. A veritable blast of sandalwood and patchouli assails my nostrils. Unlike those in Martha Brown's home, furnishings here are lavish and plush. Purple beaded curtains billow in the breeze wafting through two French doors on the other side of the room. Mrs. Scott-Thomas points me to a velvet sofa with moss-green cushions. I shake my head, preferring to stand.

"Did you notice anything unusual about the Evanses?" I say. "Either yesterday or the day before? Did they get any visitors?"

Mrs. Scott-Thomas frowns.

"Nope," she says. "I don't think so. But then again, I can only see their front door from here. Not their side door."

"What about this woman?" I thrust a color photocopy of Sophia's driving license in her direction. "Seen her before?"

Mrs. Scott-Thomas studies Sophia's face with great interest. But she shakes her head again.

"Nope."

I ought to try a different questioning tack. Because tiny departures from the norm can sometimes be significant.

"Was there anything that *didn't* happen as usual, then?"

Her eyes light up.

"I don't think Mark left the house yesterday. But maybe I just didn't notice him leaving."

"Is it unusual for him to stay put at home?"

"Let me check." She walks over to a handbag lying on the sofa and extracts her iDiary for confirmation. "Ah, yes...my diary says that Mark *always* goes for a long run on Tuesday and Friday mornings. Goes to Waterbeach and back each time. I once asked him why, why he's always pounding pavements on these two days. He said that writers need to keep on the move, to keep ideas moving in their heads. Fascinating, eh? That's probably why I wrote this down."

This is indeed interesting. If Mark's Friday runs are such an integral part of his weekly existence, something unexpected might have detained him at home yesterday. He said he wanted to keep an eye on his wife. But there may have been more to it. Something he didn't tell me.

"Anything else that didn't happen as usual?"

"The Fiat passed by two days ago. But it didn't come by yesterday."

"An old black Fiat?"

She nods, surprise coloring her face.

"When was that?"

"Sometime early evening. It was headed in that direction." She points to the west end of Grantchester Meadows, the direction of the pull-off area where the public footpath to Grantchester starts.

"Did you see who was inside?"

"A woman, for sure. Blond, maybe. Couldn't quite see her face, as the windows were tinted."

"Does she go by often?"

"Oh, yes." Mrs. Scott-Thomas nods vigorously. "She usually slows down in front of their home before speeding up again. Weird, eh? But a fact for sure. Oh, look, there's Mark again."

She points out the window. Mark Evans is pulling up outside his mansion in a dusty black Jaguar. He jumps out of the vehicle, casting a long suspicious glare at my driver and the patrol car parked just yards away. He scans the surroundings with a deep frown before walking to the back of his car and pulling a door open. My eyes widen as he retrieves a gigantic bouquet of burgundy-colored roses from the backseat. There must be at least a hundred of them.

"Oh, my God, Inspector." Mrs. Scott-Thomas draws in an incredulous breath, her eyes as round as the crystal plates on her wall. "That must surely be the largest bunch of roses I've ever seen."

"Quite so."

"Mark must be in trouble with his wife. Like, real trouble. Serious shit."

"How do you know?"

"The darker the shade, the deeper the shit. The larger the bouquet, the bigger the shit pile. Just two random facts that stick in my mind. Mark's prone to grand gestures, just like my mother. Theatrical ones. I wish my husband could be more like him. But my husband never buys me flowers—"

"Please excuse me," I say, heading for the door. "I would *really* like an urgent word with Mr. Evans."

There are three types of men in this world: womanizing bastards, sophisticated cads, and grotesque slimeballs. I once had the misfortune of meeting a man who turned out to be all three.

—Diary of Sophia Ayling

Chapter Ten

MARK

A man should never carry a hundred roses when he's struggling with his own front door (and I thought it was a good idea to empty the racks of the only florist in Newnham on my way back from the Guildhall). The key's refusing to turn, and the flowers are threatening to fall out of my arms. I can already picture them hitting the ground in an eruption of flying stalks and decapitated buds. To make things worse, their cloying, sickly sweet odor is causing my head to spin.

"Good afternoon, Mr. Evans," says a familiar voice. "You have a lot of flowers. They look nice."

My key clangs to the ground. I spin around; my nemesis is marching up to me with a slightly amused expression on his face. Fear surges to my chest. What's Richardson doing here? Surely the detective hasn't already found out what happened to…is he here to arrest me?

I will not tremble. I won't.

"What…what are you doing here?"

"I just wanted to ask you another question about *On Death's Door*," he says.

The detective must surely be pulling my leg. It's entirely his fault that one hundred roses are weighing my arms down, smothering me with the desperation they represent, their tumescent blooms epitomizing everything that has blown up spectacularly since the morning. After all, I owe the imminent collapse of my marriage and longed-for political career to Richardson's pointed remark about Sophia, the one he was tactless enough to make in front of my wife. The man's making me terrified and annoyed at the same time.

Maybe it's deliberate.

"I've already told you everything I know about Sophia." I'm gritting my teeth so hard that my words spill out in a hiss.

"Oh." He shrugs. "I wasn't planning to ask you about Miss Ayling. I wanted to find out why Gunnar and Sigrid went all the way to Svalbard during their honeymoon in 2000, *just* to see the northern lights."

"What's wrong with that?"

"Svalbard's *too far north*. It isn't the best place in the world for auroras at the height of the solar cycle. Statistically speaking, they were more likely to see the northern lights in Gunnar's own hometown of Valberg than in Svalbard."

Damn it. I'm going to have to improvise.

"They *thought* they could see the aurora there. I never said they *did*."

The detective pulls out a dog-eared copy of *On Death's Door* from his briefcase and riffles through it.

"But there's a line in the book that says: 'The sky came alive as Gunnar took her into his arms.' Page sixteen."

"It was just…er…a figure of speech."

"Then why does the next line say, 'Dark emerald pennants flickered above their heads, cleaving the heavens with golden-opal scythes before dancing away as billowing curtains of green fire'?"

A bead of sweat is forming on my forehead. It isn't caused by the exertion of carrying a hundred roses. I should be thinking faster and harder, otherwise the detective will definitely get the better of me.

I have four options:

(A) say that I can't remember everything I've written—that's why I always page back when writing my damned novels;

(B) admit that I know absolutely nothing about Svalbard, let alone the likelihood of seeing the northern lights there;
(C) tell him I was just being poetic;
(D) all of the above.

But a sudden brain wave strikes me.

"The only people who subject my books to such careful line-by-line analysis are Monos. But surely you can't be a Mono, Inspector."

He flinches. Did something dark just stab his eyes? But he yanks his shoulders back.

"If you think I'm a Mono, Mr. Evans, I'm clearly not doing my job very well. Which is a shame, because I hope to pin down *the person who murdered Sophia Ayling* before the end of the day."

I gulp.

"Have a good afternoon, Mr. Evans," he continues. "I'll be sure to keep you posted on my investigation."

"Very well, Inspector." My words tumble out in a squeak.

"I hope you'll make it to Waterbeach at some point, by the way. Shame you didn't manage to get there yesterday morning. But bad things sometimes detain us at home, don't they?"

Sweat now pours down my forehead; the detective has somehow managed to wriggle his way under my skin. How on earth did he find out that I didn't go for my usual run yesterday morning?

I take in a deep, ragged breath. I will not panic. Even though terror is thumping at the back door of my mind, begging to be let in. I ought to concentrate on the task at hand. Do what Rowan insisted I do. Save my marriage before it's too late. Stop my wife from destroying herself and us.

Claire must surely be in the master bedroom, because I can't find her anywhere else in the house. I stagger to the closed bedroom door, rearranging my face into a suitably contrite expression. The roses are still swamping my arms, filling up my nostrils with their cloying miasma of scent.

"Claire."

She does not reply.

"Please, Claire. I'm sorry."

Still no answer.

"Please talk to me." I decide to beg. "Please. Let's start all over again."

I can't hear anything. Not even the slightest muffled breath or rustle. Perhaps she isn't inside.

I turn the doorknob. It yields at once.

The room is shrouded in darkness. The curtains are still drawn, although a tiny gap separates them. A triangular shard of afternoon light streaks across the floor in a forlorn dash. The bed's still unmade. The duvet is tossed in a large messy stack on one side.

My wife has vanished.

I walk over to the curtains and drag them apart before yanking open the wardrobe doors to check that she isn't inside.

Horror scenarios flash through my mind. Claire having coffee with that *Daily Mail* journalist (the one with the four ex-husbands) while I stand here next to our rumpled marital bed in helpless silence, a hundred nauseating roses in my arms. A heartfelt afternoon tête-à-tête between two wronged women, culminating in a front-page exposé of Mark Henry Evans's nocturnal misdemeanors. The newspaper's largest scoop of the year, with my disheveled, wild-eyed mug shot plastered across the front page. Or the equally alarming scenario of Claire holding court in a press conference of her own, reiterating that a divorce is most certainly in the works and that she has *no* intention of taking her straying husband back. Especially since he'd been sleeping with a woman whose body has just been fished out of the Cam.

I must find my wife.

I pull out my mobile phone and speed-dial her number.

There's no reply. Her phone switches into automatic answer mode: "You've reached Claire Evans—"

I terminate the call.

Where the hell has she gone?

I should scour the possibilities. Use them to pin down my wife's current location before it's too late. Beg her to forgive me before these twin evils of divorce and a dead body get out of hand.

Emily Wade. Of course. My wife could be pouring out her grievances to her best friend. Fact: Emily is an ex–Varsity Blues waitress who lives in a council flat somewhere along Grange Road. I marveled in my diary that Emily packed away seven éclairs when she dropped by for tea with Claire three weeks ago.

I pull out my phone again to search for Emily's number. But she is not on my contact list.

I groan.

Yet all is not lost. Her number—or home address—could be stored on the computer in my study. I could have written these details down somewhere. Abandoning the roses on Claire's dressing table, I hurry out of the bedroom, down the stairs, and out the door leading into the garden. The wind outside has turned into a howling shriek, one painful to my ears.

I approach my study. The door is ajar.

Shit.

I swear I locked it after Claire came to fetch me this morning.

Could the police have raided the room in my absence? Richardson, after all, was lurking about on Grantchester Meadows when I got back. But he surely would have needed a search warrant to do so. It must have been Claire. She must know where we keep the spare keys to all the rooms in our house, including my study.

I push the door open. A screen saver featuring a photograph of the aurora borealis is playing on my laptop. Damn it. I forgot to turn off the computer when Claire knocked on the door earlier. I hit several buttons to check if she has been snooping through any of my digital files, including my e-mails. But it appears not. Fact: My e-mail account, like my iDiary, self-locks after two minutes of inactivity. My writing table also appears untouched. At least my papers, files, and stationery look pretty much as I'd left them earlier.

But my intuition tells me that Claire was looking for something else.

I scan the rest of the study. Nothing seems out of the ordinary. My gaze settles on the built-in bookshelf at the other side of the room.

Damn it.

I keep my file folders—as well as the spines of all of my books—aligned neatly on each shelf. It bothers me if they are not in perfect order (Richardson must suffer from a similar form of OCD, judging by the immaculate contents of his office). One of my file folders is jutting out on the bottommost shelf. Someone must have removed it and shoved it back again with unthinking imprecision.

I don't even have to check the label of the folder to know what's inside. Fact: Some of its materials have haunted me for twenty years. That's why I keep it on the lowest shelf, so that it stays out of sight and out of mind.

I pull it all the way out and peer inside. The folder's empty. Someone has removed its contents.

Hell. I think I'm screwed.

Just as Rowan had predicted.

"The brain that accompanies you to bed each night is never the same as the one that wakes you up in the morning," Rasmus said, fixing an earnest gaze on Gunnar.

Gunnar had to suppress a groan. His best friend had a tendency to state the obvious.

—Mark Henry Evans, *On Death's Door*

Chapter Eleven

SOPHIA

11 November 2013

Bloody exhausted.

Head fucking hurts.

Private investigation is damn overrated, as it turns out. The past two weeks of "surveillance" have been excruciating. Especially if one ends up loitering behind an inert steering wheel for hours on end. A run-down Fiat with dodgy climate control. I should have bought a nice little BMW. But shiny BMWs attract too much attention. I need a nondescript vantage point from which to spy undetected.

Fuck this Fiat.

I'm sick of yawning and twiddling my thumbs. Painting my fingernails to kill time. Squinting through the car's frosty windows. Hoping someone will emerge from that mansion in the distance.

Plus I've learned nothing about *her* so far. Except that she likes walking her dog in the mornings. That she drives to the Cambridge Flower School in Linton on Wednesdays, presumably to stick flowers into pots in the company of other bored housewives. That she likes visiting someone who lives in a council flat along Grange Road. That she has questionable clothes sense. Fucking awful. She goes around in a baggy shirt and loose-fitting khaki trousers most of the time. Like a woman twice her age.

So money buys things but not taste.

No wonder her husband has an eye for other women.

But that's more or less it: her life. Pathetic.

Funny how much of a difference a fortnight makes. Two weeks ago, I thought that moving to Grantchester was a good idea. I had to monitor the people who mattered.

But it's amazing how *little* you can find out about a person. My online searches have merely thrown up the earth-shattering revelation that she's a Mono housewife. There are a few images of her online. All taken at book signings or charity galas with her husband. Events way beyond her rightful station in life. Draped in ill-fitting pieces of garbage. Always in the background or hovering behind her husband. Wearing a pained, wide-eyed expression. Looking like a terrified doe caught in the headlights. Yet one does not glean anything useful from photos of a woman clad in expensive but frumpy gowns at parties. Apart from the fact that it was her husband who paid for those fucking dresses.

Dirt's hard to find under such squeaky-clean conditions. But I should keep digging. There's got to be dirt somewhere.

Nobody's perfect.

Everyone has shit in them.

Including *him*. And his stick-in-the-mud Mono wife, who has less of a brain than her golden retriever does.

There's got to be dirt.

I should stay motivated. Keep going. Deal with the demons from my past. Ghosts I once tried to forget but no longer can. Confront them head on. Reach out and throttle them with my hands.

I should start by *focusing on the positives,* as they used to tell us at St. Augustine's. Because I now have the following:

Shoes. The most flamboyant stilettos I can teeter on. The higher the merrier (I don't know who invented killer six-inch heels for the ladies, but I hope that he—or was it a she?—has since been elevated to supremacy in the heavens).

Fancy lingerie. Lace and silk slips. The more decadent the better. It must be the effect of wandering down hallways in a plain white shirt and white elastic pants for years. Arse draped in massive cotton knickers. The sort Granny would wear. Tits in no-nonsense strapless bras. No metal underwire—so inmates can't stab each other. Feet shod in cheap socks and thin paper slippers. No belts or shoelaces—so patients can't hang themselves.

Other people's secrets. I'm uncovering them slowly, but surely. My dossier's getting thicker.

Everyone has secrets. Two types of secrets, precisely. The ones they keep from others and the ones they keep from themselves. Assisted in this regard, of course, by their pathetically defective memories.

They say that in the land of the blind, the one-eyed man is king. So in a world full of hapless, memory-deficient people, the memory-enhanced woman has a shot at becoming queen.

I'm going to make Mark Henry Evans discover his own secrets.

Brutally.

29 November 2013

The Kandinsky again last Sunday. Foyer all Christmassy, complete with a tree full of glittering baubles. The receptionist handed me a key to room 261. Said Mr. Matthew Adams had not yet arrived. Turned the handle to discover she was right. No one inside. Stepped to the window and surveyed the streetlamps twinkling on the pavement below. The fog swirling around distant lampposts. Like one of those ethereal wraiths from my past. The ones that have returned to haunt my soul.

I suddenly felt *lonely*. A long night of shagging lay ahead. Yet I still felt lonely.

Sex, after all, is merely a meeting of bodies. An exchange of fluids. An outlet for animal desires.

An instrument of blackmail.

But only after I've assembled more tools to bring him down, of course. One does not demolish a building with a hammer and a chisel. One needs a proper bulldozer. A nice big wrecking ball. Lots of fucking dynamite.

I've thought about killing him. Snuffing out the light in his eyes. Oh, I have. When I first emerged from St. Augustine's. I've even mulled over some appropriate methods of slaughter. Smashing his head with an ice pick, Sharon Stone–style. Tying a noose, constructed entirely of G-strings, round his neck. Watching him choke in response. Bashing his head with a sledgehammer. Hearing the satisfying crunch of his skull. Grinding his cheeks with the steel heel caps of my Christian Louboutins. Seeing his blood pool in crimson droplets, his life fizzing out of them.

I might even get away with it. Detectives would struggle to piece together the fine details of my dastardly act, especially after waking up to discover that they only have a few skimpy facts in their diaries. Because there's no way they'll be able to write everything down. And my victim will no longer be around to explain what happened.

But vengeance is best administered in stages.

Pain is best meted out in increments.

A protracted spell in prison is what he deserves. A drawn-out, mentally agonizing confinement. After he has been stripped of everything he has, including his miserable marriage. The slow, inexorable decay I would have faced in St. Augustine's if Mariska had not opened my eyes. If I did not have the subsequent presence of mind to extract myself from purgatory.

At any rate, I did feel lonely at that precise moment. Window of room 261 of the Kandinsky on Sunday.

I couldn't help it.

Nor could I figure out why. Perhaps it was the realization that I'd turned forty-three a few days before. That no one knew. Dad and poor Mum were no more. Stepmum Aggie wouldn't have given a shit about my birthday. And I couldn't exactly tell the man I'd been fucking for months that I'd turned forty-three, either.

I'd celebrated by knocking back half a bottle of vodka that day. With only a ginger-haired cat named Rufus as company.

A cat that wasn't even mine.

Forty-three. An age that makes you think about what you've failed to accomplish in your lifetime. An age when even the smallest cut—or controlled scalpel incision—takes forever to heal. An age that makes you think seventeen years in a mental asylum was perhaps not the best way to spend the bulk of your adult existence. An age when you realize you're not getting any of those years back.

At that point, I swore out loud. At the unfairness of it. The sheer fucking injustice of it all.

But I gritted my teeth. Decided to stop pitying myself.

Because loneliness is for wimps. And self-pity is for idiots.

Life had dealt me unfair blows and kicked me in the gut. Yet I should stop feeling sorry for myself.

I should merely take my pleasures as they come.

From now on.

It was the sound of a creaking door that distracted me from my thoughts. He walked in with the usual lust playing on his face. A beautifully wrapped, ribbon-adorned package in hand.

"Early Christmas present," he said, giving it to me with a chuckle.

I unwrapped the box. A bra-and-knickers set from Agent Provocateur, it turned out, in size 36-26-37 (after all those hours spent exploring my curves, he did get my measurements right). Scarlet lace as fine as filigree. A garter belt with thigh-high black garters.

Of course. I should have known he was into *garters*.

He gives his wife roses. I saw him disappearing into his Newnham mansion a week ago with an impressive bunch. Half were pink. The rest were white. They were surely meant for his wife. But he gives his mistress garters.

Naughty, provocative garters.

Mark Henry Evans leads such a clichéd existence. No wonder his novels are brimming with clichés.

"Model it for me, darling."

It struck me, at that point, that Mark Henry Evans also knows something about modeling, but in an altogether different way. His novels are full of lying villains. Even his heroes have duplicitous tendencies. He must model his characters after *himself*.

I obliged, of course. It worked. Within seconds, he was on top of me, thrusting away. Sweating like a pig. He flipped me over. It's amazing how some men fuck like wild animals. Several minutes later, he pulled out. Satiated. Crashed straight onto the pillow next to me and began snoring. Postcoital bliss etched on his face.

I reached for his wallet, tossed on a side table. Nine crisp £20 notes, a stack of credit cards, and a strip of paper bearing the words "The birth date of the love of my life, and mine."

YESTERDAY

I scribbled the words down on a notepad (you never know what might be useful someday) before studying his profile in the dim lamplight. I could have reached out to throttle him with my hands. Or twisted my stockings and bra straps into an unforgiving noose for his neck. Or slit his throat with a penknife.

Patience.

Patience, Sophia. Patience is the virtue of saints.

And sinners.

And so I got up, walked to the end of the room, and switched off the pin-size camera I'd hidden in the corner.

A detective should work out the truth of a person, even though the truth may be obscured by false facts.

—*Textbook of Criminal Investigation*, volume 4
(Oxford University Press, 1987)

Chapter Twelve

HANS

10 HOURS UNTIL THE END OF THE DAY

She's mad. Positively rabid. Also clueless about the way good detectives operate. But her diary's strangely compelling. Unfathomable vitriol, when coupled with a healthy dose of insanity, has a way of making even a hardened inspector turn pages. I'm inclined to read on, even though her diary has taken up another twenty minutes of my precious time.

But I need some coffee first. My head is crying out for an injection of caffeine. I get up from my chair, grimacing at the pins and needles shooting up my legs. Just then, Toby comes rushing in with a pile of papers.

"Hans," he says. "I've tracked down her Barclays records—"

"Let me guess. She's flush."

"She received monthly payments of £4,179.23 from a trust fund managed by Swiss Inheritance Services," he says, running a finger down the uppermost sheet. "The transfers began on the first of April in 2013. The most recent was on the first of June, five days ago."

"Who's the payer?"

"I called the Swiss to find out. They were uncooperative. Said they take their clients' privacy seriously."

I groan. Damn those recalcitrant Swiss. I pull out my diary and type in "Swiss + contact" before squinting at the result.

"You need a Swiss to talk to the Swiss," I say. "I've learned this the hard way. Call Heinrich Heinz, Swiss Federal Department of Justice and Police. I've helped him before. He owes me one."

"I'll get on it." Toby nods. "I also spoke to Edward Perry, Ayling's landlord. Her monthly rent is £1,795. The cottage had been vacant for thirteen months before she phoned him in October of 2013 and said she wanted to move in the next day. A model tenant, he says. Gave him no problems whatsoever."

I recite the two sums and the date to my Dictaphone before returning my attention to Toby.

"St. Augustine's."

"Ah, yes." Toby nods again. "There's indeed a private institution named St. Augustine's Priory Hospital in the Outer Hebrides. It takes up five acres on the island of Hellisay. They were as unhelpful as the Swiss. Refused to say whether Ayling had been treated there."

He riffles through the papers in his hands before reading from a sheet.

"Their website says: 'We provide discreet inpatient medical care of the highest quality for women with psychiatric challenges. We have exclusive five-star residential facilities for up to twenty-five patients.'"

He hands me a photograph. I peer down; it's a shot of an imposing concrete building framed by gnarled bushes and stunted trees. The landscape that surrounds it has a desolate, windswept air. A forbidding gray ocean shades the horizon, its surface shot through with white crests.

"Money buys secrecy," I say with a sigh. "Keep your nose on it."

As soon as I step outside for coffee, I'm waylaid by Fiona Allerton of the computing services department. Today's outfit, I notice, features preppy spectacles with thick rims and skintight leopard-print trousers.

"Peter's managed to hack into Ayling's memory stick," she says, face taking on an agitated fluster (as it did yesterday morning when we ran into each other at the coffee vending machine). Though the contents of Sophia's memory stick might also have something to do with the look on her face.

"Took him more than twenty minutes to crack her password," she continues. "She used a really complicated sequence of letters and numbers, it seems. But he got there in the end."

"What's on it?"

"Maybe you should come down and take a look."

While coffee is tempting, the prospect of following Fiona to her lair is twice as appealing. She leads me down two flights of stairs to the basement, her trousers creasing under her buttocks with every step. The ripe odor of sweaty socks and cheese-and-onion Monster Munch greets my nostrils as we walk into her office. Large screens are flashing everywhere under harsh fluorescent lights. Fiona's two young assistants are hunched over a computer terminal in the corner of the room. Both are gaping at its luminous screen. One is shaking his head, his mouth an exaggerated circle. The other, a gawky youth with several days' worth of stubble on his chin, has eyes mushrooming out of their sockets.

"Peter," says Fiona. "Could you play a video for Hans, please? Let's say the one dated the twenty-fourth of November, 2013. It's one of the most illuminating."

I think I know what's coming.

The youth chuckles in response. He pulls up a file, hits the Play button, and reaches for a crisp.

A giant bed emerges on-screen. Its white sheets, duvets, and pillows are pristine. A man walks by with a briefcase in hand, on the left-hand side of the screen. He's wearing a dark suit and a slate-gray tie. A beribboned parcel fills his left hand. He sets his briefcase down next to the bed before moving out of the camera's view.

"Picked this up from Harrods earlier," a male voice says. Its tones are familiar; I heard the same clipped inflections merely a few hours ago.

"Early Christmas present, my darling."

The sound of ripping paper is followed by a small squeal of delight.

139

"Gorgeous." A woman speaks, breathless and husky. But a hint of cynical amusement colors her tone.

"Scarlet's your thing, isn't it?"

"Oh, you spoil me, baby," she says. Her voice has turned into a gushing dulcet ripple, but I detect a note of insincerity in its depths. "I *love* Agent Provocateur. Especially if it fits."

"Model it for me, darling."

A woman appears and begins walking past the bed, her back turned to the camera. She is wearing a kimonolike robe; her peroxided hair is swept up in a bun. A swath of red lace dangles from the box in her hands. She vanishes beyond the camera's view. Several seconds later, a disembodied hand tosses a black wallet onto a side table, then flings the gray necktie onto the bed. The fabric unfurls as a long gash on the sheets.

The man emerges into view again. His jacket has vanished; the top two buttons of his shirt are unfastened. He steps in the direction of a cupboard next to the bed and pulls out a bottle of Champagne bedecked in gold foil. He moves towards the camera, then falls out of range again. A cork pops several moments later, followed by the trickle of liquid.

The woman is now stepping back into the screen, minus the kimono. Her body is sheathed in a sheer scarlet bra and barely there knickers. Her thighs are encased in black garters and stockings.

I can finally see her face. Most of it, at least. Its upper part is covered by an eye mask crafted from black lace. The exposed lower half is familiar, albeit with a few minor differences. The chin I saw at the Paradise nature reserve was a ghastly shade of white, while the one on Peter's screen is flushed with sultry determination. The face in the recording is also more angular; she'd put on a bit of weight since the video was filmed. And while the lips I saw this morning were twisted in the contorted rictus of death, a dangerous-looking smile is playing on the lips on-screen.

They are also painted a murderous red.

"You look stunning," the male voice says.

The woman does not reply. Instead she sashays to the bed, positioning herself in the middle of the screen. She settles on the sheets, draping the unfurled gray tie around her neck. She raises a hand to release the bun on her head; blond hair ripples around her shoulders seconds later. Fixing her eyes at a point beyond the camera, she flicks her hair back with a coquettish toss. She runs her tongue between her lips before licking her thumb all the way to its hilt.

"You little minx," says the man as she begins sucking her thumb. His voice is taut with desire.

The woman still does not speak. Instead she parts her thighs and lowers her well-licked thumb to the scarlet-laced cleft below.

"You can guess what happens next," Fiona says in a dry voice.

Young Peter, however, is gulping at the screen.

"She knew a trick or two," he says, cramming another crisp into his mouth.

Fiona rolls her eyes.

The man on-screen hurls himself at the woman, shirt still undone, choosing to dispense with seductive foreplay. He has not even bothered to remove his trousers; they're scrunched up in a heap below his knees. The entrance he makes is abrupt, even brutal.

"I think you get the picture, Hans," Fiona says, rolling her eyes again.

"It's explicit," I say. "Are there more videos on the stick?"

"Six in total. Two in the same place, while the remaining ones were filmed in a different bedroom."

"Featuring other props and positions."

Fiona nods.

"A French maid's uniform, a paddle and whip, and some vigorously vibrating things. She's wearing a mask in all the videos. He must have a fetish for lacy eye coverings."

The man on-screen removes his tie from around the woman's neck and binds her wrists. He pushes her back onto the bed before resuming his thrusts. His groans are accompanied by a chorus of high-pitched, exaggerated gasps from the woman.

"I wonder who he is," says Fiona, pushing her horn-rimmed spectacles up her nose.

Young Peter turns round to look at her, half-eaten crisp sticking out of his mouth.

"He's Mark Evans," he says. "Someone shoved a propaganda pamphlet under my door two mornings ago. He looked much better in his photograph, I must say, than the candidate in the Labour leaflet did."

"I brought him in for a little chat earlier," I say. "He behaved like a canary that refused to sing. I need to figure out a way to make him talk."

The man on-screen is flipping the woman over.

I wince.

"But why did she film these videos?" asks Fiona.

"Isn't it obvious?" I say. "To destroy him."

I return to my office with a large cup of coffee in hand only to discover that Hamish has parked his arse on my desk. He's slipping something into his breast pocket. I stiffen, narrowing my eyes. Was my deputy snooping around in my office just now, hoping to obtain concrete evidence that I've been masquerading as a Duo?

Probably not. I should stop being paranoid. Hamish is merely brimming with information, judging from his puffed-up chest. But this is, unfortunately, the only redeeming feature of his reappearance.

"Hans," he says, not budging from my desk. "I dropped by twenty minutes after Evans's press conference, but you weren't in, so I decided to have lunch."

"Ah, yes," I say. "I ran into him soon afterwards. He was burdened by blooms. Also looked frazzled. What *really* happened at the Guildhall?"

"They quizzed him about all sorts of things. Including your chat with him earlier this morning."

"How on earth did they know about that?"

"Beats me." Hamish throws his hands up. "Bruce Bernard from ITV sniffed that one out. He's the guy with the large quiff who kept getting in our way at the nature reserve this morning."

I groan before settling down in my chair and swallowing the coffee in one gulp.

"They must have wanted to know why I brought him in."

"He tried to deflect the question. Even had the chutzpah to say that he wished to help us with Ayling's psychological profile. Added that she'd been institutionalized for seventeen years and was only released two years ago. This created quite a stir in the audience."

I suppose I have only myself to blame for telling Mr. Evans those little snippets of information.

"The press will be hounding us for more," I say, sighing. "If they aren't already."

"Bernard proved a real pest when I left the Guildhall."

"Ignore him," I say. "And the others."

"A journalist from *Woman's Weekly* then dropped a bombshell. It blasted everyone out of their seats."

I flick an eyebrow up at Hamish.

"She'd received a text message from Evans's wife. Claire Evans apparently wants a divorce."

"What?"

"Yes. All hell broke loose after that."

"I must have triggered it. What did Evans say?"

"He mumbled that they had a little spat earlier this morning. But he thought that everything would be all right soon. You ought to have seen the expression on his campaign manager's face. Redford, I think his name was. The poor man looked as though he was about to vomit."

"I'm not surprised."

"He stepped forward and bundled his client out before Evans could say anything more damaging. That was the end of it. No more press conference. Disappointed faces all around, of course. There's nothing like divorce to get journalistic pulses racing."

"Fascinating," I say, casting my thoughts back to my morning encounter with Mrs. Evans. Especially the shock that registered on her face when I implied that her husband had engaged in certain extramarital shenanigans. So that's why Mark Evans was carrying a hundred roses into his home. I should have guessed. I fish out my

Dictaphone and say: "Outraged wife Claire Evans tells journalist she wants divorce."

"One of our patrol units has found Ayling's Fiat," says Hamish.

My mouth is dry; I should remain calm. Damn that overefficient patrol unit. I should say something. Anything.

"Your arse is blocking my way," I say.

"Sorry." Hamish moves over to a chair.

I ought to do something with my hands. I take in a deep breath before reaching out and shoving the white queen forward in a random direction. Hamish watches my antics with a long-suffering frown.

"I still don't understand why you bother with that chessboard." He shakes his head in mock exasperation. "Anyway, her Fiat was found in Newnham. Parked in the pull-off area at the far end of Grantchester Meadows. The one full of potholes. Right next to Skaters' Meadow, before the start of the public footpath to Grantchester."

Something clicks in my head.

Sophia's diary says she conducted several reconnaissance missions on the Evanses' home from the uncomfortable confines of her Fiat. Carmen Miranda Scott-Thomas saw the Fiat two evenings ago. So Sophia must have been spying on Mark and Claire then. That's the reason why her Fiat was parked at the end of Grantchester Meadows. But why was she snooping around? What was she after? And what was the precise sequence of events that culminated in her watery demise?

I recite "Deceased's black Fiat found at far end of Grantchester Meadows" into my Dictaphone.

"Forensics is on it," says Hamish. "Like Marge, they hope to get a report to us before the end of the day."

"The Kandinsky."

"Slow down, Hans. I was just coming to it. There isn't a Mark Henry Evans on the Kandinsky's guest book. But a couple named Matthew and Veronica Adams were indeed regular guests between September of 2013 and July of 2014. Stayed there twelve times in total, mostly during the weekends. In room 261, as you've said. Always for one night."

"This is much better," I say, before reciting "Twelve Kandinsky encounters, two filmed" to my Dictaphone.

"Veronica Adams must have been Sophia Ayling," says Hamish. "If so, she was definitely Evans's mistress."

I raise a surprised eyebrow. Perhaps my deputy is capable of thinking outside the box once in a while.

"Well done," I say. "That's precisely why Evans stinks to the skies. I picked up a memory stick from Ayling's cottage during my second visit there. It contains six videos of her engaging in various bedroom acrobatics with him."

"What? She filmed them having sex?" Hamish's mouth is a wide chasm.

"Indeed," I say. "Blackmail, I reckon."

"But why?"

"I should finish reading her diary."

"Evans is damned fishy, all right," says Hamish. "Which makes it tempting to point the finger at him. But we should wait for the post-mortem report before concluding it's a murder. We haven't yet found any signs of external injury on Ayling's body."

"Oh, come on, Ham—"

"The *Textbook of Criminal Investigation* says we shouldn't be making snap judgments about the nature of crimes and the identity of their perpetrators."

I sigh. Hamish has retreated back into his myopic, rule-bound box, which suggests that I would merely be wasting my time arguing with him. I should give him something to do.

"I need more on Ayling," I say. "Her background in particular. Details of her parents, probably deceased. She may have had a stepmother named Aggie. I want full details of her schooling, university education, et cetera. She may have studied at Cambridge around twenty years ago."

"She was a Cambridge student once?" Hamish blinks at me.

"Perhaps."

"So our busty blond bombshell had some brains after all."

There are four variables on the path to success. Unfortunately, no one knows what they are.

—Mark Henry Evans, draft of
The Serendipity of Being

CHAPTER THIRTEEN

SOPHIA

1 December 2013

Think I've struck paydirt. Shivered in my Fiat for fifty-five fucking minutes this morning. Waiting. Yawning. Cursing. Keeping two bleary eyes on that mansion in the distance. To my surprise, she emerged from the house. Jumped into her Range Rover and sped off. I revved up my own engine and followed at a safe, discreet distance as she drove out of Newnham. Down Fen Causeway and along Trumpington Road. Was sure she was going to Waitrose to do some shopping.

But she swung left into Long Road and veered right into Robinson Way. A street I knew well. Because it led to Addenbrooke's Hospital. The place where I once spent twenty-two days of my life under sedated surveillance after Dad found my diaries in the bin. I did, after all, scream until my eyes and throat were on fire. As soon as I found myself back in one of its wards.

She parked her car and got out. Walked through the front doors of the main building. I hesitated. Terrible demons were lurking beyond, right behind those double doors. Dark splinters that shredded my soul. But I gritted my teeth. Told myself that I had to do it. I had to know what she was up to.

So I took a deep breath and pushed my way through those doors.

The foyer was large, its decor unfamiliar. Must have been renovated since I last saw it. But the people still looked the same. Doctors in white scrubs were marching through. Nurses in blue uniforms were scuttling about. The air inside was still the same. It reeked of antiseptic. That cloying, sickly sweet scourge of hospitals everywhere, masking immanent decay.

Cloaking the slow rot of human existence.

On cue, I began to hyperventilate. Couldn't breathe. Flashes of my Addenbrooke's ordeal danced before my eyes. Memories of hands pinning me down. Doctors peering at me with disapproving expressions. Nurses stabbing sharp needles into my arms and thighs. Wondering out loud if they should put a muzzle over my mouth. The straitjacket they deployed to restrain my struggles. Muttered exchanges outside the room where they had locked me. Hushed conversations insisting I was a lost cause: Addenbrooke's could do nothing for me. But a proper psychiatric institution might be able to sort me out.

Pull yourself together, Sophia.

I leaned against the nearest wall and gulped in deep lungfuls of air. Attempted to calm my racing thoughts. Quell the waves of panic breaking over my soul. Flush away the past. Yet it did take every ounce of my willpower not to run screaming from that foyer into the fresh air outside.

Thankfully, my mind soon cranked back into operating mode. Right afterward, I saw a nurse bearing down on me with a concerned, quizzical expression. Knew I had to start moving again. Act normal. Not hysterical. Because the last thing I wanted was to be flung onto a gurney and strapped down again by some enthusiastic Addenbrooke's staff. Pumped to the brim with sedatives.

Looking ill in a hospital isn't a good idea. It's as bad as looking guilty in a court of law.

Even had the presence of mind to figure out she'd long disappeared. Door at the end of the foyer. Long, harshly lit corridor. Passage leading to an adjoining annex. One I knew only too well.

The Liaison Psychiatry Service.

I forced myself to run after her, even though hysteria was still bubbling up in my throat. Aware of the ludicrous irony of the situation: I was *voluntarily* entering the psychiatric annex in my quest for information. The precise location where my slippery slope into seventeen years of ignominy began. Where my hopes and dreams drifted away into the shadows, way beyond reach.

Keep moving, Sophia.

But I soon realized she'd vanished into a labyrinth of corridors. No idea where she had gone. Staggered up and down for minutes, doing my best not to howl. Certain I had lost her. Then I saw her out of the corner of my eye. Far end of a passage. Breathless, incredulous relief burbled forth.

A distinguished-looking man with a silvery mop of hair, welcoming her into a consultation room. The door closed after them.

I hurried towards it.

ROOM 27: HELMUT JONG, MB, BCHIR, MRCPSYCH, PHD, the sign said.

So Helmut Jong, MB, BChir, MRCPsych, PhD, will be engaging in two types of consultations soon. Only some of them will be taking place within the sterile discomfort of room 27.

Consultations with cuckoos. Or the mentally disturbed, to put it more delicately. One does not visit a psychiatric consultant if one has a sound mind. The woman who had walked through that door must be suffering from dysfunctional neuronal connections.

He will also be engaging with *me*.

Like Mark Henry Evans, Helmut Jong, MB, BChir, MRCPsych, PhD, has set himself up for a good time in my company.

Lucky man.

10 May 2014

It's been ages since I wrote. Months, in fact. But there's little incentive to write when good things are happening. Writing's much more cathartic when there's something to rant about. Conversely, it's much more enjoyable where there's something to gloat over. That's the whole point of keeping this little iDiary going, really. Monos and Duos need their diaries in order to survive. I don't. My diary has a loftier, more noble purpose. Because it's a *fucking revenge journal*.

I'm entitled to smirk today. Because things are going my way. The dirt I'm seeking is emerging.

Not just dirt, as it turns out.

It's serious muck. Gooey, squelchy filth.

Her medical records say as much. Freshly harvested from the recesses of Dr. Jong's hard drive.

Suppose I should thank Dad for the inspiration. Despite his multiple failings, he did say something useful when he was still alive.

"Success is determined by two variables," he said.

Will. And *money*.

Or "determination and dough," as he had phrased it to Aggie with a flamboyant twitch of his eyebrows. Not realizing I was eavesdropping.

"Problems evaporate when you throw enough cash at them," he had added for good measure.

Aggie took his words to heart, and with vigor. She must have bribed the doctors at St. Augustine's in the winter of 2008, a few weeks after Dad's heart attack. A generous payoff resulting in the diagnosis she preferred. A terse but authoritative certificate confirming that I was still unfit to administer Dad's estate, causing me to rot in the Outer Hebrides for several more years.

I do not lack either will or money at the present time. I have lots of determination. And much more dough than I did when I was back at St. Augustine's.

But Dad underestimated the importance of a third variable.

The power of *seduction*. Especially when combined with slinky black stockings and saucy scarlet knickers.

Men are all the same. It doesn't matter if they are novelists or psychiatrists. They are all driven by their dicks. To gain access to their hard drives, one merely has to endure a few hard drives of a different nature (or vigorous thrusts, to be more precise). Dr. Jong's password was easy. Simply his dead wife's name. It also helped that most physicians have remote access to their work records these days. Nifty palm-size e-devices that they carry around in their pockets.

How convenient.

I didn't even have to suffer too much as far as Helmut Jong, MB, BChir, MRCPsych, PhD, is concerned. The man had not lost his looks, despite being a venerable sixty-four. He'd not lost his hair, either (the silver in it made him quite a sexy snow leopard). Nor had he lost his prowess in the bedroom, for that matter. Even though he had been widowed for a year and was a little out of practice.

It's amazing what psychiatrists hide, by the way. Like the fact that he accidentally placed a geriatric patient on 25 milligrams of Valium per day for four weeks, instead of 2.5 milligrams. He later wrote a groveling letter to the poor woman, begging her not to sue him for professional negligence.

He was damned lucky she didn't get addicted. Or tell anyone. They settled at £25,000.

Claire Evans's medical records, by the way, are equally fascinating. She has been on antidepressants for a long time. This is where it gets even more interesting. She has a tendency to self-harm, especially when she doesn't take her prescription pills. Cut herself with a knife on two occasions. Both episodes were bad enough to land her in Addenbrooke's under Helmut's watchful eye. Two stitches during her second visit, in April of 2013. Kept under close observation for a night, just so she didn't try it again. Antidepressants upped to a more powerful daily dose.

She's still going strong.

Aha. That stick-in-the-mud bitch has been hiding a dirty little secret.

She's a *wrist-slashing, suicidal depressive*.

Fascinating.

Incidentally, I know quite a bit about suicides.

Suicides—and botched attempts—were commonplace at St. Augustine's. I once saw an inmate trying to jump out a window. Even though we were only three stories up. A passing orderly was quick to react. Tugged her back before medicating her to kingdom come. The brunette three doors down had greater success. Banged her head on the wall in her room until it broke. Her head, not the wall. The honey-hued blonde seven doors away even did it in style. Tied the strap of an Hermès Birkin handbag to a bedsheet. God knows where she got the bag (but at least she had good taste in functional accessories). Slipped out from her room before dawn. The time when the warders are least watchful. When the sun rose, they found her hanging from a stunted poplar in the back garden. After that, only the lesser cuckoos were permitted to roam there. Individuals deemed not to be threats to themselves or to those around them.

Like Mariska Van Dijk and me.

Not that I ever attempted suicide. Even though I had once plumbed the darkest of depths. Even though I'd hated every second of my incarceration. I'd never once thought about killing myself.

I must be, instinctively, a survivor at heart.

A *stayer*.

Unlike that pill-popping, wrist-slashing Claire.

Her medical records are enlightening. It is indeed possible for a Mono who has everything to be unhappy.

It's taken me ages to work out why. But I've figured it out. Those online images of her supply the answer. She always looks as though she's out of her comfort zone. Even terrified at times, at gala parties and other events frequented by *Duos*. Wealthy, well-educated Duos of her husband's league. People above her class. Folks with twice her capacity for remembering—and understanding the universe. Enlightened, *sophisticated* people. People who must surely make her feel inferior.

She's a Mono married to a Duo. She can't fit into her husband's world. She never will. Monos and Duos cannot cohabit. One of them is likely to go cuckoo. Even suicidal.

I'm looking forward to using this piece of muck to my advantage.

At the right time, of course.

Patience, Sophia.

Patience. It's the *fourth* variable on the path to success.

After seventeen years of St. Augustine's, I can afford to be patient.

31 July 2014

What luck. I can't believe my windfall. Fortune clearly favors those who wait.

He called earlier this evening. First to apologize for the fact that our next rendezvous will be in late August. He's taking Claire to Nevis again for two weeks, he said.

I know why. Dr. Jong, after all, had prescribed regular visits to warmer climes as a means of curbing his wife's depression. "Sun, sea, and sex," he wrote, "may help her more than Lexapro and Pristiq in the long term."

Was briefly tempted to scream at Mark for putting his wife over me. That stupid little suicidal Mono. But I comforted myself with the knowledge that he surely hasn't been doing his bit as far as prescribed sex is concerned. After all the sex he's been getting elsewhere. There's only so much a man can take. Even a satyr. Dicks are not made for constant pounding. And men coming back from the Caribbean with shit-hot tans on their torsos are much nicer to bonk.

So I clamped my mouth shut. Listened to the next thing he had to say.

He's decided to do *it*. After years of yearning to be a politician, he's finally taking the plunge. Running as an independent candidate for South Cambridgeshire. After all, he has achieved everything he's ever wanted as an acclaimed novelist. Fame, fortune, and all that jazz. But it's time to move on to something bigger, better, and more satisfying. The world of politics, where he can make a difference in people's lives. Perhaps even change things for the greater good.

These developments mean two things, he added.

We'll have to be extra careful about our liaison and take pains to ensure that no one will find out about us. A more discreet location is a must. The Kandinsky, with its public foyer, will no longer be suitable. He'll look into renting a fancy apartment in London. Somewhere in Chelsea, perhaps. Will give me a key to it at the first possible opportunity.

How different from Horatio Nelson, I thought. Nelson openly

flaunted his mistress in London. But political aspirant Mark Henry Evans clearly intends to keep *his* in a covert Chelsea closet.

We won't be able to see each other as often as we have in the past, he added. He's likely to be campaigning in Cambridge during the weekends.

That's fine, I cooed.

He said good-bye minutes later, relief in his voice. I must have sounded reassuring enough. Ah, the role of the understanding, discreet mistress. I'm going to play it to the hilt. Yet I had to hide the glee in my voice before I hung up the phone. What a stroke of luck. I couldn't have hoped for anything better.

So Mark Henry Evans is entering the lion's den known as the political arena.

What splendid news. The savage and unforgiving world of politics. Where aspirants are dissected by the national and local media. Their campaign platforms. Their track records. Their fashion sense. Their conversational gaffes. Their private lives. The skeletons they've been keeping in their closets.

Mistresses, amongst other things.

And depressive, suicidal wives.

So Mark Henry Evans has presented me with his own head. Served up on a platter. His gruesome downfall, I now know, will begin with the general elections in 2015. Much sooner than I'd hoped and from a much higher perch than I'd ever envisaged. Ambitious people tend to fall from greater heights. Ah, the cut-throat joys of politics. The delightful possibilities. The sweet act of demolition. I'll be watching the process in slow motion. Frame by frame. Brick by brick.

Good things come to those who wait. Ghastly things, too.

I've waited long enough.

Study a man's eyes, and they should tell you all you need to know about his intellect and acumen. Whether he is smart enough to keep hiding his secrets from you.

—*Textbook of Criminal Investigation*, volume 4
(Oxford University Press, 1987)

CHAPTER FOURTEEN

HANS

9½ HOURS UNTIL THE END OF THE DAY

This psychiatrist must make a lucrative living from listening to other people. He's nodding his head to indicate that he's paying attention, never interrupting once, while displaying an open body position with his palms turned upwards.

His hair is indeed a spectacular shade of silver, as Sophia's diary says.

I cast another glance round the man's office; it boasts sleek furniture and muted lighting. Glossy coffee-table books top a credenza. A comfortable-looking couch occupies a corner of the room, replete with fluffy pastel-blue pillows. The space even smells of pleasant white musk. It's the sort of venue that puts people in the right frame of mind to chat about themselves. Perfect.

"Now, Dr. Jong," I say, deciding to cut to the chase. "You're a Duo psychiatric consultant at this hospital."

"Indeed."

"Do you have a patient named Claire Evans?"

Surprise darts across the psychiatrist's face.

"Er...yes. If I learned my diary correctly, she was one of the first patients I took on when I was a junior consultant."

"What kind of psychiatric problems does she suffer from?"

"I can't tell you." He shakes his head, his lips a resolute twist. "It's confidential."

"The answer is depression," I say. "Involving two minor incidents of self-harm. The second time she slashed her wrists, she ended up here for a day. You put her on a double dose of antidepressants in April of 2013, and she's been on them ever since."

The psychiatrist's eyes are as round as bullet holes.

"How…how do you know these facts?" he says. "Did she tell you herself?"

"We stumble on things."

"So why did you come here?"

"To confirm what I already know."

The psychiatrist blinks.

"I know, for instance, that you put a patient on twenty-five milligrams of Valium per day for four weeks. You also persuaded her not to sue you by writing her a check for twenty-five thousand pounds."

He gasps.

"It won't be difficult for me to write to the authorities here, pointing this little fact out," I say in my kindliest, most reassuring manner. "The facts also say that I've corresponded with your bosses before."

"What do you want, Inspector?" His eyes are narrow slits.

"I would like you to be frank with me. After all, I already know Mrs. Evans's medical history. But your professional opinion on a few related matters would be helpful. What's the cause of her depression?"

"I cannot answer precisely." He shakes his head, albeit with a slight frown. "Even after years of treating her."

"What type of depressive disorder does she have, then?"

He is still hesitating.

"Twenty-five milligrams, Dr. Jong," I say, quietly but clearly. "That's quite a bit of Valium, isn't it?"

He emits a weary groan, raising his palms in acquiescence.

"I should log on to my medical notes, to be sure," he says.

"Of course."

The psychiatrist pulls out a palm-size electronic device and taps away before replying.

"Claire Evans isn't a textbook depressive, although she displays symptoms of clinical depression," he says, reading from his device. "Nor is she classically bipolar, although bipolar medication has helped. I've tried some tricyclic antidepressants on her in the past, but they caused side effects—"

"You haven't answered my question."

"Mind diagnosis is tricky business, Inspector. It's still more art than science. I believe that she has a NOS-type—not otherwise specified type—of mood instability."

"One resulting in occasional suicidal tendencies."

"*Suicidal* is the wrong word, Inspector." Jong shakes his head with considerable vigor. "I do *not* consider Mrs. Evans suicidal. Her two self-harming episodes are a way of coping with deeply buried emotional issues. Or a means of releasing pent-up frustrations."

"Those caused by her personal circumstances?"

The psychiatrist remains silent.

"Like a difficult relationship with her partner? Exacerbated by the fact that she's a Mono married to a Duo?"

His eyes widen briefly.

"You could say as much," he says with a sigh. "She has a tendency to compare herself to her husband. Her memory limitations in particular. This has resulted in, shall we say, a chronic state of low self-esteem."

So Sophia's suspicions about Claire Evans may be accurate. The dead woman was more astute than I'd suspected.

"By the way, did you ever have sex with a woman named Sophia Ayling?"

Shock streaks across Jong's face. But he pushes his shoulders back and tightens his jaw.

"How does my sex life come into this?" he shoots back, flipping his palms over into a more defensive position. "What sort of investigation are you conducting?"

"Murder."

"But—"

"*Sophia's* murder."

"*What?*"

"She was found in the Cam earlier this morning."

The psychiatrist is gaping at me.

"No." He shakes his head, face drained of color. "This isn't possible. Sophia can't be *dead*."

"If you could tell me more about your relationship with her, that might help us track her killer down."

"But how could someone murder a woman as lovely as Sophia?" he says, throwing up his hands.

"Excellent question, Dr. Jong." I give him an approving nod. "This is what I intend to find out before the end of the day."

"How did she die?" His question ends with a tremor; he looks as though he may be in need of his own comfy couch and fluffy pillows.

"We're still waiting for the postmortem report," I say. "When and where did you first meet?"

He pulls out his iDiary with trembling fingers and types something in.

"I…er…the facts say that we met at an afternoon tea dance. Cambridge Guildhall, December of 2013. I took up ballroom dancing a year after my wife died. Sophia really stood out in the hall that day. She was younger than most of the women there. Twice as pretty. I was flattered when she came up to me and asked for a dance."

So that crafty little woman waltzed her way into the psychiatrist's bed. As her diary implies.

"The dancing developed into something more, didn't it?" I decide to spare him my knowledge of the tools she may have employed in the process, which could well have included saucy scarlet knickers.

"It did." The psychiatrist looks a little abashed.

"How long did it last?"

"Around three months."

"And how did it end?"

The psychiatrist taps his diary with a frown.

"I wish these facts were otherwise," he says, sighing. "But she phoned me in March of 2014. Just when I wanted to take her to the Chiltern Hills. A weekend in the countryside, that sort of thing. She said she 'enjoyed the time we spent together.' But she wished to 'move on.' That's what she said."

"You were stunned."

"Of course. I thought that things were going well. But the age gap might have been a problem. She never told me her age. She was pretty secretive about it. But she must be...have been...at least twenty years younger than me."

Sophia must have dumped him after she got what she wanted. As her diary suggests.

"I...I don't blame her," he says, eyes morphing into imploring circles. Our shrewd little psychiatrist must have realized that he's not exempt from police suspicion, especially after admitting to being Sophia's ex-lover.

"I only have positive facts of our time together," he continues, waving his iDiary at me for emphasis. "Sophia is...was...a vivacious and outgoing woman. She made me a happy man. I hope I made her just as happy."

Her novelist-lover called her "desperately unhinged." Her neighbor found her "sweet" and "charming." And her psychiatrist-lover has just described her as "vivacious" and "outgoing." It's amazing how the same dead woman can be perceived so differently.

"She was pretty happy with what she got from you," I say. "Did she ever mention Claire Evans?"

Astonishment flickers on the psychiatrist's face.

"No," he says, his surprise quickly giving way to a blank frown. "I don't think so. I haven't learned this fact. But I'll look at my diary again."

He clicks away at his iDiary before shaking his head.

"My diary is silent," he says. "Why do you ask? Were they friends?"

"Reckon not." I shake my head. "Definitely not *friends*. By the way, you ought to change your password on that handheld device of yours.

The one that grants remote access to your patients' records. Your dead wife's name is a bit too predictable."

The psychiatrist is frozen solid in his seat. His reaction supplies the precise confirmation I require. I should go through the remaining entries in a particular diary on my desk with a fine-tooth comb. After all, I hope to work out why Dr. Jong's erstwhile lover was obsessed with his troubled patient.

Men can be real arseholes.

—Diary of Sophia Ayling

Chapter Fifteen

CLAIRE

My hands are trembling. Even though Emily has done her best to calm me down. She has made me a mug of hot chocolate and fed me some carrot cake. Its moist sweetness lingers on my lips. But tears are still trickling down my cheeks, tears I somehow managed to hold back when I confronted Mark.

The words I used were calm, even measured. The clear assurance in my voice surprised me.

"I want a divorce," I said.

He blinked in response, not registering my words at first. But then his mouth fell open. I ran upstairs with a sense of smug satisfaction, knowing I'd hit him hard. Right in his cozy philandering gut. Minutes before his appearance at the Cambridge Guildhall, too. But as the seconds ticked by, I wanted to punch him even harder. I saw the perfect opportunity when Jane McDonald texted to say that she was at Mark's press conference.

I texted her straight back:

"My soon-to-be-ex-husband's press conference, you mean. We're divorcing."

In the heat of the moment, I thought it was an inspired idea. I couldn't have brought Mark down in more dramatic fashion. The journalists at the Guildhall must have disemboweled him right afterwards. But then my mobile phone began ringing nonstop. I even answered one of the calls, from a number I didn't recognize.

"Hello," I said.

"Good afternoon," said a high-pitched female voice on the other end. "May I speak to Claire Evans, please?"

"Speaking."

"Fabulous." The voice became a chirrupy trill. "This is Gemma Goddard from *The Sun*. You got us all excited with that text message of yours. What's going on? Did your husband cheat on you?"

I was tempted to tell her everything. But something held me back. Somehow the admission that Mark had strayed from our marital bed seemed like a slap in the face. My pride as a wife and a woman was at stake. After all, I'd been unable to keep my own husband in check.

My silence must have been interpreted as a yes, because Goddard began to gush:

"Perfect. You must surely be bursting to tell me more. We're delighted to offer you fifteen thousand pounds for an exclusive. A no-holds-barred exposé of what went wrong in your mixed marriage over the years…"

The smugness in my heart evaporated. My thoughts dissolved into a churning mess. I hung up and switched off my phone. What I needed, I realized, was a sympathetic friend, someone to listen to my woes. Certainly not a kiss-and-tell interview with *The Sun*.

So here I am an hour later, still crying. I must have used up an entire box of tissues since arriving at Emily's. The generous sympathy on her face is causing everything to bubble over.

I dab my eyes again.

"I shouldn't have allowed Mark to fool me for so long," I say, stifling a sob. "I should have smelled a rat when he began traveling to London. Should have realized he had a mistress there."

"It isn't your fault," says Emily, patting me on the shoulder. "Don't blame yourself."

"But the writing was on the wall," I say, unable to stop my voice from choking. "The facts were there from day one, Em. Mark's not to be trusted. He never loved me, not even at the start. I can't believe I convinced myself otherwise."

"Rubbish," says Emily, handing me another tissue. "No way you could have seen this coming. Stop blaming yourself, sweetie. It only makes things worse. It's Mark who deserves to feel like shit, not you."

"So what do I do now?" I say, dabbing my cheeks.

"Start thinking about your settlement," says Emily, dispensing one of her matter-of-fact solutions with a sudden smirk. "How much you can wangle out of that arsehole. Fifty percent should set you up for life. Do contact that lawyer O'Sullivan. I've just read in *The Sun* that he's managed to get seventy-five million for Petronella Cruise."

"Who?"

"That actress who found her husband in bed with another woman."

I sigh.

"Come to think of it, a lie-down might also do you good," she continues, giving me another sympathetic pat on the back. "You've been crying for an hour. You look terrible. Come with me, sweetie. We have a spare bed. You should have a rest."

I ought to heed Emily's advice. I can't think of anything better to do. I grab my handbag and follow her down the hallway. She leads me into a poky little room containing a tiny bunk bed.

"Get in," she says, plumping up the pillows and drawing back the thin covers.

I fling my bag onto a nearby table and dive into the bed. It smells of ancient mothballs and dust that has not been touched for weeks. Emily tucks the covers over me before kissing me on the forehead and bustling over to the window to draw the curtains.

"You'll feel better soon, sweetie," she says. "More carrot cake will be waiting for you in the kitchen when you emerge. Definitely more hot chocolate. I'll bake your favorite scones."

She shuts the door.

Despite what Emily thinks, the lie-down isn't calming me at all. Her dusty, mothball-reeking bed only makes my head spin. I rise and stagger to the window. I pull the curtains back and fling the shutters open, only to be greeted with a grand view of Trinity's Burrell's Field student quarters.

The Trinity May Ball, I think with a groan. The night when I should have first understood the writing on the wall.

I stumble to the table, open my handbag, and pull out the contents of the "Summer Term 1995" folder I'd removed from Mark's study. It didn't take me too long to find that particular file, thanks to Mark's obsessive habit of putting everything in chronological order.

I riffle through the yellowing papers before me, trying not to choke at the mottled dust particles rising from their surfaces. The stack consists of miscellaneous receipts and correspondence. I flick past several planning sheets relating to May Week performances of Shakespeare's *Twelfth Night* at the ADC Theatre, a production Mark must have been involved in. I pause at a letter from the Trinity bursar. It confirms Mark's fellowship allowance (£975 for the summer term) and his dining rights (three meals per day, including High Table).

I pull out the stub of his ticket for the May Ball.

"Strictly white tie," it says. "Survivors photo: 7:00. Carriages: 7:30."

A folded page from the *Times* lies behind the ticket stub. I unfold the sheet, spreading out the stubborn creases with my hands. It's dated 15 June 1995.

I gasp. The date coincides with the twelve missing days in my head.

DUO BOY, 5, FOUND ALIVE AFTER CORNWALL AIR CRASH KILLS HIS PARENTS, the largest headline says. I skim through the story, but I'm unable to see the relevance of its contents. Why did Mark retain page 11 of the *Times* in his file folder? I scan the other stories. My gaze settles on a small column at the bottom of the page.

FEMALE STUDENT MISSING, the title says. The accompanying text reads:

The police have appealed for help in finding a Duo female who has been missing since the evening hours of 12 June. Anna May Winchester, 24, a graduate of Lucy Cavendish College, was last seen by her housemate dressing up for the Trinity May Ball. The police were notified after Miss Winchester failed to show up at the event. She is white, slim, about 5 feet 7 inches tall, and has dark brown hair and hazel eyes. She was last seen wearing a peach-colored ball gown and elbow-length white gloves.

I freeze. Didn't my diary entry for 12 June 1995, say that I saw Mark holding the hand of a girl in a "stunning peach dress and white gloves"? I riffle through the remaining papers in the pile before pulling out two more folded newspaper articles. The first is page 3 of the *Cambridge Evening News* dated 17 June 1995. The main headline reads: WORRY GROWS FOR MISSING CAMBRIDGE ALUMNA. The text is flanked by a photo of a thin brunette with laughing eyes.

Was she the girl I saw holding Mark's hand all those years ago? I clutch the page, my knuckles turning white, before devouring the accompanying passage:

Fears are increasing for a Lucy Cavendish alumna who has gone missing in the Chesterton area during the evening hours of 12 June.

Duo Anna May Winchester, 24, was last seen in her room on George Street. She had been planning to attend the Trinity May Ball that evening with her friends. Miss Winchester completed a postgraduate degree in art history last year and has been undertaking an internship at the Fitzwilliam Museum since January.

Miss Winchester's Duo ex-classmate Laura Patterson has expressed deep concern for her friend's welfare.

"I don't understand why Anna is missing," she says. "It doesn't feel real at all. She was supposed to arrive at the ball by 22:00. We'd agreed to meet at the Trinity Bridge at 22:45 so we could watch the fireworks together. But Anna never came.

We are all desperately hoping she's safe. She's loved by so many people."

DC Hans Richardson, of the Cambridgeshire Constabulary, says: "Anna's parents are distressed by her disappearance, as it's out of character for her. If anyone knows anything, please come forward."

My mouth has run dry. Hans Richardson? Isn't he the gray-haired detective who showed up in my garden this morning and turned my life upside down?

I set the article aside and pick up the third folded page. It's also from the *Cambridge Evening News*, the issue dated 18 June 1995. Now I know what I'm looking for. My eyes settle on the bottommost piece, entitled MISSING GIRL'S HANDBAG FOUND. The text reads:

A diamanté-encrusted Chanel handbag belonging to missing Duo Anna May Winchester has been located at the piling of a pedestrian bridge over the River Cam, next to the Fort St. George pub on Midsummer Common. It was found by Duo undergraduate James Tempest-Stewart of the Peterhouse Boat Club during a training session.

"My mates and I had just set out for Baits Bite Lock when we saw something floating in the river," he says. "We rowed over for a closer look. It turned out to be a lady's handbag. Its strap was impaled on a steel spike on one of the bridge pilings."

DC Hans Richardson, of the Cambridgeshire Constabulary, confirms that the handbag contains a Trinity May Ball ticket in Miss Winchester's name. Anyone with information as to her whereabouts is urged to call 999 at once.

Multiple questions surge through my head. Why did I fail to learn twelve days' worth of entries from that post–May Ball period? And why did I cut out those pages from my diary? Was I traumatized by the discovery that Mark had been sleeping with another girl merely days after he took my virginity? Was I heartbroken to discover that he had merely pursued me for sex? Or was there more to my desire to forget? Something more sinister? Perhaps a missing twenty-four-year-old girl named Anna May Winchester?

First a *dead* woman. And now a *missing* woman.

But perhaps I shouldn't read too much into matters. Maybe Anna was merely Mark's friend. After all, they both went to Cambridge. I would be alarmed if a friend of mine disappeared into the blue. That must be why Mark kept these newspaper articles. Granted, I did see him with a girl in a pretty peach dress and white gloves on the night of the May Ball. But this must have been coincidental. Two other balls took place in Cambridge that evening. There must have been at least a dozen girls roaming around town in peach dresses and white gloves.

Anna May Winchester cannot be the girl I saw that evening. The one holding Mark's hand. The girl he slept with.

Or could she?

Another disquieting possibility strikes me. If Anna was indeed the girl Mark slept with, her housemate was *not* the last person to have seen her that evening. *I*, Claire Evans—Claire Bushey back then—saw her on her way to the ball. Holding Mark's hand and fighting with him minutes later.

In which case, Mark must have been the last person to see Anna that evening.

A sudden black desperation floods my soul; I'm now frantic to pull up some facts from that twelve-day vacuum. Anything at all. Moving away from the table, I begin pacing around the room, trying to jolt the information into my head. I grimace at the cobwebs in a corner of the ceiling, hoping they might trigger a revelation or two. I squint at a redbrick building outside the window. But there's only darkness inside me, a frustrating void. I suppose it's impossible to dredge up what I never tried to learn in the first place.

Sighing, I return to the table and continue riffling through the remaining items from Mark's folder. I pause at a couple of invoices from the Cambridge law firm Harrison & Co. for "services rendered." The documents are dated 20 and 24 August 1995, and show the amounts of £135 and £229. I wonder why on earth Mark needed the services of a law firm. There's also a receipt for a two-carat solitaire diamond ring from the jeweler Ernest Jones, dated 13 July 1995, for the sum of £1,888.

I suck in my breath before collapsing on Emily's bed.

Didn't Mark propose to me at 21:07 on 14 July 1995, on the upper balcony of the De Vere Hotel, whipping out a solitaire diamond ring as he fell on one knee? Unlike the twelve-day void in my head, this little fact rushes instantly to mind. Additional fact: I reacted by gaping at the dazzling ring, speechless for once. But as soon as my astonishment wore off and I realized that Mark truly intended to marry me, I was over the moon (though I did my best not to appear too giddy).

Incidentally, the diamond is still on my left hand. After years of wearing my engagement ring, I'd forgotten to remove it when I told Mark I wanted a divorce.

I stare at the glittering gem on my finger, chewing my lower lip. The solitaire sparkles even in the dim light, its multiple facets piercing the gloom of the room. I should be flattered that Mark paid a whopping £1,888 for the ring twenty years ago. Didn't I learn from *Cosmopolitan* magazine that a man should be willing to part with at least double his monthly salary for an engagement ring? If Mark's Trinity fellowship allowance was £975 that term, he must have either begged, borrowed, or dipped heavily into his personal savings to buy this one.

For *me*.

But did he ever love me in the first place? Or was his proposal driven by other reasons? If he wanted me purely for sex on the first day we met, why did he eventually ask me to marry him?

I think I know the answers to these questions. I can't ignore the facts I've learned.

Taking a deep breath, I begin tugging at the two rings on my finger.

The engagement ring slips off at once, but my wedding band refuses to budge. Twenty years of marriage has resulted in ten pudgier fingers, left ring finger included. Gritting my teeth, I yank harder. To my relief, the gold band comes off in a sharp, chafing rush.

I set the rings down on the table. It feels as though two enormous weights have been lifted off my hand. Even my shoulders seem lighter.

I feel strangely liberated.

But there's still a sense of disquiet in my stomach. Doubting questions still circle my mind like vultures, refusing to be shooed away. Earlier this morning, I was confident that Mark had nothing to do with the death of Sophia Ayling. Mark isn't a murderer, I thought. He's a *cheat*. A man who has sex with other women to the detriment of his wife's happiness and sanity.

But a missing woman has now entered the fray.

A thought slips into my head.

Maybe I should speak to that gray-haired detective. He might be able to shed light on the reasons behind Miss Winchester's disappearance. Maybe even illuminate that troubling void of darkness in my head. And while I'm at it, I could ask him a few probing questions about my husband's nocturnal shenanigans.

Anyone with information as to her whereabouts is urged to call 999 at once. Call 999.

A call twenty years overdue, but better late than never.

I reach for the phone in my handbag. As I do so, someone knocks on the door.

"Come in," I say.

The door creaks open; Emily is at the threshold. Her face is a flustered shade of red.

"Sorry for disturbing you, sweetie." She bustles in, wiping floury fingers on her apron. "You must be up to something, with those papers around you. Is everything all right? Did you get some rest?"

"Not really."

"Mark... er... Mark called the landline," she says. "He wanted to know if you're here."

I gasp.

"What did you say?"

"I said yes."

"You told him that I'm *here?*"

"Er...yes...I did. He said he's coming over to talk to you."

"He said *what?*" I stare at her in horror.

"I'm sorry." Emily raises her hands, spraying flour on the carpet. "But we don't have to let him in. Even if he makes a scene outside my door. He wouldn't dare to anyway. Not when I have two nosy neighbors right across the corridor who'll be itching to report him to the press."

I leap to my feet and begin stuffing Mark's papers back into my handbag.

"I'm so sorry, Claire." Emily's forehead contracts into a mass of wrinkles. "It was silly of me to tell him that you're here. But I did say that he's the last person in the universe you wish to see, after everything he's done."

I reach over and squeeze my best friend's arm to indicate that I'm not upset.

"There's nothing wrong with the truth, Em. I'm getting really sick of lies. I need to leave anyway."

"Where are you going?" Surprise floods Emily's face.

"I'm seeing a detective who might help me figure out what happened twenty years ago."

"Twenty years ago?"

"Yes. The summer of 1995."

The United Kingdom Human Rights Act 1953
(Amendment)
Art. 8(1) and Art. 8(2)

Article 8: Right to respect for privacy and memory

1. Monos and Duos have the right to privacy in their family lives, homes, and diaries in life and in death. Unless a person's will specifically states that a private diary should be preserved after death, electronic and written diaries shall be destroyed upon the death of each individual.

2. There shall be no interference by a public authority in the exercise of this right except in accordance with the laws of a democratic society and in the interests of national security, public safety, and the mitigation of disorder or crime. Public authorities may therefore be empowered by warrant to inspect the diaries of deceased persons to ensure the continued protection of these interests.

Chapter Sixteen

HANS

8½ HOURS UNTIL THE END OF THE DAY

The clock on the wall tells me that it's half past three in the afternoon. My lunch is long overdue, and my stomach is growling, forcibly reminding me that I've been on the Ayling case for ten consecutive hours. I should step outside for a quick bite. But the phone on my desk is erupting with a shrill clamor; I pick up the receiver with a sigh.

"Hans," a female voice says. "Front desk. A woman here wishes to see you. She says her name's Claire Evans. You apparently visited her garden this morning."

I sit upright in my chair.

"Get someone to bring her up."

"Fiona, then. She's passing by."

What an unexpected development. I wonder why Claire Evans has come to Parkside to see me. Fact: My hunches about people are usually right. And my intuition says that Mrs. Evans is a woman with secrets. Of course, I already know that she's on antidepressants and has tried to damage herself in the past. However, my gut also tells me that I'm merely scraping the surface.

Two female figures loom at the door, just a few yards away. Mrs. Evans's lavender eyes have turned a couple of shades darker since this morning. They are also framed by puffy eyelids.

"Step right through, madam," says Fiona before giving me a pointed wink and disappearing outside.

"Ah, Mrs. Evans." I stand up to greet her. "Nice to see you again. Please have a seat."

She settles down on the chair previously occupied by her husband. Her hands have acquired a nervous fidget since we first spoke. They also look different to me. They are now devoid of jewelry, although there is still a gold bracelet around her wrist. I could have sworn I saw a diamond ring and a wedding band on her left hand earlier this morning. I squint; two pale flesh circles have replaced the rings on her finger. So Hamish's report about what transpired at that Guildhall press conference was accurate.

"What can I do for you?" I say.

She does not answer. She merely studies her naked fingers. Fact: Silence can be just as revealing as an extended gabble of speech. Her reticence tells me that she's struggling with something tumultuous within.

"Does Miss Ayling's diary say they started their affair around two years ago?"

She lifts her head and fixes her eyes on me. Turmoil rages within their depths.

I nod.

She sighs. "I thought so. Mark began spending more time in London then. That's what my diary says."

"I'm sorry. Telling wives their husbands *may* have strayed isn't my favorite part of the job."

She shrugs.

"I should have smelled a rat when Mark began disappearing from Cambridge. But I failed to read the signs. Even though they were there from the start."

So Mark Henry Evans is a *serial* adulterer.

"You've since decided to divorce him."

Astonishment surges to Claire Evans's face. But she pulls her shoulders back, lifting her chin.

"Word gets round fast in this town."

"My visit must have prompted this decision. Otherwise you wouldn't have known, would you?"

"If your wife was unfaithful, would you still want to stay married to her?" Her eyes flash red.

"I'm not married. My job takes up most of my time."

"Lucky you," she says before falling silent again and staring down at her hands.

I wait for her to speak once more. Fact: Most people are uncomfortable with prolonged silences. They usually become desperate to fill the gaps with words. And sentences born out of desperation, as I've learned over the years, can be pretty damned revealing.

"Did Miss Ayling's diary say that Mark...was in love with her?" she says in a sudden rush.

"I can't answer that question."

Did I just see a glimmer of relief in her eyes? A distinct flicker of hope that her husband was never in love with his mistress? If so, she must still be subconsciously holding out for a reconciliation.

"Are you still investigating Mark, then?"

"We're following up all possible leads. They include the men Miss Ayling *may* have been intimate with."

"Have you found anything?"

"Again, I cannot say."

"You're like a stone wall." She rolls her eyes at me. "It must come with the job you're married to."

"But you didn't come here just to tell me that I resemble a stone wall, I presume. What *really* brings you to Parkside, Mrs. Evans?"

She opens her mouth only to close it a few moments later. Again, I wait in companionable silence.

"I've...er...I've come to ask you about a girl named Anna May Winchester."

"*Anna May Winchester?*" It is my turn to look surprised.

"Yes. She was a Cambridge alumna who disappeared on her way to the

Trinity May Ball in June of 1995. You were the DC on the case. At least, that was what the newspapers said at the time."

Of course. Fact: Anna May Winchester did indeed vanish on her way to a ball in 1995. It was one of the first investigations I took on as a DC. But why is Claire Evans interested in the Winchester case? I rack my brains, trying to pull up a factual connection between Claire and Anna. But my mind's an utter, abject blank.

"Why are you interested in *her?*"

"Much of the period between the thirteenth and twenty-fourth of June that year is a black hole in my head," she says, sudden sheepishness shading her face. "That's why I dug up a few newspaper articles from that period. Anna is featured in some of them. I'm hoping you could tell me more about her."

This is both odd and intriguing.

"Did you not keep any diary records of those twelve days?"

"I...er...did. But I...er...may have lost them."

I'm gobsmacked. Diary loss is serious business. People do not normally lose their lifelines to the past if they can help it. Fact: The Protection of Personal Diaries Act (1995) has reduced the number of thefts and extortion rackets by obliging citizens to install safes in their homes for the storage of hard-copy diaries (though thefts from people carrying diaries in public places is still a problem).

"Lost them? Did you report the loss, as required by the Protection of Personal Diaries Act?"

"Er...no." Embarrassment floods her eyes. "Let's just say...I may need to search my home again."

"But surely you must have worked hard at learning those pages before losing them."

Her lower lip trembles.

"Maybe not hard enough," she says with a sigh, refusing to meet my eyes. "I've misplaced those pages, that's all. That's why I'm here. I'm hoping you could tell me what happened to Anna."

"Mrs. Evans." I heave a sigh in return. "I'm in the middle of a criminal investigation. I'm up to my neck in the case. You know what I'm investigating. I'm sorry to say that my current job description does not extend to a historic disappearance."

"Please, Inspector." A shrill note of desperation jangles her voice. "Could you at least tell me what happened to the girl? Did you find her in the end?"

Maybe I should answer her questions. Claire Evans, after all, is a Mono, as I am. Monos ought to be nice to their own kind—otherwise, who else will be nice to them? Fact: I also understand how missing girls, the embodiment of unanswered questions, can gnaw away at one's psyche.

"I'll check," I say, turning to the shelf behind me and reaching for a purple notebook entitled "Enforced or Voluntary Disappearances: Lessons Learned." I flip through its pages and run my finger down the column labeled "U-V-W." My eyes gravitate to the main entry, highlighted with a fluorescent marker.

Von Meier, Liesl: What more can I write about poor Liesl, apart from the terrible, soul-destroying realization that I had an opportunity to solve her case within a single day and that I will forever be haunted by my failure to do so? (NTS: I should—

Pain stabs me, curdling my heart. I can barely breathe. I drag my gaze away from Liesl's entry to the next paragraph in the column.

Winchester, Anna May: Vanished on her way to the Trinity May Ball in June of 1995 before making a surprise reappearance at a friend's apartment nineteen days later, looking disheveled and starved. Her doctor said her stress levels had gone through the roof. Clammed up like an oyster when asked about the reasons for her disappearance; I unfortunately got very little out of her. (NTS: Came away from the Winchester interview feeling that

I should learn better questioning techniques. I ought to try to get a place in the next "How to Prise Useful Information Out of People" course in London.)

I look up at Claire Evans.

"Yes, we did find her," I say.

"You did? *Really?*"

"Nineteen days after she vanished."

"Thank God for that." Relief fills her face. "What happened to her?"

"We never found out."

"But why did she go missing in the first place?"

"She refused to say."

"How odd."

"Odd things happen in my line of work," I say, shrugging. "Because people are odd. They do odd things all the time. This is an unfortunate fact, which gives poor detectives like me a perpetual headache. Were you once acquainted with Anna?"

She shakes her head.

"Then why does her case matter to you?"

She turns her eyes to my chessboard for a few seconds before replying:

"It struck me as being unusual, that's all. Its timing also coincided with those missing days in my head."

I sense that Claire Evans hasn't been entirely forthcoming in her reply. Only a desperate person would come all the way to Parkside to find out more about a girl who temporarily disappeared twenty years ago.

I decide to probe further. "Do you know someone who was bothered by Anna's disappearance?"

"I don't know if Ma—" she says, swallowing. "No, I don't."

A flash of insight strikes me.

"Your *husband*, perhaps? Wasn't he a postgraduate at Cambridge around the same time?"

Her mouth is pinched shut. But she pushes her shoulders back and mumbles:

"No. I don't think Mark knew her."

"You're sure?"

She nods, but I sense she's hiding something darker.

"Could you tell me what your husband did yesterday, by the way?"

She blinks at my rapid change of subject.

"Do I have to answer your question?" she fires back, eyes darkening again.

"No, not at all." I keep my face even. "But I've answered your questions about Miss Winchester. And *my* question has to do with a man you wish to divorce."

She sighs.

"Very well," she says. "Mark was at home yesterday."

"Did he not leave the house?"

She shakes her head. "No. I felt poorly and spent most of yesterday in bed. Mark kept checking on me all day long. He also made me lunch and dinner. But I had little appetite for either."

"What was wrong?"

She hesitates for a long time before replying:

"Felt a bit down in the dumps."

Her answer has the unmistakable ring of honesty to it.

"Any idea why?"

She presses her lips together for a few seconds before shaking her head.

"No."

Fuzziness clouds her eyes; Claire Evans may well be telling the truth.

"What about the day before yesterday? What did your husband get up to?"

"One moment."

She opens her handbag—it's jammed full with yellowing papers—and pulls out her iDiary. She hits a few buttons with a frown.

"Mark took lunch in his study so he could continue writing," she says, glancing up at me. "He went back there after dinner to do more work. I don't think he left home on Thursday either."

I sense that Mrs. Evans is indeed telling me the truth about what's written in her diary. The details also tally with what her husband said when I questioned him earlier this morning. Alas.

"Thank you for clarifying," I say.

"I must go," she says, replacing her diary and shutting her handbag with a snap. She gets up, looking slightly happier than when she first settled down. But before she begins moving in the direction of the door, she fastens her eyes on me.

"Mark didn't kill Sophia Ayling," she says with a determined tilt of her chin. "He sleeps with other women, for sure. That's why I'm divorcing him. But he isn't a murderer. He's not one to hurt others. This is a fact I'm convinced of."

"I hope you're right."

She sighs.

"Thank you for your time, Inspector," she says before walking out the door.

Anna May Winchester? What the hell?

I'm about to pelt down the stairs to the records storage room when I realize that Fiona has reappeared at my door. The broad smile on her face matches the size of the wrapped object in her hand.

"I see you're rushing off somewhere," she says, holding out the item in my direction. "But you should investigate this sandwich first."

"You're a star, Fi." I grab the packet from her hand. "How can I ever repay you?"

"You looked starved earlier," she says with a chuckle as I rip the foil open and begin cramming the sandwich into my mouth. "I realized from my diary that it was way past your normal lunch hour. So I took pity on you. Repayment's easy, by the way. Just buy me lunch later this week."

I'm impressed that Fiona has bothered to write down and learn the time I normally have lunch. I should also marvel at her artful attempt at engineering a date with me.

"Claire Evans is quite a character, isn't she?" Fiona says, giving me another pointed wink. "But I'm not surprised her husband decided to seek greener pastures…"

"Meow. You're being catty."

"I'm being *honest*. She's no match for the woman on Peter's screen earlier. Claire's curves are in all the wrong places."

"People tend to pile on the pounds when they get married. This is a fact."

"My, oh, my." She rolls her eyes at me. "Are you defending Claire Evans?"

"Course not." I shake my head, trying to gobble down the rest of the sandwich in a dignified manner. "I'm merely pointing out the obvious."

"Hah. You have a thing for busty blondes, don't you?"

I'm tempted to groan, but my mouth is stuffed full of crispy bacon. I'm inclined to think that Fiona is flirting with me. Or she could simply be trying to work out my precise tastes in women.

"How are you getting on with the case?" She chuckles at the expression on my face.

I swallow the rest of the sandwich before replying:

"Still more questions than answers. Mrs. Evans's unexpected visit has added to the riddles in my head. Multiplied them, even."

"Busty blondes can be problematic." She gives me a sudden smirk. "You might fare better with skinny but tamer brunettes."

"Not necessarily," I say, unable to stop my eyes from straying to Sophia's photo album on my desk, the one containing multiple images of her previous incarnation as a skinny brunette. "Not when a raven-haired beauty is standing before me, one with a heart big enough to buy me lunch."

Fiona is working hard to stifle a smile. I must still be on the good books of the head of computing services, although I shouldn't be encouraging her too much. And I should write these facts down in my diary tonight: *It's time for me to stop flirting with my colleagues, even if they have lovely eyes and mesmerizing leopard-print trousers. Because this is dangerous. Especially as I'm still hoping to be promoted to detective superintendent before the age of forty-five, which would be an unparalleled achievement for a Mono like me.*

Brain recharged by bacon, I hurry down to the room in the basement where our old case-file reports are stored. Although no one knows how many folders are languishing there, I reckon there must be at least ten thousand. Fact: Digitization costs money, and the constabulary suffers from perpetual budget cuts. These musty old folders will still be plaguing the basement when I retire.

The cavernous room smells of mildew and dampness; I wrinkle my nose as I rush to the far end. I turn the wheel at the end of the row of shelves, causing them to rumble along the rails on the floor. Within thirty seconds or so, I've opened up a gap between two adjoining rows labeled "W–X" and "Y–Z." I sprint down the newly emerged space between the shelves, scanning them for the relevant drawer. I yank out the compartment marked "Wi–Wo" before rummaging through the folders inside. To my delight, I see a folder marked "Winchester, Anna May," sandwiched between "Winch, Harry" and "Windall, Bertrand."

I open the folder to discover a report at the top:

FAO: DETECTIVE CHIEF SUPERINTENDENT GEOFFREY MONAGHAN
INTERVIEW WITH WINCHESTER, ANNA MAY

(Missing Person Serial No. 14745)

9 July 1995

I conducted an interview with Anna May Winchester (of 288 Brook Lane, Coton) on 9 July 1995, at Addenbrooke's Hospital. She was reported to have gone missing for a period of nineteen days (12 June to 1 July 1995).

My notes say that my first attempt at interviewing Miss

Winchester, on 2 July 1995, was unsuccessful. She shook her head and refused to explain what had happened to her. She also yelled at me to leave. Her doctor bundled me out of the room and told me to return the following week, saying that Miss Winchester's stress levels were still abnormally high. I shouldn't delay her recovery by making her more agitated, he said. I therefore returned a week later to conduct another interview. It lasted ten minutes; although she was more lucid the second time, she remained just as reluctant to describe her experiences. I did, however, receive a verbal assurance from Miss Winchester that she was not robbed, kidnapped, assaulted, raped, or held against her will.

As Miss Winchester has expressed a clear preference for keeping her location and experiences during those nineteen days "a secret," we are obliged to respect her wishes. She is an adult, and her doctors have not yet issued a formal diagnosis of mental illness. My sense, however, is that Miss Winchester suffers from a severe psychiatric disorder, which probably accounts for her disappearance. Her answers, though coherent, made little sense to my ears. I have already drafted a letter to her doctors at Addenbrooke's raising my concerns about her mental condition.

After subsequent consultation with DI Simon Harris, we have decided to close the Winchester case.

DC Hans Richardson

10 July 1995

I shake my head with a groan. I didn't realize that I was in the habit of writing such pompous-sounding reports during my DC days.

I flip through the other yellowing papers in the pile, the ones documenting the investigation I'd conducted all those years ago. I groan again when I reach Anna's photograph. Her image is barely discernible; the contours of her face have been reduced to faint spectral outlines. The

Polaroid must have discolored over the years because of the persistent dampness in the basement. All I can see of the ghostly Anna is that she has a thin face and long hair that flows to her shoulders.

Setting the faded Polaroid aside, I speed-read through the papers in front of me. Before long, I have reacquainted myself with some key facts about the Winchester case:

1. Anna was white, stood around five feet seven inches tall, and had an extremely slim figure. Her eyes and hair were dark brown. These details were released to the press.

2. Her Duo housemate, Mary Elise Saunders, was the last person to see Anna on 12 June 1995. Anna had moved into Saunders's spare room two days after· her father remarried, in October of 1994. At around 19:15, Mary Elise passed by Anna's room and saw her applying gloss to her lips. By then, Anna had already donned an ankle-length peach ball gown and a pair of elbow-length white gloves.

3. A search of Anna's room had revealed nothing suspicious. Anna's father and friends were adamant that her behavior had been entirely normal.

4. Her Duo classmate Laura Patterson stated that Anna had promised to meet her at the Trinity Bridge at 22:45 so they could watch the fireworks together, but never turned up.

5. Anna did not appear to have a regular boyfriend, although Laura said she went out on frequent dates with boys from the university.

6. Anna's sodden Chanel handbag, spotted by Peterhouse rowers in the river near the Fort St. George pub on 17 June 1995, contained her Trinity May Ball ticket (which bore her name), a mascara wand, a tube of pink lip gloss, and a powder compact. Although these details were not released to the press, her handbag also contained her diary and a pregnancy-testing kit. The ink on her diary had washed off in the river, making it

impossible to decipher its contents. I'd sent the diary off for an expert analysis of pen impression marks; the report was still pending when Anna reappeared.

Unfortunately, I'm unable to spot any connections between Anna May Winchester and Claire Evans. So why did Claire come to Parkside to ask me about Anna? And why did she look so relieved when I said that we found the girl nineteen days later?

I scan through the contents of the folder again, but a link between the two women remains frustratingly elusive. This diversion into the antediluvian affairs of the once-missing Anna May Winchester may well be a colossal waste of time. Perhaps Claire was telling the truth: she was interested in the Winchester case simply because it coincided with the twelve days of factual oblivion in her head.

I ought to get back to Sophia Ayling. Especially as I hope to pin down her murderer before the end of the day.

I'm on the verge of slamming the Winchester folder shut when I notice some minuscule letters and numbers. They are scrawled in pencil at the bottom right-hand corner of the uppermost report:

ITR007

Fact: I'd invented a crude code for my own reference soon after I joined the force. The code tells me that I must have retained something related to the Winchester investigation in the locked bottom drawer of my office. An item with a small sticker bearing the number 7.

An item for my eyes only.

This looks promising. I suppose I can afford to spare a few more minutes on the Winchester case. I cram the folder back into the drawer and rush up the stairs to my office, grabbing another cup of coffee from the vending machine along the way.

I shut the door, unlock the bottom drawer of my desk, and riffle through the objects in it. Before long, I've dug out number 7.

It's an unlabeled cassette tape.

Fact: ITR007 is shorthand for "Interview, tape-recorded, number 7."

Of course. Fact: I'd surreptitiously recorded a handful of interviews during my early days on the force. My first mentor had confessed— after he had too many beers one night—that he once solved a case after secretly taping his interview with a seemingly incoherent thug and listening to the recording afterwards. I was inspired to wear a voice-activated recorder beneath my shirt to a few subsequent interviews, especially when I knew I would be dealing with difficult people. This was, of course, not an action sanctioned by the powers that be. But I was convinced, back then, that these secret tapes were a useful precautionary measure. I could cover my arse if questions were ever raised about my work. I could also fall back on their contents in case I missed anything during my interviews. In hindsight, I marvel at my insecurities.

But I suppose confidence comes with experience.

Number 7 must be a secret tape recording of my conversation with Anna. My 10 July report says that the interview was ten minutes long. Maybe I can spare the time. Perhaps Anna mentioned Claire Evans during our exchange, but the name failed to strike me as significant all those years ago.

A microcassette player occupies a corner of the same drawer. I fish the device out, place the tape inside it, and hit the Play button. The resulting crackle of static is followed by a male voice. I wince (I didn't realize I sounded so green when I was younger).

Male: Could you tell me where you were? Between the evening of the ball and when you showed up at Laura's door?

Female: It's a secret.

Male: What happened to you during those nineteen days?

Female: Things. All sorts of things.

Male: Like what?

Female: Things happen. Whether you like them or not.

Male: But what were they?

Female: Haven't I just said it's a secret?

Male: We found a handbag in the water, stuck to the footbridge near Midsummer Common, a few days after you disappeared. It contained a May Ball ticket in your name. How did your bag get there?

[Silence]

Female: Things float, don't they?

Male: Did someone take your handbag away from you?

Female: I'd like to see someone try.

Male: Did you lose your handbag, then?

Female: No.

Male: So how did your handbag get separated from you?

Female: I didn't need it anymore.

Male: And why didn't you?

Female: I already have enough baggage on my shoulders.

Male: I don't get you.

Female: Cash is all you need.

Male: But what did you spend your money on?

[Silence]

Male: We also found your diary inside your handb—

Female: Diaries are damned overrated.

[Brief silence]

Male: How did you go about recording things? Did you write them down elsewhere?

Female: Do I look that desperate to remember?

Male: We found a pregnancy-testing kit inside your handbag. Did you think you might be pregnant?

[Long silence]

Female: I don't feel like talking...anymore. The nurse stuck something in my arm again this morning.

Male: But we need to work out what happened to you. Please be honest with me.

Female: Everyone's been asking me the same fucking questions. Dad was at it again this morning.

Male: That's because he's worried. He thinks that something bad may have happened to you.

Female: Yeah, right. Dad only cares about himself and the women he shags. Always has, too. I should have known that a long time ago.

Male: Why did you disappear for so long?

Female: I didn't feel like doing anything for a while.

Male: You know you didn't feel like doing anything for a while and that nothing bad happened to you. You also know you had some cash. This tells me that you wrote these facts down somewhere. Could you tell me what else you've written about that period?

[Silence]

Male: [Audible sigh] Laura said that you were supposed to meet her later that night to watch the fireworks together. Why didn't—

Female: Laura's a bitch. A scheming, vain bitch. Always has been. Should have realized that earlier.

Male: You did show up at her door, though, nineteen days later. Where were you before that?

Female: [Loud groan] Stop pestering me, will you?

Male: Why did you decide to go to Laura's?

Female: Once a bitch, always a bitch. And you're getting to be a real pain in the arse, like her.

Male: How did you survive? What did you eat?

Female: I wasn't hungry.

Male: What did you do on your way to the ball? Did something bad happen to you then?

Female: Men are bastards. Especially that one.

Male: Who's "that one"?

Female: Arseholes, they all are. Particularly Mark. He led me on big-time.

Male: Mark who?

[Silence]

Male: [Audible sigh] Look here. Did anyone harm you? Like this Mark, for instance? Were you robbed, kidnapped, assaulted, raped, or held against your will?

Female: No. For fuck's sake, *no*. I wasn't robbed. Or kidnapped. Or raped. Or held anywhere. The answer is *no*. Have I made myself clear? What happened is a secret. Can you just fuck off and leave me alone?

Male: I'm glad to hear you weren't harmed. I'm leaving now.

Female: Thank God for that.

[Beep of recorder being switched off]

I turn off the microcassette player, face flushed with embarrassment. Sounding green is bad enough. But it's much worse to discover that I've committed every single mistake in the 379-page *How to Conduct an Interview* manual. In particular, I've violated the principles that "active listening should be used to establish a rapport" and "leading questions should only be employed as a last resort."

So I wasn't just a naive constable. I was also a pathetic one.

I ought to be mortified. Perhaps I should be less demanding of my assistants today. I can only hope that my interrogation skills have improved over time.

The coffee in my cup has turned stone cold, but I take a giant gulp anyway. It trickles down my throat like rancid cough syrup. Anna mentioned a man named Mark. An "arsehole" named Mark, more precisely. I made little of her remark during the interview, but I should have pursued the issue further. I should have worked harder to extract Mark's last name from her stubborn mouth.

Why didn't I do so? Silly younger me.

The long-ago errors in my 1995 investigation keep piling up like dead flies.

"Mark" must be Mark Henry Evans. It can't be anyone else. He must have been Anna's boyfriend, too, otherwise he wouldn't have "led her on," as she claimed. So that's why his wife, Claire, came to Parkside an hour ago to question me about Anna.

Mark, Anna, and Claire were entangled twenty years ago. But how exactly? Did Mark do something terrible to Anna on the night of the Trinity ball, causing her to vanish for nineteen days? And why did Claire not retain any facts from around the same period?

Mono-Bashing Psychiatrist Pleads Guilty

Budapest, 2 February 2015—A British psychiatrist has admitted to beating Hungarian Monos on their heads with a stick and subjecting them to severe emotional abuse in a bid to improve their short-term memories.

Duo Steve Temple, 47, has pleaded guilty to twenty-five counts of simultaneous physical and verbal abuse. He moved from London to Budapest ten years ago to conduct his research on Monos after receiving a grant from the controversial Equality for Monos Foundation (EMF).

In his defense, Dr. Temple argues that all Mono participants had signed full waivers agreeing to his unorthodox methods. All of them, he insists, had been eager to acquire better memories. Most individuals, he says, were frustrated by their low-status occupations and the discrimination they had endured, especially when it came to opportunities for higher education and better salaries.

Dr. Temple believes that he has managed to replicate in humans the results of a 2005 Harvard University study conducted on mice and that he should be praised and not censured for his groundbreaking efforts. He claims in particular to have converted a female Mono into a Duo through repeated head-whacking and emotional abuse. He also says that he has managed to transform a male Mono into a person with a memory that is "far superior to that of Duos."

Legal experts have pointed out that Dr. Temple's defense has been severely hurt by the fact that the so-called Mono turned Duo has refused to testify in court, while the male Mono with a "far superior" memory mysteriously vanished on his way home from work last week.

The trial continues.

Chapter Seventeen

MARK

Emily Wade is standing at the doorway of her apartment. Clotted cream is smeared on the apron around her ample waist. The heady smell of melted butter and caramelized sugar floats around my nostrils. She must be baking something in the kitchen.

But her lips are drawn back in a grim, unforgiving sneer. She is also brandishing a spatula in my direction.

"Claire isn't here," she says.

"But you said she was with you."

"She was indeed." Emily narrows her eyes. "But she's gone off now. Left ten minutes ago."

"I don't believe you."

"That's not true." Her words roll out in a quiet growl. "I don't lie. Unlike. Some. Other. People."

"Please, Em." I decide to beg, despite the pointed nature of her dig. "I need to speak to Claire."

"She isn't here," Emily says with a snarl, pointing her spatula straight at me. "Left the apartment after you called. Said she needed to get somewhere to figure out the past. Even if she were here, she wouldn't be speaking to you. Not after what you've done. She's told me *everything*."

"You said 'the past.' Did Claire mention the summer of 1995?"

I detect a brief flicker of surprise in Emily's eyes a split second before they're flooded with hostility again.

"That's none of your business. You've hurt her enough. Claire's totally serious about divorcing you, by the way. You'll hear from her lawyer in a couple of days. He's going to hit you with a fat bill."

She slams the door with a bang, cutting off the toasty aromas drifting into the corridor.

I need to find Claire at once. To stop her from doing any further damage to herself. To me. To both of us. But I still haven't got a clue as to where she has disappeared to.

I need to think.

Maybe I should put myself in Claire's shoes. If she had been snooping around in my "Summer Term 1995" folder, she must be desperate to reacquaint herself with some details about that period. Fact: If she swept it bare, she was either in a hurry to leave my study or she wasn't entirely sure what she was looking for.

But why is Claire suddenly interested in the summer of 1995?

I tap the steering wheel of my Jaguar in desperation.

But insight remains elusive.

Fact: Claire and I first met in the summer of 1995. Could she be determined to track down a significant detail or two from the earliest days of our relationship? Something that preoccupies her more than this dreadful business over Sophia Ayling? If so, what exactly is she trying to work out? Could she...could she be troubled by the tumultuous sequence of events that culminated at the altar of the Trinity chapel? Those drastic triggers for our enforced march down the aisle even before the leaves turned into a riot of red and russet-yellow? I thump the steering wheel even harder, only to conclude that I should consult my *own* diary records of that fateful, long-ago summer. Reacquaint myself with the necessary facts.

Damn. The contents of my old ink-and-paper diaries are not retrievable at the simple push of a button. Cursing Mr. Jobs for not inventing the iDiary earlier, I start my Jaguar and step on the accelerator as soon as the engine roars to life. I race down Grange Road, paying token attention to the speed limit.

It takes me only four minutes to get home from Emily's apartment. I slam on the brakes with a screech, jump out of the car, and hurry down the garden path in the direction of my study. Flinging the door open, I head straight for my custom-built platinum safe at the far end of the room (I guess we are all paranoid in our own little ways). Fact: The safe's twelve-digit code is 280276140669. I key in the number, prompting the solid metal door to glide silently from left to right.

Like my file folders, my ink-and-paper diaries are arranged in neat chronological order. I run a finger along their carefully aligned spines, settling on the volume marked "May–September 1995." While I haven't the faintest idea as to where I should begin reading, I suppose I should start from the day when Claire and I first met. Fact: That was on 26 May 1995. I flip through several pages of cursive scrawl before finding the relevant entry.

Its latter part reads:

I took Hannah Astor-Darlington to Varsity Blues for dinner only to have her storm out a few minutes later when the waitress dropped a pen onto her lap, causing splotches of ink to spray out on her skirt. I should write down the scintillating conversation that ensued. I read Professor Highsmith's "Ten Tips for Writers" yesterday; she said that all aspiring novelists should record snippets of real-life conversations in their diaries if they wish to write good dialogue in their books. Only writers who keep meticulous and truthful records of their daily experiences will become successful authors. Highsmith must be right (though I have a sneaking suspicion that good written dialogue isn't real conversation, the same way good porn isn't real sex).

—Oh, no. I'm so sorry, miss.

—Shit. Look what you've done to my skirt. I only bought it last week.

—I'm really sorry, miss. I'll pay to have it cleaned. Or replaced.

—You stupid bitch. There's no way you'll be able to afford to replace it on your measly waitress pay. God, I'm already sick of this place. It's just bursting with inept Monos.

—Calm down, Hannah.

—You should have taken me to the Hotel du Vin, Mark. My diary says it's more civilized there. This bitch has gone and ruined my Dior. God, I've just lost my appetite. . . .

Personally I thought that the splotches of violet gave the fabric an interesting avant-garde appearance (even though the skirt did look more Banksy than Dior). Unfortunately, my date did not share this sentiment. She gathered up her skirt and flounced out of the restaurant after filling the poor waitress's ears with more colorful curses. I can't say I was sorry to see Hannah go. Her company can be asphyxiatingly cloying at times. She also has a tendency to be melodramatic; I suppose she expected me to follow her with a placating expression on my face. But I decided that I couldn't be bothered to go after the histrionic Miss Astor-Darlington. After all, she was a dreadful disappointment in bed earlier today. She lay there in silence like a dead fish, expecting me to do all the hard work. Her sagging boobs were as enticing as two sandbags.

The Mono waitress, however, was an altogether different matter. Her cheeks still bore the rosy flush of a teenager; both childlike innocence and naive charm radiated from her face. To make things better, I also got a clear view of her generous cleavage as she bent down to retrieve the pen. Her breasts were barely concealed by that tight-fitting top of hers (this is partly the reason why I like coming to Varsity Blues, I suppose; they love putting their Mono waitresses in tarty outfits). Her arse was equally impressive, even monumental in scope. Her eyes, despite brimming over with mortification, sizzled like a scorching summer day. If I were a poet, I would be tempted to wax lyrical about their lavender properties. She apologized, offering to pay for my ruined dinner out of her own pocket. I accepted with glee, knowing that it would give me an opportunity to admire her ample assets for a little longer.

I watched her bustle up and down the room for twenty minutes or so, noticing that several other male diners were also casting lustful glances in her direction. The Bordeaux she brought me proved to be unfortunate cat-piss plonk; it must have been one of those lowly fifth-growths Dad will not deign to buy in his lifetime (or the next one). Varsity Blues should learn a thing or two about stocking decent Bordeaux. But I somehow managed to finish the entire carafe. Life's too short to drink bad wine, but dreadful wine is more palatable in the presence of a pretty woman. . I left a small tip and a note inviting her to dinner at the Hotel du Vin at 19:30 this Monday, which the other female server, Emily, confirmed was her day off.

I'm sure Charming Curvaceous Blonde with Sizzling Eyes will show up at the appointed time. She looks like an easy catch. I'm even inclined to think that cherubic Mono waitresses might make a refreshing change from hoity-toity Duo broads (with double-barreled last names) who keep mumbling Kafka in their sleep. Especially if said waitresses are endowed with delicious breasts that are crying out for a quick jiggle.

A quick jiggle? I gape at the faded words on the page. Did I really spout such appalling garbage in my diaries when I was younger? I must have been drunk out of my mind that evening. On bad Bordeaux, too. There may be some truth in the aphorism that a writer's youthful indiscretions and bad prose will return to haunt him in old age. I groan before flipping a few more pages to the final section of the following Monday's entry:

Dinner at the du Vin was great. Charming Blonde (NTS: Her name's Claire Bushey) showed up in a cocktail dress with a plunging neckline, and I spent most of the evening ogling what it promised below. The conversation wasn't too bad, although intellectual topics eluded us. For some reason or other, I told her all about my struggles to get published, particularly my repeated failure to be longlisted for the *Times*'s short-story competition. I don't know what brought it on, why it just spilled out over that rectangular plate of lobster tail. Maybe it's because my subconscious has been secretly loath to confess these things to the fellow Duos who populate my life for fear they'll think I'm an ultimate loser in the writing department. Or maybe her big, charming lavender eyes just loosened my tongue. She definitely radiated some sort of sympa-thetic inner grace, a quiet yet sensitive empathy. I left dinner feeling much happier than I had when I first arrived at the du Vin. Maybe it isn't such a bad thing, after all, to be in the company of unsophisticated Mono girls with refreshingly simple existential outlooks because they are less likely to judge you for what you haven't (yet) accomplished.

She'll yield sooner or later. Especially if I keep giving her roses and ordering bottles of vintage Champagne. I did manage to impress her with the Krug '77. Which was nice, because the Duo chicks I keep running into at Trinity are seldom impressed by anything. (NTS: We should do caviar the next time. I bet she hasn't had caviar before. This might put me in pole position to conquer those delicious twin peaks.)

Another groan escapes my lips. *Delicious twin peaks?* This is going from bad to positively cringeworthy. I reach out to flip the page, but the start of the next diary entry (30 May 1995) catches my eye:

Anna May Winchester was most insistent over coffee this morning that I will be a politician someday:

—You have the air of a politician about you. I see it in your eyes.

—A politician? You must be kidding. I've always wanted to be a writer.

—And a writer you will be. But writing won't give you the true satisfaction you crave.

—Really?

—Your eyes tell me that you're a man who constantly needs to prove himself. Both for your own sake and for those around you. Politics might just fill that void within you.

—We've only known each other for a few days. How do you know a thing like that?

She chuckled before replying:

—We're soul mates, Mark. Soul mates know what's best for each other.

(NTS: Should seriously consider the possibility of becoming a politician someday. Anna may be right. If she's able to work out such profound things about me in just a few days, it might well be written in the stars.)

I probably wouldn't have been at my own damned press conference this morning if Anna had not uttered those words twenty years ago. It's amazing how the effects of seemingly insignificant long-ago conversations continue to reverberate years later.

But I should be focusing on Claire at the moment, not Anna. With a sigh, I turn the pages to my entry for 3 June 1995:

Claire Bushey yielded yesterday evening, after I plied her with caviar and Champagne (so my master strategy worked). I did drink a fair amount of that bottle of Ruinart rosé myself—about three-quarters of it. It's a wonder I managed to get it up in the first place.

I even had a surprise along the way. A simpering virgin, as it turned out. But I should have suspected. That rosy, childlike innocence must come from somewhere.

I'm now convinced that nothing could be more satisfactory than the act of "deflowering an unsullied maiden" (saw that little phrase in the *Textbook of Medieval Duo Literature* yesterday), especially one as charming and well endowed as Claire is (perhaps that's why I got it up in the end). I now understand why certain martyrs are promised ninety-nine virgins in heaven—or is it seventy-two? Woke up this morning to discover that she'd crept out during the night, sometime after I fell into a postorgasmic stupor. I hope she didn't meet the head porter along the way.

I wince at the entry's lackadaisical tone. While I suppose a hot-blooded male of twenty-five is entitled to be boastful about a worthy conquest or two, young Mark Henry Evans was officially an idiot.

Fact: My subsequent encounter with Claire wasn't as pleasant. I should read my account of what happened, as it might help me understand her current preoccupation with the past. I flip a couple of pages to the entry for 12 June 1995, swallowing hard:

Waited outside for forty minutes; a girl came out to tell me that Anna had made a trip to her parents' home in Coton to pick up some jewelry and was running late. Anna eventually emerged in a magnificent peach dress and a pair of gravity-defying stilettos (there weren't any jewels around her neck; either she or the girl must have been fibbing). Her face was an agitated shade of red. She did not apologize for keeping me waiting; she merely grabbed my hand and remained silent for the first fifteen minutes of our walk to Trinity. Then she blurted out, to my surprise:

—I need to get away for a few days.

—I don't see why not.

—You said you would love to take me to Cornwall for a weekend. You'd hire a boat so that we could spend a balmy afternoon on the water, making ripples behind us.

—I don't have any such facts in my diary.

—But you said all that. I wrote these facts down. Shall we go to Cornwall on Friday?

—I can't do a whole weekend there. Not on such short notice.

—Let's spend a night in Norfolk, then. You did say you would love to take me for a picnic on the dunes someday. We'll open a bottle of Champagne and watch the sun setting over the marshes.

—Er . . . right. I don't have those facts, either.

—You are fucking selective in the facts you choose to learn, Mark.

I shrugged before replying:

—I can't be writing down everything I say.

—I need time away to figure out what to do about Stepmum. She's driving me nuts with her threats.

—Sorry, Anna. But you can't expect me to drop everything and head off. It's May Week in Cambridge, after all. There's loads going on here this weekend.

—But you said you'd do anything for me. Even the smallest thing. Especially if I need your help.

—Did I really say so?

She came to an abrupt halt and glared at me, placing her hands on her hips.

—You didn't mean any of that, did you? You were just lying to me.

—Stop being so emotional.

—How dare you call me emotional? How dare you?

—Calm down, Anna.

—Fuck you, Mark.

And so we went from holding hands to fighting in a matter of minutes. I didn't realize that Anna had such an explosive temperament until she raised her hand to slap me. I don't know why she got so upset with me in the first place, but I suppose what I said was unpalatable to her ears. I had to defend myself from her determined assault, because the last thing I wanted was to arrive at the ball with a black eye to match my tail suit. Anna lost her balance at one unfortunate point, toppling sideways over her stilettos and hitting a nearby lamppost with a sickening thwack. I gasped in alarm, only to hear her shout moments later:

—*Oh, my God. What the hell?*

I bent down to help her up, but she refused to take my hand and even tried to hit me again. Thankfully, I managed to shake her frenzied palms off. I eventually left her crouching on her knees next to that lamppost, clutching her head and still shrieking away.

I strode down Portugal Place and along Magdalene Street only to receive another shock. Claire Bushey had planted herself in front of me with folded arms and fiery eyes.

—I saw you earlier, Mark. Holding her hand. And I saw everything on Jesus Green. Everything. You're sleeping with her, aren't you? I don't ever want to see you again.

I was tempted to retort that a fling's a fling and that

Claire and I were never a proper item in the first place. However, she stalked away before I could open my mouth, sparing me from having to reply. Cursing the foibles of the women in this town (they're all crazy in their own little ways, it seems), I headed down Trinity Street and groaned at the snaking queue of ballgoers outside the college. I saw Eleanor Rothschild waiting in line, looking stunning in her yellow dress, and decided to join her. . . .

Yes, that was the evening when all my problems with the two women began. Sighing, I flip a few pages to the entry for 15 June 1995:

I read in the *Times* this afternoon that Anna failed to show up to the Trinity ball on Monday. She was last seen in her room, dressing up for the ball.

My jaw dropped. A cold chill ran down my back. What the hell happened to her after I left her in hysterics on Jesus Green?

I was tempted to ring the police, to blurt out that I'd escorted Anna partway to the ball. But something held me back. It would be awful if everyone knew that the two of us had fought before she vanished. To make matters worse, we had also quarreled the night before her disappearance (as my diary entry for 11 June states, although it also says that we enjoyed some fabulous make-up sex afterwards). If I'm held responsible for Anna's disappearance, this would be a disaster. If someone had, say . . . harmed her soon after I left her on Jesus Green, I would surely be castigated for abandoning her—in a distraught condition on her knees—on our way to the ball. And if she had done something rash in her catatonic state (like throw herself into the river), I might similarly be blamed.

My conviction that I should remain quiet about our affair

was reinforced when the phone rang an hour later. A female voice introduced herself as Laura Patterson, Anna's classmate.

—My diary says that Anna decided to ditch me on the evening of 3 June because she wanted to have dinner with a guy named Mark Evans. Have you seen her recently?

I gulped, not knowing what to say at first. I decided to admit that while Anna and I had dined together that night, I'd not seen her recently (the word *recently,* as I interpreted it, applies to the limits of my short-term memory, namely, to what happened yesterday and the day before). Laura sounded disappointed, but she explained that she was trying to help the police with their investigation. I promised to ring her if I discovered anything relevant about Anna, begging her to do likewise. I placed the receiver down with a trembling hand, hoping that Laura was not aware that Anna and I had slept with each other three times since 3 June.

Then it hit me. My entry for 12 June says that Claire Bushey saw my entire altercation with Anna.

—And I saw everything on Jesus Green. Everything.

That's when I realized that Claire could be in a position to say something incriminating about me if she's ever questioned by the police about Anna's disappearance. I have to find a way to ensure that she will never discover the girl's identity. And even if she stumbles upon Anna's name (and the fact that Anna has disappeared in a thick fog of mystery), I have to ensure that Claire is on my side.

At 18:30, I grabbed my wallet and ran through the back gate of Trinity in the direction of Varsity Blues (unfortunately, I had no idea where Claire lived). She shot me a dirty look when I appeared at the door. I pleaded with her for a quick word outside, realizing that a few customers were turning their heads to look at us. She refused, pursing her lips and folding her arms. I proceeded to beg at the top of my voice, causing the proprietor of the restaurant (Jenkins, I think his name is) to give me a severe ticking-off for harassing his staff. I returned to Varsity Blues after Claire finished her evening shift, at around 22:30. She strode past me when she emerged from the restaurant, refusing to acknowledge my existence. Her eyes were stony pits of lavender. I followed from behind, apologizing for the way I'd treated her. But she jumped onto her bicycle and pedaled away with rigid shoulders.

I should return to the restaurant tomorrow. Because I need Claire on my side, not against me.

I sigh, shaking my head. Fact: Claire did indeed forgive me twelve days later. To confirm this, I flip to my entry for 24 June 1995. It reads:

Claire emerged from the restaurant at around 22:45. Her eyes lingered over the enormous bouquet of crimson roses in my hand. But she pursed her lips, flung her shoulders back, and continued striding in the direction of her bicycle. I followed her, spewing apologies in my most humble tone. To my surprise, she emitted a loud sigh before turning back to look at me with narrowed eyes.

—Don't ever cheat on me again.

—I'm sorry, Claire. Please give me another chance, and I'll prove you're the only one who matters.

I thrust the bouquet of roses into the basket of her bicycle. She gave me a curt nod before pedaling away, but I could see that her shoulders were no longer held back in a taut line.

While I suppose that she's on the verge of forgiving me, I should continue to do my best to get her on my side. I'm going to hover outside Varsity Blues again to-morrow evening, armed with yet another giant bunch of flowers. She did seem partial to those crimson roses; I'm convinced that dogged pleading is the key to her heart.

I stifle a groan as I flip a few pages to my 4 July 1995, entry:

The day brought a double whammy of bombshells. The phone rang at 10:00; it was Laura Patterson on the line.

—I just wanted to tell you that Anna appeared at my doorstep three mornings ago.

—Really? Thank God for that. What happened? Why did she go missing?

—Your guess is as good as mine.

—Huh?

—She didn't say. Refused to tell me anything.

—I don't get it.

—She looked ill and scruffy in her ball gown.

—What? Was she still wearing that dress when she showed up at your door?

—She was. Though it had been reduced to shreds. The scratches on her lower arms made me worried. Her hair was tangled and greasy. But I was more bothered by the look in her eyes. She appeared . . . unhinged. So I called an ambulance.

A feeling of relief swept over me, although I still feared that I could be blamed for Anna's temporary disappear-ance. I questioned Laura further. She said that Anna had refused to explain anything to anyone thus far. My relief deepened; if Anna is remaining silent about her experi-ences, I'm unlikely to be incriminated in any way.

But when I met Claire for lunch at the Olive Tree after-wards, my relief proved short-lived. She had arrived at the bistro with flushed skin and bright eyes. I should have suspected from the start that something was amiss. But I was too preoccupied with the dicey challenge of finishing with her without breaking her heart too badly. It had, after all, dawned on me that Duos and Monos have no long-term prospects together.

When the waiter brought us our crème brûlées, I was on the verge of blurting out that Claire deserved someone much better than the likes of me. It's funny that I was on the brink of using one of the most tired clichés in the "How to Break Up with the Girl You've Been Fucking Recently to Save Your Own Vulnerable Arse" handbook. I suppose that men have a way of resorting to overused phrases in moments of desperation. But before I could open my mouth, Claire placed her spoon down, wiped a shaking hand on her napkin, and blurted out something I would not have wanted to hear in a million years.

—I'm pregnant.

My fork clanged onto the concrete floor. I must have gaped at Claire for several seconds in openmouthed horror.

—Don't just stare at me like that, Mark. Say something, will you?

I blinked as black spots of disbelief were still dancing before my eyes.

—Are you sure?

My words spilled out in an agonized jumble. Claire nodded vigorously in response. She explained that she had fiddled about with a pregnancy kit the day before, after throwing up in Mrs. Perkins's bathroom for five consecutive mornings. The resulting blue line on the strip (and the fact that she missed her period two weeks ago) prompted her to see a doctor earlier this morning. He confirmed that she was pregnant. About four weeks along, he said.

All I could think of was: Damn all fertile Mono virgins. But while I was tempted to flee the bistro, a niggling sense of responsibility held me to my seat. It pinned me down. Right at the knife-edge precipice of the yawning chasm of obligation.

—So what are we going to do about the baby?

Abort it at once, I was tempted to say. The Duo-Mono bastard who's going to ruin my life. If it hasn't already done so. But I held my tongue. If it ever emerged that I'd aborted my offspring, my reputation would be in tatters. How dare I even think of killing my child?

My prolonged silence nevertheless caused Claire's eyes to darken with anxiety.

—Aren't you at least pleased by the news?

I plunged a spoon into my crème brûlée and shoved a giant dollop into my mouth.

—Are we getting married?

I nearly choked out the custard in response to her question, but I somehow held myself together.

—Let's discuss this later, shall we?

My reply caused a deep frown to emerge on Claire's face. Grasping about for a suitable course of action, I promised her that we would meet again for lunch tomorrow to discuss things further. Claire did not look satisfied by my response, but she agreed to show up at the Backstreet Bistro at 13:00. I then walked back to my college room in a daze, narrowly escaping a bicycle heading down Trinity Street the wrong way.

What the bloody hell am I going to do? I'm screwed from screwing a virgin during the wrong time of the month.

I frown. Is Claire trying to reacquaint herself with any of the facts I've read? If so, what, exactly? That entire sorry business about Anna, perhaps? This is most unlikely. Claire, to the best of my factual knowledge, never figured out the name of the girl who fought with me on Jesus Green.

It was such a long time ago, too.

Could she be trying to work out what *really* happened on the morning of our wedding?

Our wedding day. Damn. Fact: I was nearly late at the altar. What a ghastly mess. If only I'd managed to sort things out with Anna before that. If only I'd been kinder to her, a little more delicate with my words (and I dare to call myself a wordsmith). With a sigh, I turn to the entry for 8 July 1995:

I decided to visit Anna in the hospital this morning. I tip-toed through the door leading to her room, terrified of her reaction to my arrival. But I need not have worried. She gave me a timorous half smile, as if our quarrel never happened, before lowering her eyes back to the book in her hands (*Alice in Wonderland*). I sat down next to her bed, noticing that she looked both gaunt and withdrawn. Definitely not her usual fiery self. After all, didn't one of my previous diary entries describe her as a "veritable tigress in bed with claws to match"?

—I'm sorry we got into a stupid little fight that night. I deserved all the punches I got.

Anna merely kept her eyes on the book in her hands. Her muteness implied forgiveness, which emboldened me to ask why she went missing in the first place. But she merely sighed in response.

—I hope I'm not to blame, Anna.

—You made me so mad that night. I hit the lamppost. Everything just came back.

Her lower lip began to wobble.

—What came back?

—The past. All of it. In a surge.

—Huh?

—Truth's a burden. Especially the truths you've hidden from yourself after your twenty-third birthday.

—What do you mean?

—After you left, I just sat on Jesus Green and howled. Too much to digest at once. Way too much.

—You aren't making any sense to me.

—Yet something good might have also come out of it. Some memories are shit. But others give you hope. The devil's in the detail, Mark. Because small details matter.

—I really don't get it.

—I remember the day we first met. In the foyer of the Fitzwilliam Museum, at the bottom of that long flight of stairs. I saw a sparkle in your eyes when I walked up to you. You knew, even then, that we had something between us. We were kindred spirits, even though we were strangers. The sparkle lingered in your eyes as you shook my hand, holding it for longer than you should have. It's come back to me now. Your sparkle.

—Maybe you're right about the sparkle, but . . .

—The curl of your lips. I remember that, too. You begged me for my phone number, your lips curling in desperation, as if you couldn't bear the thought of losing me.

—I'm amazed you wrote all these facts down.

—I remember your smallest gestures of affection. Each and every one of them. Like the way you once brushed a lock of hair away from my face, your fingers caressing my skin like a butterfly's breath. No guy—not even Alistair— has showed me such tenderness before. I see that now. You do care about me, Mark. Deep down inside.

—You must spend all your time writing down facts.

—I love you, Mark. And you love me, don't you? Tell me. I need to hear the words from your mouth.

A fact darted into my head at that precise moment: I'm due to marry Claire Bushey a few weeks from now. That was followed by a second bleak certainty: I shouldn't be leading Anna on any further. Even if it was flattering to hear that she loved me.

And so I sighed before saying in an awkward, desperate rush:

—I've...er...met another girl in the meantime. And I'm...er...going to marry her soon. I'm sorry, Anna. Really sorry.

She gasped, eyes darkening in shock. I spent the next few seconds fumbling for the right words before coming up with the gentle but lame:

—It wasn't supposed to be like this. But I'm so relieved you're no longer missing. Please take care of yourself, Anna. Please get well soon.

I clambered to my feet and departed from her room, not daring to look at her face. Yet a torrent of relief flooded my soul as soon as I stepped out into the brilliant sunshine. I think I'm off the hook; Anna isn't holding me to blame for her temporary disappearance (though I still wonder why she vanished for nineteen days).

I should have suspected from our exchange that something wasn't right. And I shouldn't have blurted out—in such an abrupt, unkind fashion—that I'd met another girl in the meantime and was about to marry her. Factual hindsight is a curse when it's accompanied by the awful realization that one could have done much better. Especially when viewed in light of what happened on the day I married Claire. With a groan, I turn to the entry for 30 September 1995:

The phone in my room rang after I finished buttoning up my dress shirt. It was Pippa.

—I made a last-ditch attempt at persuading Mum and Dad.

—Let me guess. Dad's still refusing to budge.

—'Fraid so. He won't attend a Duo-Mono wedding in his lifetime, he said, even if it involves his only son.

—Did he go on another long rant about my stupidity?

—Er...yes...he did. To be honest with you, Mark, he said that only a stupid son would marry a stupid Mono, and he wants nothing to do with stupid sons. Just so you know, Mum had been thinking of defying him and traveling up to Cambridge today. But Dad has since won her over.

—That's all right. I'll see you later this afternoon, won't I?

—Well...actually...

—You're no longer coming, are you?

—I'm sorry. But Dad will disinherit anyone who attends your wedding. That includes me. He apparently doesn't suffer failed fools, stupid sons, and daft daughters.

—That's fine. You don't have to come. Not if it makes Dad angry.

—I'm so sorry, Mark.

I hung up the phone. Sighing over my sister's lack of backbone and the narrow-mindedness of my entire family, I continued dressing. I began tying a bow tie, squinting at my harried reflection in the mirror. It struck me then that my forehead had acquired a few more lines since Claire broke the news about her pregnancy. But I've made my decision, and I'm going to stand by it. Even if the rest of my family has decided to turn their snobbish, uppity backs on our mixed union.

At that point, I heard a soft rustle behind me. Before I could turn back to investigate the cause, I saw the reflection of a second face emerging in the mirror. The face was pale and gaunt, with mesmerizing scarlet lips.

—So you're getting married today.

I should have done something at that precise moment. Something to defend myself. But I merely stood there, fingers still frozen in the act of tying my bow tie, like a mouse in front of a snake. A hissing killer cobra with crimson lips. The next thing I knew, she'd placed an icy-cold knife blade at the base of my throat.

—I also hear that she's a Mono. A stupid little Mono. What's gotten into you, Mark?

I felt the tip of the blade grinding through my skin, causing a jolt of pain to radiate across my throat. I watched, transfixed, as a determined rivulet of blood began snaking downwards. It pooled onto the band of my white bow tie, staining it a bright red.

—What are you doing here?

My words spilled out in a quivering whisper. I could only gape as she transferred the cold metal to an unblemished spot a few millimeters away.

—I'm here to offer you my congratulations. And my commiseration, if you need it.

—With a large knife, it seems.

—Pinched it from the Fort St. George pub when no one was looking. A couple of hours after it all came back in a rush. After you left me behind. Even thought of using it to kill myself. Because it was all too much to take in at once. But I didn't. Not after I realized that you do care about me, underneath it all.

She paused for breath, lips trembling. I realized that I should keep her talking before she decided to puncture my throat in a second spot.

—I'm glad you didn't do anything stupid.

Anna merely rolled her eyes in response.

—I'm a stayer, Mark. I'm going to stay on track.

I was tempted to ask her why she was still holding the knife at my throat, but I decided that it was a bad idea to draw attention to the weapon in her hand.

—Definitely on track, I see.

—You'll never understand what happened, Mark. That evening on Jesus Green.

—I thought you'd forgiven me.

—I thought you loved me.

It hit me, right then, that a girl wielding a knife belonged to a particularly dangerous species of humanity. Especially as the weapon was still placed across my throat and had already drawn blood.

—You're an arsehole, Mark. One who goes off and falls for a pretty face. Even if it belongs to a stupid Mono.

—But Claire's preg—

—All I could think of, after you left my bedside, was that "other girl," the one you're marrying. Memory makes you play things over and over again in your head. Makes you angry.

—I'm sorry I was so abrupt. I really am.

—And there I was, dreaming about my perfect white dress just before you showed up at Addenbrooke's. . . .

Tears began to streak down her face.

—You like screwing other people, don't you, Mark?

I was tempted to launch into a spirited defense of my position, for if anyone was screwed at that point, I was (after all, as she'd helpfully pointed out a minute earlier, I was about to wed a Mono). But I'd also realized that Anna had lowered her knife and was frowning at her own tear-stained reflection in the mirror, as if she were seeing herself properly for the first time.

My elbow shot out, slamming into her ribs. She staggered a yard or so backwards, face contorting into a grimace. I spun round and threw myself forward, catching her shoulder and sending her crashing backwards. She hit the floor with a thud, nostrils flaring in shock.

—Help! I shouted.

But she was still holding the knife despite her fall. I dropped to my knees, desperate to extract the weapon from her hand. She squealed as I dug an elbow into her right shoulder, reaching forward for the knife. I was on the verge of extracting it when she twisted her arm away and brought a knee upwards to meet my groin. I winced, momentarily incapacitated by the pain. Just then, I saw the knife glinting upwards in my direction, its blade reflecting the rays of sunlight streaming through the window.

—Help!

I threw myself sideways, attempting to dodge its path. But I was too late. A searing pain shot across my lower arm. I looked down to discover that Anna had managed to cut me a second time. Her knife had torn a neat path along the lower sleeve of my white shirt, penetrating the skin below.

Something bright flashed in my direction again. I looked up; Anna had raised herself to her knees and was aiming the knife at my head. Her face was flushed red. Her scarlet lips were drawn back. Her teeth were bared in a snarl. Her eyes, I could have sworn, had turned into raging whirlpools of madness.

This time, I couldn't move at all. Nor could I breathe. I merely stared at Anna. Perhaps it was the shock of seeing my white sleeve turn red and feeling the pain surging through my arm. Or perhaps it was the horror of realizing that she wanted me dead.

The knife arced downwards.

I remained frozen, like a sacrificial lamb destined for slaughter.

Yet the knife veered sideways before clanging onto the floor. I wrenched my eyes into focus only to discover that Anna and I were no longer alone. My best men, William and Paul, had rushed in to rescue me. William, bless him, had reacted by knocking the knife out of Anna's hand while Paul pinned her to the floor (it helps that he is still the scrum-half for Trinity's rugby team).

—She tried to kill me.

I raised myself back to my knees and pointed my forefinger at Anna.

—She's mad!

—I'm not.

She spat her denial from the floor, still trying to wrestle herself free from Paul's grip.

—I was just trying to prove a point. We're soul mates, Mark. We had a chance together. I saw it in your eyes the first day we met. The sparkle of recognition. But you've gone and ruined everything.

William pointed at my right arm. I looked down. My lower sleeve was soaked red.

—She's gotten you already, Mark. I'm going to call the police.

—I did not try to kill him. Please don't call the police. Please. I just want things to go back to the way they used to be. But I know they won't. Not when I remember everything. And that's what makes it worse.

I struggled back to my feet and looked down at Anna. She was still trembling with the force of her tears. Her scarlet lipstick had smeared. Her mascara had streaked all over her face. She looked haggard and skeletal. A shell of the once vivacious girl who (as this diary says) had walked up to me in the foyer of the Fitzwilliam Museum and said with a wide grin that I must be either a poet, a politician, or a polecat-slaying ax murderer. A sense of pity began to envelop me. A flicker of recognition—but only a passing one—that we once had a physical connection. Even a flash of regret—but only a minuscule one—for what could have been. What we could have possibly enjoyed together if circumstances had not intervened. Anna, despite her mental instability and her foul temper, was still the most intelligent, perceptive, and quick-witted woman I'd ever met (this diary indicates as much; I've documented quite a few heated discussions we've had about the relative merits of Ibsen, Wagner, and Woolf). My entry for our fateful first encounter even says that "there was something truly mesmerizing about Miss Winchester's personality despite her slightly protruding ears," although there was no way I could have admitted this to Anna this morning. Not when I was due to marry another woman later the same day.

But the thoughts that flashed into my mind were soon drowned out by an overwhelming sense of relief. While Anna is smart and sassy, she may well be a closet psycho. I'm definitely doing the right thing by marrying the woman bearing my child. I'm also 100 percent certain that the sweet and charming Claire Bushey isn't crazy.

—Let her go.

The frown on Paul's forehead indicated that he thought I was just as mad as the girl.

—She tried to stab you, mate.

—Let her go, Paul.

Paul released his grip.

I walked over to Anna's side. I did feel sorry for her when all was said and done.

—Leave. Just leave. And please don't bother me again. If you do, I'm afraid I'll have to report you to the police. After all, my friends have just seen you pull a knife on me.

I held up my right arm with its sodden red sleeve.

Anna recoiled, as if she'd just seen my bloody arm for the first time.

—I didn't mean to hurt you, Mark. I really didn't.

Her words came out as a whimper.

—Just get out, Anna.

She pulled herself up and stumbled out of my room, shoulders heaving with sobs. William, however, began clucking as he strode over to inspect the damage she'd inflicted.

—I can't believe you let her go. Look at what she's done to your arm. But you're lucky. The cut looks shallow.

—I was kidding about the police, actually. But I'll call Addenbrooke's tomorrow. She's gone mental. They should get a doctor to look at her head.

(NTS: I should indeed ring Addenbrooke's first thing tomorrow morning. Poor Anna's definitely gone cuckoo. I should tell them that she pulled a knife on me and may be a danger to those around her. It's for her own good.)

Paul, however, was frowning at his watch.

—Aren't you due to exchange vows in about five minutes from now, mate?

—Shit.

I ran over to the wardrobe and pulled out my morning suit coat. Both Paul and William gasped as I threw it over my bloodstained shirt and pinned a boutonniere on it.

—No one's going to see the bloodstains. We must run. Chaplain Walters will have a fit if we're not at the altar when Claire arrives.

So we did. We got there at 12:29, scampering by the

stone statues of Newton, Bacon, and Tennyson in undignified fashion. Thankfully, there was no sign of Claire and her father; I should have been grateful to her for being fashionably late. As the three of us pelted down the aisle, we saw Claire's mother and her four sisters—all seated on the left, wearing the most gaudy-looking hats I ever had the misfortune to encounter at a wedding—turn to look at us with relief on their faces (I suppose there was always the possibility that the desirable Duo groom would bail out at the last minute). The right-hand side of the aisle, predictably, was devoid of people. Chaplain Walters was pacing up and down with an enormous frown on his forehead. The poor man was probably not used to grooms arriving at the altar a minute before their appointed ceremony times.

I came to an abrupt halt before him, trying to catch my breath.

—Sorry, Father. We were held up on our way here.

—I was beginning to wonder if you'd changed your mind.

As Chaplain Walters eyed me with disapproval, I realized that the man must have never presided over a Duo-Mono marriage before (well, I suppose there's always a first time for everything).

—No, I haven't.

—You sure?

—Of course.

There was a sudden flurry of movement in the antechapel. The doors burst open. Emily began walking down the aisle in a frilly mauve dress, carrying a bunch of pink and white roses. She was followed by Claire and her father, dressed in a morning suit three sizes too small for him. His face was an alarming shade of red; he was bursting either from excitement or an overdose of whiskey. A radiant expression filled Claire's face. She looked stunning, despite the slight bump beneath her surprisingly tasteful dress.

—You look beautiful.

I meant it. At least I'm marrying a looker with indisputable inner grace and charm, even if she is a Mono. At least I'm marrying a woman who radiates refreshing, down-to-earth unsophistication. A simple finesse that warms my heart. She must have heard my whisper as she gave me a beaming smile. Thankfully, the ceremony proceeded without incident (although it was interrupted at times by loud sobs from the left-hand side of the aisle).

—Mark, will you take Claire to be your wife? Will you love her, comfort her, honor and protect her, and, forsaking all others, be faithful to her as long as you both shall live?

—I will.

—Will you remind yourself, each morning of your life, of the fact that you love Claire?

—I will.

Yet I saw my new wife's eyes narrowing when I bent over to kiss her, just before our guests erupted into cheers. The first thing she said to me, right after we'd stepped out of the chapel doors to the refrains of Mendelssohn's "Wedding March," was:

—What's happened to your collar, Mark? There's blood on it.

—I cut myself shaving. A small nick. No big deal.

The words tripped off my tongue with ease. I even produced a glib shrug.

—There's also red lipstick on your forehead, Mark. It's partially hidden by your bangs. But I'm sure it's lipstick.

My mouth fell open like a gaping wound, which was the worst thing I could have done in view of the circumstances. It signified guilt, at least in Claire's biased opinion. To make matters worse, I reached up to touch my forehead with two fingers, causing the lipstick to rub off on them in an accusing smear of scarlet. If only William and Paul had spotted what Anna had left behind. But I suppose that most men—including me—tend to be oblivious to the small things that matter to women.

Claire's eyes began exuding fire.

—You were with a girl earlier, weren't you? She kissed you on the forehead. What have you been doing this morning, Mark? Have you been sleeping with yet another woman? Minutes before you were to marry me?

—This is ridiculous.

Right then, I felt a tap on my back. I turned round to discover that Claire's father was behind me. Our guests had caught up. Two beefy arms encircled me, crushing my ribs.

—Welcome to the family, sonny boy.

His words boomed into my ears; I could smell the hot, pungent odor of whiskey on his breath. I also realized that there was a tattoo of a naked woman on the back of his neck. When he released me, I saw that Claire had been besieged by her sisters and mother, all gushing over her unprecedented success at snagging a Duo. The storm in Claire's eyes had, thankfully, abated; she looked pretty chuffed by the attention she was getting.

—Praise the Lord! I've married you off!

Even the pigeons in the rafters must have heard the squeal that emanated from the venerable Mrs. Bushey. I winced as she flapped her arms under that giant gaudy hat of hers, before pecking Claire on the cheek and reaching for a service booklet to fan the sodden circles around her armpits.

229

Thank God, I thought. Disaster has been averted.

The subsequent festivities passed without too much incident. William, predictably, gave a best-man's speech designed to embarrass. Claire's father had to be scraped off the floor in a stupor at the end of the evening. My bottles of Château Margaux 1982 (which I'd procured at the bargain-basement price of £59 per bottle from the Trinity cellars, thanks to my excellent relationship with the college bursar) were wasted on him. I'm not sure the man even knew what he was drinking. I should have put out half a barrel of the cheapest plonk from the co-op. And I lost count of the times I saw Claire's sisters making eyes at William and Paul.

Claire and I eventually parted ways outside the front gates of Trinity at six minutes before midnight. The black cab I had summoned to take her back to Mill Road was already waiting outside on the cobblestoned street.

—I'll see you on Thursday. I'm sure you'll love the house I've found for us: 23 Milton Road. Which makes it convenient for you to get to Varsity Blues each evening. The house is a little on the small side. But it looks comfy. I'm sorry we can't move in tonight, but the lease only begins on Thursday. I promise to send the moving men over to Mill Road to get your belongings as soon as they finish moving my things from Trinity.

Claire opened her mouth. But nothing came out of it. Instead, I saw her lower lip beginning to quiver.

—We'll be happy in Milton, Claire. We'll try to be, at least. And I promise to find work as a writer, instead of swanning around Trinity pretending to be a clever academic.

Tears began welling up in her eyes.

—I'm tempted not to write down that business in my

diary tonight, Mark. The lipstick on your forehead. I'd much rather forget what I saw. Because it was otherwise a perfect day.

Exhaustion hit me at that point. It had been a long day. A crazy girl I once dated attempted to stab me in the morning. And I married a Mono in the afternoon, to my family's disgust. All I wanted to do was to go back to my room and collapse on the bed.

—I didn't cheat on you, Claire.

I kissed her on the cheek and began trudging in the direction of my room. I'm secretly glad the officious head porter had trotted out the rule book and insisted that my college room is for single occupancy only, even if I'm married. Because I still have five more blissful nights of having my own space to think.

What a way to begin life as a married man, though. This must be the longest diary entry I've ever written. It's twenty-two pages long. But it must also be the most eventful day of my life thus far.

I'll have plenty to mull over tomorrow. I wonder what marriage to a Mono will bring (judging from the behavior of Claire's family today, I'll have quite a bit on my plate). But I have done the right thing by marrying the woman bearing my child. It's the only honorable thing to do. A real man has to face up to his responsibilities. And I should go to sleep knowing this fact, even if the rest of my family is still blinded by their class prejudices. Someday they will see how wrong they were.

I look up from my diary. It all makes sense now. Claire hasn't changed, even after twenty long years of marriage. She was jealous because she saw me holding Anna's hand on our way to the ball. She was quick to reach the conclusion that I'd been sleeping with Anna (and her assumption was right). But she also became jealous of an imaginary sexual partner on our wedding day simply because she saw a lipstick smear on my forehead.

I now know the reason why Claire emptied my 1995 folder. She's trying to obtain evidence that I was unfaithful on our wedding day. She's hoping to claim that she's been putting up with my infidelities from day one. So she can smash my political aspirations to smithereens, given that I've staked my campaign on our solid, unbreakable Duo-Mono union. Perhaps even cast herself as a long-suffering Mono housewife, one with a heart large enough to put up with a philandering Duo husband for years.

But does Claire understand what's happening to us right now? And should I tell her what *really* occurred the day before yesterday?

IMF Summit Ends Early

Saturday, 11 October 2014

The International Memory Fund (IMF) has ended the sessions of its scientific summit on memory improvement a full day earlier than scheduled, following protests by activists in Prague.

The campaigners managed to block movement to the convention hotel by staging a peaceful sit-in on the road. They had earlier issued a statement: "The IMF should be deterred from funding research on memory improvement because more memory only creates more hatred and misery."

The Czech minister of memory research, Pavel Novak, delivered his concluding remarks to an almost empty hall, saying: "It's a pity this conference will be remembered for its unhappy ending."

CHAPTER EIGHTEEN

SOPHIA

1 February 2015

Talk about fucking progress. So Mark Henry Evans had the misfortune to run into me in York. We then struck up a mutually beneficial arrangement. He gets plenty of sex. I get loads of dirt.

It's funny how love can mutate so easily into hate. It's like flipping a coin. The penny either lands on one side or the other. Heads *or* tails. Love *or* hate. Nothing in between.

Small things add up. Tiny slights add up.

All memories fucking add up.

I once remembered more good than bad about Mark. Now I recall more bad than good. And that's the whole bloody problem. Because it's the *sum total* of minuscule remembered gestures that makes love powerful. It's the *agglomeration* of tiny recollected grievances that makes hatred potent.

My dossier's thick enough. I already have everything I need on his suicidally depressive wife. Thanks to the nice, obliging Helmut Jong (shame it had to end between us). I even have everything I need on Mark. Thanks to my strategically positioned pin-size video cameras.

I suppose I can go to the press with my dossier anytime. Brandishing a 144-GB memory stick full of gripping bedroom escapades. Scintillating scenes of sex and punishment. One phone call is all it will take. I don't even have to show them the videos. The mere suggestion that they exist is good enough.

When hell implodes, even the heavens will melt. Particularly that snug little "Evans heaven" in the village of Newnham. One untainted with the slightest whiff of scandal thus far. But I should wait. For the right time. Because timing is every-thing.

Patience, Sophia, patience.

Revenge only comes to those who wait.

And scandals are only scandalous if the timing is right.

11 February 2015

So Mono Housewife has been hiding another secret. The Cambridge Flower School isn't really a flower school. It's a *fucking front* for budding sorts. Delusional Mono writers, to be precise.

She didn't go this morning. Drove by Newnham and saw her Range Rover parked outside. Must have been ill. So I went to Linton instead. Just to check what kind of flowers she's been sticking into pots on Wednesday mornings. You never know what sort of dirt can be attached to shrubs.

A man with a leprechaunlike demeanor greeted me when I strolled into the lily-infested foyer. A space that both looked and smelled like a funeral parlor.

How did you find out about us? he asked.

Claire Evans, I said.

Ah, he said, tapping his nose and winking in response. I'd fully expected him to say, Blooms or greens? Instead, he said:

Novel or short story?

I stared at him in surprise.

Whatever Evans normally goes to, I managed.

Short story, then, he said, pointing in the direction of the basement. Room B112.

I couldn't bring myself to walk back out again. Not when I was hooked by this unexpected turn. So I went to the basement. Twelve hazy, dim-witted faces swiveled in my direction as I sauntered in and sat down at a large table that groaned under the weight of writing pads.

Welcome, said a man at the head of the table. Rheumy eyes and wispy mustache. We are always delighted to welcome new members to our Mono writing group. The last time someone new joined was three years ago. What's your name, and what are you currently writing?

I blinked, my mind a brief void. Before coming up with the inspired: My name is Mariska Van Dijk, and I'm writing a story about a woman who was incarcerated in a mental asylum for seventeen years before seeking her revenge.

Nice, a woman said. That's thematically similar to the story Claire's writing. A Mono who was imprisoned in a claustrophobic marriage for twenty years before breaking free from her shackles.

I gaped at her. So Dear Mono Housewife has literary aspirations inside her pitiful little brain.

How do you keep track of what inspires you? someone asked. We're always open to new suggestions.

Inspiration just sticks in my head, I said, prompting incredulous expressions all around the room. The questions went on and on, during which I progressed from squirming in my chair to being thrown out of it. Especially after a man asked: Do you write in your diary *twice* a day, just to give you an edge?

I don't even bother writing at the end of each day, I said. Let alone twice.

Big mistake, as they say.

Huge.

She's a *Duo* trying to infiltrate our precious group, a woman gasped. Eyes big and horrified. If so, we should throw her out.

I'm not a Duo, I said. I don't really need diaries, either.

She's crazy, someone yelled. Utterly bonkers.

Definitely a Duo, someone else shouted. But a mad one.

We have no room for delusional Duos in this writing circle, said the man at the head of the table, wispy mustache twitching mournfully. If you could kindly leave now, Miss Van Dijk.

You are the delusional ones, I said, rising from my chair. *Not me*. Trying to write when you can barely read. Thinking someone will publish your Mono drivel.

If looks could kill, I would have dropped dead in Linton. But I was smart enough to evacuate. After all, the last time people discovered I wasn't keeping up my diaries, I ended up in the Outer Hebrides.

So Mono Housewife's attempting to cure her suicidal depression by putting it all down on paper. How wretched. Or maybe she's trying to mimic her husband's success as a writer. How illusory.

Shame I didn't get any extra dirt today. Only a miserable little secret. But it's reassuring to learn that she's both pathetic and delusional. I bet he didn't realize that when he married her all those years ago.

Which makes him just as pathetic.

14 February 2015

I can't believe this. More dirt is indeed lurking out there.

What a revelation. What a delight.

It all began when he called this morning. To cancel on me. To apologize.

He can't spend Valentine's Day with me, he said. Though he really wants to. Even if he has fantasies of tying me up to *that* four-poster bed.

Why? I asked.

A representative from the city council rang minutes earlier, he said. The Cambridge mayor has taken ill. Will no longer be able to open the Valentine's Day charity masquerade ball at the Guildhall as planned. Could Cambridge's famous resident author perform the honors instead? Part of the ball's proceeds will go to the author's chosen charity.

This is huge, he added. His political campaign will benefit from all the local publicity it can get.

Of course, I purred. Great things seldom come planned, do they? One should embrace opportunities as they come along. I'm sure you'll enjoy the ball tonight. Aren't authors pretty damned good at masquerading, anyway? They have a tendency to hide their incompetence behind flowery, adverb-infested prose. Make sure the *Cambridge Evening News* takes a flattering photo of you, my darling. Don't forget to show off your political pecs—or literary creds.

You're the most understanding woman I've ever met, he gushed in response. The most perceptive. *And* the most intelligent.

The man, despite his multiple sins, definitely has a way with words.

Now, don't you try buttering me up, I said.

Can we meet at the usual place next Saturday, then? he asked.

That's fine, I said.

I terminated the call, multiple questions burning in my head. I pulled out my smartphone. Typed in Mark's name followed by the word *charity*. A link to a website called Action for Sudden Infant Death Syndrome (SIDS) emerged, with Mark and Claire Evans listed as two key donors.

Sudden infant death syndrome? How did I miss this before? Why would Mark Evans and his wife be supporting this particular charity? Out of thousands in Britain? Mark and Claire don't have any children. Or did they? How could I have missed this crucial detail?

Shame on you, Sophia.

Just when I thought I'd dug up all the dirt I could find.

Yet this may well be the filthiest of them all.

15 February 2015

Bloody Action for SIDS. Called them up this morning, claiming to be a journalist from the *Sunday Times*. Said I was writing a story on the motivations behind generous philanthropic endowments. An article intended to strike a chord amongst our wealthy readers. So they will give more money to worthy charities like *yours*.

I took care to emphasize one word. *Money*.

But the woman on the phone refused to budge. Refused to tell me why Mark has supported her organization over the years. We can't reveal anything about our donors, including their personal motivations, she said. Privacy regulations.

You unhelpful, regulation-obsessed Mono twat, I spat into the receiver before hanging up.

Yet all is not lost. There should be birth and death certificates out there. Somewhere. At the very least.

I just need to keep digging.

Technology defines us, whether we like it or not. These days, we are utterly dependent on external devices as repositories of facts, assumptions, and memories. We are but the sum total of our digital presence. We use iDiaries and social media networks to define and delude ourselves because they contain what we prefer to remember. What we want the outer world to see. Yet our carefully curated public personae frequently bear little resemblance to our true inner selves. The two faces of our remembered lives are disparate and often contradictory.

—"The Curse of Modern Technology,"
The Guardian, 2 April 2015

Chapter Nineteen

HANS

7¼ HOURS UNTIL THE END OF THE DAY

She's right about two things. The man at the reception desk does indeed look like a leprechaun surrounded by lilies. His face is framed by a spiky mop of red hair and a luxuriant ginger beard. She's also right about the place smelling like a funeral parlor. There's even a faint whiff of incense in the air.

"We're a flower school," he says, peering at the identification badge in my hand. "It's all about the flowers here."

"Oh, come on, sir."

"We teach people arrangements."

"Look here," I say, tucking the badge back into my pocket. "I know what sort of arrangements you *really* have. Like, say, Mono writing groups on Wednesday mornings."

His lips take on an obstinate twist.

"There aren't any Mono—"

"Two options. One, you can tell me a few things about one of your writing group members. Informally. Right now."

One of his eyebrows shoots up, almost reaching his spiky bangs.

"Or you can come back with me to Parkside, just so I can put my questions more formally to you. That might take…a while. You know, the hassle of proper witness statements and all that. Arrangements

243

at police stations tend to take longer than arrangements at flower schools."

He exhales, a resigned hiss.

"What do you want to know?" he says. "There's nothing illegal about what we do here. We just don't like Duos spying on us, that's all. Laughing at us in a condescending way. Or telling us how to write. You are a Duo, I presume?"

"No…yes…er…"

The man's eyebrow is now higher than his spiky bangs. Damn.

"Er…Claire Evans. How long has she been a member of your short-story writing group?"

He flips a folder open, pulls out a sheet of paper from a clear plastic holder, and scans the large handwriting on it.

"Fifteen years," he says. "Since we first started meeting here, I guess."

"That's a long time. Could I have a look at the sheet, please?"

"You can't just look at—"

"Arrangements at police stations sometimes take forever, you know."

"But—"

"Yesterday a man came in and left only nine hours and twenty-seven minutes later. He missed both his lunch and his dinner."

With a sigh, the receptionist hands the sheet over. I peer down at it:

ANNUAL MEMBER QUESTIONNAIRE

January 2015

Name: Claire Evans (née Bushey)
Writing Group: Short Story
Date Joined: 28 March 2000

1. What do you hope to achieve as a writer?

I have long wanted to win the *Times*'s short-story competition, a prize that has eluded my husband since 1989. Unfortunately, my chances of winning this award are less than zero, even though Monos are technically eligible to enter the competition. Despite what they say about encouraging diversity, it's never going to happen.

2. How has this writing group helped you in this regard?

The group takes me out of the home each Wednesday morning and gives me a sense of direction and purpose, even a sense of hope. It has helped me improve my technical skills as a writer, though I'm aware that I still have so much more to learn. It makes me feel more cheerful, perhaps by giving me a small sense of accomplishment and worth. Because it's always reassuring to receive positive feedback about my writing (I don't know why the other women in the group keep saying that I'm more likely to get published than any of them—I guess they are just being generous).

3. What has inspired you recently?

My husband. His amazing accomplishments. They have always inspired me, although I don't think I've ever told him that. He looks after me well, despite his frequent rants about Monos. Sometimes I wonder why he continues to do so much for me. But then I look into his eyes and realize that the pain of not doing so, of stopping what we somehow started, may hurt him even more. Our marriage has given me much inspiration for the short story I'm currently writing, entitled "Tender Is the Day." It's about a woman attempting to break free from a claustrophobic twenty-year marriage, only to cause her husband to drink himself to death after she succeeds.

4. How can this writing group continue to serve and inspire you as a writer?

Through its continued existence, especially when I have very little to look forward to each week (my diary says that I have only ever missed meetings because of holidays abroad or illness). It gives me a break from gardening. And it's always nice to have a secret.

It would be great if the group could discuss the works of Virginia Woolf and Henrik Ibsen at some point, though, because I never understood why my husband is so obsessed with those two writers. Maybe we could do a line-by-line analysis of some key passages from *Mrs. Dalloway* or *A Doll's House*.

Aha. So Mark Henry Evans is indeed obsessed with Virginia Woolf. This confirms my suspicions about those black and white pebbles.

I scan the other replies on the sheet of paper. They are, unfortunately, not as illuminating, being mostly earnest answers about her writing process. But they somehow make me secretly pleased. Because Claire Evans is a Mono who's still trying hard despite the forces aligned against her.

Maybe I should be nicer to her when we next meet.

"Did Claire Evans ever mention her husband to you?" I look up from the sheet. "The novelist Mark Henry Evans?"

His face is blank.

"Could you check your diary, please?" I say.

He nods, whipping his diary out from a bag. I wait as he performs the necessary keyboard acrobatics.

"Let me see…we've only discussed Mr. Evans once, when I asked her why she doesn't want to tell her husband that she writes. She was afraid that he would laugh at her, she said. Or he might tell her that her aspirations are pointless and that she will always be hopeless at it. That somehow resonated with me, because my wife has a tendency to laugh at me whenever I—"

"Did a woman named Mariska Van Dijk ever come in here? Claiming she heard about you through Mrs. Evans?"

"Ah, yes." He nods, frowning. "I learned from my diary that Mariska was mad. She also got me into trouble. But let me check."

He taps his diary again.

"Okay…she came in one morning and stormed out from the basement minutes later. I went down to ask what had happened. They said that she was a crazy Duo masquerading as a Mono. That I was an idiot to let her in without checking her background carefully. That I deserved to be sacked."

"The perils of frontline fire," I say. "Did you mention this Mariska episode to Claire later?"

He inspects his diary again.

"I did. Claire claimed never to have heard of the crazy woman before."

"I'm not surprised," I say, handing the questionnaire back. "Not at all. Thank you for your time."

I turn to leave.

"Wait a minute," he calls after me. "What is this all about? Why did you come here to ask me these questions?"

To figure out a murderer's identity, of course. Though I still haven't worked out the murderer's motives. But there's no way I can say these things to a man who looks like a leprechaun.

"Because I'm still looking for my pot of gold," I say. "And I have only found some blooming pebbles so far."

Toby is waiting in my office with a large grin, armed with two promising-looking sheets of paper.

"Didn't take us too long to get these," he says, striding over and handing them to me.

I peer down at the uppermost sheet. It says:

Registration district: Cambridgeshire
Time, date, and place of birth: 15:41, 5 March 1996, Rosie

Maternity Hospital, Cambridge
Name: Catherine Louise Evans
Sex: Female
Class: Unconfirmed
Father's name, date of birth, class, occupation: Mark Henry
Evans, 14 June 1969, Duo, unemployed
Mother's name, date of birth, class, occupation: Claire Evans
(née Bushey), 28 February 1976, Mono, waitress
Address: 23 Milton Road, Cambridge CB4

My throat constricts. So Mark and Claire Evans did indeed have a child. I turn to the second piece of paper:

Registration district: Cambridgeshire
Date and place of death: 18 June 1996, 23 Milton Road,
Cambridge CB4
Name: Catherine Louise Evans
Sex: Female
Class: Unconfirmed
Date and place of birth: 5 March 1996, Rosie Maternity Hospital,
Cambridge
Name and surname of informant: Alan Bisseker
Qualification: Coroner
Cause of death: Sudden infant death syndrome

I whistle under my breath.

"Quite the revelation," I say. "Well done for getting these so quickly. Pull up the coroner's report, too, will you?"

"I had a feeling you'd want it," Toby says. "I called Bisseker's office a while ago. They're going through their files at the moment. With luck, the report will be winging its way to us soon."

"Excellent work, my boy."

Toby looks pleased as he hurries out of the room. I grab a black knight and use it to scoop a white pawn off the board.

I turn on my computer. Its search screen eventually flashes up; I navigate my way to the Action for SIDS website. A "Donors" link emerges into view. I click on it to discover the following:

We are delighted to have the bestselling author Mark Henry Evans and his wife, Claire, as two of our most ardent supporters. They have funded our work with great generosity over the past nineteen years. In 2007 they set up an endowment for a professorial fellowship on research into sudden infant death syndrome based at the Cambridge Biomedical Campus and the European Molecular Biology Laboratory in Heidelberg. The fellowship was named the Walter Bushey Fellowship in memory of Mrs. Evans's father, who died the previous year.

I tap my way to Evans's campaign website and type the name Catherine Louise Evans into its search box.

Nothing shows up.

I try again, just to be sure. I do a blanket Web trawl for her name. But the Internet is silent on "Catherine Louise Evans." There is absolutely no mention of the girl's name online.

This is odd. Really odd. Doesn't Catherine's existence, though brief, work in favor of Mark's political strategy? Won't the tragic tale of her premature death buy him a few more sympathy votes from the mothers of South Cambridgeshire? Yet he never mentioned Catherine during our interview this morning. Neither did he mention her to Sophia, the woman he'd been shagging for months.

Silence might result from scars. Deep scars. *Terrible* scars.

Or it might be caused by fears. Dark fears. *Terrifying* fears.

Mark and Claire Evans appear to have done their best to forget the daughter they once had. Poor Catherine Louise has been erased. Wiped clean from the factual slate of Mark's existence. From his own campaign website, even.

But why keep her a secret? Was Catherine's death so terrible that it scarred her parents for years?

I'm on the verge of reopening Sophia's diary when Toby barges in, waving another sheet of paper.

"Gotcha," he says, handing it to me. "Coroners are efficient sorts."

"That's because their clients are dead and can't argue with them. Anything yet on the bank transfers?"

He gives me an apologetic shake of his head.

"We're still working on it," he says. "Bankers are damned annoying."

"That's why so many people wish them a quick death. And that's why coroners are still in business. Keep trying, will you?"

Toby nods before disappearing out of the room. I turn my eyes to the report in my hands.

CORONER'S REPORT INTO THE DEATH OF EVANS, LOUISE CATHERINE

A detailed autopsy revealed no anatomical cause of death. Toxicology and expert consultations with neuropathology and developmental pediatricians did not identify a cause of death, either.

Anthony Paget, MD, a Duo consultant on complex behavioral conditions at Addenbrooke's Hospital in Cambridge, was asked to comment on the case. His report, dated 24 June 1996, states: "The findings of the postmortem examination indicate that Catherine's death is consistent with a diagnosis of sudden infant death syndrome (SIDS). At this point, it remains unclear how a two-week period of prenatal exposure to the selective serotonin reuptake inhibitor (SSRI) antidepressant Prozac during the first month of conception might have contributed to her death, if at all."

Cause of death is therefore listed as: No anatomical or toxicological cause of death. The significance of a two-week period of exposure to Prozac in utero has yet to be established.

Manner of death is natural, and no recommendations are made.

6 July 1996

Something doesn't add up. If the coroner confirmed that Catherine Louise Evans did indeed die of *natural causes*, why have her parents remained so secretive about her? Why hide her brief existence? Wouldn't she be perfect fodder for Evans's political campaign?

I can only see disjointed fragments of possibility instead of full, convincing answers. I glare at the chessboard on my desk. I prod a couple of pawns forward on both sides. I drag a black castle out of its corner and send a white knight scuttling backwards, wishing that solutions to real-life mysteries were as easy as those on my chessboard. But the answers remain elusive.

With a sigh, I turn to the iDiary on my desk. Perhaps the crazy woman might have an answer.

"What happened to her?" Gunnar rushed forward, mouth a tormented twist.

Thunder hissed outside their home. It wasn't the magical auroral crackle they had heard during their honeymoon in Svalbard. It was a sonic boom resulting from a rapid expansion of temperature and pressure, one that epitomized everything that had gone wrong in their relationship since then.

Sigrid sobbed as she opened her fist. A baby's bib fluttered to the floor.

—Mark Henry Evans, *On Death's Door*

CHAPTER TWENTY

SOPHIA

25 February 2015

Things are falling into place. I should be pleased with what I've managed to piece together. The coroner's report was as pricey as hell (shame private snoops don't come cheap). But it was worthwhile. Because it offered delicious reading. Interesting bedtime entertainment better than a fucking dildo.

So Claire Evans took an antidepressant for two weeks, even before she married Mark. Days after conceiving Catherine. I'm not surprised. Once a depressive, always a depressive. How fucking depressing. Probably unaware of her pregnancy when she first started the pills. Must have stopped taking them after realizing she'd been knocked up. By Mark, obviously. I'm sure that Mark was the father of her child.

So that's why he married her. He wouldn't have married a stupid Mono otherwise.

It all makes sense now.

If only I had known this earlier. I wouldn't have made such a fool of myself that morning all those years ago. Maybe I would have chosen a blunter knife. I certainly wouldn't have nicked his neck to make my point.

But did Claire's pregnancy antidepressants eventually trigger Catherine's death? Or did something more sinister occur?

Anthony Paget, MD. It's amazing what online searches can reveal about a person these days. It didn't take me too long to dig up a few fascinating facts about the man. An alumnus of Trinity. Just like Mark (although Paget graduated ten years before Mark's matriculation). Director of studies in medicine at Trinity in 1994, the same year Mark became a junior research fellow in English literature. Now a leading expert in the field of SIDS, based at the European Molecular Biology Laboratory in Heidelberg. One of Paget's groundbreaking papers on the biomolecular pathways leading to crib death is likely to earn him the next Nobel Prize in Medicine.

How fucking illustrious.

Also the first recipient of the *Walter Bushey Fellowship* in 2007.

How fucking suspicious.

I'm capable of making links. Memory, if anything, gives you the ability to see the big picture. To perceive things with greater accuracy. To pick up subtle hints and cues. To understand possible connections. To put things into context. To work out how disparate things fit together. To integrate fragmented snapshots into a unified whole. To make creative linkages between the past and present. Which, in turn, leads to all sorts of interesting possibilities. Fascinating insights, even.

If two things line up, it's a coincidence. But if three things coalesce, it's a fucking *pattern*.

I can see quite a few links between Paget and Evans.

Enough to form a garish little design.

Keep digging, Sophia. Keep digging.

YESTERDAY

Doctors are so fucking easy. Especially vapid male physicians. Helmut Jong was simple. But I didn't even have to seduce Paget. I merely e-mailed Mr. Nobel-in-Waiting, asking him to meet me for coffee. Claiming to be Mrs. Jessica Livingstone, a long-lost friend from his Cambridge days who's thinking of donating to SIDS research. An e-mail that oozed promise, sweetness, and light (I'm capable of turning on the syrup when I need to).

I'm entitled to gloat. About what I found out from little Mr. Brainiac. It made flying those 1,100 miles to Heidelberg and back worthwhile.

The sun disappeared behind the Königstuhl as I walked into that charming café along the banks of the Neckar River. The professor looked worse than his outdated online photographs. He was wrinkly, squat, and had lost most of his hair.

Fabulous to see you again, Anthony, I gushed. It's been years, hasn't it? You look amazing.

Thank you, he said. So do you.

It's incredible how people play along in conversation. How they are so fucking *trusting*. Even though they have written down zero facts in their diaries about you.

We spent the next five minutes exchanging pleasantries. Before I blasted my first salvo of the evening.

Do you have any facts on Mark Henry Evans? I asked. Nonchalantly, as if we were discussing the lovely Heidelberg weather.

Ah, nodded the professor. I first met Mark Evans when he was a Trinity undergraduate. That was years ago. He's now a famous novelist hoping to be South Cambridgeshire's next MP.

Shame about baby Catherine, I said, deciding to be reckless.

So you know about her, he mumbled. Eyes darting away from me, as if he were guilty of something.

Course I do, I said, deciding to improvise. My diary says that Claire Evans and I used to be close friends, I added. Bosom buddies, even. Until I got married and moved away from Cambridge. I held Claire's hand as she sobbed at Catherine's funeral. Claire also confided in me about what *really* happened to Catherine. It wasn't what it seemed, was it?

What are you getting at? the professor shot back with a tremor in his voice.

Aha, I thought. So the man's hiding a juicy little nugget or two.

I'm making the point that you were instrumental in concealing the truth, I said, struggling to hide the glee on my face. That little business over the Prozac was merely a smoke screen, wasn't it? For what *really* happened to the daughter of Mark and Claire Evans?

Are you trying to blackmail me? The professor gulped, face sapped of color.

Blackmail. Such a lovely, evocative word. A word that oozed all sorts of delicious possibilities. If the professor wrote in his report that the infant died of SIDS, it was probably *not* the case.

It *wasn't* sudden infant death syndrome, my dear professor, I said, newly found conviction surging through my voice. By the way, you have a lofty reputation as a world-leading expert on SIDS, don't you? A reputation that hinges on the research you've done in the past. *All* of it. The entire corpus. And if it ever emerged that your report on Catherine was flawed...

The resulting flash of fear in the man's eyes said it all.

You have no proof that Claire.... he trailed off, bottom lip quivering.

That's when I realized I'd finally struck paydirt. About the true manner of Catherine's death. *Claire Evans* had something to do with it. The problem was: What the hell did Claire do to her daughter?

Course I do, I said. I have all the fucking proof I need to go to the press tomorrow.

Another glimmer of fear in the professor's eyes. His reaction triggered a further revelation in my head. What Claire did to Catherine was right there before my eyes all along. I was too blind to see it earlier.

Claire must have killed her own baby. In a fit of postpartum depression. After all, she suffered from depression even before she got married. Those mentally crippling blues must have returned with a vengeance soon after she gave birth. And Mark must have helped cover it up. By begging his old Trinity friend to issue a SIDS diagnosis. Professional confirmation that it was a sudden, unexpected, and unexplained fatality. A death from unknown causes. A diagnosis to absolve Claire.

From *murder*.

But how does one kill a three-month-old baby without leaving a trace?

I gripped the coffee-cup handle. My mind a whirl of possibilities. Then it hit me.

I'm glad I spent a bit of time at St. Augustine's reading. Novels have a tendency to broaden one's mind. By offering insights into the minds of the damned people who wrote them in the first place. Especially certain novels written by certain authors. Who make shitloads of money describing what happened in their *own* lives.

As thinly veiled fiction.

Claire might have *smothered* her own baby to death. With something soft. Something innocuous. Like a pillow. Perhaps a bolster. Or she could have simply flipped Catherine to a facedown position. How gruesome. And how like her. If this was the case, the dark, dire deed would be almost impossible to prove. There must be only two written records of what really happened that day:

Claire's own diary.

And Mark's diary, as well.

I have *video* evidence that Claire smothered baby Catherine, I said. Calmly. Confidently. Even though I was making it up. Taped evidence that proves your diagnosis of SIDS was wrong. *Quite* wrong. Was your report influenced by certain parties? People whose lives hinged on your findings? You covered up the ghastly deed committed by Claire Evans all those years ago, didn't you?

Covert homicide.

Which makes you an accessory to murder, Professor.

Or simply an inept SIDS researcher.

The professor sagged back onto his chair. His response told me what I needed to know. I'd nailed it.

Right down.

How much do you want? he asked, voice trembling. Looking as though he was on the verge of hyperventilating.

Me? I opened my eyes wide. I don't want your money, Professor. I have enough money to keep myself in the style to which I've become accustomed. I have spartan tastes, as a matter of fact. I put it down to years of enforced deprivation. Granted, I do have a thing for fancy lingerie. And bright killer stilettos. But a world-class scientist really ought to think about the Nobel Prize, shouldn't he? Wouldn't it be tragic if that precious plum disappeared beyond reach? Especially as it's within your grasp. Right there, at the tip of your pudgy little fingers. But proximity is often an illusion, isn't it? Because the things closest to us are often the farthest away.

Like love, for instance. Or vengeance, for that matter.

What do you *really* want, Mrs. Livingstone? The man's face was wan. The color looked good on him.

I want you to help me, Professor, I said.

12 April 2015

How am I ever going to get hold of Claire and Mark's nineteen-year-old paper-and-ink diaries? Both items must surely be kept inside safes. Gigantic barricaded steel contraptions within that Newnham mansion of theirs. Everyone's paranoid about old diaries these days. After all, hasn't diary blackmail and extortion become a multimillion-pound business? The tabloids are always running stories about thefts. Criminals demanding obscene amounts for the return of those little pieces of shit.

If only Steve Jobs had gotten his act together earlier. At least three years earlier. Life would be so much easier. Definitely less complicated.

I have a plan. It's fucking crude. But it should work.

I need to find the right person. To extract the two diaries for me. In the middle of the night.

Without leaving a fucking trace.

The philosopher Kierkegaard wrote: "Life can only be understood backwards." This quote also applies to death. Although life progresses linearly, homicides are understood backwards. You can only solve these murders by scrutinizing the past in careful reverse chronological order.

—*Textbook of Criminal Investigation*, volume 4
(Oxford University Press, 1987)

Chapter Twenty-One

HANS

5½ Hours Until the End of the Day

I still think she's mad. No one in his or her right mind would concoct such a crazily convoluted scheme. A plot of such perverse proportions merely to destroy a man. Sophia's diary will never hold up in a court of law. Fact: Diaries written by ex-inhabitants of mental institutions tend not to go down well with juries. I'm also beginning to doubt if Sophia's diary can even be admitted as legal evidence in the first place. Its contents are definitely straying in the direction of the absurd.

But what if... what if it contains a small kernel of truth?

Just a tiny one.

This kernel may shed light on the identity of her murderer. And it's my job, after all, to find out *who killed Sophia Ayling*. A detective should never lose sight of the *crime*. That was what Mr. Grizzled Professor said within the first minute of walking into his Introduction to Criminal Investigation lectures all those years ago. It's easy to get sidetracked by irrelevance, he said, waving an unlit cigar for emphasis. Haven't twenty years of investigating murders taught me not to discount even the faintest possibility? Isn't this one of the main facts I've learned about police procedural work over the years?

Should I believe the diary in front of me? Chiefly, Sophia was determined to get her hands on some pages from diaries belonging to Mark and Claire Evans. Pages she thought would illuminate the fact that Mark had bribed a medical expert to conceal the true cause of his daughter's death.

The premise is so preposterous that it's ridiculous. It defies all rational, factually driven understanding. But lunatics who claim to have minds that remember *everything* might well be capable of elaborate and outlandish schemes. Tactics fueled by an equally extreme desire to destroy.

I examine the chessboard on my table for a couple of moments before reaching out to move the black queen forward. The move ratchets up sudden pressure on the white king.

A brisk knock sounds at the door. I look up; it's Hamish again with a large crease on his forehead. The size of his frown matches the one I've developed after my most recent incursion into Sophia's diary.

"I tracked down a clerk at the admissions department of the university," he says. "He was kind enough to go back to his Trumpington Street office to have a look at their alumni records, even though it's a Saturday. Sophia Alyssa Ayling isn't on the database. I made him check various permutations of her name, just to be sure. But he's found nothing. He's certain she was never a student."

"Aha."

"I also spoke to the forensics who have been examining Miss Ayling's Fiat. They've found a few interesting things."

Damn. My heart sinks to my Oxford brogues with a thud. Why is the forensic unit so hyperefficient today?

"The car's boot is a little damp, they say. But that's probably from the thunderstorm we had two mornings ago. They've found bits of grass in the backseat."

"That's not particularly interesting," I say, struggling to keep my voice neutral. "There must be bits of grass in all cars in Cambridge."

Hamish shrugs.

"They've also found several clumps of dirt on the driver's seat and on the rubber mat below," he adds. "Some are still a little sodden. Ayling must have been walking about in the rain."

"Hmm...."

"No clear fingerprint samples, I'm afraid. But they did find a couple of long hairs in the boot. Both were dyed blond and had dark brown roots. The DNA matches Ayling's."

"So she *is* who we think she is," I say.

"Indeed."

"I need two more things from you, then. First, could you track down the whereabouts of a Duo named Anna May Winchester? A Lucy Cavendish alumna who disappeared for nineteen days in 1995 before resurfacing. I wish to know what's become of her. If she's changed her name, in particular."

"Okay."

"Second, could you exert pressure on Marge to get her postmortem report to us as soon as possible? We desperately need something before the end of the day."

"Why are you so eager to solve the case before the end of the day?" Hamish narrows his eyes at me. "You've been banging on about this all day long."

"Because..."

Damn. My mind's a sudden blank.

Hamish is staring at me. Damn. I'm taking too long to come up with an answer. I need to say something. Anything.

"Because I have...er...a reputation to uphold."

He whips an eyebrow up at me.

"If you've given a murderer a day to flee, then you've given them two," I continue, trying to inject confidence into my voice. "And if so, they will never be caught."

"Ah," says Hamish with a nod. Yet I can't help but notice that a dangerous-looking curl is playing at the corner of his lips.

"You must have surely written these facts down somewhere."

"Of...course."

He disappears through the door, lips still in a skeptical curl.

Damn. Damn. Damn. This is going from bad to worse. Two near

slipups within two days may well equal career suicide. Hamish did look suspicious when he left my office. Or am I imagining it?

I walk back to my chessboard and make four fairly random moves in an attempt to calm down. I should stop fretting about Hamish, although it's tempting to wallow in justifiable paranoia. Perhaps I should think about what he just said.

I wrench my mind back to the case.

A pattern is indeed emerging. Official records of a woman named Sophia Alyssa Ayling are few and far between. The admissions department at Cambridge claims never to have heard of her. Neither have the General Register Office, the Home Office, and the local Electoral Registration Office. Even the Ministry of Memory and the Department of Duos have nothing on her. The only two organizations that possess records of Sophia's existence are the DVLA and Barclays. I suppose I could ask my Bermudan counterparts if she exists in their files. If she was born on the island and has a Bermudan passport. But I suspect I will draw a miserable blank there, too. Anyway, it'll take ages for the Bermudans to get back to me.

I work on a different clock.

Who the hell is Sophia Ayling, then?

My gaze falls on the photo album at the end of my desk. The one containing numerous photographs of a Cambridge student in her twenties. A gawky, bespectacled girl with slightly protruding ears. Who on earth is this brunette? And who the hell was the blonde we plucked from the river this morning? Could Sophia Alyssa Ayling be a *fake* identity? Or an *altered* identity? Like, say, a new identity for someone once named Anna May Winchester? Did that flat-chested brunette transform herself into a curvy blonde after emerging from St. Augustine's? And then somehow get herself killed by Mark Evans?

I sigh.

The white king is definitely in a precarious position. I nudge a knight forward to defend it. Two cheerful taps sound on my door. I look up; Toby is back again.

"You may be interested in what we've found, sir," he says, marching in with a wide grin on his face.

I raise a hopeful eyebrow.

"I had to move heaven and earth to get the person's name," he says. "The one responsible for the transfers to Ayling's Barclays account. If not for your Swiss contact, I would have got nowhere. Heinz applied pressure on—"

"And the name is?"

"The trust fund was set up by a Duo named Alan Charles Winchester. A bank tycoon of British-Bermudan origin."

I freeze.

"Thought you would like more information about the man," continues Toby with a grin. "So I looked him up. Some of it is online, anyway. Alan married a Portuguese-Bermudan Duo named Lily Ferreira in 1967. They decided to move from Bermuda to England in 1981. Bought a large country house near the village of Coton, three miles outside Cambridge, at 288 Brook Lane."

He pauses for breath.

"Go on."

"Alan and Lily were involved in a terrible car accident on the M11 motorway in 1983 while driving back to Coton from a performance of *La Traviata* at the Royal Opera House. Alan got away with a broken arm, but Lily suffered multiple injuries and was proclaimed dead at the scene. Alan remarried in 1994, taking a Mono Belarusan dancer named Agnessa Ivanova as his second wife. He eventually died of a heart attack in 2008..."

Toby emits a sudden chuckle.

"...while having sex with his personal assistant, Nola Barr, at the Ritz hotel. But what might interest you, sir, is this: Alan Winchester had a daughter with Lily Ferreira. She was born in 1970. Her name is Anna May."

"Dear Lord."

"I also called St. Augustine's back," he says. "Pretending to be an accountant at Swiss Inheritance Services. Said I was going through some old accounts and found a discrepancy in payments. Probably due to confusion over the actual period of Ayling's residence. I asked them to confirm the precise dates of her treatment there. Guess what?"

Triumph spreads over his face.

"Ayling was at St. Augustine's between May of 1996 and January of 2013."

"You're a whiz, Toby," I say. "I'm going to recommend you for promotion. This is sterling work."

"Elevation seldom hurts," says Toby, chuckling again. "The view is always better from a higher floor, as I've learned. Can I do anything else for you?"

"Not at the moment. I'll ring if I need anything. Well done, Toby. Well done."

"Thank you, sir." Toby gives me a mock salute before vanishing through the door.

I stride to the window, hoping for a blast of fresh, neuron-enhancing air. I suck in a deep breath, only to realize with disgust that I've filled my lungs with torrid fumes from a passing bus. I grimace at a pigeon on the ledge below; the bird eyes me back with an equally disdainful expression. The wind has picked up since the morning; a stray paper bag is whirling in vigorous Brownian circles along Parkside. A few boys and girls are running about on Parker's Piece, the large patch of green outside the police station. One of them is flying a yellow kite with an orange tail. It's bobbing on the air currents like a vulture buffeted by soaring thermals.

Sophia Ayling and Anna May Winchester are, of course, the same person.

I should have worked this out earlier. How embarrassing. In fact, I would have figured it out a couple of hours ago if not for that damned discolored Polaroid.

It all makes sense now. Especially if Sophia's iDiary has more than a kernel of truth in it. The dates match, at least.

Maybe the diary isn't only leading me to the truth; the diary may in fact *be* the truth.

So Sophia's desire for revenge must be caused by something that transpired in the months leading up to her prolonged residence in the Outer Hebrides. Something that sparked a burning, vicious hatred for Mark Henry Evans and continued to fester over the long years of her institutionalization.

But what could have triggered this terrible grudge in the first place? Surely not a broken heart.

Perhaps I should suspend all rational thought by putting myself in Sophia's distorted, memory-filled shoes. Those warped stilettos of hers. Try to think like her, a one-time Duo who remembered *everything* after the age of twenty-three. Accept that she's telling the truth, especially if I wish to understand her motivations for wanting to destroy Mark Henry Evans. Scientists have, after all, found the genetic switch for short-term memory. Any Off switch can perhaps be flipped back on again. Wasn't there a recent newspaper article about a crazy psychiatrist who went round hitting Monos on the head to improve their memories? Maybe there's a chance, a minuscule possibility, that an odd human might just gain full memory someday.

Now, if I could recollect *everything* (never mind the fuzzy bits and pieces), what would be the most traumatic memory of them all?

The yellow kite in the distance cuts a tortuous upwards diagonal above the children on the green.

The recollection of being dumped by Mark in favor of Claire? Possible but unlikely. Even if Mark decided to swap a Duo brunette for a Mono blonde in the most unkind, thoughtless manner possible, that must have happened at least twenty years ago. Most people would surely have moved on by now. Fact: The *Textbook of Possible Criminal Motives* states that love-related grudges don't usually last long, although money-related antipathies tend to linger. A diary line that says "The idiot dumped me for a pretty girl with large boobs twenty years ago" isn't as emotionally potent as a sentence that says "The idiot owes me a massive amount of money, and I can't afford to pay my rent today."

Unrequited love can't possibly be a factor.

I glare at the yellow kite as it conducts a merry zigzag dance above the children's heads.

The memory of Mark being involved in Sophia's extended incarceration at St. Augustine's, say? Mark could have written to her doctors twenty years ago, insisting she was mad (as I did after I interviewed her back in July of 1995). Her psychiatrists could have used our letters to back up their diagnosis of her mental condition before transporting her to the Outer Hebrides. But the woman's meticulously engineered revenge plan spanned two long, patient years. There must be something more. Something drastic.

I sigh. My groan is so loud it scares the pigeon off the window ledge. I grimace at the clouds scudding overhead.

I should be thinking more creatively. After all, I'd laughed at Hamish earlier for not being able to think outside the box.

Light sparks off the edge of a cloud.

The yellow kite dives downwards, like a vulture swooping on a carcass.

Oh, God, no.

It must be the memory of how one acquired the burden—or the perceived curse—of memory in the first place. Didn't that crazy psychiatrist claim to have converted a Hungarian Mono into a person "far superior" to Duos? A radical combination of physical and emotional traumas apparently did the trick. Mark might have done something just as drastic to Sophia twenty years ago. On the evening of the Trinity ball, for instance. An act that brought back all sorts of undesirable memories. She was still agitated during my first interview with her, for sure.

Sophia must have held Mark responsible for her memory surplus.

Bingo.

I reckon I've worked it out.

But did Mark harm this desperate, calculating woman two days ago? And how did she die?

I walk back to the chessboard on the table. I study the pieces for a couple of minutes before moving the white king backwards to dodge the rampaging black queen.

YESTERDAY

I need that postmortem report before the end of the day. But Marge and her assistants are likely to take their time over it. It's a Saturday evening, after all. Marge and company might have even packed up by now and headed to the Flying Pig for some beers. I can't blame them. Anyone who spends a Saturday peering into the insides of a waterlogged corpse deserves a few drinks. Multiple drinks. But because tomorrow is Sunday, the report will only be forthcoming on Monday.

I need that damned report today.

Who remembers more than they are letting on?
Who is lying to others, and who is deceiving them-
selves? What happens when truth cannot be
recalled? Can we truly know ourselves or others?
—Mark Henry Evans, draft of
The Serendipity of Being

CHAPTER TWENTY-TWO

SOPHIA

15 April 2015

Saw a delightful piece in the *Times* this morning about the Mixed Marriage Act. The scheme so dear to Mark's heart, forming the cornerstone of his political campaign. A piece of bullshit designed to unite a divided country. A delusional attempt at increasing the number of Duos so Britain can regain her long-lost glories. It's amazing what the government is capable of these days. Thinly veiled attempts at social engineering. This country reminds me of the fucking Third Reich.

The act is due for royal assent soon. It will go into effect next February.

Neat.

If only they knew. Mono-Duo marriages result in depression. Oh, yes. But I still need proof. I have ample evidence of pill-popping feminine hysterics. The problem is finding proof of *murder*.

Thieves and robbers are damn difficult to locate when you actually need them. They have a way of disappearing into thin air.

I should be working harder.

Much harder.

16 April 2015

Things are heating up; the general election will be deferred to Thursday, 25 June. Mark is going to be campaigning like mad. Plenty of press attention on him over the coming weeks, I reckon.

I should keep my eyes and ears peeled. For the right time to unmask him to the world.

When love turns to hate, even Hades will melt.

The melting point is nigh.

He fully deserves it, too. I wouldn't have collided with that bloody thing on Jesus Green if he hadn't made me so furious in the first place. I was already damned upset to begin with. He could have shown a bit more empathy, a bit more under-standing. Instead he made me twice as angry.

It's amazing what an encounter with rigid, unyielding metal can do to a hapless brain. It makes blinders slide off. It causes barricades to crack open.

When you have lots of time on your hands at St. Augustine's, all you can think about is the people who triggered your mis-ery. The tiny but significant things they did to you, how these added up.

I have all the tools I need to engineer his political demise. The sharp chisel of full memory. The razor-blade edge of solid perspective.

The time is near. I can see it. Feel it. Smell it, even.

The man's imminent downfall.

Almost there, Sophia.

Almost.

YESTERDAY

2 May 2015

Mr. Burrell has nimble hands. Nimble feet. Nimble enough not to leave a single trace of his nocturnal visit to Newnham last weekend. The tranquil time of night when one long-term resident of 303 Grantchester Meadows was fast asleep. The other had his dick outside his pants in London. A pair of lips between his legs. A pin-size camera recording his every groan and moan.

But nimble Mr. Burrell failed to deliver the goods. He dropped by yesterday. Wearing a worn and holey T-shirt with the words HERE'S TO A SAFER CAMBRIDGESHIRE printed on it. Carrying only *half* of what I wanted.

Sorry, he said, tapping the side of his cap. Filthy fingers probably stained from wanking. I'm so sorry, love.

The man's old diaries are housed in a platinum safe in his study at the end of the garden, he added. A metal contraption that requires a whopping *twelve-digit* combination code. A device that looks bombproof, darlin'. Probably is. It resisted all my sharp tools. The best professional devices on the market, mind you.

For fuck's sake, I said.

The man's *paranoid* about his old diaries, said Burrell, spreading apologetic nicotine-stained palms. I've never seen a safe like that before. I'm sorry, darlin'. No professional will ever be able to break into *that* reinforced concrete bunker. It's impossible. A siren, my love, is programmed to squeal if one enters the wrong code three times in a row.

This is the most I can pay you, I said, shoving half the agreed amount into his grubby paws and showing him to the door.

But...but...he protested.

You're losing your touch, Burrell, I snarled. You pinched my underwear twenty years ago and got away with it. But you delivered only half the goods this time. So you're getting only half the money. You'll get the rest if you manage to retrieve *everything* I want. I might even throw in a fat bonus.

That's one bonus I ain't getting, he said with a shrug. Flashed his gold-capped teeth at me and vanished through the door.

I filled a glass with a triple shot of vodka. After all, Dad once said that one should always celebrate—or commiserate—with the right dose of booze at hand. Sat down at my dressing table. Tore open the envelope Burrell handed me. Several pages were stuffed inside. Fished them out with a smug chuckle. The handwriting that greeted me was large. Childlike, even.

I gasped. The date on the first page was *13 June 1995*, instead of *13 June 1996*.

Burrell could not fucking read.

I was tempted to hurl the pages at the wall. Kick myself for being stupid enough to hire an illiterate crook. Perhaps I shouldn't have turned to Lucy Cavendish's former odd-job man. The person who stole my knickers off a clothesline twenty years ago. Though he did owe me one after I saw the funny side to what he'd done and decided that I was too lazy to tell the college to sack him.

But I flicked through the rest of the pile anyway. To my surprise and relief, I discovered that the thirteenth sheet of paper bore the date 13 June 1996. Burrell must have cut twelve pages out from the wrong diary before realizing his mistake and grabbing the right one from the shelf.

So the wanker could read, after all.

I toasted myself with the vodka before spending the next ten minutes reading the correct pages from 1996. Damn carefully, too.

Before hurling my vodka glass at the wall.

Fuck that woman.
I should have known.
Better.

3 May 2015

I'm entitled to complain. To moan, even. About how some people have fucking selective memories. As demonstrated by this passage from the woman's diary, dated 18 June 1996:

15:15: Checked on Cath after it began pouring outside. Still sleeping. Looked peaceful in crib. Temperature in room seemed too low for comfort, so placed blanket over lower body. Went back to knitting in living room.

16:30: Storm worsened; worried thunder might wake Cath.

17:01: Returned to see how Cath was getting on and if she needed feeding. Eyes still closed. Face seemed paler than usual. Touched her cheek. It was cold. So cold that it froze both fingers and mind.

Don't know what happened next. Really don't. When world came into focus again, I was on all fours on carpet of nursery. Hands shaking, tears streaming down face. Couldn't breathe. Mark was kneeling yards away, cradling Cath in arms. Her head was flopping downwards.

What did you do, Claire? He was shrieking.

World went out of focus again. Next thing I knew, there were paramedics everywhere. One had attached something to my baby. The other was shaking his head at Cath's gray face. A third paramedic was using his arms to hold me back. Long scratch mark across his face. Mark was standing in corner, gripping top of Cath's crib. Face white, pain in eyes.

It was then I understood what had happened to my darling baby.

Can't write anymore. They've placed me under observation since. Am exhausted. Senses numb. Mind in pieces. An abyss has swallowed me up. May never be able to climb out of it. But I should write this down before I go to sleep.

I'm so sorry, Mark.

How pathetic. A Mono hiding from her past. Covering up her misdeeds. Obscuring her sins. Tweaking the truth. Inserting false memories into her diary. Choosing to believe what she wishes to believe. Convincing herself she was not to blame. Absolving herself from shame.

It's funny how some people refuse to admit their guilt. Even to themselves.

It's odd how amnesia provides solace.

It's amazing how people forget what they've done.

There's not enough here to prove that Claire Evans killed her own daughter, alas. To convict her in the light of public opinion. To convince the world (and a jury) that she was a murderous mother.

One who killed her Cath. Her three-month-old baby.

I've gone over each word in that passage. With a fine-tooth comb. Even to the extent of copying it out here. The only phrase that faintly damns her is Mark's anguished question:

"What did you do, Claire?"

But that could mean anything. It's not along the lines of: "You've just smothered poor Catherine, my sweet honeybun, to death."

"I'm so sorry, Mark."

That could also mean anything. It's not an admission of guilt. It's not enough.

Fucking hell.

I am back to square one.

4 May 2015

Wait a minute. There's more to the story. I've gone through that little stack of musty papers again. There's an earlier diary snippet (dated 14 June 1996) that says:

8:15: Woke up drenched in sweat. Same dream as in earlier diary entries, but with horrible, horrible difference. The face wasn't that of Jenkins. It was Cath's this time. An eighteen-year-old version of my darling baby. Brown eyes like Mark's, long blond hair like mine. Mouth curled in anger. You've screwed me, Mum, she kept screaming at me. You've made me Mono. Cursed me with your blood. Set me up for lifetime of failure, of being laughed at, of being second-class citizen like you.

A snippet from 15 June 1996 (the following day) reads:

6:27: Woke up shaking, sweat on palms and forehead. Same dream as night before, but with terrible twist: my grown-up Cath wasn't Mono. She was Duo instead. Yet she was still yelling at me. You embarrass me, Mum, she kept saying, over and over again. Because you're stupid and pathetic. Useless and inept, unlike super-cool Dad. Why has Cath replaced Jenkins in my dreams? Why aren't these crazy nightmares going away?

Which explains the woman's rambling, disjointed entry for 16 June:

17:15: Stared down at baby Cath in crib. She wasn't crying for a change. Gurgled at me with smile, reaching for my finger with happy whimper. Looked beautiful. Innocent and angelic. So perfect I began to cry. What if she turns out Mono like me? What if I've inflicted lifelong discrimination on her? And if she turns out Duo instead, will she think that her ex-waitress Mono mother is beneath her? Will I lose her love and affection because I'm not Duo like her? Will she treat me with contempt? What if she says each day, in same patronizing way as Mark did this morning: "You ought to write that down in your diary tonight, Mum, and learn it more carefully"? What if I will never understand her? And what if she never understands me? Will my daughter still love me when she turns eighteen and discovers she's Mono? Will she hate me for condemning her to such a fate? Or will she hate me even more if she turns out like her father?

The triggers for Claire's postpartum depression are evident. The slippery slope of hormone-induced irrationality is clear. No wonder that moment of madness happened on 18 June, merely two days later.

Bloody hell. I'm starting to feel a little sorry for the woman. Even if she took the love of my life away from me twenty years ago. My love has since morphed into hate anyway. Love *or* hate. No middle ground.

Forgive *or* forget. I can't forget, though it's tempting to forgive her. Poor little tortured woman. I feel sorry for that little baby, too. But her husband still conspired to cover up murder. I'm not letting *him* off that easily. I should still drive home the point that he was stupid enough to marry a Mono in the first place. The precise point I tried to make when I paid him a courtesy call on the morning of his wedding day. The man's a bloody idiot to choose her over *me*. How on fucking earth do I get this message across?

It will be lovely when they get a divorce, by the way. Deeply satisfying.

When they finally see just how right I was.

5 May 2015

Maybe I'm not back to square one after all. I should think. Vigorously. Even if I can feel another skull-splitting headache coming on. Mark Henry Evans could well have adopted a selective approach. He could well have retained carefully curated facts about what happened in his home on 18 June 1996. Like his cowardly Mono wife, he could well have lied in his own diary.

But people who lie to others seldom lie to themselves.

I'm sure of this.

Lies have their basis in truth. Because they are deviations from the truth.

To lie, one must know the truth.

Especially if one is a Mono. Even a Duo.

I'm convinced that Mark wrote a truthful account of what happened to his only daughter. Of what his wife did that rainy afternoon. I sense this in my bones. This is why he's so protective of his old diaries. Keeps them in a bombproof safe.

Mark Henry Evans lies to his wife. Unashamedly. And he lies to me with equal verve. But he is incapable of lying to *himself*. As a Duo, he must be intelligent enough to know that he can't.

He can't afford to.

Not if he is a fucking *novelist*.

Most novelists write to make sense of the things that happen to them. They bring all their worldly experiences to their writing.

They translate facts into fiction. Grief. Longing. Horror. Fear. Love. Loss. Facts they've learned from their diaries. Snippets of conversations they've recorded. All beautifully reimagined in descriptive prose. Brought to life again in touching, heartbreaking fashion. Most novels are subtle reflections of the people who penned them. Their personalities. Their pasts. The facts they've learned about themselves. In one way or another.

But it's *hell* that inspires a novelist.

Not heaven.

A good novelist translates personal adversity into literary opportunity. Mark is a good novelist, despite his multiple sins. I meant it when I complimented him about his literary genius at the writers' conference. Consider *On Death's Door,* for instance. His most critically acclaimed novel. The one that catapulted him into the literary stratosphere. The one that almost won him a Booker prize in 2013.

In particular, consider the scene touted by critics as a tear-jerking masterpiece. The protagonist, Gunnar, discovers the death of his nine-month-old daughter. Mark would not be able to write that scene with such conviction. With such vivid poignancy. With such brutal accuracy.

If he'd obscured the truth from himself.

I now understand why he became so successful. How he managed to convert himself. From a penniless, unemployed ex-academic disinherited by his parents for marrying a stupid Mono. To a bestselling, wealthy novelist adored by millions. Because things began happening to his humdrum Duo existence. All sorts of terrible, brutal things. And he wrote about them with great sensitivity.

This always resonates with readers.

I need those pages from Mark's diary.

But how does one get into a fucking bombproof safe? A contraption that has already defeated the craftiest underwear crook in Cambridgeshire? Short of holding a gun to Mark Henry Evans's head? Or pressing a knife with a serrated edge against his throat?

Just asking.

25 May 2015

The clock's ticking. On me.

He called this morning to say sorry. It's amazing how he has turned apologizing into an art form. A chronic condition. He will no longer be able to get away from Cambridge next Saturday. Rowan is staging a noontime press conference at the Guildhall because the Mixed Marriage Act receives its royal assent the day before. Next Saturday morning is perfect timing, says Rowan. The right opportunity for more political capital and publicity. But this development also throws an unfortunate spanner into the plans we've made for the weekend. He's *so* sorry.

One thing hit me right then.

The press conference at the Cambridge Guildhall would be my perfect opportunity to bring Mark Henry Evans to his knees. In an altogether different way from the frenzied action depicted on my 144-GB memory stick.

I now know the date and time of his unveiling to the press corps of Great Britain.

Next Saturday.

When the magnificent bells of Great St. Mary's church begin to peal twelve times in a row, just a few yards away from the Guildhall.

But there's a small problem. A tiny but significant one. I already have plenty of hay. An impressive, sumptuous pile. But my haystack needs its crowning glory. Like a Norwegian spruce crying out for its uppermost crystal ornament. I need more icing on my cake. I need Mark's diary entries for the days between 13 and 24 June 1996. The period between the death of Catherine Louise Evans and Paget's report. Because they will make all the videos on my 144-GB memory stick redundant.

I can picture the journalists assembled at the Guildhall next Saturday. Poring over these photocopied pages from Mark's diary, which I will of course be distributing with the appropriate level of relish. The right amount of glee. Lapping up Mark's unvarnished account of what *really* happened in the nursery of 23 Milton Road nineteen years ago. The shocked expressions on their faces. The ensuing horror in their eyes, the matching newspaper headlines the following day.

The blissful satisfaction that is bound to well up in my heart. Because that moment in the Guildhall will be the dramatic culmination of two years of hard work. In the bedroom. And out of it.

My grand, jaw-dropping finale.

When Mark Henry Evans is exposed.

As an adulterer. A liar. An accomplice to murder.

The first two revelations will merely raise eyebrows. Ruin his political career. But the third will destroy him. Completely.

I need those pages from his diary.

Before. Next. Saturday.

But how on fucking earth do I get hold of them?

Looks can indeed be deceiving.
                    —Diary of Sophia Ayling

Chapter Twenty-Three

HANS

5¼ HOURS UNTIL THE END OF THE DAY

Let me get this vitriolic little diary right. So Mark made Sophia so livid that she ended up colliding with some "bloody" metallic thing on Jesus Green. This, in turn, triggered a surge of "full memory," a condition she ultimately blamed on Mark. So my deduction was right. I should be pleased that I managed to work it out. But did Sophia truly intend to unveil pages from Mark's diary at a Guildhall press conference in a bid to bring him down? The one at noon *today?*

This is pretty insane.

I reach forward to demolish the white queen with its black counterpart. Another knock reverberates on the door. I look up; it's Hamish again. A chastened, even sheepish expression shades his face.

"You're right," he says. "I take back what I said earlier."

"Uh-huh."

"Marge got her act together," he says. "This came through a few minutes ago."

He hands a sheaf of papers to me. The uppermost one reads:

Office of the Cambridgeshire Coroner
Date and Hour Full Autopsy Performed: 9:49, 6 June 2015, by

Margery Sheldon, MBBS, FRCPath, DMJ (Path)
Name: Sophia Alyssa Ayling
Date of Birth: 20 November 1970
Race: White; Sex: Female; Class: Duo
Coroner's Case #2015-289

"I'll leave you to mull over Marge's findings," he says. "There's some fascinating stuff in there. Looks like you were right all along. I'm still trying to confirm if Winchester changed her name. I'll let you know if I dig up anything. I've a feeling I'm almost there."

I'm tempted to tell him that the task is no longer necessary. But then again, I should keep him busy.

"Very well," I say.

He vanishes from the doorway. Perhaps Hamish isn't such a pompous idiot after all. At least he had the decency to admit he was wrong. I grip the papers before me, gobbling up the print with hungry eyes:

EXTERNAL EXAMINATION

The autopsy commenced at 9:49. The body is presented in a black body bag. The victim is wearing a gray trench coat (Aquascutum, extra large), with its front, side, and internal pockets filled with polished black and white ornamental garden stones averaging 50 mm in diameter. She is also wearing a black sleeveless turtleneck shirt (Alexander McQueen, size 8), long black trousers (Alexander King, size 8), and black flat-soled boots (Lanvin, size 6). Her underwear consists of a black lace bra and a black lace G-string (Agent Provocateur).

The body is that of a white female measuring 175 centimeters and weighing 116 pounds. Its features are consistent with the stated age of 44 years. The victim is wearing light-blue contact lenses and has dark-brown irises. The corneas are cloudy. The victim's hair is dyed platinum blond, layered in curls, and is approximately 250 mm in length at the longest point. The color of the roots indicates that her natural hair is dark brown. Toenails are painted a bright crimson. The victim's lips bear traces of bright red lipstick. Extensive plastic surgery has been conducted on the victim's chin, nose, ears, and cheeks. She has hyaluronic acid lip fillers and has received Botox injections to her forehead. She has also undergone major breast augmentation. The genitalia are that of an adult female, and there is no evidence of physical injury. Pubic hair has been partially trimmed.

There is a bruise on the right-hand side of the victim's skull measuring 15 mm x 5 mm. It is located beneath the victim's hair about an inch behind her right ear.

The victim's body is covered with river dirt, sludge, and plant detritus. Dirt encrusts her fingernails. A strip of green aquatic weed encircles her left leg. There are superficial scrapes and travel abrasions on the victim's elbows, knees, and backs of the hands. The red nail varnish on her left index, middle, and ring fingers bears scuff marks. The varnish on all fingernails of her right hand is similarly chipped. There are small cuts and skin abrasions on the tips of the victim's left thumb and on her index and middle fingers. The skin on the fingertips of her right hand is also lacerated in places.

INTERNAL EXAMINATION

CENTRAL NERVOUS SYSTEM: The brain weighs 1,307 grams, within the normal range. There is acute subdural hemorrhaging beneath the skull under the area of external bruising and contusions to areas associated with the overlying injuries, chiefly to the medial temporal lobe and hippocampal area.

GENITOURINARY TRACT: The kidneys (right, 117 grams; left, 120 grams) are unremarkable. Pelvic examination indicates that the victim was not pregnant at the time of death. There is no evidence of recent sexual activity…

I look up from the black print, my thoughts a whirl. So I was right about Sophia Ayling. Someone smashed her head in, causing an internal brain hemorrhage that ultimately resulted in her death. The person then draped an oversize trench coat filled with garden stones around her shoulders and dumped her into the Cam.

That someone could have been a panicky author. A writer who thought of Virginia Woolf in desperation and who hoped to mask the true manner of Sophia Ayling's death. After all, except for the bruise Marge found under the dead woman's hair, there were no marks of physical violence on her body.

But the murderer's an idiot. A veritable fool. There were not enough stones to weigh Ayling's body down. He—or she—clearly never heard of Archimedes' principle. That a massive number of stones is needed to counteract the buoyant nature of a 116-pound corpse. Certainly many more stones than a few pathetic ornamental pebbles from one's garden. I saw a few stones missing from the borders of Evans's outdoor path when I visited his home this morning. Leaving behind dark, grassless indentations on the ground. What's more, the stones are a precise match for the ones in the pockets of the dead woman's overcoat.

I think I have enough on Sophia's murderer to clap the person into a cell at the back of this police station tonight.

I prod the black queen forward before excavating a pair of handcuffs from the upper drawer of my desk. You never know with authors. Especially those who write about other people's deaths for a living.

* * *

I scramble into the patrol car outside the station. But before my driver flips on the engine, I see Hamish running in our direction at full pelt.

"Hans," he says, panting as he approaches us. "I couldn't find you at your desk. You weren't answering your mobile phone, either. Fiona said she saw you rushing out of the office."

"I'm going to bring someone in," I say. "For the second time today. I should have just kept him here this morning."

"Anna May Winchester disappeared for nineteen days in the summer of 1995," he says. "Guess what? She changed her name to *Sophia Alyssa Ayling* by deed poll before vanishing again a few months later—"

"I know all that already." I wave him off.

Hamish's mouth is agape.

"How?"

"I've got a way of finding things out," I say. "I'm heading off to get Sophia's murderer, by the way. But I'm going to drop by a house in Coton first."

"You're confusing me."

"I should inform Miss Winchester's next of kin about her death."

"Shouldn't you be nabbing her killer first?"

"Don't worry. Her murderer won't have enough guts to do a runner out of Cambridge this evening. Besides, the person doesn't yet know that I've managed to work *everything* out."

"I'll come with you. Especially if you're going to be arresting someone."

Beware of Hamish. Keep him at arm's length at all times today. I managed to shrug him off this morning and get away with a couple of unaccompanied visits. But protocol insists that two officers are needed to conduct an arrest. I grimace; an unorthodox solution, thankfully, surges to mind.

"It's all right," I say, pointing to the sergeant at the front. "He'll back me up."

We pull away from Hamish in a shriek of wheels, leaving him in a large cloud of exhaust fumes.

Alan Charles Winchester was a rich man during his lifetime. The driveway of 288 Brook Lane is impressive. We zoom past magnificent gateposts crowned by statues of golden lions and pull up under a lavish portico supported by gilded columns. I get out of the patrol car only to spot a green peacock strutting behind a manicured bed of marigolds. I walk to the front door and reach for the knocker. It's in the shape of a devil's face; a gold-plated circular knob functions as its tongue.

I rap the metal down, twice. Two sharp knocks sounding like bursts of gunfire, both loud enough to rouse the dead.

I wait, shuffling my feet on the porch and examining the gilt mosaic of a buxom nude woman beneath my shoes. But no one comes to the door. I stare at my watch for precisely sixty seconds before tapping the tongue down twice more.

My exertions are greeted with resolute silence.

I wait for another two minutes before stepping back from the porch and inspecting the facade of the house. Everything is latched shut, including the multiple bay windows on the upper floor. All the blinds are drawn; the house looks as if it's gone into hibernation. Agnessa Winchester must be miles away from home. I pull out my mobile phone and punch in the number Toby gave me.

"Hel-lo," a muffled female voice says.

"Good evening," I say. "May I speak to Mrs. Agnessa Winchester, please?"

"Speak-king. Who's zis?"

"DCI Hans Richardson from the Cambridgeshire Constabulary."

"You are ze po-liss?"

"Yes. I'm standing outside your front door, but you aren't at home."

"I'm visiting a zpa on ze zouth coast at ze moment. Vy are you standing at my door?"

"I'm sorry to bring you bad news. But I'm afraid that Anna May's body was found in the River Cam this morning."

"Anna eez *dead?*"

"Yes."

"Oh, Gawd."

The line falls silent for a few seconds.

"I'm sorry to be telling you this," I say.

"Vy are you *sorry*, Inspector?"

"Er...that's what I usually say when I speak to the deceased's family." A snort issues over the line.

"Anna isn't real famil-ee. She's ze daughter of my second husband, Alan. He died a few years back. My diary says I've not seen Anna for a very lonk time. She's became crazy mad, you see, and zey put her in ze hospital for cuckoos. Did she kill herself?"

"We think she was murdered. But our investigation has thrown up some major leads, and we're close to pinning her killer down—"

"Kil-ler? You mean someone shoots her? Like—bang?"

"No, no, no. She wasn't shot. But I cannot say more at the moment."

"Poor leetle Anna. You *must* find ze person who mur-der-red her."

"I *will*, Mrs. Winchester. I promise. Anyway, the medical services will be in touch soon so that you can make the funeral arrangements."

"Zank you, Inspector."

I turn off my mobile phone before striding in the direction of the patrol car and jumping into it. Agnessa Winchester sounds like a ditzy Belarusan who spends most of her time preening her feathers in spas. But she is still the victim's closest "family member," and I've done my duty by informing her.

"Newnham," I say to my driver.

He nods, revving the engine. The patrol car lurches forward with a screech, spitting clods of gravel.

"Make it fast," I add.

He twitches his mustache before jumping on the accelerator. We shoot down Brook Lane, scattering dead leaves across the road. I'm going to do exactly what I'd promised Agnessa. And I'm going to start by extracting a person from the depths of a particular house in the neighboring village of Newnham. He did, after all, say that he spent the past two days writing in his study. Something gruesome must have happened in that room the day before yesterday.

I'm sure of it.

Revenge. Blackmail. Seduction. Obsession. Murder.

What if the short story you're reading was a precise description of the facts in your own diary?

This is the tale of Gunnar, who picks up a dog-eared book in a charity shop in Valberg only to discover that he has been hiding terrible truths about his past from himself.

And someone else knows it...

—Back cover of *On Death's Door*
by Mark Henry Evans

Chapter Twenty-Four

CLAIRE

I wish I hadn't cut out those twelve pages from my diary. Especially as Inspector Richardson has failed to shed any light on that twelve-day void in my head. But it's still a relief to discover that Anna May Winchester resurfaced after a few days. At least Mark didn't do anything to that girl all those years ago. I'm certain he didn't cause Sophia's death. I'm confident I did not marry a murderer. I don't know why Richardson remains adamant that Mark killed Sophia.

But Mark is still a shameless *cheat*, and I'm still going to divorce him.

I'll start by packing a small bag of essentials. And I'll retrace my steps to Emily's guest room so I can spend the night there (even if the bed's damned uncomfortable and reeks of mothballs). I'll also figure out my options, with her help. As Emily had pointed out in that matter-of-fact tone of hers, I ought to start thinking about the size of my divorce settlement. She's right.

I turn the key. The door gives way; I step into the living room. A burst of late-afternoon sun is spilling through the French doors, casting rosy-gold rays across the polished floor. I can't believe I rushed down that staircase earlier this morning to attend to Mark's injured hand. It seems like a lifetime ago. A different household, even a different existence. So much pain since. I feel like a different person altogether. I have plenty to write in my diary tonight. So many terrible and unsettling facts to type out and learn.

301

Nettle trots up to me, his brown eyes sympathetic. I pat him on the head before stroking his floppy ears.

"Apart from Em," I say as a tear slides down my cheek, "you're the only friend I have."

Nettle gives me an approving wag before disappearing behind the sofa. I walk into the kitchen and turn on the kettle.

Footsteps echo behind me.

"I'm sorry, Claire." Mark's voice sounds weary, even exhausted.

I walk to the cabinet and pull out a Lady Grey tea bag. My tears have dried up. I can feel Mark's eyes on my back.

"I tried to protect you," he continues, a stricken note creeping into his voice. "Save us from what we've done—to others and to ourselves. But it's not enough. Everything's falling apart now."

The kettle begins whistling a little. But its persistent hum fails to fill the void left behind by Mark's words. A sudden anger rises up in my throat, almost to the point of choking me.

"You slept with her," I say with a snarl, turning around and stabbing my eyes at him. "You kept it going for months behind my back. *Two long years*. I thought you were spending all those weekends away from Cambridge because of work. Instead you were banging another woman in London. You're a liar, Mark. A *cheat*. From the first day we met. I've read my diary entry about that girl you slept with, even after we got together. The one you were taking to the Trinity May Ball. God knows how many other women you've had since. I've been such a fool. For trusting you. For keeping up the pretense. For convincing myself that I can't afford to leave this marriage. Despite knowing that we'll never make each other happy."

Mark merely shakes his head. Instead of looking contrite, he seems consumed with self-pity. His reaction is galling; surging fury threatens to blind me. I'm tempted to step forward and sink my fingernails into his shoulders. Shake him hard.

"I did lie," he says, spreading his palms and taking me by surprise. "About *her*. When Richardson showed up at our doorstep this morning,

I thought it would be best to deny any connection to Sophia. Tell him that I had absolutely nothing to do with her. It was the only option left, I figured. In view of what we've done."

"We?" I say, choking on the word. "It was *you*, Mark. It was you who had an affair with her."

"I'm sorry, Claire," he says. "For getting carried away by my stupidity. I'm not proud of myself. I can't change what I've done. But there are worse things than my affair with Soph—"

I can't believe my ears.

"What could be worse than your husband having an affair behind your back?" My voice escalates to a shriek. "The discovery that he's a liar who's been telling the world that we've been in a happy mixed marriage for years? What can be worse than that?"

Mark does not answer. Instead he collapses on a kitchen stool, his head slumping forward.

"I'm going to Emily's tonight," I say, spitting my words out. "To work out the terms of our divorce."

Mark sighs.

"You have every right to be jealous," he says. "And now you've every right to ask for a divorce. Hurt me back in the way I've hurt you. You've already succeeded, anyway, with that clever text message of yours. My political credibility has been destroyed in just a few words. You should be a novelist, Claire. You've managed to create a ruckus greater than any of the books I've written. But you're also on the verge of destroying us. Even yourself."

"Stop talking in circles."

"If only you knew."

Mark's innate sense of Duo superiority makes me bristle even further.

"Quit your smug Duo act. And stop implying that I'm ignorant. That you know much more than I do. I've endured twenty years of patronizing bullshit from you. This is a fact I know all too well."

"I only have myself to blame," he says with a mournful sigh. "For sparing you the agony of knowing. For telling you to *forget* what happened. I thought you would be much happier that way. But the truth is within you, Claire, whether you realize it or not. It's lurking inside your subconscious. Like a disease. You must have taken hundreds of pills over the years. But there's only so much they can do for you. You can no longer go on hiding from the truth. It's killing you from inside. I'm sick and tired of covering up for you."

"I went to see Inspector Richardson earlier," I say, ignoring Mark's senseless ramble.

"You what?" Mark seems flabbergasted. "You did *what?*"

"I wanted to ask him a few questions about Anna May Winchester."

"*Anna?*" Bafflement enters his face. "But why?"

"She was the girl you were taking to the Trinity May Ball, wasn't she? The one who went missing for nineteen days afterwards before reappearing again. I've connected the dots, thanks to what Richardson said. *Anna May Winchester.* That was her name, wasn't it? The first in the shameless string of mistresses you've kept over the past twenty years. A list with Sophia's name at the bottom."

"I can't believe you went all the way to Parkside just to ask about an ex-girlfriend of mine," Mark says, incredulity spilling out of his eyes. "You're preoccupied with the wrong things, as usual. As fucking small-minded as ever. Even with things collapsing around us. Now I know why you've been poking about in that folder of mine."

I freeze, like a child caught red-handed in the act of stealing sweets from a shop. So Mark knows I've been snooping around.

"I don't blame you," he continues, taking me by surprise. "For wanting early proof that I've slept around. That I'm a *serial* adulterer. So you can humiliate me even further in public. But I can't believe you went to talk to Richardson, of all people. With him closing in on us."

I freeze again.

"What do you mean *us?*"

Mark does not reply. Instead his head sinks forward into his hands.

"Mark?"

He does not look at me.

"Why is Richardson closing in on *us?*"

My husband's silence is ominous. A sudden chill strikes my heart.

"What have we done, Mark? Does it have anything to do with Sophia?" A quiet tremor has crept into my voice. It is not from anger.

Mark sighs again, getting up with slumped shoulders. He slouches in the direction of the kitchen door. But before leaving the room, he turns and says:

"I've done you wrong as a husband. But I did try to protect you from the consequences of your actions. First Cath. Then Sophia. But the inspector's not one to be deterred. I sense this in my bones. He let me go this morning, but he'll be back again soon."

He disappears into the darkened hallway outside. He must be heading for his study. Fact: Mark beats a hasty retreat to the bottom of the garden whenever our conversation reaches a dead end. This phenomenon has happened with increasing regularity in recent years. But this time, the dead end is much worse. Sophia Ayling is dead. And our marriage has come to an end.

But how did Sophia die?

Is Mark trying to say that *we* were involved in her death?

I must have spent fifteen minutes typing "Sophia + Ayling" over and over again into my iDiary. But nothing shows up on the screen. Nothing at all. I've even tried various permutations of her name: Sofia, Sophie, Sofya, and others. But my diary's a blank.

First Cath. Then Sophia.

What is Mark trying to say?

Fact: Catherine Louise Evans was my poor baby. My only baby. Who was taken away from me after three months by that scourge known as sudden infant death syndrome. I found her one afternoon, looking pale in her crib, causing everything to dissolve into a terrible blur. My diary says as much.

Fact: Mark has not mentioned our child in recent years. She has become something of a taboo topic in our household. He prefers to say "I'd much rather not talk about her" whenever I bring up the subject. To confirm this fact, I type "Cath + Mark" into the search box of my iDiary before tapping the SORT BY DATE—DESCENDING icon.

The hit that surfaces first is dated 21 October 2012. Part of it reads:

Asked **Mark** over breakfast if he would like to try for another baby. After all, I'll be turning thirty-seven soon. **Mark** shot me horrified look, one suggesting I was mad to bring subject up. Almost dropped spoon into bowl of cereal. Trying not to be discouraged by **Mark**'s response, I said **Cath**'s death had left terrible void in our lives, one that has grown wider over years. We should try to fill it with another child. A little one to care for, cherish, and love.

It'll be terrible for both you and baby if we have another, said **Mark**. And I'd much rather not talk about **Cath**, he added, abandoning cereal and stomping out. Spent next two hours moping in bed, shattered by **Mark**'s brusque response. But I soon felt more resigned after conducting search for sudden infant death syndrome on computer. Turns out that scientists in Heidelberg have proved the existence of genetic predisposition to SIDS. Woman's second child has more than negligible probability of dying from syndrome if first child suffered from it.

Mark could be right: it may be bad for both child and me. After all, didn't Dr. Jong once say that my depression was exacerbated by **Cath**'s death? The death of second baby would devastate me. Ought to banish all thoughts of having another. But I still want a baby, irrational as it may be.

Why did Mark decide to talk about Cath? After dodging the subject for years?

First Cath. Then Sophia.

Why did he list the two names in quick succession?

First Cath. Then Sophia.

I can think of only one connection between the two. They are both dead. Could their deaths somehow be related?

My mind spirals back to what *really* happened yesterday. I woke up in the morning and cried my eyes out for an hour before staggering out of bed. Mark was nowhere to be found; as the morning wore on, I became increasingly worried. I let myself out of the conservatory and stumbled down the garden path to his study. The wooden door was ajar; I flung it wide open. Mark was sprawled on the sofa, face contorted in sleep, torso twisted at an alarming angle above the waist. His fingers were curled around the neck of a half-empty bottle of whiskey.

"Mark," I said, rushing forward to remove the bottle from his hand.

His eyelids trembled. He groaned. I winced; his breath reeked of stale alcohol.

"Wake up, Mark."

His eyes flickered open; they were lined red, just like mine. His pupils gained focus; they settled on me.

"Claire…"

"What…what did you do to *her* in the end?"

"I…she…" His voice was a hoarse crackle.

"How can I live knowing that…" My hands began to shake; hot tears spilled from my eyes.

Mark pushed himself up on the sofa.

"How can I even—"

"Look here, Claire," he said, a sudden sharp edge to his voice. "You did as told, didn't you? You wrote in your diary that you watched television yesterday night. That you spent the evening at home."

"But…"

"Please say you did."

"I did."

"Good," he said. "It will be better tomorrow. For you, at least."

"But you can't just cover up—"

"I can." His voice was hard, shot through with steel. "And I *will*."

"Oh, Mark."

"Don't ever raise the subject again."

"But..."

"Go back to the house, Claire. *Now*. I'll join you soon."

So I did, with tears pouring down my cheeks. I rushed up the garden path, shot through the door of the conservatory, and propelled my legs up the stairs. I ran into the bedroom and dug out the birthday present I'd prepared for Mark, stashed at the bottom of my wardrobe. I grabbed the carefully wrapped parcel and ran down the stairs, back in the direction of his study.

We met on the garden path. His eyes were as tortured as before.

"Mark," I said, sobbing. "I wanted to give this to you for your birthday. But you can have it now. Before it's too late."

"But..."

I thrust the parcel into his hands.

"Open it. Please."

"Oh, God..."

"I don't know how else to thank you. I really don't."

"Why do you always try so hard, Claire?"

"Just open it. *Now*."

Mark frowned as he tugged the ribbon off. His mouth fell wide open when the wrapper slid away to reveal what I'd bought for him: a signed first edition of Virginia Woolf's *Mrs. Dalloway*.

"What..." His eyes were incredulous. "You've got to be kidding, Claire."

"Do you not like the book?"

"Hell—"

"But...but...I thought you've always wanted a signed first edition of *Mrs. Dalloway*."

"Oh, God. The irony."

"Mark?"

"Cath. Sophia. Virginia Woolf. *You*."

308

My mind reels back to the horrible, clueless present moment. Yesterday's exchanges with Mark make no sense at all. We must surely have been talking about something that happened two days ago. Something terrible. If only I were a Duo like my husband. If only I could remember things like he does. So this is why Duos have an edge over Monos. So this is why they think they are superior. Because I now understand the difference an extra day of memory can make.

I need to confront Mark at once. I'm going to hammer on the door of his study. But this time, I am not fetching him for a chat with the police.

I'm going to interrogate him myself.

I step out into the fresh air. The sun has slipped below the horizon; the first shadows of twilight are creeping over the garden. A coal-black raven hunches on a nearby sycamore; it eyeballs me with suspicion, angling its wedge-shaped tail between the boughs. The wind has died down after howling most of the day. The bushes along the garden path and the leaves on the trees are motionless. Even the birds in the distance have fallen silent. Deathly quiet, even.

It feels like the calm before the storm.

I reach the end of the path and pound on the door of Mark's study.

"Go away, Claire," he says. "I'm writing."

I heard that excuse this morning. Fact: The phrase "I'm writing" is Mark's favorite stalling device, the one he dredges up whenever he wishes to avoid conversing with me. At any rate, I'm certain that writing is the last thing he is doing in his study at present.

My husband must be lying again.

"Open the door."

"Stop it, Claire."

"I want to know how they are linked. Cath and Sophia. You mentioned them in the same breath. I want to understand why Richardson is closing in on *us*. If this has anything to do with Sophia."

I can hear Mark sighing behind the door.

"Forget it." A deep weariness shades his muffled voice. "Just forget what I said. I got a bit frustrated earlier. That's all."

"Oh, come on, Mark—"

"You said you were going to spend the night at Emily's. Just get going. You'll be happier there."

"Open the door. I know where the spare key to your study is kept anyway. I used it earlier today to get in."

My words are greeted with a long silence. But the door creaks open. Mark looks even more agitated than he did this morning. He's clenching and unclenching his right fist. His hair is tousled, even standing up in places. Fact: Mark only runs his fingers through his hair when he knows he's in a terrible pickle.

"Claire..." he mumbles as I step into the room, brushing past his body. Whiskey fumes plague his breath.

I scan the study. Nothing much has changed since I visited it earlier in the day, apart from the bottle of cheap whiskey on his writing desk. The bottle is almost demolished; an empty shot glass stands next to it. Fact: I last saw Mark drinking whiskey nineteen years ago, during those long, dark months after Cath's death. If he's on hard booze again tonight instead of his usual fancy Bordeaux, something must have gone dreadfully wrong.

I shift my gaze to his laptop; the aurora borealis screen saver is repeating itself. So my husband hasn't been writing at all. Instead he's been swigging down large amounts of whiskey. He was lying when he said he was writing. Granted, he was merely telling me a small white lie. But if a man's a liar, he's always a liar. The same goes for adultery. I'm tempted to stride forward and slap him for fibbing again, but I grit my teeth and hold my hand in check.

Because there are more important things I need to know.

"I want answers."

"You're better off not knowing."

"You said you were sick of protecting me from the truth. I want the truth. Now."

"Forget what I said earlier. It was a facetious statement. You may know for a fact that I specialize in coming up with self-indulgent twaddle."

"Cut the crap and give me the truth. Why did you say those things when I woke you up in here yesterday? Why did you look so troubled when you opened your birthday present?"

Mark is silent.

"For heaven's sake, Mark. Why did you link Sophia with Cath?"

He stumbles over to his desk. He fills the shot glass to the brim before downing the whiskey in one gulp.

"They're both dead," he says.

"I already know that."

He takes in a deep breath. Under the glare of the overhead lights in his study, I realize that he looks exhausted. His face is haggard and drawn. His forehead is a mass of troubled creases. He must have aged about fifteen years since I put a bandage around his finger this morning.

"It was *you* who did it," he says.

Truth is often the hardest thing to discover about yourself.

—Diary of Sophia Ayling

Chapter Twenty-Five

MARK

Claire recoils backwards, as though she has been physically struck by my words. Her irises are stripped of color. Her face is a pallid shade of ash. Her mouth opens only to close again. She extends a trembling hand, as though she's seeking a means of support. But there's nothing in the vicinity that will prop her up.

The corners of her lips are beginning to quiver.

"I...what..." she says.

A tiny fraction of me is both delirious and smug. It's time for my wife to face up to the truth of what she's done instead of hiding behind the blissful cloak of forgetfulness. It's time for her to enter the realm of reality, having been protected for so long.

I have three options (their number is, unfortunately, decreasing as the day progresses):

(A) start with the truth about Catherine;
(B) reveal what happened to Sophia;
(C) none of the above.

"No," she continues. "Not Cath..."

We might as well start with what happened to Catherine. After all, I would still be a father today if not for Claire's brief descent into madness nineteen years ago.

You can't change facts. Some will never be forgotten, especially the excruciating ones.

"You wrote in your diary that you found her in her crib," I say. "Looking pale. You touched her cheek. It was cold. So you called for help."

"I did," she says. "My diary tells me that…"

And this is what I say:

Your diary only tells you what you'd much rather believe. What you can bear knowing. Truth was, you must have placed a pillow on Cath's face during one of your black fits. She'd been crying all morning and afternoon. All day long. The day before. Two days before, too. Cath was a weepy little baby. No one could figure out why she howled all the time. You were frustrated by the fact that you didn't know how to stop her from bawling. It didn't help that you'd slipped into one of those syndromes common to new mothers. They now have a proper term for it: postpartum depression. I later found out a relevant fact from Dr. Jong. You were on antidepressants for a couple of weeks soon after you conceived Cath. But you stopped taking them when you discovered you were pregnant. Your depression came back with a vengeance after you gave birth…

Claire's eyes are whirls of horror.

"I didn't…"

Denial, I suppose, is a natural reaction to harsh truths. But it's time for Claire to confront the past.

I entered Cath's nursery that afternoon. I saw you cradling her. A pillow lay at your feet, limp and accusing. Your jaw was clenched. Your mind seemed light-years away. You fixed your gaze on me. Your eyes looked as though they had been occupied by demons, dragging you to a terrible new place where no one had ever ventured. They looked as though they'd been stripped of their human essence. But they were also disconcertingly vacant. It was an alarming combination, one unlike anything I'd seen before. I froze in my tracks, not believing what I was seeing. I merely

gaped in horror. You told me, in a small voice, that you'd finally man-
aged to stop Cath from crying…

"No…" Claire is on her knees now. Her eyes are awash with tears; a couple of drops have begun to streak down her cheeks. She has also covered her ears, as if to stop my bleak words from flowing in.

"This can't be…"

Her mouth is a tortured circle. Like the mouth in Edvard Munch's *The Scream.*

I rushed over to save Cath. I pulled her from your hands. Her body looked
like a marionette's. Like a frail, broken puppet. Or a rag doll without its
spine. Her head was drooping downwards, as if it had been detached from
the rest of her body. Her face had turned a pallid shade of gray. Her pupils
were a blank void, like those you see on a shop mannequin. Something vital
had been snuffed out of her eyes. In their place, a silent and unseeing scream
of darkness. Those were the precise sentences I wrote in my diary, all those
years ago. You were right. Cath had indeed stopped crying. But it was also
clear that she would never cry again…

"I didn't kill her," Claire says, still clamping both ears with her hands. "I surely couldn't have…"

It's time for you to face the truth. After concealing it from yourself for
such a long time. They placed you under observation in Addenbrooke's that
evening. I saw you lying on that hospital bed, your face scrunched up in
misery. You were whimpering to yourself. Shaking your head to and fro.
Mumbling the words Cath *and* sorry *over and over again. Chewing your*
nails until nothing was left. I waved the nurse out of the room, saying that I
had to talk to you in private. You looked up at me, a sudden flash of clarity
in your eyes. You said you didn't know what overtook you. You didn't mean
to hurt Cath. You merely wanted to stop her from crying. You couldn't live
with the knowledge of what you'd done. The truth, you said, would destroy

you for the rest of your life. That was the moment I decided to help you: I felt sorry for you. After all, you were the woman I chose to marry. We'd just lost our daughter. I didn't want to lose my wife to insanity. You were already close to the breaking point. In sickness and health, for better or worse, through good times and bad. Sickness, I reasoned to myself, applies to the mind, too.

But the guilt in my heart trumped everything else. I blamed myself. I should have suspected that things weren't right with you soon after you gave birth to Cath. I should have written a stern Note to Self in my diary, telling myself that I should take you to see a psychiatrist at once. I should have read the signs; they were there before my eyes. My diary, after all, said that you had terrible nightmares after Cath was born; I saw you crying and wringing your hands in her nursery several times. I should have acted at once, based on what I wrote down. But I did nothing. Absolutely nothing. Back then, I was too preoccupied with the draft of my first novel; I was blinded by the act of creation, oblivious to the destruction within my own household. My guilt shattered my soul. Because I could have saved Cath from you.

Claire is hugging her knees on the floor, her face a vista of desolation. Her forehead is furrowed with lines of pain, sorrow, and guilt. She looks like a tiny, hunted animal. The sight is heartbreaking. Sudden, unexpected sympathy slides into my heart; I'm tempted to walk up to her and squeeze her hand.

But I should continue with my relentless exposition of harsh facts before I lose my nerve:

That's why I suggested you forget what happened that afternoon. With hindsight, it was the most foolish thing I've ever done. But I was the person who suggested you write a sanitized version of Cath's death in your diary. Saying you found her pale and unmoving in her crib, with cold cheeks. It was a credible story. After all, she bore no marks of physical injury on her body. It was a story you could believe yourself. You looked up at me with gratitude, tears welling up in your eyes. You whispered: "Thank you,

Mark." I felt that I'd given you a second chance. An opportunity to regain your sanity, the peace you so desperately craved. When you woke up two mornings later, I still thought I did the right thing. You were a different person. Your cheeks were swollen. Your eyes were puffy. Grief colored your pupils. But the guilt was gone. I felt vindicated. But then I realized that the truth of what had happened to Cath was still buried somewhere inside your head. That it was killing you from within, whether you realized it or not. One never truly forgets.

Claire emits a sudden agonized bleat. It sounds like the gasp of a drowning person.

"Mark," she says. "Oh, Mark..."

"I taught you to lie to yourself," I say. "When it mattered."

Claire shakes her head.

"This lie, as I later discovered, forced me into several more. It's amazing how quickly one becomes a committed liar. Lies beget lies. But I knew that we needed professional medical opinion on our side. Proof that Cath had died of a *natural* cause."

"You succeeded." Her voice is small.

"I begged Dr. Anthony Paget, the director of studies in medicine at Trinity, to help us. Back then, I didn't have anything to offer him. Not when my dad had disinherited me for marrying you. The tabloids, I said, would have a field day if it ever emerged that the daughter of a Trinity alumnus had died of a terrible *mistake*."

Claire winces.

"Paget studied my tearful face for a long time in silence. The English literature DOS, he said, had once mentioned my name at Formal Hall before passing the port. Mark Henry Evans was one of the most promising students to ever pass through the front gates of Trinity, it seems. It would indeed be a shame if my future were tarnished by an *accident*."

I detect a sudden flash of comprehension in Claire's tear-filled eyes. She might even be making a few relevant connections in her head. Such as the reason why I decided to contribute half my first novel's advance to Paget's research work. Fact: The problem with Monos is that they are unable to see the big picture. Their little brains tend to run on limited processing power. So you have to be patient with them.

"I'm sorry," she says, tears streaking down her face once again. "I thought that…my diary said that…"

"Your diary says what you want it to say. Memory equals the facts you *choose* to retain. We are all victims of the pasts we *prefer*."

"So I lost my mind…"

"While I've been dying a slow, painful death for nineteen years. Truth equals suffering, Claire."

Perhaps Dad was right in the end. Fact: He insisted all those years ago that marrying a Mono was an act of madness and that it was my stupidity that prompted him to disinherit me. I now understand why he did what he did. But even he did not think I would be dense enough to marry a Mono with an *occasional* tendency to madness. That makes it twice as bad.

"So I'm a monster," Claire says, her eyes burning crucibles of pain. "Who killed her own daughter."

I have nothing to say in reply. What could I possibly tell her now?

My wife crawls to the sofa before pulling herself onto the cushions. Her slow, tortured movements are those of a woman who has lost everything. Her eyes are still filled with tears. But I sense a new inwardness to their depths. They are enveloped by a dull opaqueness, turning them from lavender to larimar. It's the glazed-over look one sees in the eyes of a fish that has been dead for more than a week.

"I'm sorry, Mark," she says. Her voice is a pitiful whisper. "I now understand why you strayed."

I freeze. That's one connection I hadn't made myself. Perhaps my wife isn't as dense as I've always thought.

"But I don't understand why you stayed."

I remain silent.

"Why did you stay with me for so long?" Claire continues. "After what happened to Cath?"

Lust makes you stray, but love makes you stay.
—Mark Henry Evans, *On Death's Door*

Chapter Twenty-Six

CLAIRE

My question hangs in the void between us. Horror blinds my vision. Sorrow grips my heart. I look down at my hands, the hands that caused the death of my own daughter.

The hands of a *murderer*.

I will never be able to forgive myself for as long as I live. Maybe I should slash my wrists again, hang myself from a rope, redeem Cath's death with my own. I ought to punish myself each day for the rest of my life, spend each waking hour in atonement for my terrible sin.

But why hasn't Mark punished me more? For killing his only daughter? Why did he not leave at once? Why has he stuck with me—his wife, the evil murderer—for so long?

"You haven't answered my question." My words spill out in a tremble. "Why did you stay?"

"I had to," he says. "My brain kept telling me facts I couldn't ignore. Like the fact that it was *you* who kept us going at first."

I stiffen.

"The fact that I was stupid enough to resign from my Trinity position. I thought it would be easy for me to publish my first novel. I was wrong. Horribly wrong."

"I know this, but—"

"Trinity didn't want me back. Those snooty Duo fellows at High Table were appalled that I'd married a Mono."

"That doesn't mean—"

"Your Varsity Blues earnings kept food on our table. When our savings ran out, you forced yourself to return to work. Only three months after Cath's death. You then kept us going for another fifteen goddamned months before I got my first advance. You even offered to sell your engagement ring when things got really bad, but I said no. These are facts, too."

"But I still don't understand why you stayed."

"Facts, Claire. Facts. It was all down to the facts I've learned: we came to depend on each other. Helped each other stay afloat. Alive in this hostile world. I had no one at my side after my family disowned me. Apart from you."

"I guess we promised Chaplain Walters that we would stick with each other."

"Deeds outweigh promises. You've tried so hard to please me for years. That's what my diary tells me each time I read it. It also says that I feel twice as guilty whenever you try to be nice."

"So you wrote these facts down. But why did they make you stay after Cath...after she died..."

A loud sob drowns out the rest of my sentence. Mark frowns.

"I don't know," he says, shaking his head. "I really don't. The *what* is often easy. Yet the *why* is usually elusive."

I remain silent.

"I know what *you* gave up to marry me, Claire. We *both* fought to be together, right from the start. That's a fact, too. A fact that may well trump everything I've just said."

I freeze.

"How on earth..."

With a sigh, Mark stumbles to his built-in bookshelf on the opposite wall and pulls out a thin folder labeled "Miscellaneous Documents." He opens the file and extracts an old dog-eared document.

"I accidentally found this letter," he says. "Back in October of 1995, after we moved to 23 Milton Road. I made a secret copy of it so that I could keep reminding myself of what you decided to forgo. For *us*."

He hands me the sheet.

"I've read it so many times that I can practically recite it in my sleep," he adds with a sigh.

I look down at the photocopy, its edges brittle and yellowing with age. The authoritative-looking handwriting on it reads:

Ainsley Manor, Buckinghamshire
18 August 1995

Dear Miss Claire Bushey,

I understand that my only son intends to marry you next month. I cannot give my blessing to this union. I'm sure you know the reason why. I propose a simple yet effective solution to the problem on our hands, one that I hope will satisfy all parties. If you were to leave my son alone and undergo an abortion, I will gladly transfer £500,000 to your bank account the same day. The money should keep you in comfort for the rest of your life. I hope that you will accept my generous offer. It will do you—and us—a lot of good. Please give me an answer before 1 September 1995.

Yours sincerely,
Philip Edward Evans, Esq.

I take in a deep breath before looking up at Mark. My head is spinning. So Mark has known all along.

"You never replied to Dad's letter, did you?" His voice is soft, gentle.

I shake my head.

"Why not?" he says.

I shrug. Our eyes meet. A tear wells up at the corner of his right eye; he tries, unsuccessfully, to blink it back.

"The sacrifice was mutual, then," he continues, voice quavering ever so slightly. "We *both* gave up something in the first place. That's what I *really* tell myself every day. Instead of what I promised Chaplain Walters—to mechanically remind myself each morning that I love my wife."

"But all our sacrifice has only brought disaster." I spread my hands, anguish stabbing my heart again. *"First Cath. Then Sophia."*

"I'm sorry, Claire. I really am. I just got carried away with Soph—"

"You said so earlier today. But..."

Another question quivers on my lips; I know I have the option of swallowing it back. But it tumbles out anyway:

"Did you ever...*love* her?"

"I don't think I ever wrote that in my diary."

"I don't believe you."

Mark wrenches his shoulders back in a confident swoop and pulls out his iDiary from his pocket. He types something into it with brisk fingers and walks over to show me the result of his search:

Sophia + love = 0 HITS (0 LINKS)

I blink in surprise. I can barely believe what I am seeing. But the jolt of an unpleasant possibility punctures my heart.

"What if...you used a different name for Sophia in your diary?" I say. "A pet name or something like that. Could you just type in the word *love?* I want to know what shows up."

"I don't think I ever used a pet—"

"Do it."

He exhales, shaking his head.

"Just do it, Mark."

With a sigh, he reaches forward and types in the word *love*, albeit with reluctant fingers. I stumble forward to peer over his shoulder. The screen glimmers; a few words flash up on it:

love = 12 HITS (3 LINKS)

Mark's eyes are round, even fearful.

"Click on the first link," I say.

He hesitates for several moments before complying. Our eyes lap up the words simultaneously:

7 April 2013

I unlocked the front door and walked to the kitchen only to discover that Claire was standing at the sink, back turned toward me. A kitchen knife lay at her feet. I thought she had dropped it by mistake. But she turned around, eyes wild and unseeing, wrists held up to the ceiling as if in supplication. I gasped. Blood was trickling down her left arm, a gruesome red rivulet snaking down to her elbow. Both the suitcase and the large bouquet of roses in my hands fell to the floor with a thud; I gaped in disbelief for a couple of seconds before rushing forward.

—Oh, God, Claire. What have you done?

—I didn't mean to. I didn't . . . I just felt awful this morning, this black thing pressing down on me, my chest hurt. . . . then I saw the knife . . .

Her words were interspersed with wretched dry sobs. I grabbed her by the shoulders and steered her to a stool before running over to the kitchen counter. I tore a long strip off a paper towel roll and pelted back in her direction to mop up the blood. The cuts across her wrists, I noticed to my relief, were superficial. But they were still self-inflicted.

My gaze fell on the gray medicine jar on the kitchen counter, the one containing Claire's antidepressants.

—Did you take your pills last night?

Her eyes flickered in their direction. She shook her head, hanging it limply.

—I thought I could do without them.

—Oh, God, Claire. I should have phoned yesterday night to tell you to take them.

Tears began sliding down her face; I knew that I should take her to Helmut Jong at once. So I shepherded her in the direction of my Jaguar (she followed meekly) and drove to Addenbrooke's. She remained silent during our journey there, holding the towel to her wrist. So did I. What more could I say?

Thankfully, Dr. Jong was in. I waited outside the consultation room for at least thirty minutes. As I paced the corridor, I realized that I shouldn't go away on two-week-long writers' conferences again, even if I'm paid a shitload of money to do so. I dare not imagine what might have come about if I'd returned a day or so later: if anything terrible happens to Claire when I'm away, I will never forgive myself. The pain of losing her to something awful would be beyond anything I could bear. (NTS: I should limit trips away from home to just one night and take them only when they are completely necessary.) Maybe that's why I've willingly devoted my existence to pulling her back from the brink, to ensuring her eventual rehabilitation, to saving her from herself. Even though the journey is sorrowful and soul-damaging, corrosive to the core. Because it will cost us more if I don't give her everything I possibly can, everything within the range of my ability. Because it will destroy us more if I don't.

Dr. Jong eventually came out of the room.

—Two stitches. We'll keep her here for a night, just in case. She'll probably need a stronger dose of antidepressants from now on, but she's going to be fine. Absolutely fine.

I exhaled in relief.

—You **love** her, don't you?

His question took me by surprise. I nodded.

—I've seen many married couples over the years. Most of them think that **love** is either black or white. But you think about **love** differently, don't you, Mr. Evans? What is the color of **love**?

The word escaped my mouth even before I could think about it:

—Gray.

—And if **love** had a taste, what would it be?

—Bittersweet.

He nodded; my answers clearly did not surprise him. He reached forward to pat my shoulder.

—This is why both of you are going to be fine. It may take a while, but you will get there someday. Eventually. Happiness may be elusive, but **love** might just bring you closer.

I suck in my breath; I can see Mark's pupils widening as he takes in the sentences he wrote.

So this was what went through his mind that horrible, black morning when everything became just a little too hard to bear. Maybe regular diary keeping isn't such a wearisome blight on human existence. I would never have realized Mark's true feelings about me if he hadn't immortalized them in his iDiary. I would never have understood the deep sorrow he has endured, how he has suffered because of me. My suspicions were right all along. He stayed because it would be more painful for him to leave. So did I. *The cord that binds us will only tighten into a fatal noose if either of us tries to break it.* This is why neither of us has left.

He sighs, probably realizing these facts himself.

"Let's have a look at the second entry," I say. My voice is soft, shot through with sudden understanding.

Mark obliges, clicking on the link. We crane our necks forward to study the result together:

7 July 2013

Claire looked pretty happy as she wandered along the white sand beach picking up seashells. It struck me, as I took in the cheerful upturn of her face at a distance, that we should definitely come to the Caribbean more often. The sun, sea, and salt air definitely do her good. My thoughts were interrupted by the abrupt arrival of an elderly woman in a fluorescent green swimsuit clutching a battered copy of *On Death's Door*. While she must have been at least eighty, her eyes were lively and bright.

—I **love** your novels, Mr. Evans. I **love** the way you combine mystery with domestic noir.

You can't escape fans of your work, not even in Nevis. We chatted about our favorite novels for ten minutes or so before she pointed to Claire with a smile.

—Your wife, I presume.

—Indeed.

—You must definitely **love** her.

Her statement took me by surprise.

—We all **love** our spouses, don't we?

—Not in the way you do. It took me a long time to work out if you are indeed Mark Henry Evans. While you've been sitting on this blanket for just as long, staring at her with a worried look on your face. As if you might lose her or something.

—Ah, well . . .

—How do you show your wife that you **love** her?

—Er . . . I don't know . . . I bring her roses, I guess. In different colors.

—Really? Do you use a color code or something? Different colors to mean different things?

—I do, actually. Crimson for "I'm sorry" and burgundy for "I'm really, really sorry."

—What about pink?

—I don't know. The first time I gave Claire roses, they were pink and white.

—The subliminal meaning is clear, then. If that was your first time giving her roses.

—Come to think of it, I gave Claire a lot of roses in those colors when we first met.

She winked and smiled at me, face creasing into an impressive set of wrinkles.

—It usually takes an outsider to see the obvious. You'll figure out the meaning of pink and white someday.

I look up at Mark.

"I never realized the colors meant something," I say. "Twenty years and I haven't worked this out."

"I still don't know what pink and white means," he says, looking a little sheepish as he clicks on the third and final link:

14 September 2013

I walked in through the front door only to be greeted by a delirious Nettle and a beaming Claire.

—I missed you, Mark. It's a shame you had to spend yesterday night in London.

I flung my coat onto a hook before walking in the direction of the kitchen, not daring to meet her eyes.

—Did you take your pills yesterday?

—I did. I feel all right today. I really did miss you. I'm making your favorite rabbit stew.

I wasn't sure if I could trust my voice, but I felt compelled to say something in response.

—Oh, Claire. You didn't have to. I feel bad for . . . er . . . missing the last train back to Cambridge yesterday.

And I felt twice as bad when I walked into the kitchen and took in the rich, piquant smell of rabbit and bay leaves rising from the pot simmering on the stove. The secure, comforting aroma of daily domesticity. A huge contrast to the scented magnolia candles that perfumed room 261 of the Kandinsky yesterday night. Mingled with the musky bergamot that woman had sprayed liberally onto her wrists and neck.

The smell of lust.

If magnolia and bergamot are the smell of lust, could rabbit and bay leaves be the smell of **love**?

It must be. It can't be anything else. Rabbit and bay leaves in the kitchen fill a man's stomach. But they also nurture his soul. They keep him going, both literally and figuratively, whether he realizes it or not. Maybe this is why I instinctively come home to my wife each day, much like a homing pigeon, despite the terrible things that have happened. (NTS: I should learn and retain this fact.) And that's why I feel guilty as hell: how could I be cheating on Claire? How could I?

Our eyes meet again. Mine are soft, dewy. Because something has just melted away in my heart. Jealousy and resentment made it brittle a long time ago. But newly found understanding is driving away the angst, the bitterness, my long-held factual misconceptions about Mark.

My hands are still covered with blood. I never will be able to wash them clean, no matter how hard I try. My soul is flooded with grief, horror, and guilt. *Terrible* guilt. Yet something might just mend my heart by the tiniest of a fraction, making everyday life a little more bearable.

Not just something. *Someone.*

My husband, the man who never left my side. The only problem was, we never really found each other in the first place. Not in the way we just did over the past hour. But it may already be too late.

I sigh.

"So tell me, Mark." My voice is a whisper. "What happened to Sophia in the end? How did she die?"

I have never understood Virginia Woolf. There, I've finally admitted it. Maybe I'm so intrigued by her because I don't understand her. Or maybe I'm just morbidly fascinated by how the spiral of darkness within her soul eventually led her to the swirling eddies of the River Ouse.

—Diary of Mark Henry Evans

CHAPTER TWENTY-SEVEN

MARK

My wife's question lingers in the air. Silence coats my lips. Why have my words suddenly dried up? Maybe it's the shock of realizing that lust has blinded me to the troublesome realities of love, to the bittersweet complexities of our marriage, to my true feelings about Claire. It's amazing how old diary entries can take on new meaning years later, when viewed in the distilled light of the present day. And it's staggering how myopic I have been to the truths about us.

A couple divided by memory yet forced by responsibility to the altar. But we were never truly obliged to remain with each other despite our vows. We both stayed because we wanted to, deep down inside. Because we have always been bound by the silken yet solid thread of *willing* self-sacrifice, despite the pain it has brought us.

Because any other alternative is worse.

"What *really* happened to Sophia?" Claire interrupts my thoughts, plunging me back into the harsh moment.

Minutes ago, I managed to unleash nineteen years of bitter bottled-up facts about Cath in quick succession. But my recent *memories* of Sophia are an altogether different matter. Especially in view of what happened after Claire found her snooping about in this room two evenings ago.

My options are reduced to only two possibilities:

(A) tell the truth;

(B) say nothing at all.

I'm inclined to pursue option B. But the whiskey surging through my bloodstream is heightening my instincts instead of dulling them. My intuition insists that if I do not tell Claire what happened to Sophia two evenings ago, I'll live to regret it. I should explain what happened when I can still *remember* it. When I still have vivid memories of what occurred the day before yesterday, instead of cold, sterile facts. Because nothing beats the poignant immediacy of memory. It's like seeing the past in crystalline color instead of in factual black and white.

If I don't begin talking right now, I might never summon the courage to do so again. I also reckon that Richardson will return to our doorstep before long. He's become a horrible rash that will never go away.

The wind has picked up once more; its mournful howl echoes outside the windows. I glance at my desk. An empty bottle of whiskey sprawls on its side, devoid of even the tiniest drop.

I clear my throat, causing Claire to jump. This is what I say:

We were having a late dinner two nights ago because you returned from Emily's around seven. We got into a quarrel about something silly— namely, which Caribbean island we wanted to go to for Christmas. You wanted Nevis, because your diary says you always feel good there. Mentally, emotionally, and physically. I said I wanted to visit a different island for a change, like neighboring Saba. Our discussion degenerated to the point where I stalked back to my study halfway through our meal, abandoning you and my half-eaten roast beef. My rudeness, in hindsight, shames me.

When I drew closer to my study, I realized that the door was ajar. I also heard the soft patter of footsteps inside. I froze in my tracks, stunned by the realization that there was an intruder in the room. But I also became curious as to what the person was up to. Why would anyone be poking about my study in the first place? So I flattened myself against an outer wall and peered into the window to find out what was going on.

I almost collapsed onto the flowerpots below me when I realized that it was a woman who had broken in. The figure was moving about with an ethereal, feline grace that could only be feminine. Yet she was also circling the room in a slightly agitated manner; she resembled a hungry, desperate panther. I squinted; she was clad from head to toe in midnight black. A sinuous sable scarf concealed most of her face.

I pause before walking to my diary safe and tapping in the combination code. Its door slides open. I yank out the Versace scarf; Claire shrinks back as I fling it atop my desk. It unfurls as a long, accusing gash of black over a dog-eared printout of *The Serendipity of Being*.

With a sigh, I continue my story:

The woman strode up to my safe and tapped its platinum door. She pulled out a small piece of paper from her pocket and studied it. I gasped as she tucked the paper away and began fiddling about with my safe's combination-code lock. She tapped something into it. A red light flashed in response. She tried again. The red light flickered once more. This time, I heard her cursing vigorously under her breath. She hesitated for a long while before reaching forward and tapping in a third set of numbers.

A foghorn tore into the night, shredding the silence.

She froze, raising her hand to her lips.

The siren mutated into a shrill two-tone clamor, alternating between loud and twice as loud. She began backing slowly away from the safe, hand still covering her mouth.

The alarm grew even louder.

It drilled my ears.

It went on.

On and on.

At some point I couldn't bear it anymore. I burst through the study door, shot past the woman, and tapped in the correct code. The door of the safe slid open, cutting off the siren.

I turned around to face her. We stared at each other in suspended animation for what seemed like an agonizing eternity. Somehow the ensuing silence seemed twice as deafening.

"You're such a disappointment, Mark," she said, pulling out the piece of paper again and waving it at me. I blinked; the words on the note said: "The birth date of the love of my life, and mine."

I couldn't believe my ears. Or my eyes. Because it was Sophia Ayling who was speaking to me, behind that black scarf.

"How did you get that—"

"Thought I'd worked it all out," she said, shaking her head with a disapproving tut. "That you used my birth date. Or that of the daughter you once had. Your poor little Catherine Louise. Shame it wasn't either one. I even tried your own birth date, repeated twice."

"What the hell—"

"But you rescued me in time," she added. "The safe's open now. That's all that matters."

Multiple questions surged to my head. How on earth did Sophia know that we once had a daughter named Catherine Louise, let alone Cath's birth date? And why was she trying to raid my safe? Nothing made sense to me. Nothing at all. I blinked in bewilderment as she strode back up to the safe, ran a finger along the rows of my old diaries, and pulled out the volume labeled "June–September 1996."

"I hope you won't mind me borrowing this moldy little masterpiece of yours for a couple of days," she said with a chuckle.

"What on earth . . ."

Just then, a soft rustling sounded at the door. We both turned around in surprise. My mouth fell open when I realized that you were standing at the threshold with a covered dinner plate bearing the remains of the meal I'd abandoned on the dining table.

"I heard an alarm," you said, taking a couple of steps forward and trailing off into petrified silence.

You stared at Sophia. Sophia stared at you. And I stared at you both. It became an unblinking three-way exchange. Between three people frozen by

circumstance. By the horror of their colliding paths. By the agony of know-
ing that things would never be the same again.

Color slid away from your face, turning it corpse white.

What have I done? I thought. What have I done to you? To us?

Sophia was the first to recover. She yanked her scarf off and dropped it
on the floor, revealing her face and her glossy mane of blond hair. It struck
me just how similar the two of you looked.

"Had your man for two long years," she said to you, her lips curling up
into a mocking sneer. "All to myself. After all, there's only so much fucking
a man can do."

She smirked as she began sauntering to the door, diary still in hand.

"But all good fucks must come to an end. Unfortunately, the same goes
for faithful husbands."

I saw comprehension in your eyes. The realization that it was my mis-
tress who was striding past you. Taunting you with her words. Deliberately
making you angry. She succeeded with aplomb; your face crumpled up in
fury. The rage in your eyes was mingled with a chilling vacantness. I should
have understood the meaning of that look. After all, I'd learned from the
diary in Sophia's hands that I had seen it before. On the rainy afternoon
when Cath died...

Claire emits another strangled sob. It prompts me to return to the sofa.
But this time, I reach for her hand. My fingers curl around hers gently,
forming a protective sphere.

I should have done something at that point. Anything at all. But I didn't.
I only have myself to blame. I merely gaped at the two of you, para-
lyzed by the terrible realization that I had failed in all possible ways. I
had slapped you in the face with evidence of my infidelity; you couldn't
have discovered the existence of my mistress in a more horrible way. I had
thrown away what we had shared, substituted lies with truth, exchanged
meaning for a meaningless tumble in the hay. Jeopardized everything
we had fought for. My recklessness of flesh, my first moment of puerile

weakness in York, had unleashed a terrible sequence of events resulting in this three-way encounter.

My litany of sins and failures pinned me down; I just stood there, broken and unmoving. Cowed by my wrongs. Desperate to make things right again, yet knowing that would never happen.

"Bitch," you said.

She flinched.

"You horrible bitch," you continued, spitting the words at her.

I saw a steely red mist flooding Sophia's pupils as she paused in her tracks to glare at you.

"You ugly bitch."

Everything happened in disjointed freeze-frame motion after that, like a broken film reel.

Her nostrils flared.

My diary somersaulted into the air, tumbling down on the floor. She rushed forward in your direction, a cry bursting from her lips. She reminded me of a feline predator closing in for the kill. Her palm landed on your face with a crack, leaving a sharp trail of red across your cheek, prompting you to squeal. I gasped. Her hand reared upwards again like a viper's head, vicious and poised for another attack. You instinctively lifted your arms to protect yourself from her next slap. My dinner plate crashed to the ground, erupting into a dozen ceramic shards and spraying thick gravy all over the floor. The beef thudded off my wastepaper basket before landing under my desk. You thrust your hands forward, eyes still vacant and unseeing. Your palms connected with her shoulders, merely inches away.

The contact was wild.

Desperate.

She crumpled backwards, her lips forming a surprised scarlet circle. Her eyes widened; I saw both her pupils dilating in shock. Her right hand shot out for support, fingers curling into a desperate claw, but there was nothing to cushion her fall.

Only vacant air.

Her head struck the edge of my desk with a crack, a second or two before her body slid to the floor.

I point to the precise spot where Sophia collapsed two evenings ago. The one that left Claire with more blood on her hands, even if no actual blood was shed that night.

My wife flinches in response. I suspect she knows what's coming next.

It was our turn to stare at each other in shocked silence. With Sophia's body sprawled between us, her back twisted in an alarming knot. Realization struck: she was not moving at all. She had been rendered unconscious by her fall. The anger in your eyes melted away. My limbs unfroze; I raced over to Sophia's side. So did you. Her face was pale, even pallid. Her chest was still. Ominously so. She did not seem to be breathing. I bent down and placed my cheek against her nostrils. I felt nothing. Not the slightest reassuring flutter of breath against my skin. I knelt down and reached for her wrist. I felt no pulse at all. Not the faintest beat. You crouched next to her and placed two trembling fingers below her ear, trying to detect a throb. But you couldn't find anything, either.

Minutes passed. We looked at each other again, our faces colored by horror. Your eyes had turned into raging pools of fear. The terrible realization of what had happened to Sophia hung above us, bleaching our souls. After what seemed like an eternity, you whispered that you didn't mean to hurt her. But your words trailed off into the ether when you realized that you hadn't just knocked Sophia out.

You'd killed her.

I don't know what came over me. But I just wanted you out of my study. Somehow I couldn't bear seeing you and Sophia together in the same room. The fact that you were crouching over her dead body made it worse.

So I told you to leave. To go away and forget what had happened here.

To get the hell out at once. To leave me alone to sort things out. To write in your diary that you'd spent the evening watching television after I retreated to my study. To stay put at home the next day.

You blinked at me at first, not understanding what I was trying to say. But you soon realized I was offering you an easy way out. I knew you would listen to me. Sure enough, you mumbled that you were sorry and would do exactly what I said. You then dashed out of the study, tears streaming down your face. The door slammed behind you as you vanished into the darkness outside.

"I can't believe you tried to protect me twice." Claire shakes her head, her face a tangled knot. *"Twice."*

I have nothing to say to this. Despite the absurdity of the situation, my heart is breaking for her. It must be terrible to discover that you've been responsible for *two* deaths. Especially if one was your husband's mistress and the other was your own baby daughter.

I'm itching for more whiskey. But nothing is left in that bottle. I need the reassuring weight of alcohol on my tongue. I walk to the cupboard at the far end of the room and pull out the finest bottle of Bordeaux in my collection: Château Mouton Rothschild, 1945. Fact: The bottle had cost me £7,800 at a Sotheby's auction in January of 2012. I'd bought it in a fit of delirious extravagance two weeks after I received the fourth installment of my advance for *On Death's Door*. But if I'm going to jail for what happened to Sophia, I might as well drink my best bottle before someone else gets to it.

I uncork the wine. A whiff of wet newspaper and muddy golden retriever greets my nostrils.

The smell of a big, costly mistake.

I groan before collapsing back onto the sofa next to Claire. The problem with extravagance, I now understand, is that it's nothing more than a money-wasting form of delusion.

Claire coughs. I glance at her.

"So...what did you do with Sophia's body?" she says, with a frown that suggests she'd rather not know the answer. "How did she end up in the Cam?"

"I picked her up from the floor," I say. "I staggered out into the garden with—"

A knock sounds at the door.

I stiffen. So does Claire.

"Oh, no," she says.

I know who's at the door. Claire knows it, too. A cold chill streaks across my heart, gripping it with frozen fingers. The whiskey I knocked back earlier must still be amplifying my senses.

The person taps again. Twice.

"No…" Claire's voice is a terrified whisper.

I turn to her. She reaches out for me, blindly.

Our bodies collide.

All the facts in my head have evaporated. They are no longer relevant; I've stopped caring about them. My brain has stopped processing possibilities and flitting between unpalatable options. It has also given up trying to make sense of things. Because the cerebral part of me has been drowned out by something inexplicably irrational. Something deeper and more instinctive.

Something visceral.

All that matters is the woman in my arms, my here and now. My past, present, and future.

Nothing else.

I never realized that Claire's hair smelled of beautiful jasmine. I never knew that her skin was so soft, so inviting. I never understood that her warm chest, beating next to mine, could be so delicate, so fragile. I should have known that the person I'd been hoping to find was with me all along. It's amazing what a single day's worth of recovered memories can do to your heart.

What is love if not the sudden surge of certainty? What is love if not the desire to experience this terrifying magic again and to remember even the tiniest sparkle of stardust it leaves behind?

I reach out to brush a tear from her cheek. Time and facts stand still for a couple of blessed moments.

They no longer matter.

Another knock.

The intrusion slices into us like a knife. A brutal surge into the horrible present. Yet this time, we know we don't have a choice. We prize our bodies apart. I drag myself up from the sofa; Claire does the same. She takes a first, tentative step forward; the expression on her face is that of a woman walking to the gallows. I move quickly to plant myself between her and the door.

"I'll get it," I say.

She shoots me a silent, grateful glance.

The distance between the sofa and the door to my study is about seven yards. But it feels more like seven miles tonight. Seven excruciating miles. I get to the door and turn the latch; Claire steps up behind me and encircles my waist with her arm. The door swings open with a loud, hollow creak. A vicious gust of wind bursts in, slapping me in the face and scattering dead leaves from the garden onto the floor. Sure enough, the very person we'd expected to see is silhouetted against the darkness outside. A tall uniformed man stands behind him, face concealed by shadows.

A raven caws in the distance.

"Did you hear everything?" I say.

My question elicits a grim nod. I should have known better. Yet I didn't really expect the man to return to our doorstep this evening, despite what he said. I thought that we would have a grace period of a few days before everything fizzled into smoking oblivion.

"We've been standing out here for a while," he says. "Your garden's really lovely, by the way."

Claire flinches. I reach for her hand; her fingers encircle mine like a vise.

"I have only three things to say in response to what I've overheard," he continues. "First, your wife may have indeed smothered your daughter nineteen years ago. Yet we have no evidence of that. The only difference between suffocation and SIDS is a confession. And this is one confession I reckon we're not going to get. That isn't the case I'm working on today, anyway."

Claire's hand is trembling. I squeeze it.

"Your wife is off the hook, as far as our current investigation is concerned. What she has just discovered must be torture enough. I would be pretty traumatized, too, if I found out that I'd killed my own daughter. It's not a fact I would want to have on my own conscience."

Claire is clinging to my hand so hard it hurts.

"The second thing is just a curious question. You used Mrs. Evans's birth date for your safe, didn't you?"

I nod.

Claire grips my hand even harder.

"Third, it *wasn't* your wife who killed Sophia Ayling. I have solid evidence of this fact. Irrefutable proof."

I freeze. Claire gasps. But the sound that escapes her lips is mingled with the unmistakable trill of relief.

"The person who killed her was *you*," the man continues, his eyes drilling into mine. "Mark Henry Evans, you're under arrest for the murder of Sophia Alyssa Ayling, previously known as Anna May Winchester."

One should always expect the unexpected.
Yet shit still happens. Even when you expect it.
—Diary of Sophia Ayling

Chapter Twenty-Eight

HANS

2¾ HOURS BEFORE THE END OF THE DAY

Their faces are as white as my snowy button-down shirt. Claire Evans is still attached to her husband. She's gripping his hand so hard that her knuckles are practically devoid of blood. While the expression on the man's face suggests that I've just introduced him to his worst nightmare.

"If you could kindly come with us, Mr. Evans," I say as my driver scoops up Sophia's black scarf with his gloved hands and puts it into a tamperproof bag. I'm glad he's good at following instructions.

"This can't be happening," Claire says.

I move forward to take her husband by the elbow; she rushes forward to plant herself between us.

"You can't take him away. Not when I've finally found him—"

"Please step aside, Mrs. Evans," I say. "I'm really sorry, but I have to perform my duty."

She spreads her arms before me, barring my way. My driver steps up to fend her off; she turns her hands on him.

"Claire…"

As my driver attempts to pacify Claire Evans, I seize the suspect by the elbow and propel him out of his study. He moves like a sleepwalker, one who has been denied any hope of waking up again. I lead him up the

349

dark path, past bushes rustling in the wind. The raven is still screeching above our heads; it's as persistent as Mrs. Evans.

We pass through the side gate; the patrol car is just yards away. I fling the back door open and point him to it. He complies without a whimper; I'm glad his petrified sleepwalking has spared me unnecessary shenanigans involving violent struggles or handcuffs. My driver and Mrs. Evans are a few yards behind us; she's yelling her husband's name at the top of her voice. The poor sergeant is still struggling to restrain her; I'm worried she may tear his mustache off.

"I promise I'll write down the truth in my diary tonight, Mark. All of it. *Everything* you've just told me."

"Claire…"

"I won't forget this time. I can't. I *won't*."

Our suspect's eyes are moist. I bundle him into the car and get in next to him.

"I'm so scared I'll forget, Mark. That I'll wake up on Monday and lose what we've realized about each other today…"

I reach for the door handle, giving her my most apologetic look.

"I'm going to stick with you, Mark. I promise."

I shut the door; I have no other choice, even though I feel sorry for her. My driver flings himself into the front seat, relief on his face. Claire Evans pounds the glass window that separates us.

"I'll do the same, Claire. I *will*."

I'm certain she didn't hear the words he muttered under his breath just before he ran a hand past his wet eyes. We pull away with a roar; her anguished face slips out of sight. But Evans's final words to his wife continue to ring in my ears during our short, silent journey to Parkside station.

This time, after dealing with the necessary paperwork, I take our suspect to the "conversation room" instead of my office. He has since procured a solicitor, an elderly man wearing a mustard-colored tweed jacket and thick circular spectacles. The spartan space is soundproof; it contains two digital recording devices, a metal table, and four chairs, all bolted to the floor. I flip on five ceiling lights, causing fluorescent glare to bounce off the room's freshly painted white walls. Our suspect winces in response. As soon as he recovers, his eyes settle on the large one-way mirror behind my chair, taking in its shiny, reflective contours. Excellent. He's aware of the possibility that someone outside the room may be scrutinizing his movements. The precise frame of mind I wish him to be in.

I point him and his solicitor to two neighboring chairs. Grapefruit-scented disinfectant wafts into my nostrils. Someone must have sprayed a liberal amount of it onto the floor tiles this morning; the room smells like a dentist's lair. Now, if only our man will open his mouth. I should begin with the usual drill.

"Procedure compels me to state these points to you," I say. "One: you have the right to remain silent. Two: this interview will be taped."

Our MP-no-more does not respond. He merely examines his shoes with sudden interest. I flip on the digital recording device before resting back on my chair and clasping my hands in front of me.

"Interview with Mark Henry Evans at twenty-two twenty-five on the sixth of June 2015. What happened after Sophia Ayling fell unconscious in your study two nights ago?"

He shakes his head in silence. This tells me that dear Mr. Evans intends to be difficult.

"Did you fill up the pockets of your overcoat with stones before putting it around her shoulders?"

Muteness greets my words. This does not bother me in the slightest. Our pleasant "conversation," after all, has only just begun. I reach into my briefcase. With a flourish, I pull out an evidence bag containing four black and white stones. This triggers a small, almost imperceptible widening of Evans's eyes.

I set the sealed bag down on the table before pulling a fifth pebble from the pocket of my trousers.

"I picked this up from your garden earlier this morning," I say, rolling the highly polished black stone between my forefinger and thumb.

"While I waited for Mrs. Evans to get you from your study. I couldn't help but notice that it was an exact match for the stones inside Miss Ayling's pockets."

I drop the stone onto the desk between us. A crack reverberates in the room; Mr. Evans reacts with a startled jump. The pebble bounces off the desk before skittering across the tiles and coming to rest against the bolted door. As Evans's eyes follow the stone's tortuous trajectory, I detect a small flicker of apprehension in their depths.

"You shouldn't scare my client," the solicitor says, disapproval burgeoning beneath his thick spectacles.

"Sorry," I say. "It just fell from my hand."

This is what I say next:

Let me describe what you did to Sophia Ayling two nights ago. You studied her body, realizing there were no obvious marks of injury on it. You then sat back on your haunches, a whirl of possibilities running through your mind.

A brain wave hit you. Fact: Virginia Woolf filled her pockets up with stones and waded into the River Ouse to kill herself. Suicide. Of course. And you might get away with it. Spurred by this delicious possibility, you picked up Miss Ayling's body and stumbled down your garden path. You fumbled with the side door, the one that opens onto the footpath at the end of Grantchester Meadows. The path that runs alongside the nudist colony and leads down to the river. Thankfully, there was no one in sight. No nudists sunbathing at night. Groaning under Miss Ayling's weight, you staggered down the path. The going was difficult, even treacherous, because rain had poured down earlier in the morning. The footpath was slippery, even boggy in places. It was also a cloudy, starless night. But you gritted your teeth and struggled onwards. Hoping that no one would see you. After all, you had everything to lose. Your hard-earned reputation. Your longed-for political career. Everything you had worked so hard for over the course of your lifetime. You knew that you didn't have a choice, that you had to keep moving forward. Your choices, after all, became fewer and more difficult the day Anna May Winchester reentered your life, whether you realized it or not.

The bleak expression on our suspect's face suggests that I have not exaggerated.

You reached the riverbank and placed Miss Ayling's body down. Hoping she did not acquire too many postmortem cuts or grazes along the way. After all, it had to look like a suicide. You returned for your trench coat, filling its pockets with stones on your way back to the river. You fastened the coat around Miss Ayling's shoulders before shoving her into the Cam. Her body made only a few ripples as it hit the water. Even the accompanying sound was muted. Her entrance was as discreet as that of a water vole plunging into the river. Which was exactly how you wanted it to be. You stared at her as she was swallowed up by the Cam, her hair forming a blond halo before it disappeared from sight. The current, you noted, was stronger than usual. A lot of rain had come down in the morning. You waited in the darkness, worried that she might resurface. But she did not. You heaved a deep sigh of relief before walking back to your study. The light shining through the windows seemed surreally welcoming in contrast to the horrors that had just taken place.

I pause to let it all sink in.

"You have a vivid imagination, Inspector," our suspect says to my surprise, speaking for the first time since we entered the room. "Perhaps you should be a novelist, too—"

"Mr. Evans," the solicitor says in a stern, cautionary voice.

I'm definitely getting there. Because our suspect has finally decided to speak. I should continue:

Fact: Virginia Woolf's body was found three weeks after she waded into the Ouse. By then it was in a badly decomposed condition. You had hoped that by the time anyone found Miss Ayling's body, it would have degenerated to a similar state. One that would mask any traces of her encounter with you and your wife. But when you got back to your study, you realized that Sophia's black scarf was lying on the floor. In your haste, you'd forgotten all about it. You wondered, briefly, if you should throw the bloody thing into the river after her. But there was no way you would make that journey to hell and back again. You'd already traveled there twice in the same evening. So you decided to place the scarf in your safe. You then grabbed a cloth and wiped down all the surfaces in your study, fearing that Miss Ayling had left her fingerprints behind.

I pull out the hermetically sealed plastic bag containing Sophia's scarf from my briefcase and fling it onto the desk between us.

"But DNA evidence may damn you, Mr. Evans," I say. "We're going to test this scarf. Traces of Miss Ayling's DNA and yours might well be found on it."

Though a shard of alarm is stabbing the man's face, he pulls his shoulders back. Mr. Evans is a tough cookie. But I have yet to play my trump card.

"Your wife's DNA may appear on the scarf too," I say. "But that doesn't matter. That doesn't matter at all. Cross-contamination happens all the time. False positives are common. As I said earlier, Claire Evans remains off the hook. Especially as far as the prosecution of this murder is concerned."

I detect a flicker of relief in our suspect's eyes. The man is clearly bent on protecting his wife. I suppose that old habits die hard. His dogged attachment to Claire, I must say, is impressive.

But it's time for a change of scene; I get up from my chair and walk over to the light switches.

"It's a little bright in here, isn't it?" I say.

I flip one of the switches, turning off two fluorescent lights at the far end of the room.

"What matters is what *you* did to Miss Ayling, Mr. Evans."

Although our suspect's face is plunged into comparative dimness, I detect a distinct shadow of fear on it. A bead of sweat is forming on his forehead. A thin blue vein is throbbing above his brow.

"I can't see the notes I'm making," the solicitor says, squinting at his notebook and pushing his spectacles up his nose. "Could you turn up the lighting again, please?"

"Of course," I say, flipping the two lights back on. But I turn them off as soon as the solicitor's pen stops moving on his notepad. He frowns at me; I ignore him.

"The postmortem report came through a couple of hours ago," I say. "It's peppered with predictable findings. First, our coroner, Dr. Sheldon, identified a small bruise on the right side of Miss Ayling's head beneath her hairline. The injury was almost imperceptible on the surface. But the autopsy revealed acute hemorrhaging beneath her skull. *Blunt-force trauma*, as Dr. Sheldon phrased it."

I flick yet another switch, turning off two more fluorescent lights, those in the opposite corner of the room. Our suspect's pupils dilate in response. He is now floodlit by a sole light above his head, as if I have placed him on a stage in a theater and asked him to sing.

"Someone caused Miss Ayling to injure her head. That person could be Claire Evans. You told your wife that her actions caused Miss Ayling to strike her head on your desk. But that person could also be *you*. After all, no one really knows what happened in your study two evenings ago. Apart from you, Mr. Evans."

I emit a deliberate chuckle.

"But facts can be manipulated with ease. To suit one's own selfish ends. To save one's exposed ass. To cover up *murder*. What you *prefer* to remember becomes a fact, doesn't it, Mr. Evans?"

He blinks.

"Yet there's much more to Dr. Sheldon's findings," I continue, walking back to my chair. "I'll read the last part of her report to you. I do relish the prospect of reading to a *published author*. A skilled wordsmith who's able to grasp the significance of certain key phrases."

I sense that my words are causing some consternation in our man's heart. I take a pair of reading glasses out of my breast pocket and fix them on my nose for theatrical effect before fishing out Dr. Sheldon's report. I begin reading its final section with an authoritative tone, lingering over certain words:

RESPIRATORY TRACT: There is a small amount of fine froth in the victim's nostrils and upper air passages. The lungs (right, 353 grams; left, 310 grams) are overlapping and hyperinflated. The oral cavity shows no lesions. The teeth, lips, and gums are free of injuries. There are no mucosal injuries or obstructions to the airways.

GASTROINTESTINAL TRACT: A large amount of water fills the victim's stomach, though not the intestines. All mucosal surfaces are intact, with no lesions or injuries.

MUSCULOSKELETAL SYSTEM: No significant injuries. There is a small diffuse bruise, measuring 10 x 5 mm, on the victim's lower back near the spine.

Drug Screen Results
Cocaine: POSITIVE
Ethanol: 295 mg/100 mL (Blood—Heart)
Ethanol: 64 mg/100 mL (Vitreous)

Opinion as to Cause of Death: Consistent with Drowning

Time of Death: Body temperature, rigor and livor mortis, and stomach contents approximate the time of death between 22:30 on Thursday 4 June 2015, and 00:30 on Friday 5 June 2015.

Injuries: The presence of small cuts and abrasions on the edges of the victim's fingers, the presence of riverbed dirt beneath the victim's fingernails, and the victim's torn and scuffed nail varnish suggest that the victim had struggled for a brief period underwater before succumbing to eventual death by drowning.

Remarks: Decedent was presented to this office as a possible suicide victim. Evidence of a brief period of underwater struggle leading to drowning, exacerbated by acute subdural brain hemorrhaging caused by blunt-force trauma, makes suicide improbable.

I look up at Mark Evans. His eyes are bulging. His face is ashen. His mouth is a "tormented twist," just like that of his protagonist Gunnar in *On Death's Door*.

"*Drowning*," I say, my voice ringing out loud and clear. "Miss Ayling was alive when you put her in the river two evenings ago. You thought she was dead. But she was still very much *alive*."

His hands are trembling. He looks as though he's on the verge of drowning himself. Like Sophia two evenings ago, he must surely understand that he is unable to save himself. This time round.

"*You* killed her, Mr. Evans. You're the person who caused her to die. By burying her in the watery grave of the Cam."

"No." An anguished cry issues from his lips. "This isn't possible…"

I've given Mark Evans a taste of the same medicine he meted out to his poor wife, Claire, earlier this evening. It must be damned disconcerting to discover that you've committed murder. Especially when you've managed to kill your mistress, who also turns out to be an ex-girlfriend.

"I didn't mean to…" he says, blubbering and shaking his head, as if this could diminish the horror of his crime. "Poor Sophia—"

"Mr. Evans," the solicitor says, raising a cautionary hand at his client. "Inspector, you shouldn't be jumping to conclusions."

I ignore the elderly man. Death by drowning is a rather unpleasant way to go. I should make our suspect aware of the physical horrors Sophia experienced two evenings ago. I sift through my mind for the facts I've learned from the pathology courses I took when I was still a constable.

"Let me continue," I say.

Miss Ayling regained consciousness after she plunged into the Cam. But things didn't seem right. Water was swamping her body. Water just about everywhere. Tons of it, pinning her down. Flooding her eyes. Causing her to see nothing but murky darkness. To make things worse, something heavy was dragging her shoulders down. Sucking her farther down into a watery hell. She held her breath, trying to convince herself that it was merely a horrible dream. A nightmare she would eventually emerge from. Maybe she should surrender to the current flowing past her limbs, as it might carry her back to safe ground. So she permitted herself to drift along the contours of the dream, just for a little while. But she soon realized that it was impossible to keep holding her breath. Her head felt dizzy, deprived of something vital. Something intrinsic to her existence. She needed oxygen. Air.

Our man seems transfixed by my words. He may be right. I may indeed have a future as a novelist. I'm not doing too badly so far; maybe I ought to join those earnest Monos at the Cambridge Flower School. I'm even getting better at it as the minutes tick by; I never realized that I could conjure so many magnificent adjectives and active verbs out of my little black policeman's helmet. Maybe it's the effect of having read hundreds of murder mysteries in my lifetime (including Evans's, though I'm never going to admit to him that I'm a massive fan of his books).

But I'm merely operating according to a key principle: one should always try to find the lowest common denominator—or a half-inch of common ground—when dealing with a suspect.

A basic tenet of any criminal investigation.

Thus if one is dealing with a storyteller, one should dispense a good yarn. Using the same fanciful, overwrought descriptions he is likely to employ himself. The same colorful excesses he favors in his own books (I should also provide ample evidence that policemen are capable of constructing good sentences). It will force him to empathize, to understand his wrongs.

It may even break him.

She took in a deep breath. But instead of life-sustaining air, water began surging into her nostrils. Cold river water, smelling of rotten algae. It traveled down her air passages right into her chest. She began coughing in a desperate attempt to expel the water. This merely drove air out of her lungs and caused water to flood her mouth. She began struggling with her hands, trying to claw her way out of the liquid darkness that engulfed her. Out of the nightmare that had swallowed her up. Her fingers struck something hard. She latched on to it. It merely cut her fingertips and shredded her nails. The pain in her lungs had become excruciating. It was as if they had been filled with sharp metal blades. She needed air. Just once. One tiny gulp. So she took in a second breath. Again, water began surging in through her nostrils and mouth, inundating her insides with more liquid hell. Her movements, she knew, had degenerated into terrible, frantic convulsions. But nothing matched the agony she felt in her chest—

"Stop it, Inspector." His words trickle out in a whimper. "Please stop it..."

Ah. Our tough cookie is beginning to crack.

"I didn't know she was still alive—"

"Mr. Evans—" the solicitor says, jumping to his feet and flapping his hands at his client.

"I didn't," our suspect says, ignoring the elderly man at his side. "I *really* didn't. She wasn't breathing at all. Neither of us could find a pulse. We thought she was dead. If only I'd checked more carefully. I didn't mean to cause her to suffer..."

A tear pools at the corner of his right eye. He tries to blink it back.

"Poor Sophia," he says, his voice a mumble.

"Manslaughter, Mr. Evans," I say. "Your sentence may be reduced from murder to manslaughter if you give me your full cooperation."

My words cause our man to stiffen. He looks at me, the anguish in his eyes giving way to the realization that he's fallen into my trap. The power of a gripping tale should never be underestimated.

I flip on all the lights again before walking back to the table to pause the digital recording device.

I study my chessboard, having ensured that Mark Henry Evans has been safely and securely locked up for the night. Only one move remains. I prod the black queen on a forward diagonal before toppling the white king and placing it in a forlorn position in the middle of my desk.

I grab my briefcase and head out in the direction of the front doors. To my astonishment, I see Fiona bearing down on me with a purposeful gait, her leopard-print trousers undulating in the semidarkness. I'm surprised she's still in the office. It is, after all, past eleven in the evening. Doesn't she have anything better to do than to hang around the dim corridors of Parkside station on a Saturday night?

"I hear you've brought your man in," she says, beaming at me. "My diary says you've solved four other murders within a day over the past six years. I'm sure you will win the special award for excellence again. For the seventh time running. I'll be surprised if you aren't promoted to detective superintendent soon."

Fiona has lovely iridescent eyes, even though they are concealed by her horn-rimmed spectacles. She has a beautiful smile, too. What a shame.

"Well done, Hans."

I shrug.

"I was wondering if you've had your dinner." She gives me a shy but hopeful look from behind her glasses.

"No."

Her cheeks are flushing a little. She tilts her head, as if she is expecting me to go on.

I oblige.

"Good night, Fi."

I give her a regretful nod before walking through the front doors of the station. I shouldn't be flirting with my colleagues. Even if they are geeky yet flamboyant raven-haired women whom I secretly fancy. Nor should I be having dinner with them. Even if my daily workload leaves me with no time whatsoever to scour the online dating sites for better possibilities. Fact: My colleagues will find out all sorts of undesirable things about me if I spend too much time with them. Things I'd much rather keep to myself, especially if I wish to get somewhere in my career.

What a terrible shame.

I get into my private car before pulling out a pack of Marlboros from my breast pocket. Fact: I offer cigarettes to suspects to make them a bit chattier, although I had no reason to do so today.

Right now, I need a smoke myself. (Fact: While I once indulged in a brief, grief-fueled cigarette binge right after Liesl von Meier disappeared, I've stayed away from them since.) I light one before drawing hard on it. The instant rush of nicotine is soothing, though not as tranquilizing as I'd hoped. After a couple of long drags, I crush the cigarette and fish out my iDiary. The remaining tendril of smoke curls and disappears as I tap my way to the final section of the entry I wrote two nights ago, the one my eyes abandoned earlier this morning:

It was your fucking letter that sealed my fate, the blond woman yelled. The one you sent to my psychiatrists. Telling them I was nuts. They used it to back up their own flawed diagnosis before shipping me off to the Outer Hebrides.

I saw the woman launching her hand in my direction again. I had no idea what she was talking about, but I did know that she was turning into something of a public hazard. I caught her right arm in midair and twisted it behind her back. She squealed. I dragged her a few feet backwards and pinned her against the back of the Fiat. She squirmed, attempting to free herself from my grasp. I instinctively pushed her back, trying to hold her down against the boot. But I must have caught her at the wrong angle, because she crumpled sideways with a yelp.

Fuck, she said.

Are you all right? I said.

That hurt, she groaned. That fucking hurt. How dare you attack me?

I was tempted to point out that she was the one who'd tried to slap me in the first place. But I may have overreacted.

You'll be fine, I said.

Just fuck off, will you? She glared at me, wincing. You've caused me enough grief in the past, you son of a bitch.

You must be all right if you're swearing so eloquently at me, I said. But don't push it, madam. Because I'm on the verge of arresting you for attempted assault.

Her eyes widened as she took in my words, including the distinct possibility that she might end up spending the night at Parkside station.

Fine, she said, pulling herself up to her feet and stumbling away to the front of her car. *Fine.* I've much more urgent things to do this evening than to bother with shitty twats like you.

I resumed my jog, wishing that verbal insults could be easily prosecuted. Nevertheless, it was daft of me to engage in an altercation with the crazy woman in the first place. After all, she did not pull a gun or knife on me. She had merely tried to slap me. (NTS: Must <u>refrain</u> from attempting to restrain lunatics in the future unless absolutely necessary.)

What a rubbish day, by the way. I still can't believe I did two daft things in a row.

I am tempted to edit—or even delete—my diary entry so that its contents will be less damning. But it's too late now. I've already read and learned these facts. I can't erase them now that I've committed them to mind. At any rate, the act of tinkering with my diary would be just as bad as what Claire Evans did. I'm not a coward, like that woman, although I understand why she did what she did. Cold hard facts, after all, are always more palatable when they are pleasant.

I turn my iDiary off and flip the ignition switch of my car. As I speed off in the direction of home, past the kebab shops and flashing neon signs of Mill Road, a little voice in my head pipes up again. It has been torturing me all day long, ever since I entered the Paradise nature reserve and studied the dead body extracted from the Cam, clad in soggy designer black.

The murmur in my mind is still going strong. In fact, it has become more persistent over the course of the evening, especially after I eavesdropped on the conversation between Mark and his wife. The voice is still telling me the same few things:

Isn't she the woman you met two evenings ago? The one dressed from head to toe in black? As your diary says, you were stupid enough to tangle with her hours before her death.
You even hurt her.

Two points emerge in my head:

1. No one is going to read my diary unless I meet a sorry end, as Sophia Ayling did, and another investigating detective is empowered by warrant to scour its contents for clues. If so, the description of what happened in that pull-off area would make little sense to the person reading my diary. I'll be long dead by then, anyway. You can damn a dead man, but you can't charge him with manslaughter.
2. Unlike me, Mark Henry Evans is indeed guilty of a crime.

The crime of killing another human being without malice afore-thought. He threw Sophia Ayling into the Cam and caused her to drown. He deserves to go to jail for what he did to her. I'm going to ensure that he is convicted (I should write this down in my diary tonight). No one is going to know what happened before Sophia showed up in Mark's study two evenings ago. Apart from me.

Yet I suppose I have to live with this persistent whisper in my head. And the dreadful little facts that the voice keeps repeating to me, twisting them like a dagger into my heart. Whether I like them or not. Claire Evans, too, must live with the factual knowledge that she killed her only daughter. So must Mark Henry Evans, after realizing that he caused his mistress to drown. But Claire and Mark can still decide whether the truth goes down in their diaries tonight.

We are all damned by the facts we've decided to learn. It doesn't matter how much memory one has. It doesn't matter whether one is a Mono or a Duo. Whether one has a single day's worth of memory—or two enviably long days. Even nutcases who claim to have superpower heads full of "memories" are damned. You can wash blood off your hands. But you can't wash facts from your mind. Not after you've made an effort to read them and learn them. Facts remain. They are inseparable from our conscience. This is why awful facts have a tendency to haunt us for the rest of our lives.

Like the fact that I was involved in a sequence of events that culminated in the death of Sophia Ayling.

The fact is killing me. I can no longer bear the thought of going home alone tonight only to be confronted by the remains of yesterday's lasagna in my refrigerator and "Ten Things You Should Know About Getting Ahead in Your Job" on my bedside table. I'm tempted to chuck one of my principles out the window. After all, I found out earlier today that I was once a naive and pathetic constable. I'm tempted to be a careless chief inspector. Just for once, perhaps.

Chiefly, an inspector who *cares less*.

I hit my brakes, making an abrupt U-turn in a loud screech of wheels.

Claire Evans told the whole world this morning that she wanted a divorce. But by the evening, she had clearly changed her mind:

"I'm going to stick with you, Mark. I promise."

That's what she said just before I shut the car door.

But I was much more surprised by what her husband said afterwards (he was, after all, the same man who had frolicked about with a woman in scarlet lingerie):

"And I'll do the same, Claire. I *will*."

People are so unpredictable when it comes to matters of the heart. So inexplicably irrational. Maybe memory does that to them. It's funny how twenty years of recovered memories (Mark and Claire Evans did dig pretty deep during the conversation I overheard) can make people feel so differently about each other by the end of the day. I suppose that if a woman brings her man a sandwich for lunch, he might feel a sudden burst of affection for her. But if he discovers that she had in fact brought him a sandwich each day for twenty consecutive years and kept him company each time he wolfed it down, the sandwich acquires new meaning. It's just possible he might fall in love with her.

Does love equal memory? Or does memory equal love?

I haven't got a clue. At any rate, I'm tempted to be as unpredictable as Mark Evans this evening. Just this once, perhaps. I can permit myself the occasional aberration of rational judgment.

My car races back past the kebab shops and flashing neon signs on Mill Road.

There's a chance that Fiona's still at the Parkside station. She may be good at keeping secrets. Women in skintight leopard-print trousers might even be *very good* at it. After more than two decades in the force, I have not amassed any evidence to the contrary. I need dinner, anyway. Definitely something more substantial than the ham-and-bacon sandwich that Fiona brought me earlier.

I'm hungry for more.

The person in control always has the last laugh. This is what I've learned from my time in jail.
—Mark Henry Evans, draft of *Revelations from Belmarsh: The Musings of an Imprisoned Author*

Chapter Twenty-Nine

A BEACH ON BORA-BORA, SOUTH PACIFIC
MANY, MANY MONTHS AFTER THE MURDER

This piña colada sucks. And so does that fucking martini. I'll take a triple shot of vodka anytime.

The man with the shaggy Labradoodle is definitely eyeing me. From behind the glossy-covered book he's reading. I recognize him. He stepped off his private yacht four days ago. I wonder why he's still hanging around this beach. I'm sure he isn't a detective of some sort.

Or is he?

Fucking hell.

But detectives don't own yachts. Nor do they own shaggy Labradoodles.

Or do they?

He must merely be admiring me.

I fucking hope so.

Like that hot dude in the pink-hibiscus shorts. From atop his lifeguard perch. Or that man sprawled out on the sand with a beer, belly flopping to one side. He has already thrown me several lusty glances whenever his female companion isn't looking. Oh, God. That pudgy bloke on the inflatable swan is practically gawking at me. I wish he would go away. He reeks of sweat and stale coconut-scented sunscreen.

Life on this sunny beach is full of hazards. I shouldn't have worn this itsy-bitsy white bikini. It attracts unwanted attention. Even in fucking Bora-Bora.

I thought I could get away from it all. From the pesky dregs of humanity. Instead I'm being leered at by a man on a giant inflatable swan.

I can't decide. Should I be worried or flattered? I'll settle for flattered (for the time being, and for my own sanity). I did, after all, fork out over £47,900 for a comprehensive round of "treatment." Necessary fixes from dear Dr. Patel. I should technically be pleased that my money didn't go to waste. I'm desirable to multiple males on this beach.

But I still look like a dead woman whom I hate.

And that's the whole fucking problem.

This sorry situation is partly my plastic surgeon's fault. I blame the idiot. For being so damned good at what he does.

For not being able to *undo* what he did.

I groan whenever I think about that day. The afternoon when I went back to Dr. Patel's office in Belgravia bearing another photograph in my hand.

The poor man, naturally, was surprised to see me.

"My diary insists that I did all I could for you," he said. "And so does this case file in front of me."

"You did. I was very pleased with what you accomplished, Doctor."

"So what brings you here today? A little touch of Botox, perhaps? Your forehead could do with some firming up."

"I want more than Botox," I said. "I want to look like this woman."

I handed the photo to Dr. Patel. The man took one look at it, double-checked the profile of the skinny brunette on the top of his case file, and nearly fell off his chair.

"But…" he said, spluttering. "But…isn't she *you?* Isn't that how *you* used to look? Before I made…er…a few improvements to your face?"

"Precisely, Doctor," I said, trying to hide a grin. "That's indeed how I used to look. Before you gave me a shit-hot makeover. But I would like to have my old self back, please. It's a bit of a mousy look, I know. But I was pretty damned comfortable with that old face of mine. Though I wasn't so happy with the slight kink in my nose. Those protruding ears. So I'll keep the ears and nose you've given me. But the chin and cheeks can go back to what they used to be."

The phrase "You must be mad" hovered on Patel's lips. But he bit his words back. Knowing that he would be insane to insult a cherished client. Especially one as well-paying as I am. A sucker who keeps coming back for *more*.

"I've never had a client tell me that she wants her old looks back," he said, incredulity etched all over his face.

"There's always a first time for everything, Doctor. Women are so awfully fickle, aren't they? Especially when it comes to their appearance. But I'll pay. I'll pay whatever it takes to revive my old self. Reverse engineering's a bit of a pain, I know. This is why I promise to pay *well*."

Patel's face temporarily lit up at the mention of money. Plastic surgeons do what they do for dough. They say they took the Hippocratic oath. But they are equally bound to the Hypocritic oath.

He sighed, defeat brimming in his eyes.

"Sorry," he said. "But there's no way I can give you your old looks back. Plastic surgery isn't as plastic as it sounds."

I frowned. I glowered. I raved and pleaded like a lunatic. But Patel remained adamant that any further work on my face would turn me into Frankenstein's monster, no matter how much I paid. So I slouched out minutes later, still looking the same. It's a shame that the only surgeons willing to perform the fixes I wanted were *all* third-rate sorts. Reckon I'm smart enough not to risk it.

Net result: *I still look like a woman I hate.*

Fucking hell.

There are some things money can't buy, no matter how hard you try. Like love and the unsolvable problem of one-directional plastic surgery.

Yet money still makes most of the world go round. Or come to a bloody standstill. As it did for seventeen years in my case. Money still makes things happen. Or not happen. It brings out the best in people. As well as the absolute worst. It makes people do all sorts of awful things. To themselves. To those around them. Like what dear Stepmum did to me. And I only found out afterwards.

They say freedom is sweet. It tasted damned syrupy in my case—but only for a few hours.

Before turning sour.

It all began when I stepped off that bumpy boat from hell. Or Hellisay, to be more precise. Blinking in the sunlight like a mole after being swathed in darkness for years. Brimming with suspicions. Fearing that the world had moved on while I'd remained stuck in a goddamned hole. That's why I went straight to Dad's lawyer, Reginald Rowe, as soon as I got to London. To find out what had happened to my father's estate during my extended absence.

Dad had passed on while fucking his nineteen-year-old PA, Nola Barr, at the Ritz hotel, I heard. So Dad *came and went*. Straight on top of poor Nola, too. The girl must have learned a good lesson from the episode: never fuck a rich old man with a heart problem. He can easily turn out to be a dead weight.

The graying and bespectacled Rowe was most surprised to see me, good old Anna May.

"How much did Dad leave behind?" I said, getting to the crux of my mission. There's no point beating around the bush with lawyers. They are arseholes who make their money on your fortunes and misfortunes.

Rowe tapped the diary in front of him for a couple of minutes. Pulled out a large file from a drawer and inspected its contents.

"Alan Winchester set up a trust fund in your name a few months after you were born," he said in a silky smooth voice. Didn't take him too long to recover from the shock of my arrival.

"You were entitled to receive a monthly income from the age of twenty-eight," he continued, squinting at the file. "The fund is managed by a firm called Swiss Inheritance Services. It may take a while for them to pay you, though. After all, you're no longer called Anna May Winchester."

I nodded. It took me a damned long time to figure out why Dad had forced me to change my name. Then one afternoon, it hit me. Like an arrow piercing the middle of my forehead. As I lay beneath those stunted poplars on Hellisay, squinting at the weak rays of sunlight filtering through them. Embarrassment, of course. His daughter "losing her mind." Throwing away her pen-and-ink diaries. This must have triggered plenty of undesirable gossip. Especially amongst the folks who frequented the hallowed inner sanctums of his private club. So he got rid of that mighty embarrassment (an act encouraged by his darling wife, Aggie, of course, who was, naturally, delighted to wash me off her scheming paws). He made me change my name to Sophia Alyssa Ayling and packed me off to a godforsaken Scottish island with more nutcases than sheep.

Sophia isn't such a bad name, actually. It means "wisdom." I even think I have shitloads of it by now. Alyssa confounded me for a while. Then I read somewhere that it means "sanity and logic. Because of its associations with the flower alyssum. The cure for rabies and madness in ancient times.

I still haven't got a fucking clue as to where Ayling came from.

"You'll need to prove to the Swiss that Sophia Alyssa Ayling and Anna May Winchester are one and the same," said Rowe. "As you've been out of the...ahem...picture for a while. But I can help expedite the process for you. You should receive your first payment soon. In about two or three months from now, with luck."

"I'm not interested in a shitty little trust fund, Reggie. I'm interested in Dad's *estate*."

Rowe began sucking his teeth in response. Tapping his notepad with his silver monogrammed Montblanc. Looking as though he'd developed a sudden bout of constipation.

That was when I knew that I'd been screwed.

Comprehensively.

"Agnessa inherited your father's estate after his death. *All* of it."

"But...but..."

My words were a strangled splutter.

"My apologies, Miss Winchester...er...Miss Ayling," said Rowe, looking far from sorry as he fingered the ruby-encrusted clip on his tie. "But your father changed his will a couple of years after you went into St. Augustine's. This is a fact. You can't change facts."

He consulted his file again, running a finger down the print. Before reading with a ponderous voice:

"In the event of my death, I bequeath all my assets to my beloved spouse, Agnessa Winchester (née Ivanova)."

His words hit me like a cannonball in the gut. I gaped at him for several moments, acid bile rising in my throat. Yet I didn't have a fucking choice. I could only beg him to expedite my first payment from the Swiss while sinking my fingernails into my palms to prevent myself from screaming.

I staggered out of his office minutes later, rage blinding my eyes.

Dear Aggie was not pleased to see me the following day. Not pleased at all. She walked in to discover that her precious little Anna May had somehow managed to escape from St. Augustine's. That I'd spilled coffee from my take-out cup on her upholstered Louis XVI–style divan. That I'd just fed her pet goldfish to her Siamese cat to stop it from hissing at me. After all, her Polish housekeeper did impart a few juicy tidbits of information. Minutes before she scurried off to summon Aggie. Like the fact that grumpy little Khrushchev had a taste for caviar, wagyu beef, and the choicest items from the Harrods fish section.

"Vat ze hell are you doink in zis room?" she said, wincing as she heard her cat crunch down the last of the goldfish bones. "Vy haf zey let you out of St. Augustine's?"

"Thought I'd pay you a courtesy visit, my little Aggie. To see how you're getting on. And you've traveled pretty damned far, I heard. From your humble working-class Mono roots in Mogilev. With pit stops in a couple of strip clubs in Moscow along the way. A longer spell as a hooker in Soho. You've even gone as far as making Dad change his will in your favor."

"Your pa decided to change his vill *himself*," Aggie said with a smug twitch of her lips, the expression she always wore when she knew I was at her mercy. "No one forced him to do so."

I was reduced to glaring at her through slitted eyes.

"You didn't need his money, anyvay," she added. "Not ven you vere doomed to spendink ze rest of your life in St. Augustine's."

The smirk on her face grew wider.

What they say about stepmothers is true. *Cinderella* isn't a fucking fairy fable. Or a miserable morality myth. It's a reality show in high definition, featuring blond Belarusans with Botoxed foreheads.

"You definitely know a thing or two about stripping," I said. "You managed to peel your G-string off in Dad's presence. While giving him that lap dance in Soho all those years ago. You then stripped him bare. Before moving on to his bank balance."

Aggie rolled her eyes.

"Now you've graduated to robbing me of my birthright. I admire you, Aggie. But I'm going to do some stripping myself. By the time I'm done, there won't be any skin left on your paws. Or on that tarted-up face of yours."

She issued an unimpressed sniff. And so I said:

"Let me tell you a couple of horrible secrets. I'll start by showing you a photograph. This is me, a long time ago. I had a flat chest and protruding ears. If you look closely, you can see that I once had hope in my eyes and fire in my soul. Today, both the hope and the fire are gone."

I rambled on and on, brandishing a second photo in her face with the words: "I'm going to transform myself so I'll look *exactly* like you. I'm going to bleach my hair and get boobs like yours."

Before finishing with:

"Vengeance would be nice. Especially in view of what *you*'ve done to me. All the terrible little things you've been guilty of over the years. I recall each and every one of them. It's the *sum total* of remembered grievances that makes hatred potent. Oh, yes. The act of revenge will be easy. Because no one will remember what I'm going to do to you. Except for me."

I got up from the divan and walked straight into Aggie's rock-crystal vase. The hideous gold one, dripping with jewels. Before trotting out of the drawing room to an accompanying gasp of horror.

It proved to be a fruitful little visit. I got exactly what I wanted a couple of minutes before Aggie marched in. I'll be forever grateful to her housekeeper for pointing out the bitch's most recent holiday photographs on the mantelpiece. The snapshots had been taken seven weeks earlier, when Aggie was frolicking about in St. Barts. The first photo offered a delightful high-resolution close-up of her face. Right down to the foundation-clogged pores on it. The second featured Aggie in a tacky green bikini, arm draped over the shoulder of her on-again, off-again Italian lover.

I removed the two photos from their ghastly emerald-and-gold frames and slipped them into my handbag before looking around for something else to pinch. Something small and easily removable. A pea-green Gucci clutch bearing the gold monogram A.W. on its clasp lay nearby. I rummaged about inside and decided to liberate Aggie's driving license from its confines. After all, the card contained a fine specimen of the bitch's signature. I then wandered to the hallway and studied the items hanging on a coatrack. Black gloves with gold fur trimmings. Hideous green beret. Black Versace scarf. On impulse, I stuffed the three items into my handbag and scampered back to the living room just before Aggie swept in.

Aggie's Versace scarf (the most tasteful and practical of the lot) has served me well.

Mightily well.

Ah, the joys of DNA testing.

They found her DNA on it, naturally. Mingled with Mark's.

Her scarf became exhibit A at Mark's trial. It was handled with appropriate reverence by the prosecutor. I read in the newspapers that the man pulled it out with a flourish, to a flurry of appreciative murmurs from the jury box.

Somehow my instincts told me to wrap Aggie's scarf around my nose minutes before I sallied forth from my Grantchester cottage that evening. My intuition had said, in a small growly voice: *The smell of shit should make you more determined and goal-oriented, my dear Sophia.*

My instincts were right.

I went straight to Dr. Patel the morning after I visited Aggie. Because I'd heard good things about the man's surgical abilities. Including his ability to transform a woman into exactly whom she wished to be.

That sounds good, I thought. That is what I want.

As soon as I got into his consultation room, I opened my handbag and pulled out the two photos I'd pilfered from her living room.

"I want to look like this woman," I said.

The doctor took the photos into his hand and squinted at them for a few moments with a large frown on his forehead.

"Are you sure, Miss Winchester?" he said, frown deepening as he continued to scrutinize the photos. "Are you aware that this woman has had many procedures in the past? Chest, nose, ear, and chin. Botox, too."

I gaped at Dr. Patel for several moments. I had long worked out that Aggie had thrived on implants and Botox. From the first day I walked into Dad's study and discovered with horror that the woman he intended to marry was *a year younger than I was* and had tits the height of towering conifers. Back then there was already enough Botox on Aggie's face to give a puffer fish a heart attack. But I hadn't realized that she had had a nose job too. Then it hit me: I'm cursed with the famous Winchester nose, and I hate the goddamned kink in it.

This made my setup twice as perfect.

Might as well fix those slightly protruding ears while I'm at it.

"How marvelous, Doctor," I said. "This makes it even better. Can we start tomorrow, please? I'll pay."

And I did pay as promised. Yet Dr. Patel will never know that I had to scrape the bottom of my piggy bank to cough up the first two installments before the Swiss paid up. Research, unfortunately, takes lots of fucking time and money.

Especially research on Agnessa Winchester (née Ivanova), Mark Henry Evans, and Claire Evans (née Bushey).

With hindsight, Agnessa proved a much easier subject than the other two. Even though there weren't any photos of her online. I should thank her chatty little Polish housekeeper again. Aggie had apparently enjoyed flitting between the bright lights of London, Moscow, and Minsk for a few years after Dad died before hanging up her traveling shoes. She'd assembled a stable of boy toys to keep herself amused in all three cities. Twenty-year-old bucking stallions with bulges in all the right places. Paid for with Dad's money, of course. She eventually fell for a twenty-one-year-old Calvin Klein model who later dumped her for a younger poodle with even more money. That's why she retreated to Dad's old country house in Coton to lick her self-inflicted wounds a mere six months before I emerged from St. Augustine's.

Thank God for that.

Because I would have been seriously screwed if Aggie had not been stoned out of her mind in Coton on the night Mark Evans decided to dump me into the Cam.

Boy, did I make several stupid mistakes that evening. Nearly destroyed myself. Almost self-imploded. My first error was to get into an unprovoked kerfuffle with that detective. As I waited in my Fiat for the right moment to creep into Mark's study. But I was damned surprised to see the man jog by. Damned furious, too. That supercilious idiot could have scuppered everything. Thanks to him, my judgment was impaired. Which led to my second grave mistake. I was dense enough to break into Mark's study while he was still having dinner with his Mono wife.

I enjoyed taunting her. Baiting her, even. But I'd never expected her response. When her furious hands connected with my shoulders, everything went black.

The metallic, coppery taste of blood fills my mouth. Pain roars through my ears. My head feels as though an ax has been buried in it. I'm slung over someone's back. A person gasping for breath from the exertion of carrying me. A man moving with a labored yet urgent stride on a woodland path. Tangled leaves whisper above. Branches rustle overhead. Twigs crunch beneath feet. I close my eyes again before he places me down on my back. The earthy smell of foliage fills my nostrils. Marshy ground squelches next to my ears. Water laps nearby, merely a yard or so away.

I hear footsteps receding. I wonder if I should pull myself up. Take to my heels at once. But I'm clearly part of some heinous, dastardly plan. One I intend to unravel. I'm certain the man will come back for me.

So I wait.

Wait.

And wait.

Muffled footsteps again, several minutes later. I slam my eyelids shut, pretending to be dead. The man yanks my torso up from the ground. Places something over my shoulders. It feels like a coat. A damned heavy one, too, as if it had been weighted with lead ingots. It drags my shoulders and chest down.

He gives me a shove.

One hard enough to roll me sideways into hell. I crash into the water like a brick. Inky, liquid darkness swallows me.

The river's cold.

Fucking freezing.

But the icy water slices into my skull like a scalpel and kicks my brain into hyperdrive. Dulls the throbbing pain in my head for a few seconds. Makes me see everything with crystal clarity, including what to do next. I struggle with the coat's pockets, tipping out some of the pebbles in them. I propel myself forward, using the slight current to help me. Through the arctic, murky hell that engulfs me. As far away as possible from where I first landed with a soft splash. Keeping my entire body below the surface, without showing even a single wisp of hair.

Air.

I need air.

I fucking need air.

My lungs are killing me.

But I should keep swimming.

I need to surface.

I fucking do.

I. Need. Air.

I swim up. A single, desperate gulp. Permitting only my lips to emerge from the water. Hoping I've gone far enough. Praying he can't see me in the darkness.

Stick your head back down, Sophia.

Keep swimming. Just keep swimming. Oh, God. This is ridiculous.

Swim, Sophia, swim.

Keep moving with the current. Keep going downstream.

Left, right. Left, right. Left, right.

I'm exhausted. I'm dying.

This is fucking killing me.

I can't swim anymore.

I think I've gone far enough.

I splash my way to the riverbank. A tree root protrudes into the water; I seize it with desperate fingers. I haul myself onto solid land, water streaming from my clothes. Teeth rattling, hands trembling. Eyes stinging from the water. I collapse facedown onto mud, a spent and sodden force.

Grit and damp earth seep into my mouth. The sickly sweet taste of mold and rotted leaves.

I lift my head with a groan, peering around. I'm surrounded by drooping willows, their thick leaves blotting out the moon and stars. A boggy riverside path snakes ahead into darkness. The current must have carried me as far as the Paradise nature reserve. I drag my body up from the mud; the ground shifts and undulates for several disconcerting moments. I stagger through the dark copse, past twisted trees tapering upwards. Their gnarled, leafy fingers tug at my clothes as I crunch my way back to the car.

I must look like a soggy vision from hell. I hope I don't meet anyone. It'll be a disaster if I do.

Move faster, Sophia.

Bloody hell. A woman is walking her puppy at the far end of Grant-chester Meadows. Do not freeze. Do not tremble. Just keep walking. Pretend everything's normal.

The woman turns into Marlowe Road with her dog. Thank heavens.

My Fiat's still in the pull-off area. Its ignition key is wedged in the pocket of my trousers. I get in and rev up the engine. I shoot down the winding country road leading to Coton, shivering in my wet clothes. A hare darts out of my way, its eyes wide and bright. I pull into the peacock-infested driveway and kill the engine before letting myself in through the front door.

Aggie's snorting a line on the black marble kitchen counter next to a half-empty bottle of absinthe. This must be why she isn't falling off her high stool. Even though her soaked doppelganger is sauntering towards her with a wide grin.

Grumpy little Khrushchev hisses at me. Tries to sharpen his claws on my foot. But Aggie doesn't even blink. I suppose one sees mirror images of oneself all the time if one survives on coke. Even if there aren't any mirrors around.

"Hello, Aggie," I say, smile growing wider.

I stride up to her. Positioning my body on her right.

My arm is tensed. Ready.

She ignores me in favor of the second line of coke. Laid out on that kitchen counter.

Why am I not surprised?

I swing my arm.

The rolled-up £50 note in her hand flutters to the ground.

I'm tempted to stand over her unconscious body and tell her in the most solemn voice I can muster:

I've waited years for this moment. Because I remember. I remember every single fucking thing you did to me. Like what happened when I dropped by this kitchen on the afternoon of the Trinity May Ball. I'd wanted to retrieve Mum's pink diamond necklace and earrings so that I could impress the young man who was walking me there. After all, I had loved him. I thought I could make him feel the same way about me.

That afternoon, I climbed the stairs to Mum's old bedroom only to discover that the set had vanished.

And so I ran down here to confront you. You were sitting at the kitchen counter, flipping through Cartier's summer catalog. Your rosebud mouth was pursed up in an air of chronic dissatisfaction.

"Where are Mum's diamonds?" I said.

You merely threw me a silent, knowing smile.

"Zey are mine now."

"That's ridiculous," I said. "They were Mum's."

"Your ma's dead."

"You have no right to take them."

"She doesn't need zem anymore."

I gritted my teeth and said:

"Hand them over. I want to wear them tonight."

"Zey von't look good on you," you said, smirking at me. "Not good at all. Not viz zat ugly leetle face of yours."

I raised my palm to wipe that smirk off your face, only to be stopped in my tracks by your next words:

"Don't mess viz me, Annie. Because your pa listens to me, not you. And if I tell him you are still secretly frowing up your food in ze toilet, he's going to be so, so angry."

"How did you know that—"

"He'll insist zat you move back in here so he can keep a careful eye on you. Zis vill be a reel shame after you worked so hard to move out in ze first place. Eez a fact, no?"

"But—"

"Maybe even cut off your allow-ance while he's at it."

"You horrible—"

"We'll be one big happy famil-ee again. You'll like zat, von't you?"

Somehow your flat, dead tone made your threats twice as menacing.

I didn't get Mum's pink diamond jewelry set that afternoon. I never did.

Memory makes you fixate. All I could think about for seventeen years were three people: Mark, Claire, *and* you.

I'm merely retrieving what's rightfully mine.

Yet I'm also doing her a freaking massive favor. If her life is filled with absinthe and coke, she might as well join her late husband in that great void in the sky. Knowing her, she'll start a strip club there at the first opportunity.

I yank off my wet clothes. Before stripping *her* bare. Her garments are in varying shades of green. What an ex-slut with no taste would wear. Tapering velour trousers with a gnome-colored see-through top. Ghastly, exaggerated sleeves. The fabric reeks of stale cigarettes and pickled gherkins.

But at least her clothes are dry.

They even fit me. More or less. Her bra is on the large side. Dr. Patel had underestimated things a little.

I kneel down again to dress her with the wet clothes I'd peeled off minutes earlier.

Only to struggle.

And struggle.

What a fucking pain. Never realized it's so difficult to put soggy clothes onto a limp body. The trench coat's easy, though. Thankfully, a few black and white pebbles remain in its pockets.

I should take a few of those lovely peroxided hairs, just in case I need to plant a few DNA-rich follicles somewhere.

I grab a pair of kitchen scissors and snip a lock off.

There's something else I need to do. Ah, yes. Lipstick and nail varnish, straight from the handbag at the back of my Fiat. I stoop down to paint her lips and fingernails a scintillating shade of scarlet.

Not bad, Sophia.

She goes into the boot. Just about fits.

I turn on the engine and race down the dark, winding road again.

The parking lot of the Paradise nature reserve, a couple of minutes after midnight. No one at all. No lovers. No campers. No nudists, either. I'm damned lucky the rain came down like a battering ram earlier that morning. Swamping the footpaths in the reserve. Turning them into a veritable bog. An unappetizing quagmire. Sending all riverside stragglers home before midnight.

I tip Aggie into the River Cam, pressing her body down with a firm hand.

Is she struggling? Or am I imagining it? Does exhaustion play tricks on the mind?

I count to a hundred before releasing my hand.

I repark the Fiat at the end of Grantchester Meadows and wipe the car clean.

I walk back to Coton. All three miles. On foot. I collapse onto Aggie's four-poster bed. Even though it reeks of Dior's Poison and boasts lurid green sheets the color of mold. When one is knackered, even Aggie-related shit doesn't stink as much.

It all goes black again.

It's amazing how seemingly useless skills become useful. When shit happens.

Like being able to hold my breath under water. Learned during those endless childhood swimming lessons in Dad's pool in Bermuda. That definitely helped me in the Cam. Or the basic Russian I picked up from the classes I took during my first year at Cambridge. Thanks to Dad, who insisted that I learn the language after he decided to marry that Belarusan stripper. He'd hoped that I would understand my new stepmother better (fortunately for me, and most unfortunately for her, I never did). That certainly helped when Mr. Inquisitive-Yet-Pathetic Detective rang Aggie's mobile phone to inform her of my untimely departure. I certainly had fun chatting with him that Saturday afternoon from behind the blinds of my rightful home (hope I didn't overdo the Russian accent).

I also dealt with several other things on the day he called. I put fifteen vials of coke into the garbage bin. I fed five liters of absinthe to a gnarled potted plant in a corner. I threw all Aggie's paper-and-ink diaries into the fireplace. I took a kitchen hammer to her iDiary. Even bought a Persian cat online. A fluffy white feline that was a dead ringer for Catapult. Like me, the new cat got used to grumpy Khrushchev. And little Catatonic also got used to her name.

Unlike me.

I hate my new name. I particularly detest signing "Agnessa" on the dotted line. Even now that I've perfected the signature (after months of practice). The name's worse than Sophia Alyssa. Definitely much worse than Anna May. But I'll have to get used to it, I suppose. There's even a delicious irony to being called Agnessa. Because the name means "pure and holy."

If anyone's fucking pure and holy, it's me.

I knew that three people dropped by Aggie's home in Coton, either occasionally or regularly. Her Italian lover, her chatty Polish house-keeper, and her green-thumb Hungarian gardener.

I began by texting the Italian lover. Using Aggie's mobile phone, of course.

My message was short and sweet:

"Fuck you," it said. "We're over."

It worked. Because I never heard from him again. I also sent text mes-sages to her housekeeper and gardener telling them that their services were no longer required.

I kept Aggie's Ferrari (even though I much prefer BMWs). I kept her gilded furniture. I kept her garments. Even wore them each day. Needed to be on the safe side. After all, people might begin smelling a rat if Agnessa suddenly started going around in a slinky scarlet Elie Saab dress. Instead of the gaudy green ghastliness she normally wore. Imagine a nosy Mono neighbor musing about the new "Agnessa" in her diary: *Blimey. I saw her earlier today. She was flouncing about in a tasteful red dress. Shock! Horror! What's happened to her predilection for lurid green? Some-thing's not right. Someone must have taken over her identity. I should phone that pompous gray-haired policeman to report my suspicions. The newly promoted detective superintendent who keeps winning awards for solving crimes as soon as they happen.*

That wouldn't do at all.

Detective Superintendent Richardson deserves more than a few punches, by the way. I'm still convinced that he—and Mark—hammered the final nails into my St. Augustine's coffin. But I should nevertheless thank my lucky stars that he's a rubbish investigator. I should sort him out someday.

I lay low for a long time.

Long enough for most of the dust to settle.

On the subject of dust, I made sure they incinerated Aggie's body with due care after I got it back from the morgue a week later. I also paid Perfect Cremation Solutions to turn her ashes into an artificial diamond. It is now tethered to a platinum ring around my little finger. Aggie should be grateful I'm so magnanimous with her remains. She doesn't deserve to be a diamond. But there's some poetic justice in turning her into one. She did, after all, deny me Mum's diamonds for years.

I bought a first-class ticket to Bora-Bora soon after I called Aggie's asset manager. He told me that Aggie's estate was worth £37 million, which included ownership of three strip clubs and shares in Playboy Magazine. I gasped when he recited the sum. I thought I'd inherited only £31 million. Then I realized that Aggie had married a Grosvenor before divorcing him six months later to marry Dad.

It never hurts to marry a rich man.

Or an even richer man afterwards.

I've since sold Aggie's Playboy shares (I wouldn't touch the Hefner empire with a barge pole). I've decided to keep her three strip clubs, though.

They are doing rather well.

Profitable, as they say.

Especially the one called Dante's Inferno, in Moscow. Her fortieth-birthday present to herself. Even if the Inferno's profits are a little dented by monthly payouts to the chief of the Moscow police. The mustached man is most photogenic and agile for his age. But his motto seems to be "We serve to extort." Innocent little Anna May thus remains the de facto employer of fifty-four pole dancers and twenty-three male strippers, including five Channing Tatum look-alikes.

Yet it's amazing how the past can come back with a vengeance. Even on a blinding white beach in Bora-Bora. Sinuous coconut palms swaying around me in the breeze, crystalline waves lapping yards away from my toes. The farthest-away place I could think of when I bought my plane ticket. I read about *him* in the *Wall Street Journal* yesterday. The man with the shaggy Labradoodle left a newspaper on the beach before taking a dinghy back to his yacht. I picked up the newspaper only to be greeted by a small headline at the bottom:

AUTHOR TO PUBLISH ACCOUNT OF HIS TIME IN BELMARSH

He is now working in the prison library. One of the choicest jobs in the facility, it seems. He hopes to publish his musings soon. Perhaps even a short-story collection. Scintillating tales of crime and punishment. Harvested from fellow inmates over endless baked-bean lunches. A model prisoner thus far. This is why he is likely to get early parole. May even be released after four years.

Bloody hell.

It's incredible how one's literary career can continue to flourish. When one's political aspirations have been shattered. When one ends up in a high-security prison for the crime of manslaughter.

But then again, that man always did have a way with words. Words tend to prevail, whether you like it or not.

The article also says that he has been granted extra visits from friends and family each week. His dutiful Mono wife has apparently been visiting him every other day, bringing him books, socks, and knitted sweaters.

Why hasn't that woman divorced him? After everything he's done? After finding out that he not only had a mistress but also managed—supposedly—to drown her in the Cam? And why hasn't he left her? He must be crazy to stay with a stupid Mono, especially one who killed his daughter. I don't get it. I don't fucking get it. I've long given up scouring the newspapers for reports of their divorce. I'm tired of waiting for something that isn't going to happen. They surely don't care about each other. Or do they?

This is bloody unsatisfactory. Deeply annoying. I'm itching to throw something at the man atop the giant inflatable swan.

The final lines in the *Wall Street Journal* article are particularly galling: "Mr. and Mrs. Evans have just renewed their marriage vows in the chapel of Belmarsh prison. Their spokesman, Rowan Redford, says that 'Claire Evans is looking forward to her husband's early parole.'"

I'm tempted to go back to Britain. Finish him off properly. Finish off their marriage, too. Just to make my point. The bit about early parole bothers me. That won't do at all. The man deserves a slow, inexorable end in prison. Or seventeen gloomy years of confinement, at the very least.

Not four.

But that's altogether a different story.

A future mission.

In the meantime, I'll sit here and order a better piña colada and chuckle at the shiny diamond on my little finger (because revenge is brilliant and easily attainable, even if love is not). Maybe move on to a triple shot of vodka. And I might just smile at that hot lifeguard in the pink-hibiscus shorts. Even though he must be a stupid Mono.

I'll take my pleasures as they come.

Because I remember them.

Epilogue

A man walks into a kitchen. He has been away from it for four years. His heart is full, shot through with the happiness of homecoming. He takes in a deep breath, savoring the piquant smell of rabbit and bay leaves wafting from a pot on the stove. His wife smiles as he hands her a bouquet of pink and white roses. Her lavender eyes are soft and affectionate; quiet elation shimmers in their depths. She has waited for his return for just as long.

He notices that there aren't any gray containers of antidepressants on the kitchen counter. There are only two items there. The first is her iDiary. She tells him that it is packed with words and descriptions. Everything she can possibly write down each day. She is careful not to forget.

He nods. He understands what she means. After all, he's trying to do the same thing himself, though it isn't easy. Yet he also knows that few things in life are straightforward. This is why they must hold on to what they have shared, both the beautiful and the tragic, because the past will eventually make them whole again. Because the pain embedded in the past makes them who they are. Helps them understand where they have come from. Where they are in the present. Where they hope to be.

Because memory is everything.

The second item is yesterday's copy of the *Times*. His eyes settle on it, taking in the large photo of a beaming blond woman on the front page. The accompanying headline reads: MONO FINALLY WINS £30,000 SHORT-STORY COMPETITION WITH DAZZLING TALE OF DOMESTIC LOSS AND ATONEMENT.

His eyes widen.

I never knew, he says, reaching for her hand. I've been so stupid and blind. To what was in front of me all along. To *who* was in front of me.

We both were blind, she says. But we no longer are.

What's the story about? he asks.

It's simple, she says. It's a bittersweet tale about love and redemption. It is always about love in the end. Because love makes us try harder. Because love makes us want to remember.

ACKNOWLEDGMENTS

I'm extremely lucky to have an incredible team of agents and editors at my side. Special thanks to my brilliant agents Jonny Geller and Alexandra Machinist for championing this project and taking it beyond my wildest dreams. It has been a real privilege to work with Alex Clarke and Josh Kendall, whose sage and incisive editorial comments have helped me develop my vision for the book. Thank you, Dream Team, for being passionate and committed, sensible and fun.

This book was entirely influenced by my time as a student at the Faber Academy. I'm grateful to my tutor Richard Skinner for directing the start of my journey. I'm equally indebted to my classmates from the 2015 cohort who read early drafts of the novel and provided astute feedback. In particular, the magnificent quintet who still meet in Bloomsbury each week to exchange work: Michael Dias, Helen Allen, Ilana Lindsey, Chloe Esposito, and Kate Vick. The Bloomsbury Five have truly lit up my path; I'm fortunate to have their regular support.

Several beta readers have generously helped me with later drafts of the work. Lydia Rose Ruffles, Sally Garner, Arabel Charlaff, and Nicolle Freni deserve star mention for their perceptive and ingenious input on the full manuscript. Many thanks, too, to Margaret Watts, Paola Lopez, Sarah Edghill, Allison Stenberg, Andrew Wille, Richard Tanburn, Erin Kelly, Richard Beard, Nacho Mbaeliachi, Tony Bicât, Selina Ukwuoma, Christian Brinsden, Amanda Saint, and My Ly for their numerous thoughtful suggestions.

I owe a large debt to Geoffrey Monaghan of the Metropolitan Police Service for his excellent advice on police procedures. Huge thanks as

ACKNOWLEDGMENTS

well to Stuart Hamilton of the East Midlands Forensic Pathology Unit, Wan Yi Min of Jurong Health, and Leslie King of the Forensic Science Service for sharing their expertise in pathology, psychology, and drug detection.

I'm grateful to my copyeditors and proofreaders for their careful scrutiny of the prose and meticulous attention to detail. Thanks, in particular, to Barbara Clark, Jane Selley, and Sarah Day. I would also like to thank Kate Cooper, Luke Speed, Rich Green, Jake Smith-Bosanquet, Eva Papastratis, Catherine Cho, Hillary Jacobson, and all at Curtis Brown and ICM Partners.

Many cheers and massive thanks to the fabulous publicity and marketing teams at Headline and Little, Brown: Georgina Moore, Millie Seaward, Joe Yule, Sabrina Callahan, and Pamela Brown. They have my immense gratitude and admiration. A big thank you, too, to Kate Stephenson and Ella Gordon at Wildfire, as well as Ben Allen and Nicky Guerreiro at Mulholland.

Finally, I would like to thank two of my most ardent supporters: Lee Han Shih, for believing in me, and my wonderful fiancé, Alexander Plekhanov, who backed every step of my journey (and who provided all the necessary diversions). Han and Alex, this book is for you.

ABOUT THE AUTHOR

Felicia Yap grew up in Kuala Lumpur and has written for *The Economist* and the *Business Times*. She has also been a cell biologist, a war historian, a Cambridge lecturer, a technology journalist, a theater critic, a flea-market trader, and a catwalk model. She lives in London and is a recent graduate of the Faber Academy's creative writing program.

Follow her on Twitter @FeliciaMYap.